Spoon in the Road

A Novel

By Ben Bonkoske

Edited by Leslee Johnson

Cover Illustration by Sarah Goodyear

Cover Design by Joseph Jirik

First Printing

ISBN-13: 978-1-7929-82118

"I just hope that one day – preferably when we're both blind drunk – we can talk about it."

- J.D Salinger

Chapter 1

All I needed was three days to walk away from everything. That was how long I took to plan to travel to New York because that was all I had. Honestly, people who ask *why* never do a damn thing in their lives. I just wondered if I could, but just because you can do something doesn't mean you should. In my mind, if I could acquire a tent, backpack, and food this journey was by no means impossible. I had basically no money and the listings for backpacks online were over one hundred dollars except one.

"Hello? Is this Tina?" I spoke into the phone lightly.

An aloof sounding woman answered. "Yes, it is. Who is calling?"

"Hello. This is Jack Wright. I am calling about the backpack that you're selling?"

"What? Oh, yes, that old thing. Are you interested?" She replied, seemingly occupied with something.

"I am *indeed*, very interested." I tried to not sound like an eager puppy.

"And what will you be using it for?"

"I will be walking across the country."

There was a brief silence of concern, which melted to excitement.

"Lovely, just lovely, only the backpack runs rather large, how tall are you?"

"Oh, I should be fine."

"Do you need it soon? The only thing is I'm in Colorado right now and the backpack is at my house."

"I was planning on leaving in two days." I was intrigued but couldn't picture her age or quarters.

"That should not be a problem, I will call my roommate Annie to give it to you tomorrow or whenever you can stop by. How's North Carolina?"

You could tell she was missing her old friend, the South.

"You know, taking her time as usual, kind, and more comfortable than home itself. Listen, I don't really have a lot of money. I was wondering if the price could be lowered from sixty to forty?"

She paused again, but this time for intentional arousal.

"I had hoped that this backpack would go to good use. Forty dollars it is."

"God Bless you. Thank you so much. This means so much to me."

"Thank *you*, sir and good luck. You will be hearing from Annie shortly."

She knew dreams were coming true when she hung up. It wasn't long before the motivation from the likelihood of getting a backpack started to wear off, and my dream of walking to New York was becoming just that, a dream. I was sure I needed a lot of other things, but I didn't know what they were. The things we really need in life come from within, and those were much harder to acquire than a spare tent. I waited for a response from Annie, but instead, I got a call from my blond curly haired stoner friend, Chad.

"Hey man, for the history final do we need to write an essay *as well* as make a presentation?" He asked.

"Yeah," I replied, rolling my eyes about a much more serious matter.

"And it's due tomorrow?" He coughed.

"Yeah man, list-" I was about to cut him off, but then I remembered that his single was filled with a kayak and all sorts of camping supplies.

"Dude, I'm actually planning on taking a long trip, and I don't have any supplies. Do you know where I could get some?" I asked in vague desperation.

"You know my dad works for REI, right?" He expressed ardently.

I didn't know what that meant, but I assumed it was a good thing.

"Do you by chance have an extra tent lying around that I could buy?"

"Maybe, I will check, come on over." We hung up.

When I arrived, his single reeked of marijuana masked with popcorn. Chad sat on his bed hitting his new bong, Daffodil. While blowing the smoke out the window, he seemingly worked on his history final. He offered me a rip, and I took one to calm my nerves. Chad was very similar to me in all the wrong ways. Irresponsible but lovable, stubborn, and knows he can get what he wants.

"So, you're gonna go on a trip?" he asked with a cotton mouthed tongue.

"I'm going to walk from here to New York City."

"Dope." He said, evidently unamused.

"I've never camped alone." I appealed, hoping he would know a little more about the subject.

"You've never camped alone before?" He looked up confused by my explanation and getting a little bit more serious, he asked, "and you want to go out alone?"

"Yeah." I said with the most amount of confidence I could muster.

"Alright just checking, you're going to need this," he got up from his chair to grab a small green bag from under his bed. "It's my old small tent."

"How much?" I asked, a little worried.

"Free." He handed it to me carefree.

My mind went into slight shock. If the backpack came through, then so could I. I listened to his advice in a hypersensitive serious sort of enthusiasm since it couldn't hurt to hear from someone who had actually done this sort of thing before.

"The first thing you are going to want to know the difference between is front country and backcountry."

He was getting more serious now that he had my attention. We were both unsteady, so it was difficult to take him or any of this ridiculous situation seriously. "If you are less than three hours away from medical attention you are in front country. Should you need it, backcountry means that you are more than three hours away if something happens. Safety is the most important thing out there." He was pacing back and forth, waving his hand like he was the tour guide for this hellish voyage.

"If you break something, you'll want a brace you can wrap around yourself to stabilize broken bones." He said.

"I could always just use duct tape and sticks." I said.

"Yeah, but you can wrap a brace around your neck if that snaps too."

A brief chill passed, but neither of us was really going to let any small worries get to us now.

"You are going to need to cook some food. Can you build a fire?"

"Yes." I answered.

He started shuffling around opening drawers in his desk, pulling out and opening gigantic tupperware out from under his bed.

"This boils water in under two minutes. It is a portable stove. If you can get your hands on one of these, do it. They are about one hundred dollars."

"Dude..." I lowered my shoulders and looked at him blankly. "I don't have money like that to spend." I said.

"Oh, well you should be fine if you can make a fire." He ignored what I had just said and went back to his cavalier attitude.

"What about bears?" I tried asking.

"What about them?" he replied, unconcerned.

"Will they attack me?"

"If they are hungry." He shrugged it off. "If you give them a reason to assume you have food, they will." He said with about as much worry that he had for his final.

"So, I should just hang a bear bag?"

"Yeah, Good. Bears come out at night. No deodorant, no sunscreen at night, if you brush your teeth, do it away from camp."

"Is that it?"

"No, but yeah, mostly. We should probably have the talk."

"What talk?"

"Do you have any form of protection on you?"

"No. Should I get a knife?" I asked darkly.

"Dude, I would get a gun if you could get your hands on one." He said with conviction.

I hadn't thought in depth about the dangers of being on the road alone. I had a little, but I didn't want to. The thought was too alienating.

"Listen, what you are doing and where you are going attracts a certain type of person..."

"Crazy people?" I grimaced.

"People who spend a lot of time *alone*." He seemed worried about something else.

"And?"

"And those people might want to hurt you."

"Do you know of any bad stories of people getting murdered while travelling?" I asked.

"Yes."

"Yes?" I responded shocked like he was explaining it to a child.

"First off, don't tell anyone where you are going. If someone seems like they are following you, they probably are. You don't want to let assume you think anything about them. You want to separate yourself as quickly as possible. Get off the road and get to population. Do you understand?"

There was a sharp pain inside of my chest like I didn't want to hear the answer I asked for. He broke eye contact lightly. Instantly, I was relieved. I had heard of a murder story in North Carolina. Someone who was strangling people and wearing people's faces in the Smoky Mountains last fall.

Chad started explaining to me what felt like a true ghost story. "My friend was backpacking in Spain, and it started to get late, so he snuck into a barn and slept in the top window on a haystack. He overheard two men come into the barn. One man started arguing and they began wrestling until one hit the other in the head with a blunt object. He was out cold. Next, he heard a gunshot. Killed him. Right there. The murderer moved the body right under the haystack where my friend was sleeping, just a few feet down from him. He said he had never been so scared in his life. If that man had just looked up and saw him there, he would have killed him. No witnesses."

I thought about the lack of a consistent flow of any real evidence of people getting murdered. People who died or were killed were more of an exception than an expectation. My goal was to get over my fears and as far as I was concerned, people didn't just kill each other in cold blood unless they were cannibals, rapists, or sociopaths.

Still trying to get a genuine rise out of me, Chad said, "He said that after the guy killed the other one, the murderer spent the rest of the night digging a grave, muttering to himself."

"Is there anything else I need to know?" I asked.

"No. There is other stuff you will learn on the way that you'll wish you knew now, but you're as prepared as you'll ever be."

"Thanks man."

"Just don't get summit fever,"

"What is that?"

"It's when you care so much about getting to where you are going that you don't enjoy the present. Remember to enjoy yourself."

"Peace." I shut the door.

After I left, I wondered if I had unfinished finals that needed to be taken care of as quickly as possible. Some of college is really rather enjoyable, but not always the things you would expect. Rigorous routine gets me adrenalized and exhausted, which is the state my body and mind like to reside. Four o'clock with a drink in my hand is a good sign to stop working but is also when the best work is done. I study people, but myself most often. My political stances go as far right as they do left, but when people look at problems in the world, I think they tend to try and help them. Sometimes there's not always a problem, and people instigate more trouble than help by getting so offended. We had to make a presentation about a band that impacted the world.

It was late or early depending on which ball in the sky you prefer, but the birds were chirping. I was restless. I needed some form of food if I was going to survive on the trip. Since it was the end of the school year, people would leave old food that they didn't eat in the hallway. I poked my head out of my door looking both ways for traffic and ran down grabbing all the bags of groceries and old fruit I could grab. I got three apples, two bananas, seven bags of Cheetos, Fritos, Doritos, ramen, and a full box of Cheerios. I thought that would be sustainable for about a week. About a half hour later, I was woken up by a phone call.

An alarming high-pitched voice hit my eardrum. "Hello? Is this Dan?" I pictured a talking porcupine haired woman on the other end. I was sure, I was Dan. "Um, yes, good morning, is this Annie?" I asked in my cocooned dream state.

"Yeah hey, I have to go to work, but does five thirty tonight work for you? I can send you my address."

"I will be there."

"Good, see ya then."

I did a little happy dance in bed. I got up and rolled a joint and went to breakfast. I had one more night before I planned on leaving. I grabbed coffee, orange juice, a waffle, hash browns, fruit and cereal before I went to my history final.

Chad waltzed into the room ten minutes later with a fierce defiance of last-day-of-school attitude. He was wearing sunglasses, and you could just see the rays of freedom shining behind him as he closed the door to the concrete cage of a classroom in June.

Afterwards, I went out of the classroom into the bright day encouraged from opening a text from Annie revealing her address. The house was about seven miles from campus, and I was willing to walk. Chad's roommate, Joseph had a car and said he would give me a lift if I smoked him up. We all kicked it while *Always Sunny* was on TV.

"How many miles a day do you think you are going to go?" Joseph asked while eating a freeze pop.

"Twenty." I said, casually.

"That sounds a bit much, especially if you are going to be climbing mountains." He looked over at Chad as though I was out of my league.

I sprawled out on Chad's bed lethargically. "If I go twenty miles a day, it will take me about a month and a half." I said, finishing sitting up with nonchalant determination.

"Maybe you should bring it down to fifteen?" Joseph uttered, trying to convince me out of my own death.

"Possibly. I am going to see what it's like."

“Do you think you are prepared?” Joseph pried a little deeper.

“After I get this backpack, all I will need is a knife to kill with.”

“Damn dude, I hope so.

Chapter 2

My phone died on the drive over, and we pulled up to some godforsaken house in a back alley. I knew Joseph wouldn't just drive me around all day if I had the wrong address, so I had to recite the address by memory. This had to work. I used an especially suspicious website, so I wasn't exactly fond of the idea of going into a stranger's house alone. Chad offered to come with me to "inspect the backpack," but I think he was a little worried as well.

She told us five thirty and nobody was home. I was getting worried that we were at the wrong address. Without a backpack, the whole plan wouldn't happen. We kept knocking, but no one answered. Chad looked at me as though there was no use. Finally, a woman pulled onto the granite driveway lined with bamboo and rolled down her SUV window.

The petite woman popped out of the car with her ponytails swinging. Once you put a nice face like Annie into the situation, everything just becomes sweet like Southern tea. She shook our hands and walked us up her porch as the sun was setting. She began to unlock five or six locks on her back door, which took about a minute.

"Sorry, my husband is a little suspicious." Whatever that meant.

We walked in, and it looked like it was for about three or four roommates. The house had a little bit of a sorority feeling to it, but an oriental style living room, aged wooden floors with wide-open windows, and a hiding cat. She went into a bedroom and came back holding what to me looked like the most beautiful thing I had ever seen.

"Here is the backpack. Go on, try it on."

As far as I was concerned, if the backpack would just *be* a backpack and fit a lot of stuff in it, simple as that, I was buying it.

"If it doesn't fit you, it's not worth your money," she said a little snarky. "You are going to want to be able to put two fingers in between where the shoulder pads are.

You are going to enjoy these straps above your shoulders, they will distribute the weight into your back."

Chad, inconspicuously stoned while wearing sunglasses in the inside of her house, was still somewhat helpful for as goofy as he looked showing me some straps and pockets.

"I hiked 500 miles last summer through South America, and the only reason why I made it was because I had a good backpack," she went back into her room and returned with her own backpack which looked like Barbie's hiking pack. When we didn't say anything, she answered herself with, "It was incredible."

"So, forty dollars?" I calmly asked.

She seemed hesitant. She had all this adultness in her stature. I didn't want to explain myself any further. If I did die, I didn't want to have her recognize me in the paper.

"Stay dry, avoid danger, and come back safe."

I put the forty dollars on the table and was already holding the backpack, so we left. Joseph apparently got intimidated by some drunk offender while waiting for us and had to move his car. Chad thought it would be a good idea to slightly intimidate the guy back while Joseph came back around. Testosterone at its finest, I rolled my eyes. I decided to play macho for the hell of it and Joseph pulled up before the situation turned into anything more serious or fun.

"You get the backpack?" he asked as we hopped in.

"Yeah man." I answered.

"You know you have to do it now."

I chuckled, but the seriousness of that mentality was starting to settle in. This was almost to the point of no return. I had told enough people that I was going to do it. That wasn't the reason why I would have risked my life like this in the first place, but why the hell did I have to be born such a loudmouth. When we got back to campus, Joseph wanted to inspect the backpack for some reason. He looked at it all silly upside down and pulled on loose straps. We went out to where people smoke, and my friend, Ellen, who had purple hair, was there.

Apparently, she had a rough hell of an embarrassing night, and Joseph and Chad were trying to avoid her.

"What's with the backpack?" an anonymous smoker asked.

"He's walking to New York." Chad said directly as though it added purpose to his own life.

"From Asheville? Oh shit. That's wild man."

"You should watch this." Chad handed me his phone, and it was actual footage of Aron Ralston cutting his arm off while stuck under a rock in Colorado. This poor guy spent five days thinking he was going to die. He actually filmed himself cutting his arm. I looked away from the macabre gore of the real video.

Ellen had heard about my little adventure already. She always gave me cigarettes when I didn't have any and reminds me of a Cheshire cat.

"I think I have a solar charger that might help you on your way," she said, trying to help as we shared a cigarette.

"That would be great, but I think I have everything I need," I said nonchalantly, more tired than anything.

"No seriously, if I have something that can help you on your way, I want to give it to you," she said it with vitality, so I met her energy.

"Ok. Let's go get it."

She led me to her room, which was messy. I thought about the last time I had sex with her and wondered if this was my chance. After we grabbed the solar charger, it dawned on me that I still had a twenty-page paper due the next morning, and along with trying to pack everything you are going to need for a month is a bit much to do in one night. It didn't matter. I was already lost and scared. Lost in my own head and scared of seeing what I was actually capable of.

I pride myself in being a social introvert. Being able to not follow the crowd if it's not what you want to do is a talent and being able to be part of one if you wish is a skill. Sitting in silent solitude is my best friend. I could have kept procrastinating with those "friends" of mine, but I had had enough. I like people, but I also hate them most of the time.

My dorm stays unlocked since I lost my key on the first day, and the replacement after a week. I put the backpack up against a chair and began to lie out everything I needed to travel with on my single bed. It was unlikely I was getting any sleep.

One small wool blanket, the tent, a yoga mat, computer, food, clothes, camera and small backpack were all laid out. I like clothes, especially shoes. I thought I was going to pack a whole suit and so that once I arrived in New York I would have something to walk around in. However, this idea was completely bonkers. For those of you who haven't carried everything you own on your back, you want the least amount of weight as possible.

I packed three pairs of underwear, a pair of jeans, two shorts, three pair of socks, three t-shirts, a flannel, a sweater, and a winter jacket. If I had brought a blazer, dress pants and shoes, there would have been no space for anything else left, just attire. By the end of the journey everything I carried probably weighed as much as all those bloody clothes I originally left with.

In many ways travelling *is* like a catwalk, but I was so accustomed to the ways of fashion I would have died for it. In college, there is an excess of everything, from sex, booze, work, porn, and drugs to any other indulgence you can think of. Everyone thinks they are the greatest things that happened to this planet, and everyone treats each other like shit. There is so much of everything that for anything to not feel meaningless must come in paramount proportions.

I was wired 24/7 on a hedonistic binge. I didn't try. College is a place where they pat you on the back just for showing up. I wanted a change. I wanted to know I was alive and actually try for once in my life. I just didn't know how to do it yet. I had barely started my essay and wrote 20 pages that night - walked away with a B. Granted, it was an art class, the only thing I was relatively interested in, but sleep evaded me for one more night.

Chapter 3

I knew if my father saw a backpack filled to the top with a week's worth of clothes, food supply, and my computer he was going to be suspicious. I did one last check to see if I had everything I needed, and I made a short trip over to my good friend Ned's apartment where I stashed my backpack. Try and see it from my point, was this a dangerous idea? Yes. Was I willing to die to do it? Why not? Does that mean that you shouldn't do something? No. My life was more worthless than the penny. If it had gone on the way it was, I would have put myself in danger intentionally sooner or later.

I've had three roommates during the three semesters that I've been here. If you end up having a roommate who is dirtier than you, then the whole dorm will go to hell. The bathroom floor was always wet with some foul liquid. You couldn't see the floor in the living room since it was covered with old videogames, slight but present stench of puke, and disregarded art projects. We fought over who would buy toilet paper next and we would often go weeks without any community paper. The whole place gave me anxiety anytime that I had to go back there and spent most of my time depressed, lying in the filth.

My Father, Don, arrived with a new grey gopher goatee since the last time I'd seen him. We loaded up the car with basically everything I owned apart from everything I needed. He got on my case about how many clothes I had. Somehow, the dorm looked relatively presentable with only a few minor dings in the ceiling for putting duct tape on it to cover the smoke alarm, which ripped off some of the paint.

I had a few books to return to the library, and a few microphones I decided to snag for the journey thinking I might need to read or record some audio. When I got back to the car where he was parked, we went out to my last meal before not knowing where any of my next meals were coming from. Sitting in that Thai restaurant keeping all of this information in the back of my head while we ate made me feel nauseous. He kept going on about my grades, my summer job, my future, and everything I just didn't give a damn about anymore. I have been to hell and back enough times in my life to realize it is always going to be all right somehow, somewhere in the end.

I couldn't listen to a word he was saying. All this business as usual was gibberish, muted like in those war movies when someone's hit with an explosion. I did not wish to waste away my life with detail, but I couldn't help but think of the idea of me starving to death somehow, somewhere. That was a big detail. I truly no longer cared about all I was ready to leave behind. I sincerely couldn't finish my meal. The waitress asked if we wanted to take our meals. I asked her if she could wrap mine in a plastic container instead of paper. My dad gave me an off look, but I casually ignored it.

"So, are you going to come back to the hotel with me tonight and leave tomorrow morning?"

"I'm going to just stay at Ned's house."

"I'd prefer if you just came back and then we could leave in the morning." He curbed the conversation.

"It's my last night here. I want to say goodbye to all of my friends. I'm just going to stay at Ned's."

"Alright. I'll pick you up at ten?"

"Sounds good."

We went back to campus because I didn't want to show him where Ned's apartment was. I felt borderline cruel. I gave him a hug as though it was the last time I was ever going to hug him again. It hurt. All of it hurt, but at least I felt something. I went to the sandwich shop and ordered two sandwiches with everything all the way and every sauce. I wrapped them in saran wrap and took two canned root beers since they are part of the meal equivalency. It was as good as it was going to get.

I walked over to Ned's apartment. A guy named Aiden, one of those super annoying tell-you-how-to-live-your-life Californians, ponytails and all was there. He had all sorts of stuff that I was initially all about, but after a few days got under my skin. He made hemp milk, and hummus that he was very stingy about it and then went bad. He used hemp wick only when smoking and was into making videos, so I offered to go with him to make a small documentary in some communities across the East Coast. He said he'd take me up on the offer, but then bailed.

I didn't really expect it to work out in the first place, but just the way he acted like he was skilled in the ways of living off the land while then revealing he had never camped alone in his life. I only mention him because this was the kind of guy that had around six or seven knives with him to the couch he was crashing on. We went through his collection and there was one that was about a foot long and had a compass in it. He came off all noble that he would give it to me for fifteen dollars but felt sort of disingenuous when he had so many knives and promoted such a communistic lifestyle for an upcharge.

He rolled his eyes and reluctantly sold me the knife. I heard he was still on my friend's couch by the time I had made it to New York. There was no place for me to sleep so I rolled out my yoga mat on Ned's floor. He was listening to a podcast with all the lights off. Fear was really starting to settle in. The podcast talked about smart people and creative people and sabotaging one's life.

Smart people look for creative people. However, being a creative person comes with a lot more risk. A smart person is assured a specific type of success, while a creative person has no limits. The greatest work of art is a happy life. Anyone can go to school, have a family, and a job, but you only achieve success if you do it with value. I don't hate money or want to be a hermit my whole life, but I do want something else.

I lay on the cold hardwood floor next to a bed filled with old dust and dead skin from a year of being uncleaned. I don't know what I was looking for. The best advice my father ever gave me was that I couldn't achieve my dreams. Perhaps I had enough to start a life with, but for that to become a reality I would have to throw out everything I had become up until now. I was scared but cried myself to sleep pondering my choice as though I was disarming a bomb.

Chapter 4

I wanted to get a head start before I got that expected phone call from Don asking where I was. It felt later than it should have. It was 7:30 am and my phone, had this horrible select language screen. Apparently, Apple decided to update my phone or something (conspiracy). I had no music, internet or information on my phone. It wanted *my* information. It was at that moment I realized if this was going to happen, I was going to have to be able to rely completely on my own. It didn't take that long to set it up but still everything was erased.

I have to thank Ned. He is not a perfect individual, but he believed in me at a time that no one else did, as do I him. In all truth, I often think drunk. Once I said I was serious, all bets were off, and nobody wanted to talk me out of it, which only proves the worthlessness of life. Although cautious and worried, Ned helped me put the money where my mouth was. He lent me forty dollars and gave me a little bit of weed and walnuts right before I left. I had absolutely no intention of smoking pot on this trip. A plant that makes you tired, hungry and unmotivated. I thought it would have killed me.

This drunken construction project was engineered to be tested. I didn't care if my phone wasn't working. I would have walked there with nothing at all. I slammed the door shut into the hard morning sun. I just used the compass in my gigantic knife. All I did was go as due north for as far and long as I could go. People waved at me from their cars and looked at me with the strangest concern on the street. The backpack was a dead giveaway that I did not belong in society anymore. A few people honked and I would give them the peace sign. There is a strong power that comes from believing in solidity as foreign as that sometimes feels.

After about an hour or two, I got off the main drive, which was littered with fast food chain restaurants, grocery stores and massage parlors. The sun began to beat down on my shoulders and the weight began to settle in. I took it off outside an antique store and went in asking for water. They said they didn't have any. I began to instantly feel like an outsider looking in at the world. What if all that was over? I thought water was the first amendment. The sparse stores began to turn into mountainous countryside and that was when I got the Phone call from my dad.

"Hey, where are you?" I was sure he had already known.

"Don, um...I have been planning a cross country trip for a little bit and I left this morning."

"What are you talking about?"

"I planned a trip, and I'm leaving for New York."

A potent long pause.

"What planning?"

"I got a tent, and a backpack, and filled it up with food."

"Oh fuck. It is over. You have ruined trust between us forever."

"I'm sorry."

"There's *no* sorry. I don't know if you can ever come home after doing something like this."

"I had to do it. I hope you understand."

"No. You are a liar. A deceitful person, who cannot be trusted."

I flicked a booger off my finger and noticed some blood on my knee.

"I'm serious. I don't think you can come home after doing this." I'm very used to these threats.

"I understand. The world is my new home."

"And all your things. Everything. It is ALL being thrown out or dropped off at the first Goodwill I see."

"Do what you have to do."

"Alright well...Goodbye." He hung up the phone.

I sat on the hot pavement for about a good minute and reflected on all that I had done. I questioned if I had sabotaged everything I had worked for in my life up until this point. Donald and I have gone to the edge of hell. He may not agree, but our relationship had been strained much worse throughout the years. He was just upset that for once, I manipulated a situation better than he always does. I learned from the best.

I felt bad, but if you can't handle the dark reality of things, you'd better stay at home. I picked up my things and felt like I had a weight off my shoulder. I kept along the road until I saw a Dollar General. My budget was very embarrassing, but there were things I needed to survive. I went into the store with my big backpack on and asked the struggling actress working there where the flashlights were.

"Aisle six for the flashlights."

I got one of those g 2D battery flashlights that was about 3 pounds. I was in the checkout pulling out the small amount of cash I had from my duct tape wallet and who do I see standing before me with his greying gopher beard and red eyes, my father. He pointed and stared like we were about to get into it right there. Even at his worst he has too much pride. The reality of his son running away was a blind hit. He didn't say anything and stormed out. I bought my items and it came out to about two dollars. I thanked the cashier for their assistance as witness. I lugged all of my crap outside where I saw the loaded car.

"How did you find me?" I said trying to not make a big deal of this, trying to be a big boy who can make his own decisions.

He shoved his phone in my face without much restraint.

"Well. I thought you had wiped my phone or something." I said wiping my blinking eyes and throwing some empty conviction away.

"No. I gotcha. Now get in the car." He yelled and pointed like a big boy.

I looked at it all for about a second and then just began walking away. What good was any of it worth anyways?

"If you walk away now, this is everything that you will ever be and all that you will ever have. Everything on your back." Everything I had ever owned was not worth giving up on this. I kept walking.

He got in the car and began to pull out of the driveway. "I'm donating everything. Trust is over."

I didn't say anything as he drove off. I just was holding back those silly tears.

Chapter 5

I was following my compass going through some backend bushes where some homeless people had congregated on an old spring mattress. I found myself looking out at the back of one of those beautiful Walmart parking lots. I still needed to buy a pot to cook food so I thought I should give it a visit. I was about 50 feet up from the concrete with a very steep grassy downhill. I didn't want to waste any time walking all the way around so I thought I would just risk a speedy run downhill. I took my first steps and realized that there were briars along the way, and I didn't assume that weight increases momentum.

I tried to step around one, but my feet were caught, and I fell forward right onto multiple thorns cutting up my wrists and legs. Once I had fallen, I decided to keep rolling all the way down to the parking lot, which was painfully efficient. There I lay discouraged for about a minute breathing deeply but sat up since I didn't want to bring any attention to myself that wasn't needed. I assessed my red stinging body to see what damage had been done. Nothing needed stitches or anything like that, but I just had a lot of little cuts all along my body. The ones on my arms didn't hurt after the initial sting, but they didn't look good. I was probably being a little dramatic, but still it sucked.

My backpack was intact but had some green thorny crap clinging to it, so I gently ripped the loose fragments off. Nothing had fallen out, so I wasn't all that worried about the contents inside of it. America's favorite store's air conditioning healed my wounds instantly. I felt refurbished by the sweet opportunity of the lowest prices on the planet. I went to the hunting section, and although a store owner earlier that day had been reluctant to give this dehydrated young man water, the gun salesman said, "Can I help you find anything?" Pointing to the guns on display.

I chuckled to myself.

"Yes, I would like a Magnum .44-gauge shotgun please."

"Excuse me?"

"Nothing."

I walked down the aisle over into the camping section.

They had everything that anyone could ever need to survive in the woods if they had the budget. Rain gear, dehydrated meals, lightweight backpacks, cooking utensils and stoves, all of it. It looked very nice I will admit, but I didn't want to see if a bunch of gear could get me to New York City, I wanted to see if *I* could make it and I still think that that is a major difference between travelers.

I saw a metallic small pot that looked about the size of a styrofoam ramen container and it was four dollars. Next, I saw water filtration systems and they ranged anywhere twenty to forty dollars. I didn't know if I needed it, but the thought of being dehydrated in the middle of the woods without any clean water was gruesome. I began to bargain that if I had the option to get water anywhere the amount of time it would take to stop to divert and get water would save me hours and miles of travel. I thought I would spring though it was almost half of the money I had. I went to the checkout line.

"Where the hell are you going with all that?" A bystander asked me.

"Oh, I'm walking to New York City." I said with confidence.

"Hmmm. Boy, are you crazy?"

"Yes sir."

"You are going to die if you do this," he said a little louder, getting the attention of the other people in line.

"Well, the way I figure I'm going to die either way, but only if I meet the wrong people will I be in any real danger."

"Well, if you meet the wrong people, you'll get murdered as shit."

"Thank you for your concern, but I think I'll be fine." I took his advice in stride.

"Whatever you say." he said shaking his head.

I checked out and got back on a main road. I saw a kid with slicked back hair driving a red convertible car and gave him a sarcastic look with my thumb up. As if I would have even taken a ride from such a snob. He shot me back with a similar look, and with the roll of our eyes he drove off. I wondered if he drove off because of the way that I initially looked at him and devalued all that capitalist crap he had from a place of so much less, or if just having so much more makes one feel so much less for others.

There was a rumor going around campus before I left that I was going to stop at every Starbucks along the way. The only reason why that would be true was because they are known for having wi-fi, otherwise, I hate that establishment and don't want to go anywhere near one. I went in to one attached to a grocery store. It was horrible to look at all the food I couldn't afford.

I went into the bathroom. My laptop was packed at the bottom of everything. I began to unload it all and put it on the floor and slowly everything filled up the whole area of the floor in the handicap stall. All of my different clothes all over the place, my computer charger wires, the food, flashlight, my new cooking pot, it was all a mess and it was everything I had to my name.

A chilling thought of if I was going to have to sleep in bathroom stalls passed. This was what my life had literally been reduced to. I made a horrible realization that I didn't have a charger cord to plug into my phone. I began to open up all of my pockets and thought I had found it but then realized it was only my headphones.

I began to freak out. My phone had gone back to its normal screen but if it's battery died it would be useless. A phone was the difference between life and death. I put everything back into my backpack and took out my computer and one of the sandwiches to eat lunch. I plugged in my computer and opened it up and saw some screen that I had never seen before. It was the equivalent of asking me for what language I wanted to pick except worse. It asked if I wanted to reboot the hard drive or some crap and wipe the whole computer. It asked if I wanted to set the time and date and I did everything I could, but the machine was completely and utterly useless. Unable to log in, I expended every single option the machine gave me. I thought it was another stupid update, but I don't think I was ever as close to giving up, as I was at that moment and it was only the first day.

My phone had been erased. I didn't have a charger. I had no money. My computer didn't work. I already was cut up to hell. The only person I had talked to since I had left told me I was going to get murdered. And I was only 10 miles from my college. A wonderful song selection played *Lean on Me,* and I felt weak, like everything I was doing was foolish and that I should probably just go home. No, I had gone too far. There was no looking back, but there could always be some support, couldn't there be? I looked at my phone while I ate the soggy squished sandwich that all the sauces had just melted into slimy bread with meat in the middle.

You'd be astonished at how underutilized my phone is even when it is working. I talk with one person maybe two on a weekly basis. I clicked on the apple store, and thankfully it opened. I checked to see if I could download any social media apps. I got Instagram and Facebook. I looked through the names of people to help talk me through this situation. What a joke. I suppose it's nice to see what people do with their lives, but it doesn't make you know them any better.

Austin Rains was the first girl I ever fell in love with. She had a wild laugh, gorgeous red hair, and it was always cloudy whenever I saw her. That was enough for fifteen-year-old me to be hormonally infatuated for life. We broke up when I tried LSD and to this day, stands as one of my greatest regrets. She taught me how to dance and is one of my favorite people. Austin reminds me there is faith in humanity, no matter what. She's quite adventurous and probably would have just the right trick to get me out of this situation. I texted her, but I kept scrolling since I was really just avoiding someone else's number.

I had recently broken up with a girl named Paris Greene for the umpteenth time. The day I met her, I jumped out of a moving car and ran up to her and that was that. We had been on and off for two years. She told me she loved me the first night we slept together, and I felt like such a battered soldier having already been in love once before. I yearned for her innocence and quickly became addicted. We were agreeable on our most recent breakup. It came down to her calling me to break up with me and by the end of the phone call I had broken up with her. We feigned how we both thought of each other as great people. I told her to not communicate with me anymore, but her Spotify selection of Mac Demarco's *Still Beating* was playing, so I knew it wasn't completely over.

I decided to give Paris a call. Just for moral support, maybe just to hear her voice. The call rang three times, each worse, and longer than the last and went into voicemail. She saw the call and that it was from me, and purposefully ignored it, further proving my point that there was no one to lean on.

I finished my sandwich and walked up to a cashier. "Do you have an Apple charger?" I asked.

"Yeah, just go past Aisle one, with the electronics."

"Thanks."

Usually, you look very suspicious when you walk around in a store with a backpack that weighs sixty pounds, but for some reason nobody really looked at me twice while I was in this hybrid grocery store, or if they did they were rooting for me. I found a charger and went back into the bathroom, ripped open the packaging and threw it in the trash, and stuffed the charger into my underwear. I would never take from a person, but major corporations are fine. I made a Beeline out of the store, swiftly but not too quickly.

Crying can make you feel a lot better, but not when you are in public. You know when you start thinking about all the times you could have done something different and why you are worthless, well that's what I did. If only I hadn't been so full of myself to think I could do something like this. I have a bad history of punching hard objects when I get mad. That poor tree I used for shade was given a rough beating, but I already had enough blood coming out of me so it didn't really hurt. I'm probably not a good enough person for any*one*, and if that's the case the world is going to turn me away as well.

We all have scars, some more visible than others. Some we show off, and some we hide. It honestly still hurts to squeeze my fist all the way closed. As I finally sat down with the tears drying, I thought about why I actually did all this. I don't know if humans are designed to only be with one person their whole life, but what about our past lives or next lives or forever? Sometimes we love someone, and they just don't seem to see it the same way. People put each other up on a pedestal all the time, but this is different. I was once married to a girl in a play in High School and from the first time I saw her until the last time I've seen her, she is the reason I live. You may be an atheist or feel alone, but true love is the constant. Until the day I die, or at least for at as long as I've lived, I did this for her.

Chapter 6

I got a call from my grandparents who were understandably concerned about the whole thing.

"What the heck are you doing? I just got a call from your father, he's very upset."

"Hi Grandma, he will be fine."

"Grandpa's here. Talk to him, Jerry." She handed the landline over.

"Oh, howdy Grandpa, how ya doing?" I spoke into the phone.

"Oh, we're swell, hehe, we heard you're going on an adventure."

"Yep."

"Have you thought it through?" He asked.

"I think I have God with me, so don't worry."

"Where are you going to sleep?" My grandma over spoke.

"I have a tent."

"Oh, well we're worried about you, but it sounds like you're going through with this." My grandpa said, "we will have you in our prayers."

"I'll be praying too."

"Atta boy."

After I had talked them down, they were in full support and understood that what I was doing came from a place of no intentional harm and thought my adventure was rad. I'm very spiritual. I meditate and do yoga almost every day and try to get to church every week.

"We just wanted to call to make sure you were ok." My grandma said.

"Not a moment too soon grandma. Love you guys."

"You too." They said unanimously.

Faith is about how much you are willing to believe in something and the integrity you are willing to give it. God is any man, woman or child, and their words are my sermon. I believe God has a good sense of humor and accepts and forgives us however we may come. All religions have value and basically preach to love one another unconditionally. If you aren't willing to invest yourself into something regardless of what it may give back, or if you expect a specific return, you don't know god; you are playing god. Artists do that all the time, especially the dead ones.

What I had was a lot of faith in this journey. I didn't know where my next meal was going to come from or where I was going to sleep, but I did believe god had my back. I acted from the heart. I was as kind to myself as I was to others. If you aren't good to others, you aren't kind to yourself because we are all one. It was good to know my dear grandparents were in support of me. Moral support was enough to pick everything up and stop feeling sorry for myself. Remember, I *was* prepared to die. I didn't want to, but a few cuts and a broken computer was nothing compared to what I truly was willing to sacrifice.

I thought if I could just get to Mars Hill by tonight I should be alright, it was a town of about 1,400 people. I could figure out a place to camp or ask someone to sleep on their lawn or something. You have to remember the South is known for their hospitality. I did what I had to do as I walked into the setting sun. The worry set in because the sun was going down much quicker than I was travelling. I walked for about three or four miles, along some busy roads. Along mountain curves, which would go up and down and bend. Slowly I really was getting away from most of society. This can be a good thing or a bad thing. If you are away from society, people don't get many visitors knocking at their door, so I liked to think they would be thankful to see a strapping young man on the road offering work to stay. It's a bad thing because you are all alone.

The sun was coming down on the wheat field surrounding a trailer home. Wonderful, I thought to myself, how sweet and simple, the true meaning of America in such simple quarters. I contemplated going up to them and ask if I could sit on their porch, but I didn't want to put them in an awkward situation when they looked so happy as a family on this evening. So, I kept going until I came across a bar. My beard had not come in and I wasn't twenty-one yet. I knew I might have been carded, but looking back, when a man walks into a bar with everything he owns on his back, they're going to give you a beer. It was my first day, so I sat outside away from everybody, in the most suspicious manner.

This was going to be a lot harder than I expected. It was hard to look at all these people enjoying themselves smoking and drinking without a care in the world, at the same time, I knew they did this probably every week and would have enjoyed something different. I sat outside for about 10 minutes to decompress and catch my breath and walked inside and up to the bar.

"Can I get you anything?" The woman working the bar asked me.

"Just water please." I held up my water bottle.

"Would you like some ice?"

"Yes please."

I felt the back of my neck and which had a stinging sunburnt feeling. She handed me back my Nalgene and the tin container I had. We nodded at each other and smiled, which meant a lot in its own way, it kept me close to all the humanness I was feeling further and further away from. When, I went back outside, took a big gulp of water, put on my backpack and kept going. It wasn't long before it was getting pretty late, and I came across a gas station. Two men with gruff on their face and oil on their shirts were having a conversation. They were pristine hick South. I could tell that their conversation was closing.

I'm no statistics major, however, I remember learning that the answer of a question is greatly affected by the way that it is asked. If I had interrupted these men, I would have come off as an outsider, but because he was already getting into his car, I knew that he was on his way somewhere and more likely to give me a ride. I ran up to him right as he opened the door to his dark turquoise truck, and we stood together at eye level.

"Excuse me sir. I am travelling across the country and I was wondering if you could give me a lift."

"Where you wanna go?"

"New York City."

We both looked at each other and laughed.

"Billy, you hear this boy?"

"Wher't he say?" Billy asked stroking his dark beard grinning.

"This boy wants a ride to New York City."

"Hell, Give it to him. Jenny'll enjoy the time off."

"Nah, I'm supposed to bring home dinner," he cracked back.

He looked at me with a face of satisfaction but held back his smile.

"I was wondering what would happen if I went to Mars Hill. I could maybe find me someone to put me up or camp along the road." I appealed.

"Well, Mars Hill is pretty small, young man, and it's getting dark. I don't think you'll find anyone who will let you stay with for the night and there ain't much anywhere to camp."

I probably either looked defeated or psychotic.

"I can take you to the state line, off the highway and the Appalachian Trail is right there. It's on my way home."

"You can take me to a trail? I never thought about that." I had jubilation running through my bones. "Which state line?" I asked

"The state line of Tennessee. It's a little bit West, but it's North of here."

I thought about pulling out a map on my phone, but the deal sounded good enough. I would be on a trail and I would be able to tent in the woods safely. If I had known exactly how far West he was going to take me I'm not sure I would have taken the ride, but I threw my backpack into the back of his truck, waved Billy goodbye and we drove off.

The car had an old musk to it. The way a lot of old cars with manual windows are. I looked over to my right and in between us there was a revolver sitting on the seat. It was black with a stout barrel. It was unsettling but not as much as you might expect since we were in the South. He noticed me eyeing the gun.

"Oh, sorry about that."

"No worries, sir. I trust you. What kind of gun is it?"

"It's a .32 magnum revolver."

"Can I hold it?" I asked.

"Hehe, go ahead." He picked it up, checked to see if it was loaded. Apparently, it was, and he held it upside down and a few bullets fell into his hands, all while he was maneuvering his stick shift, and handed me the pistol. I held the gun in my hand. It was hot and heavy. I spun the chamber and counted six holes for bullets aiming it forward.

"You wouldn't want to pass this on to a young traveler, would you?" I offered.

"You got anything to protect yourself out there?" He asked.

"I brought a blade."

"How big."

"About a foot."

"You should be fine but look out for them bears."

"I've been told."

"And mountain lions."

"How big are the mountain lions?"

"They get bigger than anything you would want to see," he reached his arms across the length of the seats, "If any animal gets ya, you shove your arm down his throat and start stabbing at his face. Ya hear me."

"Sounds brutal."

"Nature ain't soft, young man."

"Well, I'm pretty tough."

"If you need anything else, food or something, I'd be happy to oblige. We can stop at the store if you want."

"Do you have any sunscreen?"

He opened his glove compartment and looked through it and closed it. Then he shuffled through the door on his driver's seat.

"I think I've got some in here. Look on your side."

I looked through the door and found a warm old sun tanning container."

"It's your'ns if you want it."

"Thank you so much sir."

We pulled up to a drive.

"Now this is West." He pointed down a road, "the state line border and the highway is this way, which you can get on the trail is there."

"Then lct's go."

We talked in the car about the casual things people talk about. I congratulated him on his marriage of thirty years or something. That deserves a congratulations. I just wonder what a love of that length would be like; there's something very honorable with staying together. It's sad, but maybe if there was, physical rewards in this materialistic world, people would stay together longer these days. He had a son older than me, and a daughter my age. I let him know that if all this works out maybe I'd give her a call after all this. He told me he'd shoot me if I did. Although the world might be going to hell, with values and morals probably going out the window, people are still so wonderful when they laugh together. We pulled up to a dirt road off the highway and both got out of the truck. An old man with a white patchy beard was sitting on the sidelines.

"Oy! Hello." I called out to the older gentleman.

"How are you today, good sir?" he pepped up.

"I'm wonderful," I said climbing into the back of the truck to get my backpack.

The two men nodded at each other.

"What are you?" I asked the older man in a very interested tone since he was the first of his kind that I had seen.

"I am a hiker," he looked at me with question. "Have you been on the trail at all?"

"Today is my first day on the road. I'm walking to New York."

"With all that on your back?" He sounded confused.

"Yes sir. What is your name?"

"They call me Dr. Fix-it."

"Oh. Why?" I asked, intrigued

"Well, I'm always fixing things?"

"Like what?"

"Well, I've fixed flat tires, helped someone with a broken tent, the only thing I can't fix is a broken heart. It's my trail name."

"What is a trail name?"

"It's a name you are given on the trail."

"And you just get it by doing something, or someone calls you it?" I asked.

"Basically."

"Are you going any further tonight?" I wondered.

"Not tonight, there is a shuttle that gives you a bed and a shower for ten dollars."

I hate to admit it, but that was out of my price range. I didn't have any money. Literally I didn't know if I was going to get any help from anyone the whole way and expected to make it to New York.

"Sounds nice. Have you been on the trail that long?"

"Last year I went about 1,000 miles but my legs gave out in New Hampshire," he said.

"Where are you from?"

"Vermont."

"Interesting. You don't think your legs will give out again?"

"I'll stop by to see the wife, but I'm going slower this year than I went last year."

"Do you know which way the trail is?" He asked.

I looked at my driver.

"Yeah, it's jers't cut up past the freeway, walk along it and you will turn into the Appalachian." He pointed.

"Well, thanks for the lift." I gave him a hug.

"Alrighty, you be safe now."

Chapter 7

Cars raced past me at high speeds as I slowly made my journey North into the sunset. I looked forward after what seemed like miles. There was a tunnel coming up, which had not been mentioned so I must've missed the trail. This was my first experience with the very valuable lesson of backtracking. Aiden, that know it all hippy who lived on a couch talked all wisely about how he never went backwards. I realized that if I was going to succeed, I had to be less stubborn than that, so I sucked it up. A few miles back along the highway, eventually I took a turn into woods. At the first sight of flat land I dropped my backpack and knew that that was as far as my legs could carry me for the day. I laid down for a minute, which turned into five, and then ten minutes from extreme exhaustion.

"Hey." A woman called.

"Hey." She looked at everything scattered all around the small campsite.

"Are you a section hiker?" She asked.

"I'm hiking to New York."

"Oh." She looked at me with concern about how unorganized I was.

"But this is my first day." Further proving that I was not much of a hiker.

"I have a map, it might help you," she said.

She was wearing some grey yoga pants, and she was at least a few years older than me. I've always been a rather hormonal boy growing up, but I've grown out of falling for every woman I meet. Then again, I had imagined about meeting companions on the trail, and being that I was available at the moment, I was blindly excited to look at the map with this woman.

"We are here," she pointed at the beginning of the map. "The next town is Erwin, Tennessee. The next shelter is about 15 miles from here."

I was sure that I was camping right where I was when I heard that.

"How far are you going to go tonight?" I asked in a not creepy way.

"Well, it's a full moon tonight so I am going to probably night hike for a while."

"Cool, I never thought about night hiking before."

"Do you have a map on you, or the book?" She asked me.

"No."

"Well, here, take a picture of the map, it will help you."

"I think Erwin will be my next stop." I said as I took out my phone and took a photo.

"That's about 30 miles away."

"I went more than that today." I exhaled.

She looked at me so confused. "Who are you?"

"Me? Nobody. Who are you?"

"They call me Horizon. Do you need any water or anything?"

"I'm fine, maybe I'll see you up the trail," I said

She kind of looked at everything and shrugged like, alright.

"I hope so." At the time I thought she said that because she liked me, but I now know it was because she was very worried about the state of my situation and how everything looked. After she left, I kept going through my backpack, took out all the clothes, the wires, began a fire and pitched the tent. I ate the cold Thai food from the night before. Fire gives a sense of security with its movement. It was my home for the night. It showed that I had strength within what I was doing and was capable of what I believed in. You know when you are home alone, and all the lights are off and you are lying in your bed and everything is dark and silent? Your brain begins to create sounds and the next thing you know you are checking under your bed and checking that everything is locked again, unless you own a cat.

In the middle of the darkness of night, I walked about 200 yards into the deep woods getting slapped in the face by branches. Finally, I found a good tree, which would be suitable to hang a bear bag. It took me about twenty minutes to get my backpack on a branch high enough away from bears. It was horrible and this was my life. All these stupid new little exercises I had to do to survive and none of them were fun. I was on a strict regimen: eat as little as possible, go as far as you can, sleep for the shortest amount of time, diet. Anything else could be lethal.

After I finished, I realized that my bag was about three maybe four feet off the ground, but I was too exhausted to do anything about it. If a bear or a raccoon gets into it, I'll just starve to death I thought. I mustered through the leaves and thick branches back to my campground. My fire was winding down, so I added just a little bit more to it and got into my tent. The tent was not large enough for my legs to extend the full length and have my backpack in it at the same time. It got colder as time passed. I wore my flannel pajama pants underneath my jeans and my sweater on for warmth. I began to shiver since the blanket I packed was not enough to keep me warm. I grabbed my full winter jacket and put it on which helped a little bit though the hairs on my legs were still erect.

I was exhausted and scared of every sound I heard. Only 1 in 4 make it through the Appalachian Trail, everyone else quits or dies. It was a very windy night. I heard the wind push and breeze against my tent. I began making up horror stories in my head about how some crazy crackhead would come and cut my throat and loot my box of cheerios. You know when you don't really fall asleep, but you dream. That was what my first night was like. I imagined bears next to my tent and I awoke screaming.

In the midst of the night I heard too much noise going on down by where my bear bag was, so I grabbed my knife and went out into the woods. It was pretty far away so I began not knowing where I was going. The fire was out. I thought I should just get back to camp and, in my tent, and I would be safe from my thoughts. On my way back, I walked into my hung backpack. The woods were making me crazy. I ran back to my tent, bundled up the best I could and prayed for morning.

"I'M ALIVE!" I chanted to the morning sun. Ow, ouch, oh lord. My legs felt like rubber as I got out of my tent. Each step I took made me look like I was holding in a massive dump. No, my gluteus was just sore from picking up and putting down my backpack so many times in a squat formation. I took a breather as a hiker passed me and I got to work as quickly as I could. Everything was in my backpack in an hour or less. I had to refrain from any sudden movements.

I had a smooshed bagel for breakfast with nothing on it and an apple. It wasn't that bad. As I said, with college there is such an extreme amount of excess with everything that nothing had any worth. This was delicious. When you have so little, the smallest things feel the most extraordinary. I was thankful for once in my life. I can be pretty high maintenance. Although it had only been one night, and I don't think many people could do what I was doing. That is a challenge. Everything had to be put back into the backpack in the right order or else everything wouldn't fit. I wore the same clothes as the day before, but the shirt was still wet from sweat and was already starting to have a stench.

Finally, everything was put together compactly, and the campsite looked exactly the way it did when I came up to it except for a small circle of ash where the fire used to be. I looked at the backpack and the pain in my legs made me worry. I couldn't just sit around for a few days to let the torn muscles heal. I threw the backpack over my shoulder and when I did, it was like everything fell into place. I was beginning to get adjusted to the weight. I'm not squeamish of spiders but I took about ten steps looked down and there was the wildest looking centipede I had ever seen in my whole life. It was thick, had orange legs, and was crawling right towards me. That horrible feeling of spoiled milk running through my body occurred and as I looked at it, I thought all about the other creatures I would be seeing on this trip. Not the big bears, mountain lions or coyotes, but the spiders, the snakes, insects that could terrorize a man half to death if they got into his tent. Ghosts.

Luckily, I didn't have to think about going to bed for a long time now. I had just gotten up, sleeping was the last thing on my mind, I could possibly get all the way to Erwin if I moved fast enough. It was only about 8 o'clock in the morning. Walking past another couple getting up, there was a stream. I went over to the water source next to a small pond. Filling up two water bottles took me about a half hour. I didn't make small talk with the couple while they were making breakfast to not come off as suspicious or intrusive. I finished up, told them to enjoy breakfast, and kept going. Woods, woods, woods. So pretty, but then I came upon a beautiful opening from the trees and looked out at the gorgeous sight of a mountainous range. I got into every college that I applied to, but the reason why I chose to go to school in North Carolina was because the Appalachian Mountains are the oldest on the planet and I believed that if I was going to start my life anywhere, I wanted to do it where my spirit would align with a previous physical manifestation.

I looked out at the magnificent beauty ahead of me. It made the already grandiose idea in my mind look so much more romantic. Going through and over mountains, what an adventure. I was impressed with the amount of people that I passed in such a short time. First, I talked to a bearded guy who was on a section trying to complete his second "thru hike," which would mean his second completion of the entire Appalachian trail of 2,100 miles. Next, I met Teddy, an eighteen-year-old on a thru hike. Age is but a number, but that is pretty young to be doing something like this. He had long red hair, a slim frame and wore waterproof flannel wear. He had the discipline and the right attitude. We took the time to talk to each other. We were both interested in each other like two dogs.

I guess I expected to see a few people along the way, but I assumed that the forest was much less populated than cities. It made me smile and feel like I had a better chance. I looked back at my own backpack, which was a horrible load to carry. So many clothes I cared about. I knew that there were things I should let go of, but I was so attached to everything I brought. I couldn't really just let anything go. I picked it all up and buckled the belt that was meant to distort the weight onto my hips and looked out again at what lay ahead of me. There were some clouds in the sky but nothing I was worried about. I opened my knife and looked at the compass and saw the trail heading North.

It looked like there was going to be some upward climbs from where I was standing. I wasn't too worried. I looked at my phone currently at about half charge and revised the pictures of the map. The altitude changes in the map showed indeed, there was climb ahead of me. The first thing I learned on this journey was that a lot of things are going to happen that are outside of your control, and are things that you can't really change, and but all of that forces you to learn how to change.

Whatever situation you get yourself into or whatever life throws at you, that is your new situation. You have to adapt to make it better. Accept that there is a solution that may be different than the one you initially intended. That is the only way you are going to succeed and survive on this journey. Trees and leaves were everywhere surrounding me. It was a cleansing experience. There were times that I didn't know which way to go. You just pick one and hope for the best, which is another life lesson.

I was getting antsy. I get that way if it's been a bit since I'd smoked anything. North Carolina tobacco comes cheap. Nothing serious, I knew it would pass in no more than a few days, but I was not smoking anything on this trip, so help me God. I didn't want to die out here. Anyway, I thought I would stop to eat the next chance I got. However, the trail just kept going in its thin winding way. I began to get very tired and sweaty, finally I gave up and just sat down in the middle of the trail. I unzipped the bottom of my backpack where I kept all the food. Opened my pack and ate my other creamy, wet sandwich. Although it was mushy, the meat still tasted refreshing and as though it was going to give me the strength to move on. As I sat there reflecting in the silence, who else but Dr. Fix-it come to see me in my apparent state of distress.

"How are you doing, fellow?" He waltzed up.

"I'm alright."

"You look exhausted." It wasn't a compliment.

I continued to eat my excuse of a sandwich.

"So, it's your first day on the trail?" He knelt down encouragingly.

"Second day travelling. First day on the trail." I gulped.

"And you are carrying all of that?" He looked over at my backpack.

"Yeah."

"Do you know how much it weighs?"

"No."

"Well, I hate to tell you, but you are carrying far too much. You ain't going to make it to New York with all that on your back." Classic Dr. Fix-it.

"I think I'll be alright," I agreed but also knew I didn't have much that I felt like I could let go of.

"If you says so. I know what I'm talking about. Your legs will give out!"

The thought was not a comfortable one, and my legs were in agony.

"Well what should I get rid of?" I asked.

"Look at the size of your blade. It's unreasonably big."

He reached into his pocket and pulled out a blade the size of a nail file.

"The only thing I've used this blade for is cutting thread off my clothes, otherwise, a knife just ain't that useful."

Then a Hiker with long black hair came up to us.

"What's your trail name fellow?" Dr. Fix-it asked.

"Uh, my name is just Chris. Never got a trail name. You guys thru hikers?"

"Sort of. I'm going to New York." I answered pompously.

"Where'd you guys get on?" Chris asked.

"Georgia," Dr. Fix-it said.

"The last highway," I said.

"Oh, cool man. Do you guys know if it's supposed to rain?"

"Nope, sorry man."

"I don't either." Dr. Fix-it answered.

"Listen man, have you seen any bears?" I asked Chris to settle this knife situation.

I saw one once, in the Smokies. We were at camp and I was putting everything in the sun to dry after a bad storm. It got below freezing, snow almost every day."

Two horrible things to hear about in one question.

"Anyway, the bear sort of eyed me and I shook my tent, you know, to scare him off and he got the message and backed off, but he stuck around the campsite for a while," he responded, "listen guys I'm going to go up ahead." He began to hike and left me with Dr. Fix-it again.

"Now, I don't know why you are out here lad, that's none of my business. I personally am out here to *run away*."

"I'm out here because of -."

"Eph, That's no business of mine. I get out here to hide from the real world. It's not a place I find contentment. It makes me very anxious. All I am telling you is that if you want to survive and make it to New York you are going to have to let go of something. How many Pushups can you do?"

"About a hundred."

"Now imagine you have twenty pounds on your back. How about then?"

"Fifty."

"That's right. Imagine that walking to New York is a hundred pushups. You ain't going to do it with twenty pounds on your back."

I sipped my root beer.

"Look at your flashlight. A heavy flashlight is a pound just on its own. How far do you really think you are going to go in the dark?"

"I just didn't know when I left."

"Well, what I know is that when you left you were afraid that you were going to go a long while. That tells me that you had fear in the back of your mind."

Then he said something that has stuck with me.

"The more you take with you, the more fear you have."

I looked at my backpack, and from the sights of it I was horrified to go on this trip.

"Listen, a lot of the hostels out here will do work for stay. Why don't you just go to one and work there for a while, hideout, get back on your feet and go back home."

After all of his wise advice, I had never heard something so stupid.

"Oh! I'm going to New York. I don't care if I die doing it. I'll do a hundred push-ups with a hundred pounds on my back if I have to."

"Haha, alright. Just don't make yourself work harder than you have to. Trust me, there is a lot you could let go of."

He stood up, said goodbye and walked up towards the top of the next mountain. My lousy sandwich had been long consumed along with one of those small bags of Fritos. I thought about how that little bit of weight had been taken off. I grabbed my backpack and threw it on my shoulders. There was a sheering pain in my shoulders, like I had relocated a muscle or something. I walked on for about a mile until I literally said out loud, "That's it!" I opened the backpack up and looked through to see if there was anything that I could let go of. I began to unload all of my clothes in the middle of the trail, getting them all muddy and covered in leaves. I thought good and hard. There was one t-shirt and one pair of underwear that I was willing to part with.

My grandmother is a bit of a hoarder. Nothing that would get us on television or anything, but she has an attic full of antiques. I inherited this gene. I am very sentimental about even the smallest of things. Letting go of something as stupid as a t-shirt or a pair of underwear took a lot out of me. Then I looked at my pillow. It weighed about half a pound. I thought that I would just keep the pillowcase and stuff it with my clothing which could act as a pillow and save me a little bit of weight. I let go.

Chapter 8

At this time, I was still just a kid without a home, lost somewhere in the woods with a compass and a dream. I thought about what I would do in New York. Possibly apply to art school, but nothing was really waiting there for me. I felt like I was beginning to get trapped in a lifestyle that I didn't know if I wanted to be a part of. Any institution can be a cage, but the only confinement that really matters is the one inside our head.

College is bound to be filled with multi-colored haired introverts, and artists who can liberate themselves all they want in that liberal habitat. We are still all just birds in a cage. Myself included. I felt like my perspective was getting smaller and smaller in that dirty shithole hearing people fuck, under and next to me every night while I would calmly read for as long as I could acquiesce. Say what you will, caged birds are tormented safely.

I looked up at this blasphemous hill. I shoved my boot into the ground and felt each muscle in my leg as I carried the weight up about a thousand feet. By the time I got to the top I heard a bell ringing from behind me. I thought I was going mad, but I looked behind me and I saw an older couple casually walking up without any backpacks. The older man had a moustache and the woman was wearing pink and had a nice braided greying ponytail and was jingling a bear bell.

I was covered in sweat and I wanted to say hello, but they could tell I was in a bit of distress.

"Do you need some water," the old man investigated.

"No, I'm stupendous. I just have to carry a lot up the hill."

"Oh, where are you going?" the woman chimed in.

"Well, I'm going to New York without a dime on me."

I had about a dime on me.

"Oh well, that sounds impressive."

"Let's walk with him for a while."

They told me that they thought the Balds were the most beautiful portion of the Appalachian Trail. I just kept hearing them say balls. There was a big ball and a little ball, and I was cracking up just a bit to myself. Eventually, they went ahead of me because I was obviously moving at a much slower pace due to my weight. As they passed, they gave me about sixteen dollars, which felt like enough to get me anywhere at the time.

I felt like rejoicing. I felt like I was king of the world. I began to chant at the top of the mountain in the wind. I had never really looked at the beauty of this country. Feeling infinite in nature, I could see for miles and miles and miles. I believed this whole trip was going to be a breeze. I could see the way I was supposed to go. God, it looked gorgeous. But this, this was something else. I was blessed just with the sight of what was yet to come. Green pastures, and forests for me to live *among* for the next month.

To have the nerve to walk out of your dorm without an idea of what would come and then to see the most beautiful sight you have ever seen two days after relished within. This was when I saw an awful snake slither through the woods right past me. I swear I ran. The weight was no problem then. It was 100 times worse than seeing that centipede. My whole body was electrified. I thought if there was one snake there was likely to be more lurking under the leaves so, I didn't want to take any chance. I ran until I was out of breath. I came across another hiker sitting off to the side by a stream. I thought it was a perfect time to get some water. I still didn't know how to use filter system correctly, so it took about a half hour. I looked over and this kid wasn't looking so good.

He looked a little green.

"Hey man, you alright?"

"I'm feeling pretty sick," he said.

"What's wrong?"

"Just a stomach ache along with a headache. I think there is a shelter up ahead."

"How far did you go today?" I asked
"About a mile."
The idea of only going that far in a day scared me. The way that I calculated it was that if I went about twenty miles a day, I would get there in a little bit over a month. I had never had one night of camping alone let alone a month.
"How long have you been out here?" I asked.
"A month."
"Oh god, are you doing the whole trail?"
"Yeah, I took off a semester from Southern Michigan to do the whole thing. They say it takes about seven months."
"How far have you gone?" I asked.
"I think this is mile 329."
"And it took you a month to go that far?"
He nodded his head. Google maps said NYC was about 798 miles away or some ungodly number, so at his rate it was going to take me two months, which was twice as long as I had bargained for.
"Do you smoke weed?" I asked, trying to figure out why it took him so long to get such a short distance.
"Yeah."
"Doesn't it make you tired?" I asked.
"You smoke it before bed."
Just then a burly man walked up.
"You guys getting some water?"
He looked tough and a little worn.
"What are y'all trail names? I'm Raccoon," he said, though his hair was reddish.
"Sonic." the sickly boy said.
"I don't have one," I said.
"I think there is another stream about half a mile up, so I'll just refill there. It was nice to meet y'all," and like that he was on his way.
I was still refilling my water since technically I was doing it wrong.
"Have you ever been scared on the trail?" I asked.
"One time. I heard Coyotes and they were pretty close to me while I was sleeping."
"Were you in a tent?"

"Eno."

"Oh, nice, my tent is a little heavy, but it does the trick."

"I think I'm just going to go to the shelter up ahead. I don't think I am going to make it to Erwin." He said in a discouraging tone.

"Yeah, man. I don't know. You gotta get some sleep."

I left him feeling a little bad. I guessed he would be fine since he made it this far, but after I went about 200 feet I turned back around and got him.

"Hey man, listen. Let's just go together. You're making me worried."

"Ah, thanks man. Yeah, I guess I was just about ready to go anyways."

He picked up his things and we walked together. We didn't talk much, I know that feeling when you are sick and nauseous and the last thing you want is to engage in conversation you don't care about, it didn't really matter. I've seen trees and dirt my whole life, but this was unlike anything I had ever seen before. I was astonished. Every step I took I just looked around in awe. The land looked like the skin of a lion. The trees jutted out in stretching branches as if they had dried up through a scarcity of nutrient. Perhaps I hadn't been accustomed to the grace of nature in its peaceful power, and it was overpowering.

Maybe it was just nice to walk with someone, and made the journey feel less alone in its own way. Physically it was gorgeous and my favorite part of the trail, but there are plenty of parts I enjoyed a lot more than this half-mile walk. I was probably unappreciative and just thought it looked like some dried up hilly land at the time, but now I couldn't imagine America without this iconic dry patch.

We walked up to a tiny little blue shack. It was nothing special but looked like a little home. It felt like a cabin I slept in at camp, but without one wall. Sonic stumbled over to it, threw his backpack on the floor pulled out his sleeping bag and fell asleep. It was a nice but strange feeling. I had nothing to do. I didn't need to pitch a tent. I unrolled my yoga mat and laid back. I was exhausted, and just closed my eyes for a moment, and I fell asleep for about an hour.

"Ello, mate, didn't mean to wake you"

"Oh, you're fine, just try not to wake him, he seems sick." I awoke detached.

"Oh goodness, I hope he'll be fine? Do you know what he's got?"

"Stomach problems."

He introduced himself using his trail name, "iPod." and pulled out a cigarette. I wanted one but restrained. As he lit the end of his tobacco stick it reminded me that I needed to make a fire and cook dinner. I looked at my phone and it was basically dead, so I went through my bag and found the solar charger and laid it out in the setting sun and plugged it into my phone. I got up and looked around for sticks. The place was covered in wood chips, which are useful, along with leaves, which are a great start, but nothing big enough for me to cook off of.

I went down the path and found a few logs and I also found a smaller shelter. It was a toilet, or a luxury in my case. I began to create a small fire, even though I may have been able to survive on raw foods like nuts and such, I was glad I had the ability to cook. I looked through my food supply. I grabbed out a ramen. The packaging had been damaged. I filled up my small pot with water and let the fire begin to sizzle down to embers. The embers are the hottest part of the fire and optimal for cooking. My water boiled and I took the ramen out of the styrofoam container and into my pot. It was as though it was meant for that exact amount of ramen. While I was doing this, iPod and Sonic got out their pocket stoves and began to boil their water.

We sat together at a bench while I slurped my noodles.

"Earwin is only 16 miles away," iPod said with an accent.

They pulled out their booklets.

"Isn't there a hostel as well?" Sonic replied.

"Yeah."

"Uncle Jeff's Hostel." iPod said.

Sonic started rolling a joint and lit it. "You want

any?" he asked.

Apart from the fact that he was sick, I really didn't need that as an additional challenge on the trip. Anyone who smokes weed will understand it is a great way to calm yourself down. I just didn't feel safe enough to get stoned at the moment. One wrong puff could land me in the wrong place, without any food, lost or dead.

"Nah, I'm good."

They went on smoking and a chirpy fellow came through the camp. He had a long mustache, looked about twenty or so and walked very simply and quietly into the shelter.

"How old are you, iPod?" I asked.

"I'm thirty-seven"

"How long have you been smoking?"

"I calmed down around the time I was twenty-seven."

"Smells good." The mustached fellow said with a smile taking the joint.

"Have you eaten?" Sonic asked him.

"I ate up on the Balds, by the view."

There I sat with three stoned gentlemen, getting more anxious by the second and probably thinking about weirder things than all of them. I wanted to keep the conversation light as possible.

"Why are you doing this?" I asked iPod.

"Why?"

"Yeah, why? I met a guy on the trail who said he was running away." I said.

They all looked at me for a moment.

"Not literally running away. Ya know, just getting away from it all."

"I went on my first hike about three years ago and decided to do it again. My visa is up in August though." iPod said.

"I'm a Youtuber." Said the moustache guy.

"Really?"

"Yeah, I just film hiking stuff and people seem to like it."

"How many subscribers do you have?"

"I stopped keeping count a while ago, but something like 6,000."

"Damn. It's cool to meet a Youtuber."

"I've been doing it for 3 years now."

"Oh, I made some videos last fall, but really I just make the videos because I enjoy watching them and think it will be fun to look back at someday" I said.

"Are you going to the hostel?" iPod asked.

"How much is it to stay?"

They looked at each other.

"About twenty dollars or so." iPod said.

"That's a little out of my price range, guys" I shook my head.

"How much did you leave with?"

"Not much."

"Well guys, I'm going to get some sleep." The mustached fellow said abruptly. "Good luck." He said to me.

I had faith, but luck was a part of it too.

"Goodnight."

"Night mate." iPod waved.

Sonic went in after that, and eventually iPod did too. I sat by the fire, scared by their words of doubt. A mohawked man emerged onto the campgrounds stomping.

"Is that yer fire?" He asked

"Well, I built it, but you can use it."

He didn't respond and unloaded everything he had and pulling out an assortment of meats and cheeses, he pulled out a bottle of whiskey and began to take big sips of it. I just watched in awe like, is this guy for real? How is he going to get anywhere if he's going to wake up, eat cheese and spoiled meats making him shit and who is going to trust him with a hairdo like that. I did what anybody would do in this situation.

"Can I have some cheese?" I asked.

"Yeah sure. Her ya go," and he cut me off a slice of pepper jack.

It was delicious, a little warm and squishy but warmed my soul with the flavor. He began to cook a cheese stew mixed with the meats. It looked very unhealthy but delicious as hell. He pulled out a cigarette and began to smoke it, and that's when I called it quits. I liked the man, but there was no doubt in my mind he was on a suicide mission or something because nobody can just neglect their body like that and expect to get anywhere.

I went to go hang my bear bag since there were clasps to hang them. I said goodnight kindly and walked into the shelter. The shelter had a tin roof and I laid in it confused, worried, and happy all at the same time. The traveler who was out with his cheese and meat stew bundled everything he had back into his backpack and walked off, not a minute later it began to pour down rain. I was worried about him but truly impressed by the gritty nature of this man. I wasn't sure if he was prepared to go all night hiking drunk in the middle of a storm.

Alone in the woods
What a terrible excuse
To do what you love
And be who you are
If only I had
A guitar

Chapter 9

The rain did not sound calming on the tin roof. Every single drop could be felt figuratively rippling on my skin. My food was all just hanging out in the rain, so I grabbed it out of the wet woods and ran back into the shelter with it. I was sorry to have put everyone in jeopardy if a hungry bear came onto the site. However, a bear did not come through the night. It did get colder as usual and I put on all the layers I had. My muscles didn't just hurt, they felt as though something was just cutting through my skin. It was hard to fall asleep, but I was ready to dream.

I had a dream that night about being at party. I saw Paris dancing and then asking me to dance. I didn't understand why she would want to dance with me with all the other attractive men available, and declined out of self doubt. I awoke and stretched my body from head to toe. I thought since it was still raining, we would all sleep in, but I was mistaken.

Within one minute we were ready and leaving camp. I needed to shit, but I came to the horrible realization I hadn't packed any toilet paper. I tried to disguise or not think about my situation by eating breakfast quickly. It was another Apple. Sure enough iPod had to use the "loo" and I let him know that I had forgotten to pack toilet paper with me and he just handed off the roll.

I didn't know how quickly I could travel compared to them, so I thought I would get going. The trees took care of most of the light morning rain. The woods were awe-inspiring. Overgrown roots and some small delicate blue ivy, and stringent plants of all kinds were around in the morning haze. I could hold them in my hand and smell their fragrance. I didn't really want to play with anything being that they could be poisonous. I checked my compass and saw that I was heading North West. I went down some hills that had streams and waterfalls along it. Beyond a line of trees due North there was no sun behind the fog.

I stopped for water and Sonic caught up. He advised me to take it easy for a while so my muscles can adjust to everything. I took his words with care, but I was on a schedule of sorts.

"Are you not going to, you know, 'enjoy yourself' the whole time you are out here?" He asked.

"To be honest enjoying myself was not really something I expected to do. I thought this would be a grueling experience that would just make me thankful enough to stay alive."

"That's kind of sad, man."

"And are you happy?" I retorted.

"Out here, I can finally say I am."

"Well, let me get adjusted."

"You just got to lighten up man, you are out here. We have a saying, "the trail provides." You might not have any money, but you are going to be fine, try to have a little fun."

"I'll take note of that, maybe next time." I wobbled stubbornly.

"I mean people out here are usually doing that sort of thing every night."

I was still in a little bit of disbelief. How could these people survive? Isn't the Appalachian Trail known as a dangerous place?

"You take acid?" he asked me.

"Good lord."

"Well if you get the chance out here, take it."

I suggest LSD if you haven't tried it. It won't necessarily make you successful, but it'll *show* you what you need to do in order to be successful. Just my two cents, but there was no way in hell I was taking it out here. I'm sure the visuals would have been beautiful, but one wrong blink of the eye and I could quite literally end up in a different state.

"Have any good stories?" I asked.

"Yeah, I was caught in the Smokies during a snowstorm with my albino friend and his girlfriend we went into a shelter around noon. We all took it then, and what a mind-blowing experience. To be five thousand feet up, getting hit in the face with snow, hundreds of miles away from home, it was just beautifully bizarre."

"I'll keep that in mind."

I don't really mess around with the stuff anymore. It takes the part of your brain that has the ability to reason and suffocates it so anything becomes possible. This can be good if you have low self-esteem and want to reassure yourself that you are indeed capable of whatever you are after. However, it is not a stable lifestyle to live off of for multiple months at a time. And once, an idea became so real, so beautiful, that it had to be true. Everyday built off the next as I was going slowly insane. I thought everything had to happen in a specific objective way, but really we become just our thoughts.

We caught up to iPod who was taking a cigarette break, so I ate another apple and the rain had calmed. We all left at different times this morning, but I think I was the first to leave and within two miles they both got in front of me, and quickly went ahead. I was walking slowly compared to these seasoned hikers, plus they had trekking poles.

I came across pavement for the first time in two days. I didn't know what I should do. The thought was cooling. The trail seemed to be the best option for me, so I stayed on it. Eventually, I began to smell pretty bad, so I thought it was a perfect time to shower.

I dipped my toes in and prayed that nobody would walk past, but then again, I didn't really care. I'm very comfortable in the nude. I scrubbed all the stank off me and afterwards I smelled like milk and tulip honey. I worried smelling so good would attract bears. I didn't worry about it too long, I felt almost too good. I sat back and ate a few granola bars for lunch after washing my hands. Even though it wasn't much, I was fresh, and I was ready to go. As I was looking through my bag, I realized everything was a little bit damp. My computer was in a trash bag, but everything else had been relatively exposed. I had a thin poncho stashed away. I put it on and tried to stretch it over my backpack.

Another mile down the trail and I saw a guy just breaking down his campsite. It was around eleven o'clock, not an unreasonable hour to wake up, but it wasn't too much to think that people got up relatively early around these parts.

"Can I approach?" I asked him.

"Yeah, sure man."

"Oh, I know you." I said.

"Oh yeah. Sorry, I'm bad with names."

"You passed me when I was talking with Dr. Fix-it."

"Chris." He was a kind looking fellow with sullen eyes. He had long brown hair and looked to be in his mid to late thirties.

"Nice, man."

"Yeah, I thought I would stay in my tent to let the rain pass us by."

"I felt that too. I wanted to sleep in, but I thought if I did, I might die. Do you know how far we are from Erwin?"

"Let me check my map." He said pulling one out.

"Says here we are about 8 miles away."

"Interesting." I pondered for a moment.

"My phone has been dead for the past two days, so I am trying to get there today."

"Nice man, me too. You wanna hike together?" I offered taking on his spiritual responsibility as my equal at that moment in time.

"Yeah forsure, I was just about finished with packing up."

He took out something that was made for his backpack to prevent rain from getting in and pulled it over his bag.

As we began walking, it wasn't long before we got to know each other.

"How old are you man?" I asked

"I'm getting up there," he said, seemingly distant having just woken up. Where did you get on?"

"I got on at the highway a ways back." I chirped.

"Oh, by Hot Springs?"

"Possibly." I shrugged.

"Yeah, what a nice town I tell ya."

"You liked it?"

"You know. I could really see myself spending the rest of my life there."

When he said this, I was a little skeptical. What about the great goliath that everybody wants to be a part of, why would you want to settle for somewhere in the middle of nowhere?

"I have never met people who have treated me kinder in my whole life. There was a blues festival, and I was sitting at a bar, and this girl comes up to me. Ya know, we get to talking, she lives there and turns out her brother in is one of the bands playing."

"No way."

"She's staying at the hotel and says she wants to put me up." He went on.

"Did you?" I asked impulsively.

"No, I probably could've, but I didn't do anything. I didn't want to change us having such a good time or add to it. But I did get her number. My friends think I'm crazy, but I'm sort of giving up women."

I smirked and seemed unaware of any response.

"Hmmm, I feel that, but hey you should text her man. Don't give up." I offered.

"Yeah, I have been texting her, but my phone has been dead for the last two days."

"Ah damn, she probably thinks you're dead."

"She was just a really cool person, and at my age it's just hard to meet those people. I felt like we genuinely had a connection."

"I know the feeling."

"I just sort of want to go back sometime." He finished his thought.

"Do it, you're still young. How old are you?"

"Thirty-Five."

"You are fine my man. Add a little pen pal to your journey, finish up this trail and then maybe...maybe. If you guys are still talking, give her a visit at the end."

"Hahaha, I think I will do something sort of like that."

We walked a few more feet.

"What's your story man?" He asked.

"Oh Lord. That's a bit of a loaded question, man."

"Hey, all bets are off on the AT."

"No, it's fine, it might be healthy to get some of it out. I guess, I'm sort of caught up with this triangle of three girls I'm still in love with. A redhead was my first love. She had seen the world and was embarrassingly clumsy. The first feelings of sharp emotion you feel in your heart longing for someone for the first time, and believing anything is possible together. I realized with her just how innocent and impatient love is."

"Sounds lovely."

"She really was."

"What happened?"

"Well, I tried LSD. My hormones thought I figured everything out in the world, and everything I needed to do in the world. I got dressed up in a suit and wanted to go to a prom party to get laid and broke up with her. Biggest regret of my life. I ended up at some dinner party with the richest kid in town. I was just there inconspicuously on acid in suit and a tie-dyed headband. I barely knew the guy. If I got one thing out of the whole thing, he said to me, and I'll never forget, "Jack Wright, don't ever let anyone tell you you're not a badass motherfucker," and to this day that has given me the confidence to be whoever I am."

"What about the other ones?"

"Well, Paris, has been my girlfriend on and off for the past two years in college. She is beautiful, blonde, smarter and richer than me. I often feel ashamed to be who I am around her. It's complex, because she helps me be the best version of myself."

"Listen man, I was married to a blonde that was richer than me."

"What happened?" I asked.

"She ended up cheating on me with her boss."

"Oh man."

I don't think she had ever cheated on me until that point, but I started to believe it. The thought hurt but lying is what tears me apart. At the end of the day if someone still accepts me for who I am, who am I to tell you how to tell them how to live their life.

I continued, "I just feel like I come from a different universe than her sometimes. I'm a little bit out of place anywhere though. I like her family, or I respect them, but I just feel like some lower-class embarrassment. Trust me, I know some pretty trashy wealthy people that I often think of myself as better than, but her folks were astute, and I often felt stupid. Unfiltered or like I was the butt of some joke. A part of me resents their lifestyle and the other part of me really wanted to be a part of it."

"You can't lie to yourself like that man. I did that for ten years, it will kill you."

"I don't know if I'm lying or not anymore. I do love her. I'll admit, I was in love with someone else when I met her, but she has been there for me through a lot and there is something very valuable in that."

"I had been through a lot with my wife, but all of that was meaningless once the truth came out." He sounded indistinctly sour.

"Did you love your wife when you got married?"

"I did man."

"Did you ever cheat on her?"

"I didn't."

"Damn."

"Well, what happened with the blonde?"

"We actually sort of recently broke up. She said she was lying to herself about the fact that she wanted to be with me and thought of me as part of her past. We've broken up before, many times, I don't know if I should put her behind me or if I'm just doing this to win her back."

"Put it behind you, man."

"Anyways, the brunette." I smiled,

"I like the brunette already."

"Everyone likes her. She was my best friend once. We shared a locker together one year. She is just the only person who I actually feel like a deep connection with. I can't describe it, but life just feels like a big art project I just want to create with her. I can't really explain it. Just weird things have happpened man, timing things. "

"Timing things?" He asked.

"Like, what I would call God. You wouldn't believe me if I told you the *coincidences* that have occurred."

"Oh, I get it."

"Yeah, well I started developing feelings for her around the end of sophomore year. But slowly, she became less of a person I knew and more of a memory I was trying to recreate."

"Then what?"

"Then, like I am known for, I fucked it up. Like really, really, really badly. I had too much pride to ask her out on a date, because I didn't have a car, and one time all my friends forced me to call her and I didn't follow through, it was bad. The harder I tried the less I could do." I said, wanting to slap myself.

"Why don't or didn't you just talk to her?"

"Dude, I am a pretty confident person, literally people don't make me nervous because I could give a shit about what they think of me, but it's bad in front of her, man."

"It's bad?"

"Yeah, I can't even speak. My hands start shaking and I get choked up. Everything goes right out the window and I go after it all. If you saw her, you'd understand."

"I feel you, man."

"I don't think she would ever want to talk to me again, after what I did."

"You are going to meet a hundred girls just like her."

"Yeah, but they aren't her. It doesn't matter. This condition is not special. Plenty of guys have a girl that gets away."

"I hate to tell you man, but when you get older, all this stuff doesn't go away."

"You want to know at least something *funny* about all this?"

"What?"

"Well, the brunette has gone blonde and the blonde's hair has gotten much darker the longer I've known her."

"Ha."

"Eventually, I saw that I was just neglecting a person who did love me, at some point. The worst thing you can do to someone you love is make them into something they are not. Learn to love someone for what they aren't instead of what you think they are."

"Don't just give up, man. It sounds like you really have a thing for her."

"You gave up on women."

"That's after years of betrayal and lying and I'm just taking a break."

"I need a break. I'd rather be dead. I just don't have the balls, but I might as well look like I'm trying."

"It's going to be alright"

"I know, man. It always is, that's the problem."

We walked across an open area of trees, and saw a buff old man sitting in a shelter.

"Howdy," the old man said.

We nodded our heads to him.

"Gonna watch the storm come in," he chuckled kindly.

"We're going to make it to Erwin. Only about two hours away." Chris said.

"Is it uphill?" I asked, getting tired.

"Only the first half of it." The old man laughed.

"So, you're just trying to get to New York? What are you going to do there?" Chris asked as we maneuvered through the tropical landscape.

"I don't really care. I could be the best damn actor this world has ever seen and never get on stage. I dance alone. Along city streets and under the invisible stars looking back at me like an audience. I sing, for the hearts of stray cats."

"I like you, kid."

We went ahead as the sky began to get greyer and greyer. I was afraid. If there was one thing I was worried about on this trip it was rain. I took out the trash bag and put it over my bag covering everything inside. It did a poor job, but I thought it would do something. We began to get going and not soon after it began to pour. It wasn't a light rain either. It was a cold, thunderous rain. I wish I had my winter coat, but it was at the bottom of my pack and wasn't even really waterproof, it just would have been nice for the warmth.

I kept going, through it. Eventually all of my clothes were soaked to the core. I imagined how long this trip was going to take. In a month I wouldn't even remember this rainstorm. That pain is only momentary. My boots felt so wet like an uncomfortable agony.

"In a week this won't even matter." I looked out over the storm and my eyes began to play tricks on me. It was not a mirage, but the scene began to look further away and bigger. I kept heading deeper through the thick woods, the storm began to get more aggressive. I heard a loud rough unexposed crack, as though the forest was coming down somewhere not too far off. The plants began to form a tunnel and I felt safe within, but it was still soggy. I wanted to just stay in it, but I knew I couldn't. There was a chance of hypothermia, so I had to keep moving. I didn't know how long it was going to rain. I came across a huge tree blocking my path. It had fallen from a small hill and hung over a large cliff. The tree trunk was at a diagonal angle, so I had to climb over at its lower side hanging off the edge of a cliff.

I felt the weight of the backpack sort of swing me backwards and I grabbed onto that tree so fast I hurt my fingers against the bark. I was scared as all hell but got over the tree and kept going. I could see through some gaps in the trees that there were roads beginning to form among the abyss of trees.

"Hey man, do you know how far away Erwin is?"

"I would assume pretty damn close." Chris said over the rain.

"Ugh, this weather is horrible. Listen man, I didn't want to do this but I'm getting scared as hell out here. Do you think once we get into town, I could stick around with you for a little?"

"Oh man no problem. We could go to a bar. I might sound like an alcoholic, but I cannot wait to get a beer once we get back into this city."

"Nah man you're good. It's making me want to smoke some weed."

"You have weed?" He asked.

"Oh, yeah, just a little bit. I'm trying to avoid it."

"I get that, but if you let me have some, you'll be fine for the night." He said.

"I don't have any money to stay at the hostel."

"It's alright we can work something out."

The path began to wind more smoothly down into the town and eventually we came across a road. There was a big bridge that went outwards into the town.

"You think we should cross the bridge?" I asked.

"I dunno man. Let's look at the map. Look at that place, maybe we should go there. It looks like a bar."

"Alright man. We could give it a shot and look for directions once we get in there."

As we walked perpendicular to the river, there was a small wooden structure with tiki like assortments along it. It looked like a swell restaurant, but more than that, it just looked dry. I thought about how that would be a perfect dry space to sleep for the night from afar. We pulled up to the place. There was lively activity around and a group of people sitting at a table outside under a wooden roof. I didn't know where I was, but it was as if it had been dropped from heaven into the middle of nowhere. It was exactly the kind of place you would hope to see. It had a bunch of young people laughing and drinking beer eating food, playing cards, and playing music.

"This is the hostel. We're at Uncle Jeff's," Chris unloaded his gear.

Chapter 10

I didn't speak to anyone for the first hour. I had barely eaten anything all day, and I was freezing and a bit confused. I didn't understand what a hostel was. It seemed to sort of give off a communistic vibe and that is what I loved. It felt like I was at camp. On one of the tables outside, under an umbrella, there was a big bag of grapes with holes in it, fresh from the supermarket, and there was a nice bowl of trail mix. I was so starved that I snuck a few grapes.

I felt so awful doing it, until one of Uncle Jeff's goons said, "You can have as much as you like." He was a gruff chubby fellow, who wore a Harley Davidson shirt and had big sideburns.

The angels sang from the heavens. I brought them over to the table where everybody was sitting which was under a wooden structure and within two minutes all of the food was gone, mainly being eaten by yours truly. I wanted to make conversation, but my body was exhausted, and everybody just seemed so happy. I was still stuck on the idea that if I was going to accomplish all of this that I had made up in my mind, I had to keep my wits about me. These hikers, maybe fresh out of college, were downing beers like it was water.

They seemed like nice people, I just was not in a place to converse with anyone. I didn't have a plan. It was still raining hard. My best option for where I was going to sleep was under that bridge we nearly crossed, I just wasn't in a very happy mood. Chris came up behind me and put a beer in front of me. We made eye contact and he nodded like he was doing me a favor. I probably did need a drink but at the moment I was not impressed.

"Oh, here you can have this back." I said, handing back him the beer.

"Are you sure you don't want it?" He asked.

"Shuttle is leaving!" The side burned biker yelled.

Almost everyone at the table got up. Chris was about to go in the shuttle.

"Yeah, hey man, where are you going?" I asked him.

"The shuttle is taking everyone to dinner."

"You want me to get you some food or something?" He asked.

"Yes, man! Please. I don't care how little it is, but if you are getting food, please, I can always use food.

"Alright man, we'll be back in an hour or two, I'll see you then and then we can..." He motioned to smoke.

"Yeah, yeah, sure."

With most of the people gone, I felt stable enough to walk around a little bit. I left my backpack by the table and checked out the grounds. Off to the side there was a room that had a bunch of bunk beds. I went inside, just to feel the peace of a warm room and compassion of actually being inside of something. The den was warm, and nicely lit.

"Hello." A blonde-haired young man just at the length of a ponytail with a soft face and thick eyebrows peering down at a map acknowledged me.

"What are you doing?" I asked.

"I'm looking through this map to see where I am going."

"You don't know where you're going? That's interesting."

"I'm going along the mountains, that's for sure, I just don't know where I'm going to get off."

A busty woman in her early seventies with short white hair walked in.

"Hey, E.T, who's your friend?"

"Oh, I don't have a trail name yet." I said.

"You looked freezing when you came up." She said getting on a bunk.

"Yeah, I needed some time to get warmed up, but this place is great."

"I'm working for stay," E.T expressed.

"Hmm, do you think they would let me do that for a night?" I asked.

"Talk to Jeff, but there is a lot of people working for stay right now, I don't know if they need the help."

"I'm sure, I'll figure something out. There is a bridge across the road."

"You really want to sleep under there? Don't you have any money?" The woman asked, concerned.

I shook my head no. "I don't want to, but I will if I have to."

"Lord it's only ten dollars to camp. And you think you are getting to Maine?"

"Just to New York," I bargained.

"New York is a long ways away." She assured herself.

We all looked at the map we had out. New York was pretty far, although we were just looking at a map, I knew that it was going to be beautiful however I got there. Maybe not easy, but it was going to be beautiful. E.T began to sketch out the way he wanted to go. He said he was going to walk into Virginia, hitch up to Washington D.C, skip Pennsylvania, go to New York for a night, and get back on the road in New Hampshire.

"I've just heard nothing good about Pennsylvania." He said irritated.

"If you go through Virginia you have to go to Grayson Highlands," she said sweetly.

"What's there?" We asked in unison.

"Well, you go up through this mountain and then..." She built up the suspense. "There are wild ponies." She smiled like a little girl.

"Wild ponies?" I had never been so overjoyed.

"Hmm, interesting." E.T contemplated.

"Are you for sure going to see ponies?" I asked the old lady.

She looked me straight in the eye, "Oh, you are going to see ponies."

"Then I will walk from here to the Grayson Highlands! Hitch up north, then go to Washington, back to West Virginia, through Maryland, Pennsylvania, Jersey, and up to New York," I said with a plan.

"Wild ponies. Who would have thought? I kind of didn't think they existed anymore, at least not in America." E.T said.

A big woman in a flowery dress and curly auburn hair opened the door. "E.T, Pizza!"

"I get pizza?" he asked surprised.

The thought of pizza seduced my mind. What a warm slice of cheesy, pepperoni and crunchy crust would do to me. E.T left to get his dinner, reminding me I hadn't really eaten one.

"Ya know, I will put you up for the night if you want," the sweet lady said.

"I don't really want to bother you."

"Please, it's nothing. Here take twenty."

People are kind at their core. I gave her a hug and thanked her.

"I've done this trail before. Once with my son."

"Oh really?" I smiled very interested.

"Yes, he was maybe a few years older than you."

"What year was it?"

"1990." She answered.

"Did you have a favorite part?"

She thought for a moment. And then smiled.

"Probably the ponies," she was priceless, "you will like them. You can just go up to them and feed them."

The thought of taming a wild pony crossed my mind.

"And ya know that there is hike naked day," she said.

"Say what?"

"Yeah, it is on the summer solstice. My son and I did it way back when."

"Wait, what?" I asked in astonishment.

"That's not the funny part. When we were hiking, we came across a troop of girl scouts."

"And you didn't get arrested?"

"No, no. If it had been any other day we probably would have been. It's pretty well known along the trail."

I was impressed with her comfortability of her body and made me wonder why I was so ashamed of my own.

"Well, this has been truly wonderful." I said standing up. "Thank you again for what you have given me. It will make it much easier to get further along."

"Sleep tight."

"Goodnight."

It was only seven o' clock, but I wasn't really about to question her sleeping habits if I hadn't dug deeper into the former conversation about walking naked with her son. I'm sure they just come from a fairly liberal or conservative family.

I stepped outside. "Oh my god, I was so worried about you," A familiar voice called out to me.

Out of the darkness came a familiar shadow, Horizon, the first woman I had met on the trail, greeted with a hug. She had been drinking.

"Oh hey, why were you worried?" I questioned.

She got a little bit louder. "This kid. I saw him on his first night."

Everyone looked up.

"He had his shit all over the place." Horizon said obnoxiously.

People laughed, but only because they had been drinking too.

"I was really worried about you, man. I'm glad you made it here." She feigned being impressed.

"Look at me," she moved in close "You are going to make it. How old are you?" I wasn't against it, but I wasn't for it either.

"Old enough."

"TRAIL BABY. You and this other one over here, he's eighteen."

I looked through the dark porch and saw that it was Teddy hanging back on a recliner chair with his hair in a ponytail.

"Oh hey, dude," I said, removing myself from Horizon's arms.

"Yo, what's up?" I high fived him.

He was sitting next to the petite mustached man from the first shelter, who looked up from his phone. "Oh yeah, I know this guy too."

"Glad you could make it." Teddy said with enthusiasm.

"Is this your bag?" a British voice called out.

I looked behind me and it was iPod. I nodded.

"You're absolutely mad. It's heavy as shit. What do you have in there?"

"Clothes."

"Well, whatever you have, it's too much." He dragged on his cigarette.

He picked it up above his head and there was a scale hanging from the ceiling with a hook and he hung my bag from it.

70 lbs.

"Holy shit, man. How long have you been carrying that?" Horizon asked.

"About three days."

"May I?" iPod asked if he could go through it.

"Sure."

I walked over and he began pulling out things.

"Listen mate, you are going to have to let go of a lot of things." He said assured.

"I know, that's what I've been told, but I don't know what to get rid of. I can't just throw any of it out."

"Go into the store and go get a box. You can mail it home."

I didn't have a lot of money, but it seemed like this really was my only option. I went into the store attached to the hostel, and it had a kitten just waltzing around. It was filled with all sorts of camping gear, and Snickers for forty cents. I saw Uncle Jeff himself sitting behind the counter. He was a very wide and old wise man. You could tell by walking in the store and looking at him that at some point in his life he had been one hell of a of a smoker of the green stuff. He had a beard that went down to his belly button and wore an impressive hillbilly hat. I walked up to the counter.

"Evening, Jeff."

"How you doing, good sir?"

"I'm fine." The kitty jumped on the counter.

"Would you believe this was a stray cat when it came in. Just like Jeb over here."

I looked over Jeff's shoulder, which revealed an almost older looking man than himself. Slimmer, but with all the same long grey hair, bright eyes, torn jeans and a drug rug."

"Whatcha say?" Jeb asked.

"I said, you were a stray when we found you."

"Hehe, how longs it been with ya now?" He looked at me and winked.

"Oh you? Ya know, I can't remember."

"Someone said I was here in 2014, but that doesn't make any sense..." Jeb said looking away.

"What can I do for you fellow?" Jeff turned his attention back to me.

"I was just looking for a box to mail my things."

"We got two boxes, 17.95 and 20.95."

"Listen, I don't have the money right now, but tomorrow morning I'll probably be able to work something out."

"Oh, no problem. We're about to close anyways."

"Oh, and can I camp here?"

"Yessir. That'll be 10 dollars." And yer going to need you to sign this for legal purposes in case anything happens to you on the trail."

"Of course, I understand."

"Here's the deal. We have a breakfast shuttle that goes at nine o'clock. A lunch shuttle at eleven o'clock, which goes to an all you can eat pizza diner. And for dinner we either do Mexican or Italian. Here's your towel and go get an ice cream from the cooler."

I couldn't afford any of it, but I just wanted to give the man a hug for his kind grace of letting me stay on his land. I chose a drumstick and the ice cream melted on my tongue as I took each bite down to the solid chocolate bottom. I will never forget that ice cream cone. I grabbed the smaller of the two mail boxes, went outside and my things were all spread out all over the table, and everyone was laughing.

"What's your name, mate?"

"I don't have a trail name."

"Well, what the hell is this?"

He pulled out the full box of Cheerios.

"Food supply."

They all burst into laughter. Everyone was sort of tinkering with the things I had brought. It sort of made me unsettled in case they were going to steal, but if I have learned anything about hiker culture, it is your things are safe with hikers.

"This is all snack food. You don't have any meals," E.T said.

I held a ramen in my hand. "I eat snacks *and* meals."

"You are supposed to eat a thousand calories per meal. This is like a hundred." E.T replied.

"That's why I brought a full box of Cheerios." As I picked it up and the plastic bag burst open and cereal went everywhere.

Taking a bite of the crumbs, iPod smiled "Your new trail name is Cheerio."

"How about Samurai Jack?" E.T said holding up my huge knife.

"Listen we are going to go through everything, and you are going to see how much you don't need. And then we are going to go to the hiker box and get you some real food, and other supplies." iPod concluded.

"Alright,"

"Computer. You don't need it." iPod said putting it in the cardboard box.

"I need to get to an Apple store so I can use it."

"Where do you suppose the nearest Apple store is to Erwin, Tennessee? Two hundred miles? This thing weighs ten pounds, it's going to get wet and broken."

I looked at it and realized that it had already gotten a little wet.

"Alright man, forget the computer."

"That's the spirit."

We put the computer and it's a charger in the box.

"You have nearly a week's worth of clothing with you. You need one, maybe two days' worth of attire."

I began to go through all of my clothing.

"You don't need jeans, and you don't need this coat."

"Isn't going to get cold at night?"

"Summer is coming, it's going to get hot, plus, do you have a sleeping bag?"

"No."

Everybody looked up at me when I said that.

"You don't have a sleeping bag?"

"No, I have a blanket and a yoga mat."

"You have to get a sleeping bag," Horizon spoke up.

I was very restrained. I kept my cool, but I didn't just instantly agree with everything everyone was saying. I had made it this far. Sure it got cold, but I could take it.

"I am going to focus on one thing at a time. Right now, I need to let go of some stuff. If I find a sleeping bag, good, but I really don't need anything." I said.

"Alright, well then you aren't going to need this flannel."

"Woah, what about when I get to New York? Aren't I going to want something to look good in?"

"I mean, I guess, but you are not going to make it there with this weight, you have to understand." Teddy assessed.

I believed him. My body was in distress. I was happy to have been putting in the miles, but my muscles had not gone unnoticed. Every step I took anywhere hurt. My arms didn't hurt as much, but they were weak. It wasn't late but I had trouble keeping my eyes open.

"Eh it's not even a pound, I'll keep it." I shrugged.

"Alright you'll just have to bear the weight." iPod shook his head.

"Fine with me when I look good as hell in Brooklyn."

"Deodorant. Throw it away." He chucked in a wastebasket.

"Aren't I going to smell?"

"Everyone smells awful on the trail. Along with all this soap, get rid of it."

I rolled my eyes but threw it away. We whittled a lot out of that bag. I kept one t-shirt, a pair of basketball shorts, and a pair of normal shorts, two pair of underwear, my flannel and my sweater.

"What the hell is this?"

"It's my flashlight."

"This is more than a flashlight, this could light up the whole forest. This thing must weigh five pounds."

"I didn't know, man."

"Go over to the hiker box, I left a headband flashlight over there, it weighs an eighth of what you are carrying now."

A hiker box is a box or small area in which hikers leave things they don't need, things that are too heavy, or may help other hikers. Change can be left, food, gear, (chargers), gear and so forth. Remember, I had no idea that anyone was doing anything similar to what I was doing. Without hikers and their ways of "no man left behind" status quo, I would be dead somewhere right now, I assure you. I got four different kinds of dehydrated potatoes, which would serve as meals for me for a long haul. There was also a bag, which was good for compacting all of my clothes and resting my head.

My stuff was still all over the table. I slowly began to pack all of it in. There was so much room left in the backpack when I was finished. I put on the pack and hallelujah, did it feel light. I felt like I could fly off with it into the night, however there was still a light drizzle going on.

I went around back where Chris was drinking a beer.

"Hey man, sorry it took so long."

"Oh no problem, dude. Did you figure out how you were going to let go of that stuff?" He asked.

"Not everything really fits in the box for me to mail home, plus I don't know how I am going to afford it."

"You'll be fine, man. Trust me. Things always work out here."

"I hope so. I just don't get the free spirit of all of you guys right now. I'm still in survival mode."

"You will warm up to it. And once you do, you will enjoy being out here more than anything you've ever done."

I smiled. It was good to feel some reassurance.

"Do you think you are going to leave here tomorrow?" I asked.

"I dunno. It's Friday, and I kind of like it here. I haven't really decided yet."

I was thankful for the space to camp on the land, but I knew I was going to get wet tonight. Of all the things that I packed, one of them was a vaporizer. It weighed about half a pound. I like it because it gets me high, but it doesn't make me tired. I packed it with weed Ned gave me and began to feel its subtle effects.

"I don't think I'm getting anything," Chris said puffing on the contraption, looking at me finishing off another beer.

I was so high, man. I had no idea what he was talking about that he wasn't getting anything. His eyes looked a little too big for his head now.

"I'll just turn it up then." I said.

"I still don't think I'm getting much."

All of a sudden, my thoughts began to fill my mind. About this strange place I was in, these people. None of them had anything to gain, yet they were so kind. It was such a rare quality in the real world.

"Hey, you want to come hit this?" I said, a little too loud for my own good to passerby.

"Pshh. No!" A bearded mixed fellow came over. "Is it weed?"

"Hehe, yeah," I smiled. He was muscular and slim. He was still a little intimidating in his eyes. He took the vaporizer and inhaled.

"Thanks, man. What's your name?"

"Cheerio. Hehe." I had the giggles.

"Nice to meet you, man. I'm Bear."

Bear, super serious hiker man, lone ranger, bearded man, tough spirit.

"I like this thing," he said, blowing out a cloud.

My mind went back to casual.

"Yeah, I can't seem to find the charger for it. You a thru hiker?"

"Indeed, my friend. You know you either make it or you don't, that's the way I see it." He said, as he pulled out a cigarette.

"You want one?"

"Yes.... but no. I'll just take a drag."

"Cool, man."

"I'm really not getting anything," Chris continued about the cannabis.

"Just wait, you will." I said, in a niche relaxation.

I took a light hit of that cigarette it complimented that ice cream cone with the sweet taste of tobacco touching my lips as I sizzled all forethought and worry melted away.

"Oh, now I feel it. I don't feel high though, it's like I'm mentally awake or something," Chris observed.

"Yeah, it's like a light tickle of the brain." Bear smiled. "Are you a thru hiker, Cheerio?" he asked with his tough voice.

"Sort of, I feel like I am becoming one more and more."

"Ah yes, the trail will change you."

"Tell me about it, man. All these hippies and hikers are far out."

"Just wait until Trail Days." Chris sipped.

"What's Trail Days?" I asked.

Chris got a little excited. "You don't know about Trail Days, man?"

"Trail Days will be perfect for you. There are raffles where you can win equipment. People trade, it's a festival." Bear said.

"Yeah, then you could get all sorts of new gear that you need, trekking poles, a new backpack." Chris said, trying to help.

"What's wrong with my backpack?"

"Nothing. It's just old."

"So, it's a festival?" I asked.

"It's basically like a giant party in the woods and it's next weekend," Chris said puffing on the cigarette being passed around.

"There is free food, and showers, and a ride board," said Bear.

"Ride board? Where is it?"

"It's in Damascus, Virginia."

"How far away is that?"

"Only about a hundred and forty miles away."

"But there are shuttles that will take you into it," Chris explained.

"Do the shuttles cost money?" I asked

"Probably, but not that much and they get cheaper if you get closer."

“There was a group of hikers who left yesterday, who are going 18 miles a day to get there. I really wanna walk into it man,” Bear shook his head gently.

“That would be awesome, well I think I’m going to Trail Days.” I said, having discovered my next destination.

“That’s the spirit,” I was patted on the shoulder.

“Alright man, you look exhausted, you should probably go to bed.”

“Hehe, yeah.”

“Bear, it was nice meeting you, man. I’ll see you up the trail, or at Trail Days.”

“Goodnight, man.”

I looked over at my backpack, I needed to unload it and pitch my tent still. Ugh, I was so tired. I grabbed a hold of it. At least now all my clothes were together in a bag, so I didn’t have to take each article out separately. I got to the bottom where my tent was. I knew what I was doing but it still took longer than usual since it was dark, and I was stoned. I had fun with it though. You can really have a horrible time being high if you end up thinking the wrong thoughts, but all I remember was feeling safe and on my way onward.

By the time I got in my tent it was about eleven, which was the latest I had stayed up. I got a text from Austin in a usual overly excited string of texts. I told her that she would love it out here. I let her know with good people and she laughed that I was in a hostel. She used to tell me about her brother going to foreign countries and staying in cheap single hotels. We laughed at I was doing and she believed I was wild. Rains truly is an adventurous soul and we should see the world someday.

Chapter 11

The thermal pad that I had exchanged for my yoga mat for was not waterproof in the slightest. I laid back for a little bit, but not too long since I didn't really know what the day had in store for me. It's always best to get a head start if you can. I checked my phone and saw that it was dead, so I went to find an outlet. People were coming back from breakfast, so it must've been around ten. My body was overly relaxed and when I knew I shouldn't be. I saw some familiar faces, as well as some new ones. The store was open, and inside it was a tall woman in a tie-dyed dress. I was hopeful she would think the box I was mailing would be already paid for.

"Morning, man." She said.

"Good Morning."

At times like these when I feel behind schedule, I can be a pretty tightly wound person regardless of what is in my system. I was getting things done as quickly as I could. I knew I didn't want to put my wet tent back into my backpack right away. Behind the bathroom, there was a dryer and washing machine, and I put my tent in the dryer.

"Hey, you can't do that," a very high voice exclaimed.

I turned around to see one of the smallest men I have ever seen in my life.

"I'm sorry to inform you good sir, but there is a sign here that reads, and I will recite, DO NOT PUT YOUR TENTS IN THE DRYER, OR THEY WILL GET TANGLED AND BREAK. Now, do you want your tent to break, to tear, to leave you open in the wilderness susceptible to bears, snakes, spiders and raccoons?" he pierced ravishly.

"Who are you?" I had to ask.

"Ah, yes, I am a part of this fine establishment at the moment. I am going to work for stay for a few months as all the day hikers, and tourists pass through, and then when they have all passed, I will find myself alone with these woods. Mr. Rice will do."

"Beautiful. Do you think I could put some of my clothes in the dryer, they got a little wet last night?"

"Nonsense!"

He began looking at me as though I was suspicious. He had a trim golden haircut.

"When you go out into the woods, there is a poise, a sour fermentation that exists on your clothes. If I was to put one article of clothing into this dryer, the whole lot would be contaminated."

"Good to know."

"You're welcome. *I said a hip hop, hippie to the hippie, the hip, hip a hop, and you don't stop, a rock it out, bubba to the bang bang boogie, boogie to the rhythm of the boogie to the beat.*"

I liked the fellow, but my head hurt. I just walked away feeling like he deserved to marry a hell of a woman. He definitely had the energy or wisdom or something because it was hard to take your eyes off of him. I went out to the front and the skies began to clear. I hung my tent up and I saw Horizon with her pack on, looking like she was ready to head off.

"Hey, are you going to Trail Days?" I asked.

"It's not for another week."

"Yeah, I meant, like when it happens." I looked a little disheveled.

"I was thinking about it. That's why I'm leaving now."

"Oh, cool. I was going to try and get a head start myself, but I don't want to be carrying a wet tent."

"Well, you are learning." She shook her head.

"I never would have made it here without your map." I said sarcastically.

"I don't understand how you are going to hike the trail without knowing where water sources are."

"I hadn't really thought about it." I smiled. "I'll just stop whenever I see water."

"Please do."

"Well, I'll see you up the trail."

She walked off and I thought she was kinda foxy. Even if I never met her again, it was just nice to have met her. I ate a sufficient amount of the cereal left on the table for breakfast even though they were dry, and I threw the rest in the trash and cleaned off the table.

"You are going to have to get some real food." I looked up and it was an unfamiliar face.

"Who are you?"

"Kendal."

"Oh, hello."

"They were talking last night in the bunks about you."

"Is that so?"

She had light hair, a young face and spoke softly. "Nothing bad, I just heard you don't have any real food."

"Yeah, well last night I got potatoes."

Even as I said it, it was discouraging.

"Are you thru hiking?" I asked her.

"Yeah, I'm out here with my brother, and we just bought a dog."

"Oh wow."

"I think everyone is going out for lunch, but next door there is a grocery store and I'm sure we could find you some cheap food that is sustainable."

"Have you heard about my money situation?"

"I heard you were given twenty dollars last night."

"True." I shrugged, "I'll see. I kind of want to get out of here as soon as possible. The first thing I have to figure out is mailing all of this crap back home."

I knew I couldn't afford two boxes to mail so I went into the store. The woman in the flowery dress smiled at me before I got to the desk.

"Hey, listen. I can only afford this box, and I don't think that all my stuff is going to fit in it, is there anything we can do?"

She smiled a wise dash. "Oh, we can make it all fit, trust me."

I took her word at face value, went back out and grabbed all my things. We put the computer in first, then the charger, then my shirts, and jeans, by which point the box was full. Then she held all of it down with force and I stuffed my jacket in.

Mr. Rice's little head popped out from behind the corner. He went over to the desk and handed her duct tape as I held everything down. She began to put layers of duct tape around it and sealed it shut.

"Nice work," she nodded at me, almost sweating.

"Teamwork," I laughed.

"Just address the return address to the address you want to send it to."

"Hmm, I didn't know that worked." I realized there was well over a thousand dollars' worth of things in there.

"We'd just send it again if it comes back, but there usually aren't any problems. That will be eighteen dollars."

I had twenty-five dollars with what was left over from last night and I knew I had to buy some food. I paid for the package and went back outside.

"Hey guys are you going to lunch?" I asked Teddy.

"Nah, I will probably get going soon,"

"Do you think it would be a bad idea to get a plastic bag, and go to the all-you-can-eat pizza and just save a bunch of slices?" I asked nonchalantly.

"Yes, frankly, I do." Mr. Rice squeaked. "If you steal from a local business, word will travel along the trail and if someone's stuff ends up missing, then you will be the first person that they will assume took it."

"Sounds a little dark." I said.

"Nobody will help you!" He stormed off.

"I actually liked your idea about the pizza," Teddy said casually.

I sat there trying to not let too much time pass. People would come and go, and I would observe them. Not in a harsh judgment, just thinking maybe I would like to hike with them or maybe I wouldn't. Similar to the way you might want to surround yourself with someone at a party. An Albino and his girlfriend arrived together around eleven.

"I'm Snowman." He shook my hand.

"Cheerio."

"Stargazer." His girlfriend smiled.

"Are y'all going to lunch?"

"Yeah."

"Well, the shuttle is leaving." Jeb announced.

Jeb was driving the shuttle and it was little bit of a wonder to me how this man had his license. I got mine, so it wasn't really that far-fetched. The drive to the restaurant was snug. We all squeezed into the back and there were definitely more hikers than there were seats, so I sat on the wheel well. A few older gentlemen began talking about how there was a four-state challenge.

"You have to wake up around three in the morning,"

"It's 43 miles." A kind old man said with astonishment.

"I'll be able to do 43 miles no problem." The other older gentleman said.

"You're going to be tired. That is not just something you casually take on. That's almost two marathons of distance carrying your weight."

"Once you get to Pennsylvania, it is flat." He replied.

"You ever run a marathon?" The authoritative one asked.

"Yeah." I butted in.

"It's so competitive at your age," The gentler one said.

"I've done an Ironman," the man continued. "Are you going to do one?"

"I am now."

Some of these strenuous activities seem so out of reach but whenever I meet someone who has done something that seems impossible in front of me, I take that as a challenge to accomplish it, it comes from the love of doing.

"When we parked, everyone went into the parlor except for me and Kendal.

"Aren't you hungry?" I asked

"Nah, I had pizza yesterday."

"How long have you been here?"

"About two days."

"Do people often just sit nowhere for a couple of days?" I asked lightly.

"Yeah, they are called zeros. It's a day when you don't do anything."

"Oh, well, I did not plan on any zeros when I left." I told her.

We went into one of those old timey grocery stores with pastries in the front.

"Are you getting any food to pack out?" I wondered.

"I'm going to get some dog food."

We went to the edge of the store where the dog food was. She began to lead me around pointing out sustainable nourishments. She picked up the smallest food package, which was the size of a brick. I thought it was a little out of style from her previous shy attitude when she snuck a hand full of nuts, but I wasn't complaining. She was pretty, in a cute blonde Southern cut sense. She seemed afraid to not have her life figured out, but at the same time was very willing to help me figure out mine.

I grabbed peanut butter, jelly and tortillas off the counter.

"You should get some tuna, for protein." She offered.

I looked at the packaging. It was about two dollars per package of tuna. I grabbed one, and six ramen for five dollars total. It was a sufficient amount of food I had. I felt really good.

Then I got a phone call.

"Hello." My father's voice was pissed.

"Hi. I'm in Erwin Tennessee. It's a beautiful town."

"That's nice. Listen, there is a bus from Johnson City that leaves today at one o'clock, and I suggest that you take it home."

"I don't think you get it. I might not come home."

"Listen, you don't make the rules. You are in danger, you obviously haven't been thinking straight."

"Well, if that was a concern to you then you shouldn't of drove off."

"I did not let you go. You walked away. What was I going to do? Throw you in the car in some parking lot?"

"That's sorta what I expected. Wouldn't be the first time."

"No. I am talking with your psychiatrist and you need to come home, and you will not be getting any assistance on this journey of yours, from me, or my parents, understood?"

"That's not fair. I understand that you don't want to help me, but you don't determine what grandma can do."

"COME HOME NOW. You have been gone long enough."

"It's been three days."

"When all this blows up in your face, I am not going to help."

"Is that all?"

"I'm serious. You are men-"

I hung up. It is very draining to talk to Don. I love him to death, but he bullies me quite often because I do things he wishes he could. He sees himself in me. We're both ungodly stubborn, but he listened to what people told him to do. I don't believe in me doing the things he settled for. I got very quiet after this conversation, like I always do. We were at the checkout and it came out to about eight dollars. I had to put aside the tuna. It was definitely a low point on the trip. I was all out of money, and Kendal had to witness all of that.

"You good, man?" She asked once we were outside.

"Yeah, I'll be fine. I just need a minute."

We were only in the grocery store for about a few minutes. The shuttle wasn't leaving for another hour.

"I don't really feel like staring at an all-you-can-eat pizza diner right now."

"Wanna go for a walk?" She asked.

"Sure." I started to feel better. Not chirpy, let's go out skipping better, but thankful I had food, and maybe a friend, better. I looked around at this wonderful small town surrounded by hills and trees.

"Where the hell are we, ya know? Like when in a million years would you ever choose to visit Erwin, but now, I don't think I have ever felt more at home."

She looked up at me, looking down. "And you want to go to New York?"

"Yeah. I walk fast and am very important."

If you are always trying to be somebody, somebody is always going to be more than you. The only thing that is important is if you know who you are, and how well you know yourself. I could give a damn about fame. I wouldn't know anyone any better because of it.

Friends matter. Not the number of friends.

"Half of me wants to be important, not for the vanity of it, but to make a difference in the world, even just inspire one person. Change them, open them up to believe in themselves a little more." I said, kicking a rock.

"I didn't want to go to college because that is what everyone does. Is that really so wrong?" She asked me.

"Classic, leave town to see the world?" I asked at the young beauty.

"That's what I'm told. At least you tried to do something. It's better than working at some dead-end job which I'll just have to go back to when all of this is over." She seemed sort of ashamed.

"Hey, well now you're free. You don't know where this can go. You have the opportunity to do what you want. I can't even afford tuna. I'll probably die out here."

"Don't say that. I would have bought you the tuna."

"I can only take so much generosity before I feel like I'm taking advantage of people, or I'm homeless. Besides, it's not like I want to go back to college, either. It's complicated. I might not go back. I may just live in the streets of New York and start working a dead-end job until someone takes me seriously."

"You could always... never leave." She raised her eyebrow.

"That's very romantic, but I'm NOT going to die out *here*, thank you very much."

"Do it."

"I'm *actually* thinking about it." I actually was.

Looking at men in their driveways repairing old cars, we watched a dog on the porch for a while, and I tried to pet it, but she said I'd probably get shot down if I went on anybody's property. Eventually we walked in to the restaurant and it smelled good and I got hunger pains. I went and sat next to Snowman and Stargazer, who were next to Sonic who looked like he was feeling better.

"What's up, guys." I yawned.

"Nothing really." Stargazer assured nibbling on a slice.

"Is the pizza good?" I asked, obviously hungry.

"I can get you some if you like." Stargazer said in a slyly.

I could tell Sonic and Snowman were not really enthused, but there was no way in hell I was turning down free pizza.

"Pepperoni, please."

She came back with a plate with like six slices and by the time that Sonic had eaten one of his slices, all six of mine were gone.

"Thank you so much, you have no idea how much that means to me. I literally just ran out of all my money." I licked my fingers.

"No problem, man. Sonic was telling us he met you on the trail."

"Oh really?" I had a shy smile. "Listen, I'll be fine. I'm just not a hiker. I'm just a trailblazer, Stargazer." I rhymed fully.

"Well I hope we've done our part." Stargazer said warmly hugging the cold Snowman to extend her generosity to him.

I checked my phone and saw that I had gotten a message from my old schoolmate Paul from high school. He was one of my first friends in elementary school and goes to an Ivy League now. Hearing from him made me laugh and smile deeper within than I imagine he knows. I was a little worried since I sent him a very aggressive letter on a drunken spree. Our text conversation went something like this.

Paul - Hey dude! I heard you are walking to NYC. Sounds amazing. Listen I'm going to be in Washington D.C if you need a place to stay or wanna kick it.

Me - Yo! Yeah man, it's crazy out here. That would be so sweet. I probably won't be over there for a while, but I'll try to get out there.

Paul - Sweet. Hope to see you. Please don't die.

The shuttle came but we had to go back since we forgot someone and by the time we got back to Uncle Jeff's, I was ready to go. While I was packing my food into my bag, there was a guy with a blue shirt and vest on that had been around the campsite, but we hadn't formally interacted. He was making a PBJ.

"What's up, man," I said casually, stuffing my food into the bottom of my bag.

"Nothing dude."

"How long have you been here?" I asked.

"Two weeks."

"Two weeks?! Are you working for stay?"

"Yeah. But I injured my foot, that's why it's been so long." He spoke with a low voice. He was probably my age or maybe a year younger or older, you couldn't tell, but he was probably very mature in some sense, but a little hurt.

"Damn man, I'm sorry." The thought was horrifying. I hadn't even been out a week and besides a few scrapes I had, I'd been fine. One wrong step and the whole journey could be jeopardized.

"Patience is probably the most important thing you will learn on the trail. It should heal in a week."

Chapter 12

I said goodbye to the friends I had made. Kendal's brother was among them since my name had been floating around the hostel that I'd spent some time alone with his sister. For me, there is just a line of respect in the South more evident than in other places of the world. From the sound of it, they were getting the puppy later in the day so they said they would probably see me up the trail. Chris and Bear were staying another night, and Teddy was long gone. I left alone, the same way I started the trip in the first place. It is hard to feel the beginnings of comfort and comradeship with a small group and then to leave them without knowing their futures. It's not fun to be alone. However, by this point I felt like a lot of people were rooting me on or supporting me through this journey.

I went along the bridge past a small church and it wasn't long before I was facing the deep woods again. It was a chilling feeling but one of familiarity as well. I felt safe in the woods for the most part. The dirt and trees almost hugged me as the terrain engulfed me. Before the trial began, there were train tracks, which I followed for a little bit. I could hear from the off distance a train coming soon. The thought passed through my mind of hopping on, at the sign of my compass pointing due North.

The thought was frivolous and dangerous, and not only did I not want to risk legal action, I wasn't about to just risk both of my legs to be run over by the train. I found a trail-marker and went down it. Campers and new animals were along the way including a small orange salamander.

My close friends from home, George and Eve had been messaging me back and forth. It was a good feeling of being close to the ones that are close to my heart. Although they weren't there, I could still talk to them. It was at this moment I realized that harder than the physical demands of the trail, it was the emotional absence of ones close to me that made me feel like an alien, and often discouraged. The signal wasn't good in the woods, but you could still reach the internet and I used this time to reach out to Austin and other friends.

The trail was a joy to be back on. The views were beautiful, I felt like I was getting somewhere every time I climbed over a rock or looked out at the mountainous views but eventually, I was low on water and it was starting to get dark out. I came across a shelter. There were a few men in their fifties hanging around it and sipping Jameson along with a young cat who looked about a few years older than me. They were just about ready to leave once I had finished getting my water.

When I sat down, I recognized a familiar face. It was Raccoon, the burly thickset redheaded gentleman I met next to Sonic when he was sick. His beard and hair was on the verge of getting a bit wild. Next to him was a thin grey man with a moustache. They were both fixing dinner.

"How far did you go today?" I asked Raccoon, sitting down.

"I try and go thirteen a day. How bout you?" He replied.

"Not much, I think I want to try and keep a twenty a day pace."

"Well, I bet you can do it."

"I dunno, do you think I could use your stove?" I asked the greyed fellow.

He paused. "Why not." He smiled at me. "With all this gas we could start a forest fire." He had a canister of gas that was almost as big as my head.

"That thing is huge," Raccoon agreed while lighting his own pocket stove.

"It's worth the extra weight so you don't have to worry about running out or finding a place to buy a canister."

He handed the stove over to me and I went through my bag and pulled out ramen. It was the first of many. There is something to be said about taste, and enjoying what you eat, but the two men had obviously superior food choices than what I was eating. I was a little concerned by Raccoon's food option though. He took two pieces of spam and put them together with an obscene amount of cheese wiz.

"So, have you two gotten any action on the trail yet?" The pervish senior motioned.

"Not really, nope." I answered.

"I was with two girls," Raccoon said.

We both perked at him. Not because he was unattractive, just not really the type.

"Yeah, we were staying in a shelter and it was just one of those freezing nights and all of sudden these two travelling sisters, started scooting closer to me for warmth, by the end of the night they both were on my sleeping pad, but I'll tell you this, they were both ripe."

"Nice," I said, sarcastically unimpressed.

"Their mom ended up buying me Chinese food when she came to visit."

"Why do you ask?" I raised my eyebrow over to the old man.

"Well I was making this girl laugh, ya know, we were joking around, and she was talking about how she met this guy on the trail. He was Northbound, and she was Southbound, and they ended up shacking up because he made her laugh so much."

Raccoon and I both exhaled.

"Yes, but my story is not over. I was making her laugh you know, so I said, I'm making you laugh. How about a hug? And she said I would, but you smell like pee."

It was a bummer to hear.

We continued talking about things besides women for about a half hour and I learned the old man was married and Raccoon was divorced. Raccoon had been in the Navy for a few years, and the old man was a lawyer from Maine. I was just some broke hungry kid on his way to New York. They were concerned but nothing came from the conversation.

I left as the sun had just set over the Western mountains. I figured I would have a good two hours before I would have to pitch tent. It was uphill for the first mile, and the forest took a beautiful, almost tropical form. A deep maroon and set along the sky. Austin had made her way to Tanzania. She replied to my picture of the sunset with one of a lion. I think it's fair to say we were both a little jealous of the illustrious things we were doing at the time. The attitude she carries herself is a complete openness to a new world of opportunities.

I walked past one campsite, but it was on a slant. The men who drinking whiskey were there and through a tent I could hear, "Well move!"

I personally was not enthusiastic about hearing some couple yell at each other while all the blood rushes out of my toes.

"Do you know where the next campsite is?" I asked one of the men keeping slight distance

"Yeah, it's about two miles up, but be careful, it's close to a road up ahead, I live around this area. Kids go there all the time and get drunk."

"Why should I be careful about that? That sounds like a blast."

"That's the right attitude," the other fellow said.

In my head I felt up to the idea of meeting some young teens and having a good time, but I knew it was unrealistic. It was just all that talk about shacking up on the trail that made me wonder. You know, how nice it would be to meet someone on the trail, have them take me home, feed me, even sleep with me, learn and grow from one another and then give me a ride a hundred miles towards wherever I wanted to go.

The sun had set, and it was beginning to get dark and I didn't know how far away this road was. I was prepared for this since I had a flashlight headband, which worked fine, for about five minutes. It started to flicker and then it went out and everything was black for a minute until my eyes adjusted. It wasn't much use. When you are in the thick of the woods there isn't a whole lot of light around. Each step I took gave me an anxiety attack. I couldn't see in front of me and the trail had so many turns and weaves in random directions. I tripped on a root. When you fall like that in the dark, you just freak out. Holy shit was I scared. I got up and wanted to run, but I couldn't. I just had to compose myself and walk at a deathly slow rate in the dark night.

Forget the road, or trying to engage in any promiscuous activity, I just needed a place to sleep. Tennessee is known for being a part of the deep South where you don't mess with anyone, especially hick teenagers. They will just rough you up for no reason. I could see it. Boy gets beaten to death after poor life decision. I stopped and got my knife from my bag.

I walked with it in my hand. An idea began to scare me that I could trip again and the next thing I would know the blade would be in the middle of my chest, miles from help. I kept walking, the ground weaving back and forth along the roots. I wondered if I had gone off the trail, and right when I thought about turning back around to go to the previous campsite, I saw a lone tent.

"Can I camp here, please?" I called out.

A woman's voice responded.

"Sure."

I threw my backpack on the ground and the sweat on my forehead made me regret the whole trip. Just the sticky moisture of the humid air combined with my fear was enough for me to want to cry. I sulked for a moment, and then began to unload my bag. I had no light, so I was going all by touch at this point. The tarp was on top, so I laid it out and put my clothing down and got my tent from the bottom. I opened the tent bag, found the poles, and clicked them all together. I put them through respective holes, only to find out they were the wrong ones and that it was not properly set up.

It took me a while to just get everything the way it was meant to be. The process had been expedited at this point, but I still was not very efficient at any of it. Ugh, the bear bag was hard to hang. I (again, scared of my own imagination at this point) went far too deep into the woods as usual and it took me at least twenty tries to get it over a branch to hang from. I felt like a dork, unprepared and not able to set out for this world. I'm just not very sportive, but I do get competitive about very stupid things.

Finally, everything was hung and set up. I climbed inside the tent and laid back until I realized I couldn't fall asleep. I decided that some marijuana might help the situation. If I want to, I can go as long as I want without pot. However, if I have had it the night before, I'm much more prone to using it again. I was petrified when I left. Properly so, but I didn't know how to do any of this survival shit, and now I was slowly becoming trained at the ways of the trail and I knew that a little puff wouldn't harm anyone anymore.

I packed a one hitter and I smoothly hit it. As the smoke reached my brain, I fell back. I was slightly glad about my alternative sleep method, it replaced my fears but brought too much humor into the situation. I was giggling to myself for a good four or five minutes. I had never done what I was doing. I was in the middle of the woods, somewhere I had never been, and I couldn't be happier and more confused by the whole situation in itself.

Then I got a very sneaky idea. An idea that probably came from a stoned mind, as such. Why not bring a little pleasure into the mix. If I just masturbated, I could fall asleep right away and I could get up and do those twenty. Personally, once this thought crossed my mind it has a great deal of trouble leaving. Now, for some inspiration. I'm a man of simple tastes. At this point a walnut probably would have made me burst. I was so pent up about saving all of my energy since I left. I have a picture of Tina Fey on a winter's day wearing a sweater and scarf. She just looks like a hot intelligent woman. Something about an in-charge comedy writer is my taste, since funny is the biggest turn on of all. I'm not going to go into too much detail but as you can imagine I was in my tent enjoying the idea of meeting a powerful woman writer in New York City and was cut off by the woman in the woods in her tent ten feet away from me.

"You know I'm still awake." The voice called.

Oh lord, what have I done? Never have I shrunk so quickly. I was anxious to the bone. This would have never happened if I hadn't frivolously smoked. Word travels fast on the trail. Nobody was ever going to help me again echoed in my head. There was no changing the facts, I couldn't say I was just rustling around, I couldn't say anything for a moment, but of course my smooth stoner wit came through.

"You're not the only one having trouble falling asleep?"

"Cheerio?" the voice asked.

I really didn't want to respond and give away my identity in this current circumstance.

"Who are you?" I questioned.

"It's Horizon," she gulped.

"Oh shit. I am so sorry about that all that ruckus."

She didn't say anything. I tried to make small talk. "How's your Saturday night going?"

She was understandably quiet but exhaled loudly. "Nothing's happening, trail baby, but your weed does smell good."

"Trail baby? C'mon that's bullshit, you are like five years older than me."

"Try fifteen."

"I've been with older women than that."

It was quiet for a moment.

"C'mon, we could smoke. It'll help you forget about it."

"What women have you been with older than you?"

"Now who's the trail baby?"

She laughed.

"I've slept with a woman who had kids older than me."

"Kids?" She asked. "Impressive."

"Oh yeah, you should've met the whole family."

We both laughed.

"I've done a lot worse. You'd be a breath of fresh air."

"Trust me, I do not smell good." She inhaled with restraint.

"Didn't you shower at Jeff's?" I asked.

"Yeah, I don't have deodorant and I haven't been shaving. It looks like the sixties down there, but why am I even amusing this idea right now." She was surprisingly embarrassed with herself, exposing a younger spirit without its immaturity. Personally, I was surprised by how well this situation had been going.

"The sixties are my favorite era." I said, sounding too young.

"Of course it is dirty hippy boy. Goodnight."

"Ah, why you got to be like that?"

No response.

"If you want to go finish up, do it over by your that bear bag that took you a half hour to hang," she finally said.

"You didn't have to come at my bear bagging skills. I'm sort of looking to get away from judgment."

"It's just obvious you have no idea what you're doing out here."

"Well, sorry, I didn't think I was going to be walking through a bunch of mountains for months, and I didn't take a year of planning to do it like the rest of you." I said exhausted.

It was barely audible, but she pressed down a laugh as I unzipped my tent to pee.

"Good night Horizon." I said, curled up within my blanket, and was snug for the night.

Chapter 13

I wondered if I had scared Horizon off, since she left bright and early or if she had gotten her hiker name because of when she left in the morning most days. I heard her rustling around at six am and let myself sleep a little longer out of shame. In a strange way, I imagined I would probably see her again, face to face, but hoped not. When I checked my clock again and it was about nine. I had hoped I would be out of the campsite by ten, but I began to dillydally. I was still hungry after I ate a few granola bars for breakfast, but I didn't want to exploit my food supply. Less was more, was my attitude.

I had just about finished up when I heard what sounded like arguing coming from back along the trail.

"I don't *want* to eat it,"

"You are so picky for a grown man." A low feminine voice said.

"I am not picky. I just don't want to eat that."

An over prepared looking couple walked up to the campsite and stopped dead in their tracks.

"Good morning." A greying balding man with a kind smile and a light Southern accent said.

"Good morning." I rubbed my eyes.

"Howdy," said the woman in spunky jumpsuit and curly red hair.

"What's your name?" asked her partner.

"Um, Cheerio, and you are?"

"I'm Tim and this is Amanda."

"C'mon Tim, just eat one, you need the protein." She began waving food by his mouth.

"I'm sorry Amanda, but it is just a little early for dehydrated shrimp."

"I'll bet Cheerio would want some. Wouldn't ya?" She strutted closer.

"Yes please." I still needed food whenever I could get it.

The dehydrated shrimp had a tangy taste to it. It was extremely rough like you were chewing a piece of gum that had aged for a year. Still, I sorta liked it.

“You don’t like ‘em, Tim?” I asked.

“Well, they’re not my favorite, plus we just woke up.”

“If we don’t eat ‘em they will go to waste,” Amanda complained.

“If you guys have any food that is going to waste, I would be honored to eat some of it.” I offered.

They stopped at looked at each other for a moment. Then looked back at me and began unloading their bags to force food onto me.

“Oh, we got food,” Amanda said.

“Do you like Beef Jerky?” Tim asked.

I was probably given about half a pound of different assortments of dried sausage, seafood, or beef. I was extremely grateful, and I had grown tired of granola and ramen, so some meat would definitely spice things up.

“Wow, thanks guys, that is so nice.”

“Yeah, Tim wouldn’t of been able to stomach the meats anyways.” Amanda made a puking motion.

“That is not true. I enjoy the food just as much, it just seems that, Cheerio here might be in more need of it.”

You have to understand, my old backpack and the fact that I didn’t have trekking poles were still a dead giveaway that I did not belong out there and was nothing more than a runaway.

“Are you guys heading North?” I asked kindly.

“We sure are.”

“Do you mind if I come with you guys? I’ve just got to put my tarp away.”

“Take your time.” Tim said.

I stuffed my new meats into my bag along with the tarp and we began to move.

“So where are y’all from?” I asked. They seemed like fun bunch.

“Texas.” Said Tim.

“Oh, nice, man.”

“Where are you from, Cheerio?” Amanda asked with her raspy voice.

“I go to school in Asheville, North Carolina.”

"GET OUTTA TOWN." Amanda said in her aggressive tone. "Tim grew up in Greensboro."

"Oh wow, nice, I have some family that live in those parts."

"Asheville is very diverse...eh," she jabbed, and it got a little quieter.

"Nothing wrong with that." Tim announced enthusiastically.

"How did you guys meet?" I changed the subject.

"We're musicians." Tim said proudly.

"Oh really?"

"I was a drummer and she was a singer in a band and eventually I got the nerve to ask her out. Now we have shows together and have been together ever since," Tim wrapped his arm around Amanda's oversized backpack.

"That's awesome. Do you guys have any of your music on you?" I asked.

"No, but if you ask, Amanda will probably sing for you if you ask her."

"Amanda, will you sing for me?" I asked politely.

"Tim, why did you tell him that? I don't want to sing right now." She slapped his chest.

"Oh, you really don't have to sing." I smiled embarrassed.

"No, no, it's fine." She cleared her throat.

As she began to sing, and I started to regret that I had asked. Her voice was really raspy, and she would start low and then reach high levels and get loud and quiet with no continuity. I don't really know what music they played but it sounded like it rooted from people who didn't practice enough.

"Oh, wow. I really liked that song."

"Amanda, sing him the one that you wrote for me."

"Oh baby, I sing that one all the time," she blushed.

"OOOOHHH MY BABY'S GOOONNE AND I WANT HIM TO STAAAAYY." She chanted.

They were really swell talkative people though and part of me really had a soft spot in my heart for them, but good lord, I started to get a headache. You could just tell they wouldn't be very popular in social settings. I think that's what I liked about them, they really didn't care too much about that sort of thing. They were lost with each other.

"You know, I'm a musician as well," I said under my breath.

"Really?"

"Well, I don't really consider myself a musician. My friends, now those are musicians. I'm just a songwriter who enjoys singing."

"Do you write your own music?" Amanda asked.

"Well, yeah, but it's just simple chords and such.

"Why don't you sing us one?"

"I don't know if that's necessary. I sound much better with a guitar. I've been told I'm tone deaf (by Don)."

"No, I'm sure it's fine."

"Alright, your funeral."

```
        G
I can already guess what you're going to say
    Em
We talk too much but we don't agree
  D             C           G
There's so many things to do without you
                                          Em
And I can probably guess we both look like messes to
                 D            C
our friends But then again, who said things had to end
     G
this way

G                 A          D
Why the Hell do people fall in love,
              C         G
It's such a horrible thing to do
D     C
To, yourself
```

I didn't sing the whole song but when I finished Tim turned around and grabbed me by my shoulders.

"Who has hurt you?" He asked solemnly into my eyes,

"Oh please," I rolled my eyes. "I don't need to get started on *this* again."

"No, No, No. I know a song that comes from the heart when I hear one. You've got a story behind those eyes."

"And you've got a story under that bald head of yours too. We all have a story." I retorted.

"HA! Leave the kid alone, Tim. He doesn't want to share it," Amanda smirked.

"I just want you to know, I've had a lot of experience with these things," Tim said assuming the role of a mentor.

"Oh yeah, you ever been in love with three girls at once?"

He was taken aback by my question but caught back up quickly.

"You hear that, Amanda? We've got a Mormon on our hands."

"Very funny, and ain't helpful," I tried to focus on walking.

"No, I'm serious. You don't have to talk about it if you don't want to. We are just here to help." Tim offered, again.

"I understand, and thank you, I just feel like if I keep talking about it, I won't ever be able to move on from it."

"That's foolish! You need to express yourself, let it out and then you can move forward."

It was a good point, so I thought I would give it a shot. I gave them the basic storyline.

"The blonde sounds like a good balance to you," Amanda said.

"Well, you're obviously feel more in love with the brunette," Tim observed.

"Yeah, but what I'm doing is such a redhead thing to do," I contended.

"Hmmm, and you said the brunette hates you and the blonde and you just broke up?"

"Well, yeah. I'm pretty sure the brunette doesn't want anything to do with me."

"Why?"

"I just did something that was very...*strange*. There are other parts to the story."

"Like what."

"I just...was diagnosed as bipolar; that's the most *clinical* explanation for whatever happened."

"Oh, you had an episode and she saw it."

"She was the episode."

"I've been bipolar almost all my life," he said with a humbling pride. "Do you take anything for it?"

"No."

"I was on Lithium for 20 years, I've just switched to new meds."

"I've heard good things about Lithium, but I met someone about your age who changed after about that long. It makes me wonder if medication isn't a real solution to the problem but just something to suffocate whatever we are suppressing until it rises back to the surface. Do you like your medicine?"

"No, I'm probably a much better of a person because of them. I miss that impulsive spice of life, but I have better handle on things, while before bipolar really had a hold on me." He said.

We stopped walking and Tim broke out into song.

"You really got a hold on me..." he sang in tenor.

"Really got a hold on me..." I sang in a higher pitch.

"REALLY GOT A HOLD ON ME...." Amanda sang.

"I LOOOVVEE YOUUU AND ALL I WANT YOU TO DO IS JUST...HOLD ME... HOLD ME... hold meee." We all sang with anguish and splendor.

"Being bipolar is nothing to be ashamed of. Everyone goes through this at some point in their life, you're lucky to be dealing with it now." Tim said. "What did you do to the brunette that freaked her out?"

"It's a long story, but it was bad."

"Were you arrested or committed to a hospital?" Tim asked.

"Yes. Most people would stay a few days or a week in the ward, but I spent three months inside."

"Oh, well she's out," Amanda said. "You should probably move on from her."

"Haha, I shook my head. Don't you get it?" I waited for a response.

"No, I get it." Tim assured.

"If I have to explain, you don't. I would do anything to move on, but I can't. The way I feel about her shapes everything in the world into who I am, and to let go is for all of it to be in vain. She looks like everything I feel. The trees. The air. The moon. The stars and the ocean. Some of us of rare form don't act normal because there is no proper way to express what we feel. She is stuck in my heart. It doesn't matter if we are together. The fact that I feel this way about *anyone* is enough to make me feel human."

"I was committed too." Tim muttered.

"You should listen to Tim's story. I think you would find a lot of similarities between you too," Amanda spoke up.

"Yeah, enough about me."

"Well," Tim cleared his throat. "I grew up in Morton Grove where I met my first wife. I worked in a factory until I was twenty-five and had worked my way up to a better position. She was an undercover cop making a sting operation and she didn't want to blow her cover." He laughed to himself. "When I was thirty-five my wife killed herself. We didn't have any kids, but she left a letter and a mess to clean up. Herself and the things."

Any light tone had pretty much left.

"Then what?"

"Well, I was depressed for a few years, but I finally worked up the nerve to get a fresh start in Texas. I stopped focusing on work so much, started drumming and playing the stock market and now I don't work, and I play music with my sweetheart."

"Awww." Amanda smiled.

"Well, I have to give it to you, that *is* a story, but when were *you* committed?"

"After my wife killed herself."

"What did you do?"

"I freaked out at work. I trashed my office."

"I would've guessed you two had been together your whole life." I said.

"I feel like I've known her my whole life, but we've been together less than a year."

"On and off," Amanda included.

"Oh really?"

"Tim said he didn't know if he was interested in anything long term after a few months," Amanda explained.

"Yes, but then I realized I was wrong." He established.

"You made me call!" She shoved him.

"Well, you knew I was thinking about you."

"Only because you were telling everyone."

"Why do you think I was telling everyone...So you would call."

"You still could have called, it's not the woman's job to call."

"That's sexist," he said.

"It's true though," Amanda replied.

"I called the blonde up a few days ago and she didn't even pick up. All that shows is that I'm just incapable of being independent, while they can just be gallivanting around with whoever they want without feeling anything."

"That's not true. I bet she didn't want to pick up the phone because she still has feelings for you and doesn't want to hold you back on this journey." Tim said.

"She doesn't even know I'm on this journey right now." I exhaled.

"Still, I bet she is at home, upset, and thinking about you." He continued.

"Is that sexist?" I asked.

"It's true," Amanda said.

"I hope so."

We had made it to the top of some mountain.

"This has been a real interesting conversation. Do you mind if we get a picture?" They proposed.

"Oh sure, I'll take it."

I took a picture of them. There was new and clear air in the day's sky, and it was still early.

"Now, Cheerio, get one just with you and Tim," Amanda gestured.

It was a sweet moment and I felt a connection to these people, as I do all people. You could tell they were too old to have children of their own, but they both wanted one. Our photo session ended with a picture of Amanda and I posing with our muscles up on the mountain. She was just that type of strong woman on the outside, but truly kindhearted on the inside.

We sang classics through the forest. It got tiring, but Tim and I held our own truly singing out. They said they didn't sleep on the trail. They *rejuvenated* and that is exactly how I felt about my time with them. It brought a new energy of strength I hadn't yet felt on the trail. Eventually we stopped for water. Raccoon was enjoying a spam sandwich, so we agreed to stop. He told us that there was a bear nearby and that a fellow hiker, Gonzo, had been woken up by one last night on the top of that gap.

These Texans took their sweet time making lunch. They had honey in their coffee and cooked a few dehydrated meals. I only ate two tortillas with Peanut butter and jelly, so I was finished eating in about five minutes. They kept offering me more food, but at the moment I felt fine. I didn't want to make them think I was leaving because of them, but it was time for me to continue on my journey. It was still early enough that I thought I could go twenty miles that day. I enjoyed walking with people, but I felt stable like I could go another day without even seeing anyone if I didn't need to. As I walked, I enjoyed the beautiful day and hoped it wouldn't rain for the next few days to come, but sooner than I thought, I began to get winded.

Chapter 14

My muscles were just not adjusted to walking long days on end without a break. I didn't know this at the time so I just kept walking for as long as I could before I sat down for a few minutes to catch my breath. The bright heat was agonizing. I realized there was a truck with a bunch of hikers surrounding it about a hundred feet up ahead. I didn't want to approach, then I heard "Hey, you, come on over!"

I thought I would give it a shot.

"Hey, we are from a hostel up in Maine, we're just giving out some trail magic before Trail Days." He was built large man with a bronze crew cut hair and sunglasses. "You want a sandwich?"

I had already eaten, but a sandwich was like lobster.

"Do you like ham, salami or turkey?"

"Turkey." I adjusted my eyes.

"Everything on it alright?"

"Yes sir."

"Please get this young man a coke, dear."

A beautiful Latina woman had an infant asleep on her chest rose. In a little extension she reached out and handed me the cold drink. The carbonation seduced my endorphins and woke me up. The family was truly beautiful, not Hollywood, but Californian. I looked around and there were two gentlemen in their fifties, one with bright white hair and the other tie-dyed camouflage, along with a tall young redhead girl, and a toddler running around blowing bubbles.

"Are you going North?" I asked the redhead.

"Yeah, I just finished college and my dad asked if I wanted to join him out here." She pointed the one with white hair.

"Oh, fun," I joked.

"That would be me," he said emerging from the crowd. His had some trimmed facial hair and his arm had a delicate assortment of tattoos along it.

Oh lord. I shook his hand. "I'm Ghost."

"Nice to meet you." I said.

“This is my daughter Charlotte, she doesn’t have a trail name yet, but she thought she would celebrate by hiking a few hundred miles with her dad.”

“And you are?” I asked the other tall aging gentleman.

“Cyborg.” He looked skeletal besides his thick dark grey beard and bizarre hair. He had a camera attached to his trekking pole.

“Here is your sandwich, Cheerio.” The mom gave to me.

“Oh my god, thank you so much. This is so nice.” I smiled back.

“What were you guys talking about?” I sat back.

“My knees are giving out,” Ghost said.

“Oh, that's not good.” I wondered to myself about my own predicament that I had been putting myself in, and the stress I had been causing my body. It was obvious that I had started to lose weight on the trip and every night my body was in excruciating pain, but the thought of knees just “going out” was horrible.

“As I was saying,” Cyborg said in snobbish way, “What you need to do is take an elastic string band. And stretch out your leg on it before you hike in the morning. Your body just can’t hike twenty miles a day when you start out, your legs can’t handle that.”

I was a little suspicious that he might have been listening to my thoughts.

“How many miles a day do you go?” I asked Cyborg.

“Well you wouldn’t know by looking at me, but I am disabled. I was blown up in the war.”

“Oh, damn.”

“I map out every day how many miles I am going. Today I am going seventeen miles, to the next shelter. Tomorrow is uphill so I am only going nine.”

“That is a lot of precision.” I said.

“You need precision out here. It is the only way to survive.”

He was looked at me very seriously as I finished my lunch.

“Do you want a piece of pie?” The father pushed further to satisfy me to no end.

"What kind?"

"Strawberry Rhubarb."

"Oh yes. That would be very nice."

"We have whipped cream too." He said.

"I need to get in the extra miles today." I nodded my head.

The little toddler girl began to demand everyone's attention.

"Okay, I'm gonna run!"

We all watched in delight as I ate my pie. Raccoon caught up around the time I was getting ready to go.

"Well, it was nice to meetcha all. I hope the knee gets better." I nodded to Ghost and his daughter. Before I left, I shook the hand of the kind gentleman who had given me food and said, "You truly have a beautiful family, God Bless."

I was back to the grind until I realized I needed to poop. No problem. I went deep into the woods hugged a tree did my business and covered it up with leaves. It felt great. I don't think there is an activity more freeing. When I was returning from my business, I ran into a little old lady with very messy grey hair. She seemed like an omen of some sort.

"What's your name?" I asked.

"Broken Arrow."

Uh oh. She spoke rough, and as though she had been lost out here too long.

"You can go ahead of me." She wined.

"I am sore and exhausted myself, I think I'll just go at your pace." I said.

She walked very slowly, but it was rocky and uphill, so I was in no rush. All of a sudden, I *really* had to poop. Like right away. I quickly turned around without telling her went down a few rocks and off to the side and my body let go of what must've been some excess. I got back on the road and it just kept going uphill. I caught up to Broken Arrow, and I just wanted to sleep at this point, so I went ahead of her. I came across a concrete road and followed along it up the mountain until I realized I wasn't on the Appalachian Trail anymore.

Broken Arrow was waiting for me once I returned

and showed me that there was a sharp turn before the gravel road. She looked at me with her old eyes. I felt like she pitied me a little bit, so I kept going at her pace though it was the last thing I wanted to do. I had a stomachache, and my legs were ready to "give out."

"Do you know how far away the next shelter is?" I asked

"About 5 miles."

"Great."

"It's uphill for most of it," she tested me. "If I can do it, you can do it," she said peacefully daunting.

"Thanks." Old bat.

I went in front of Broken Arrow for about a mile until my stamina ran out and I had to take a nap. There was a gap and a nice view among the pine trees. I thought it would be a perfect time to just lay down, until I could make it up the next hill and finish off the last few miles for the rest of the day. I rolled out my thermal pad and just began to sleep in the middle of the day. It felt so nice, but I'll admit I also felt very guilty. I knew I wasn't getting anywhere and if that was the case it just meant longer that I was going to have to live with these conditions and be in daily pain.

"How did you get in front of me?" A very confused Broken Arrow asked. "And what are you doing down there?"

"I'm trying to procure a little willpower."

"Oh, I suppose," she shook her head and left me to rest.

After about a half hour my muscles in my legs went from relaxing to hurting. They were building muscles, but they were so tense, and unlike any pain that had reached deep into my bones.

Raccoon walked past and just chuckled to himself. Followed by Charlotte, the tall red headed girl, and by the time she came around it had been a good forty-five minutes, so I asked her the time.

"About four o'clock. We're going to stop at the next shelter since it's only about three miles past this next uphill."

"Sounds good. I'm going to get going in just a few."

"Good luck."

I laid there in my own pity, but at the same time I was switching from being in pain, to feeling guilty, to being extremely relaxed. Around one of those intervals I gathered the rest of my strength and began to move forward again. Just before the uphill I saw a tree. It was a small pine tree was covered in ornaments made of paper and some of glass. I thought it was odd, so I went up to it. The tree was decorated in memory of someone who had lost their lives on the trail the previous year. It was a sad thought. It made me think of all the horrible ways someone could die on the trail. Starvation, getting lost, falling off a cliff, even murder wasn't out of grasp. I took a moment of silence. There was a picture of her. She had dark curly hair and a big smile. She didn't look any older than me. I prayed at that moment wondered about my own family.

By this point I had started to be able to calculate how far a mile was in my head, but the road just kept going, I felt like I was going to pass out. I stopped several times, and water was scarce. Eventually a young-looking chap caught up to me. We didn't say anything when we crossed each other, but we started to play tag and I'd pass him after a while and he'd pass me again, until finally we were at the campsite.

Raccoon and Charlotte were the only ones at camp when we got there. It was still sort of early in the day anyways. It seemed like they were talking small talk. I didn't engage myself with them and I went straight into the shelter. I laid back and good God, I was tired. I slept for at least an hour, not really asleep but just laying back closing my eyes listening to what everyone was talking about with one ear. When I started to hear more people arrive, I decided that it was rude to just sleep.

I pulled my head up. The kid I had been passing had been sitting there next to me for a while, but I didn't get up just for him. Charlotte's dad, Ghost came in with Cyborg and Broken Arrow after them. They were all setting up tents around the campsite. Ghost and Charlotte were closest to the shelter, and Raccoon had a comfortable looking blow-up mattress he had set up in the shelter. My stomach problem hadn't gone away, and I hadn't adjusted to the idea that I didn't need to go any further for the rest of the day. I still was anxious.

"Are you going to Trail Days?" I asked the kid next to me.

"Everyone is going to Trail Days, I'm Gonzo, by the way."

"Cheerio. Heard you had a run in with a bear last night."

"Oh yeah, I saw this big shadow and I grabbed my knife and at the top of my lungs I yelled, "GET THE FUCK OUT OF HERE. By the way, is this your knife?"

Apparently, I had put my large knife on the wooden table where Raccoon was sitting.

"Uh, yeah."

"Dude this thing is huge. I'll buy it off you."

"I don't know man. I would sell it, but I also need a smaller knife in return."

"I have a smaller knife." He went into his bag and pulled out a nail clipper sized Swiss army knife.

"Oh, wow, that *is* a smaller knife."

"Dude, I'll buy it from you for like, fifteen dollars."

"I dunno." I said.

"He started going into his bag. He pulled out a pipe."

"And this pipe."

"Maybe. I could use the money, just let me think about it."

"I'll also give you more money at Trail Days."

"I don't know, maybe." We left it at that.

I overheard Charlotte and Ghost bickering at each other.

"Don't Be Impatient. That should be your trail name - Don't Be Impatient," Ghost nearly yelled.

I laughed out loud. I thought it was such a dad thing to say.

"Are you thru hiking?" Gonzo asked me.

"Sorta, I'm heading to New York."

"Now, why would you want to go to New York, Cheerio?" Ghost called over. "In my day, we said that, good people go to heaven, bad people go to hell, and *really* bad people go to New York City."

"You know, I wouldn't know. I've heard it's changed a lot since the 1940's."

"Good one," He snickered.

"What do you want to do in New York?" Gonzo asked me.

"I dunno, drink in the streets, smoke in the rain, see a show, fall in love."

"That sounds like a good plan."

"How old are you, anyways?" I asked him.

"I'm nineteen, you?"

"Twenty. Where you from?"

"Philadelphia."

"Philly is another rough city." Raccoon spoke up. "I went through there with a few of my boys and the women looked rough, man. Cute, but rough."

"What do you want to do?" I asked Gonzo.

"I don't know, I was thinking about joining the French Foreign Legion."

"Oh, why?" Raccoon asked astonished. Even Cyborg looked up and all of a sudden all of the military buffs came out of the woods.

"Why would you want to join them, unless you are trying to die?" Cyborg came up to the bench.

"Because after four years, you are treated like a king," said Gonzo.

"*If* you serve four years." Raccoon said.

"Did you serve?" I asked Raccoon.

"Navy. For six years."

"I just don't know why you would want to serve for them. 90% of all-American soldier deaths happen on American soil. You are putting yourself in a much different situation with The French Foreign Legion." Cyborg said.

"Maybe that's what I'm looking for," Gonzo said, trying to sound brave.

"Howdy!" Tim and Amanda bustled down the hill and into the campsite. "Phew, what a uphill battle that was," Tim butted in. "What are you all talking about?"

"Joining the army," I answered to him offhand.

"Why did all you want to fight, man, it's all about

love, man," Tim said platonically.

"I wasn't loved as a child," Gonzo comeback lighting a cigarette.

"Dear, where are we tenting?" Amanda asked Tim a little seedily.

"I don't know, maybe go find a flat spot over there." Tim said, wanting to be part of the guys.

"Well, come with me!" Amanda yelled.

You could tell it had been a long day for everyone.

"Do they let you join the Navy if you have a mental illness?" I asked.

"You'd need to get a hell of a waiver for that," Raccoon said, "But then again, I knew a drug dealer who had been to prison, and he ended up joining the army somehow. So, you never know."

"If you want to join a force, I'll let you know I was blown up in the army. I'm disabled. You wouldn't be able to tell just by looking at me though," Cyborg said.

"What happened?" Gonzo wondered aloud.

"I was in training and we were running a drill on coordinates, and some asshole wasn't doing his job correctly, and I got blown up. Spent seven hours buried in concrete."

"Do you remember any of it?" I asked.

"I was in and out." He shook his head.

"That's crazy," Gonzo's eyes widened.

"I can't work because of my disability. The government has paid for me since I left. "I was 2 years away from being in the service for 10 years," he sounded sour.

"If that hadn't of happened, would you have stayed?" Gonzo asked.

"Probably."

Everybody started to get ready for dinner. I was still just relaxing on my back, when Kendal and her brother finally arrived, along with a puppy. She smiled when she saw me. The happy investigative creature that caught my eye was the adorable cutest most adorable thing in the world. This puppy was a brownie colored baby Labrador. It was pulling at the leash to go faster and further. Kendal gave me a hug, and the next thing I knew

I was getting licked all over by the sweet dog.

"Nice to see you guys," I said glad to see some familiar faces.

"Yeah, we pulled a little over a twenty," she said, blushed in the face.

"Damn."

"When you've been hiking as long as us, you can do that sort of thing. Especially after a few days of rest," Her brother interjected.

"Aren't you guy's exhausted?" I asked.

Her brother took action. "We're fine. Kendal, let's go set up the tent."

"Alright, I'll be there in a minute," she answered. "How long have you been here?" She up looked at me.

"About an hour, maybe two. I've been asleep the whole time. I haven't even got water since I've been here."

"Let me go put down my stuff, and I'll go get water with you," she offered.

"Alright sounds good."

Her camp was really far away from the shelter.

"I'll build a fire," I said now more awake.

"I'll get the wood," Gonzo said.

Raccoon called out, "If anyone wants to build a fire, I've got a camp essential. Marshmallows!"

Kendal came up to me. "Are you ready to get water?"

"Sure." I grabbed my two water bottles and my water filter. Behind the shelter and down a long path was where the water stream was.

"So, you like the dog?" I asked.

"Err . . . I love the dog. He's perfect. I just kind of got him a little spontaneously."

"That's not always a bad thing. I spontaneously went on this walk."

"Haha, but you can back out at any time you want. I just took on the life of a creature and I'm responsible for it. Like until it dies. That is a lot of responsibility."

"Don't stress so much. That's a gift. You can still do whatever you want. I always said that if I could have a baby daughter, I would hike across the world with my little baby girl on my chest and we would become an internet sensation. You are hiking the Appalachian Trail, right now. If you can do that, you can take care of a dog."

"I know, just what if there is something wrong with the dog, and I have to decide to put it down."

"You are not a mom. It's a puppy, not a human."

"You know, that's not the way that you fill up your water filtration."

"I haven't even been out here for a week, give me a break. Look. See? You'll do a great job taking care of your dog." I put the bag under a flowing stream, and it filled up 100 times quicker than I had been pouring water to fill up the bag.

"I don't know, just what if this trip ends and I'm just back to a life I don't want." She said.

"You don't have to go home. I might not," I said.

"You wanna run away?" she looked at me

"You want to?" I smiled back and looked at each other's eyes briefly.

"You probably have a girlfriend."

I reflected for a moment and my heart hurt and became a little sullen, and it got quiet, but I didn't. While we filled up our water bottles, we noted the water bottle filtrations kinda looked like a dick, which made us laugh and pantomime, resulting in us both getting wet. It was still kinda weird, but good weird. Once we finished filling them up, I asked the next formality in this situation.

"Do you smoke?"

"Yeah, sometimes." She rolled her eyes.

"Want to get high and eat some marshmallows tonight?"

"I'm down. Just don't make it weird in front of my brother."

"Oh yeah. Do you like your brother?" We started heading back to camp.

"Yeah, he's got his own stuff going on, but I'm glad I'm with him."

"How old is he?"

"Twenty-one."

"Oh. I guess that makes sense."

"How old does he look?"

"I dunno. I didn't really think about it."

We got back to the camp.

"Well, I'm going to go make some dinner." She waved.

Gonzo had gathered a lot of firewood, but he hadn't started to build the fire. There are as many ways to build a fire, as there are ways to make love to a woman. He went with the smoosh a bunch of kindling into the bottom approach, and it didn't work. I go with a much more graceful approach of putting two logs against each other and with the right angling a fire can emerge with just a little bit of kindling and patience. Once the fire was going, we began to just throw a lot of wood on it and it began to rise and rise until it was massive. I still hadn't eaten and the exhaustion from the day was really settling in.

Tim, who was eating some stew, said he didn't really want what he was eating, so he offered it to me, and I was thankful. I was too lazy to switch spoons and the sausage was rough. Cyborg gave us a negative look as though it was not smart to be sharing food utensils. I suppose he was right. I still felt a little bit odd. Not upset or anything, just not in the mood to deal with a lot of people. I looked over to my side and Ghost was smoking a little pipe. I was intrigued. I walked over to him and he began to smile a guilty grin.

"So, what's this?" I asked casually

"You want some?"

I took the pipe and began to inhale. It tastes fruity.

cough "Thanks man. I was thinking about rolling a joint and sharing it with Kendal, but I'm running pretty low, would you mind if I borrowed a little bit from you?"

"Oh, not at all." He took out a zip lock filled to the top.

"Grab a few."

"No way."

"Way." He raised his eyebrows. "Is that enough?" he asked me.

"Oh, much more than enough, my good man. What do your tattoos on your arm mean?" I asked with my hands full.

"Well, after I finished college, I went to seminary school. I didn't want to be one of those people who go knocking on doors asking if they know who Jesus Christ is. So, what I did was I tattooed "Jesus Loves You" in almost every language on my arms so that when I'm travelling or on a bus somewhere around the world, people will come up to me and say, "Do you know what this says?" and I reply, "Do you know what it means?""

"Wow, that is a badass way of spreading Christianity."

"It makes the world a better place." He laughed and inhaled on his pipe.

"I agree to an extent, I suppose. Listen, thanks a lot."

"No problem, Cheerio."

I went over to the bonfire. Gonzo, Kendal and Broken Arrow were all sitting around it roasting marshmallows. I didn't have a stick, but I was holding something else in my hand. I showed it off to Gonzo.

"Where'd you get that?" He barked.

"It's growing over there."

He took me seriously for a moment.

"Ghost gave it to me, but don't ask him for any, I got enough for everyone." I handed him some.

"Do you have any papers?" I asked.

"Yeah, I have a few," Gonzo replied. He got up to go get them and I went over to my bag, opened up my little zip lock and mixed in the weed I had, saved a nice amount, went back to the bonfire.

I sat down. Kendal offered me her stick.

"Sure, will you grind up the weed?" I asked.

"Ok."

"Is that what I think it is?" Broken Arrow asked with a smile that revealed a few missing teeth.

"No," I said to her.

"Shame, I ran out back in North Carolina," she said.

"I left with a half-ounce and I ran out in two weeks," Gonzo said sitting back down.

"I'm just happy I have marshmallows, right now. But we'll pass it your way Broken Arrow," I said.

Eventually everything was rolled up and we passed

it around.

"So, you ever been married," I asked Broken Arrow as I roasted my marshmallow.

"Twice."

"What happened to the first one?"

"I just didn't like him anymore." She said it in a simple movement.

I looked over to Kendal and Gonzo and we all started laughing.

"That's fair, I guess." Kendal said.

"What about the second one?" Gonzo said.

"He died."

"I'm sorry to hear that." The laughter settled.

"Eh." She shrugged her shoulders, "The first one is a millionaire now."

"His loss," I said with a snarky laugh.

"We met when he was fourteen years old."

"Ahhh" Kendal and I said.

"I lied, I told him I was thirteen, but I was only eleven."

"Oh," We both were laughing pretty hard.

Broken Arrow commented again, "My son almost married this girl but she got hit by a car and got an 18,000 dollar settlement and left him. He was heartbroken." That disgusting human nature reached my core in one of those painful reflections you don't want to understand about people. He could have been just as horrible as what she did.

Cyborg called over to us, "Hey, potheads. I made a cake."

We all were interested and probably hungry, so we all walked over to the picnic table. Cyborg had a pot of boiling water and then another pot that was on top of it that had cake batter in it, which was now a soft chocolate cake. We all took our spoons and dug in. I was nursing the joint and hit it right before I ate mine.

"You want any?" I asked Cyborg, which was not an absurd question considering the dyed hair, and the fact that he was a war veteran.

"I have never smoked anything in my life." Cyborg responded tersely.

"You're missing out, man." I took a puff. "Tim, you want to try?" He looked around suspiciously. "You know, I also use pot occasionally for medical reasons. It takes the edge off when my mind starts to go too fast sometimes." I said.

"That's what happened when I didn't take my meds a few nights ago," Tim replied.

"What happened?" I asked.

"Things started to go a little too fast." He said.

"He got anxious. I could tell right away. He's usually not even this talkative." She said with her arm around him.

"Do you think pot would help?" he asked.

"I can't really tell you that, but we can always find out," I smiled.

He turned to Amanda who was like, "go ahead."

Gonzo passed it to him and he took one light inhale and began to cough. We all started laughing as it happened, except for Cyborg.

"Oh, wow," he said. "That stuff is strong."

"Just wait a few minutes."

Ghost came up to all of us.

"What am I missing?"

"Nothing, man. We're all just here having a nice shin-dig on a Sunday night."

"Amen."

"Hallelujah," Broken Arrow called out.

Ordinarily the scene might have seemed slightly cheesy, but it wasn't. It was nice and after such a horrible day. It was really great to feel such a nice group of people coming together and just having a nice time in the woods. I felt like I knew each one of them in their own way and though it was only momentary, I loved them all as though they were my brothers, fathers, grandmothers, aunts, uncles, and so forth.

"I might sleep in the shelter tonight," Kendal whispered to me. I did my best to make it seem as though I wasn't listening, but it was hard to not overhear when she relayed the information to her brother. It was getting dark, and people were beginning to go into their tents. I was sitting down by the fire and Kendal came by with her sleeping bag in her hand. Her teeth were brushed.

"What's up?"

"Hey."

I just sat and looked at the fire and she rested her head on my knees for a moment.

"You alright?" I asked.

"Tonight was pretty great. You?"

"I dunno. Maybe I'm homesick. I just have this empty aftertaste."

"That's understandable. I got really homesick in the Smokies."

"Part of me really loves what I am doing, but I feel like I've been so cushioned for so long that my body is just reacting so harshly."

"There is a motto on the trail that goes, "Never quit on a bad day." Today was hard, it happens. You haven't even been out here a week and you want to quit?" She lifted her head to eye level.

"I'm not saying I want to quit, I'm just saying. It's a lot different than I expected, and I feel like I *can't* back out."

"Only 1 in 4 make it to Katan." She grinned.

"Ha, well, maybe I'm not one of them. I'm only going halfway there, but it still feels like there's only a 50/50 chance I'm going to make it that far."

"Uh, New York is a lot further than halfway of the Appalachian Trail. It's like 300 miles past Harper's Ferry which is known as the halfway point at mile 1,050."

New York was another thousand miles way. I was defeated.

"Well, this day just got a little worse." I ran my hands through my hair.

"Dude don't think like that. You are lucky to be doing what you're doing." She wrapped her arm around the back of my head and comforted me.

"I'm just tired."

"Tomorrow will be a new day and you are going to feel a lot better."

I stood up. "I'm going to pee out the fire."

"I would help but, I can't."

"Listen, sorry, I just get this way sometimes. I'm sort of polar."

"It's all good, dude. I can be a bitch sometimes too."

I pissed out the fire and went to the shelter where Kendal set up her sleeping bag close to mine. I quickly brushed my teeth and laid down next to her. I don't know what was going on with me. I wanted to hook up with her, but at the same time, I just felt depressed. It's not like that sort of thing is just one person's decision either. I hoped would be a cold night. I only had my blanket over me. As the night progressed, I slowly got the courage to move closer to her. Eventually she unzipped her sleeping bag and I moved in. Her tiny legs were prickly, but the touch of another human being was what I had longed for all day. We held each other, because, it was indeed cold.

I didn't try anything on her at first. I was exhausted. Eventually she used me as a pillow before I dozed off. And then, I was rudely awakened by the strangest noise I had ever heard in my life. Raccoon snoring like a steamboat *and* two animals fighting. I had never heard the human body make the noises that came out of that man. It woke up Kendal too and all of sudden we were both holding back laughter. Our faces got close enough that I kissed her, and it was a good kiss. Long, but both of our eyes were closed, and I don't think either of us were really looking for any funny business next to the sounds of the grizzly man snoring that loudly into the night. We fell asleep together, which is my favorite thing to do in this world with any person.

Chapter 15

The sun rose, and surprisingly, people mainly slept in. Even Cyborg was at the bench making breakfast around nine o'clock. Kendal and I got up a little earlier than everybody else. She offered to eat breakfast with me. Everyone was starting to break down their tents and Raccoon was deflating his sleeping pad. I got all my things together, didn't change clothes, put everything away and was pretty much ready to go, apart from eating.

I was about to break out a granola bar, but Kendal came up to the bench with her stove and a few packets of oatmeal.

"I wonder why more people don't sleep in the shelters," I said my morning thought.

"Rats," Cyborg said.

"Oh, I guess that's a good reason." I chewed.

"Either that or they don't like who they are sleeping next to," he made a crack.

"I didn't mind it so much," Kendal smiled.

"Well, imagine trying to sleep next to someone and they start beating off."

I was flushed.

"That happened?" Kendal asked disgusted.

"Yeah, there was a guy around mile a hundred in a shelter."

Don't Be Impatient walked up to us. "How was sleeping in the shelter last night?" She gave Kendal a smile.

"It was nice, except this man!" She looked over to Raccoon. "I have never heard human noises come out of anyone the way you sounded last night."

"How does my hair look?" he joked.

"Natural," I responded.

Don't Be Impatient laughed like a bike horn.

"Well, I'm going nine miles today," Cyborg said, finishing up his breakfast.

"I think I'll go twenty," I planned.

"I don't think that would be wise," Cyborg said.

"Twenty miles ain't nothing," Gonzo came up to the bench, looking ready to go.

"I've run a marathon before. I'm starting to warm up to more miles every day." I tried to reason with Cyborg.

"How long did it take for you to run the marathon?"

"Five hours."

"My wife has come in first place in every marathon or race she has ever run in, except one where she came in second."

"Don't devalue what I've done. That's great. I hope you and your wife are very delighted, but some people are just happy with accomplishing something and do not have to be the best at everything."

This guy had such an undertone of authority with everything that he was doing and such a condescending nature towards everyone else.

I ate breakfast quickly and quietly after that.

"Are you guys feeling alright?" Raccoon asked.

Everyone mutually nodded their heads.

"I dunno, that city food yesterday is giving me some trouble. My stomach hurts. I think I'm going to stay at the next hostel. There is one in six miles."

"That's as far as we're going today," Don't Be Impatient said. "And that's as far as Broken Arrow is going."

"I'm trying to get to Damascus as soon as possible." Gonzo said.

"I think there is a shuttle to Damascus from the hostel I've heard," Ghost replied.

"Maybe I will check it out. Are you going to stop there?" I asked Kendal.

"Probably not," Kendal said.

"Gonzo, are you are ready?" It took him about 10 minutes before we set out. I did some yoga and stretched. Kendal and her brother were a little bit behind and we started to walk out of the campsite, but Tim and Amanda were arguing.

"Good morning, Cheerio." Tim broke their banter.

"Everything alright?" I asked.

"Oh, everything is fine. We just want to see as much as possible before we leave."

"I understand that, just remember don't take everything so seriously. The real world has enough of that bullshit."

"Cheerio. Listen, it was so great to meet you. I hope to see you up the path."

"I hope to see you too, Tim. And you too, Amanda." I gave them both hugs.

"*When I wake up early in the morning, lift my head, I'm still yawning*." I sang as I walked off.

"*Please don't spoil my day, I'm miles away and after all, I'm only sleeping*."

My legs were sore. My back was sore. My shoulders were sore. At least I was used to the pain that was to come of it. We walked for a while, Gonzo and I, but as the miles came, we began to get further and further apart, with him in front of me. I didn't mind and I wasn't worried. I thought about how if I could get six miles done before noon, I could do another twelve if I went for seven hours after lunch.

It wasn't too long before the road split. I wouldn't have known. However, there was a bonfire and someone I recognized.

"Bear? Is that you?"

"Eh? Oh yes. Hello."

"Hey, we met at Uncle Jeff's, shared a beer and some weed."

"Sounds like me, hehe. How you doing, man? I'm just getting this fire started to have some tuna mac and cheese."

"Sounds nice, but I had a good breakfast. I think I am going to stop at the hostel."

"Well, you're going the wrong way. It's down here." He pulled out a joint.

I stopped and turned around, I looked past him and saw that there was a path that diverted from the road down the ways.

"Oh well, I guess I have a moment to sit down, it's only ten o'clock."

"Yeah, take a load off." He seemed like he might come off as creepy to some people, but I really liked him.

"How old are you man?"

"Thirty."

"Nice, what made you want to go out on this trip?"

"Good people, Good times. Never done it. Thought I would."

"Fair enough."

"You smoke?" He asked.

"Lately, but I have my own, though." I started to go into my bag to get some.

"Nonsense." He handed me the unlit joint. I thought I would at least give him a show for his good deed. I took the stout marijuana cigarette and put my face up against the bonfire and lit it with the flames, inhaled deep and with one hit I was stoned.

"We're not dealing with someone from their first rodeo here, are we? Haha." He snickered.

"Apparently not," I coughed.

"Well Alright!"

"Are you gonna try to walk into Trail Days?" I asked.

"I really want to man, but it's over 30 miles a day from this point, and I'd probably arrive on Friday night instead of Thursday. I think I'm going thirty today, so I've got to eat up."

"Damn. You'll get there." I encouraged him.

I began to get a little anxious. Not uncomfortable anxious, but ready to go anxious. I knew I couldn't go thirty miles a day. If I wanted to get there on time, I was going to have to book it.

"I've got to get going if I am going to make it." I said, grabbing my hat.

"Alright, then. I think the hostel is about a mile and a half, if not two down this way."

"See you at Trail Days."

"Sounds good."

I began walking towards the hostel. It was downhill which was a good thing in one way and bad in another. It was good because it was easy to get to, but bad because I knew I was going to have to walk back up. There were a few houses very split and far away from each other. I went off trail to pee and went sort of far off, and in the distance, I saw something. I didn't really know if what I saw was what I thought it was. The woods were thick, but I was so interested, nothing could have stopped me. Deep into these woods, very deep, stood a structure. Old houses, or clubhouses were all beaten down, all just old wooden buildings. I began to walk into the area. I was noticeably affected by the weed and the ambiance of the place made me very scared. I didn't know if anyone was living in these buildings or what the situation was, but it was eerie.

I began to narrate what I was seeing. There were stacked rocks, which are called Cairns, underneath the largest of the structures, a wood cabin, balancing the building. It was unstable to say the least. One off movement could be fatal. There were other structures hidden among the trees, made of old cedar and rusted pipes. I began looking into the other ones. They were all destroyed by years of neglect and storms that had probably torn through them as they stood all by themselves without anyone to notice them. It was deep off the trail. I climbed into the cabin through a back window and it was so silent, it screamed. I've done some very stupid things before in my life. This one truly took the cake as the most life risking, just plainly idiotic entrances. Still, I wanted to explore the whole building. Parts of it were falling apart, but you could see how it was built well enough for it to be lived in, apart from what it stood on. I noticed only some old candles and a tarp in the back room along with a mirror. I didn't dare investigate further. I drifted across the floorboard and the front door had been blown off, so I climbed out through it, and thanked God nothing had gone terribly wrong during my short intrusion on what I would call nature.

I had only gone into this direction by becoming disoriented. I was indeed, in a cross of a lost world. It was like it was a small settlement that had fallen. That had failed to survive. These buildings or this small fallen town were as natural as a tree fallen in the woods. It was decayed deeply, covered in forest mulch and history. Nature had dominated any humans stupid enough to try and live out in the woods. I pushed my way through the forest back onto the trail and walked in silence. I had been deeply moved by what I had seen, disturbed in these woods in a way I had not previously understood. I was in the outskirts of the village known as Greasy Creek, Tennessee.

The trail eventually turned to gravel and then I saw a small pond off the side of the road, which I walked my way around to a porch where there was a nice row of hiker backpacks all lined up. I put my backpack next to them and walked into the hostel. It was much less of an establishment than Uncle Jeff's and really just someone's home.

"Shoes off!" A white-haired woman greeted me as I walked in.

"Oh, I am sorry ma'am." I nearly jumped out of my skin after what I had just been through.

"And wash your hands when you come in," she said all of a sudden, kindly.

"Yes ma'am." I took my shoes off in the foyer and looked up to see that they sold ice cream and hamburgers out of a little cooler. My shoes were off, and I went into the kitchen. As I washed my hands, I saw on the windowsill written in small nail polish the letters NYC on them. A symbolic momentum, which made me feel like I was at getting somewhere. It was a very nice living room, very old. It had greenish wallpaper that looked like it was from the forties. They had old books all over the place and I was interested in a Steinbeck book which when I opened and it read, "*Obviously all the people and events in this story are fictitious*".

Gonzo sat at the dinner table eating a hamburger, Raccoon was on a reclining chair, and Ghost was drinking a Coca-Cola standing over a lamp chair. They all greeted me as I walked in but were more or less occupied in their own things.

"Hello," A black man with a greying wild afro said staring at me a little blankly through his glasses.

"Hello, Sir," I said back to him.

"I'm Jimmy." He was about my size and he came up to me.

"Cheerio."

"Have you filled one of these out yet?" He handed me a sheet of paper, which informed the hostel of my phone number and emergency contact, along with what food I would like to eat. I sat down and began to fill it out.

Ghost looked concerned.

"Have you seen Charlotte?" He asked me.

"No, I haven't. How did you get here before me? I left before you." I asked.

"We've been here for a while." Raccoon said.

Ghost looked anxious that his daughter hadn't arrived yet and walked out of the room. My feet were very sore, and I felt something pulsing on it, so I took off my sock, which stunk up the small living room and it revealed a horrible blister on my foot. It was the size of a small water balloon filled up all the way. I hadn't taken my socks off in at least two days.

I looked over to Gonzo who was enjoying finishing up his burger.

"Do you have your little pocket knife?" I asked.

"Do you want to sell your knife now?" His eyes widened.

"Do you think I could just use yours for a moment?" I asked distressed.

"I'll sell it to you. Fifteen dollars and I'll put you up for the night here."

The offer was tempting.

"Well, I just have a blister on my foot and my knife is way too big to pop it with, and I was wondering if I could just use your small knife really quickly."

"Oh, I'll keep my last offer and raise you a hamburger."

I should have taken the offer. I was starving, but sometimes I don't do well under pressure.

"Sorry dude, I just can't really not have a real knife on me. I still don't know what might happen out there."

"Well then you can't use this one."

"Thanks, dude."

"1000 movies, Elizabeth!" Jimmy called out.

"Hoorah," she said a little enthusiastically.

I looked at him and over to Elizabeth, the house owner. Her and Jimmy were obviously romantically involved. They were warm with one another beyond the comforts of the South. They were both were in their mid-sixties, and she was white and he was black. Not that these things always matter, but it did once where we were. I wondered what it must've been like to love someone in Tennessee where racism still existed. If her family was supportive, or if she decided to live along a creek with the man she loved regardless. If he was ostracized just the same for loving someone different. There was a picture of them hiking when they were younger, so they must've been together a while and faced discrimination at some point in their lives together. Maybe, it didn't matter the way I think.

"She's here!" Ghost exclaimed excited that his daughter had come in and was safe.

Charlotte (Don't Be Impatient) came through the door looking very tired.

"Having fun?" I asked her once she had sat down. She looked exhausted, her hair was tied back and all sweaty.

"Did you wash your hands?" Elizabeth yelled.

"Charlotte looked at me for guidance, a little guilty and confused.

"Did you take your shoes off?" I said under my breath.

"No." She shook her head answering both of the questions thrown at her.

"You might wanna do that," I responded.

As she was getting situated, Jimmy called out, "1001 movies, Elizabeth!"

I realized they were illegally downloading films.

"What movie should we watch tonight?" Jimmy asked the group.

Gonzo said, "Psycho."

I was still a little high. "Wow, watching that out here right now that would be bizarre," I said still not used to comfortability so far away from it.

I stood up and went to the kitchen where Elizabeth and Charlotte were.

"Do you have a work for stay program?" I asked softly.

She smiled back. "Yes, one hour of work and you can tent, or two hours and you can have a bunk."

"Ok thanks." I don't know why I asked, I'm just getting a little too comfortable.

"My neighbor needs some work done in her yard. She'll probably pay you if you do some work. She's also doing a shuttle to Trail Days."

"Oh really?" Beginning to think this wasn't such a bad idea to stay a few days after all. "How much does it cost?"

"A hundred and twenty-eight dollars. A dollar per mile."

"Oh, haha." "Yeah, I don't think I can afford that, I don't have any money." All hope was lost.

"You don't have *any* money?" Elizabeth asked.

"Not today." The room got a little quieter. "Well, I have a few quarters I think," I said trying to divert some attention to break the silence.

"Do you want a hamburger?" Jimmy asked.

"I have some change, I can buy it," I said, getting a little depressed but I guess I wanted a burger. I pulled out twelve quarters because a burger was three dollars. I started thinking about how I was going to have to get going soon. On a flat screen connected to a computer desktop, which took up the entire back wall of the small house, there was a picture of a beautiful overview of a mountain gap in the fall.

"Where is that?" I asked Jimmy.

"Oh that is twenty seven miles away from here. It's beautiful."

"Looks that way." I smiled internally.

"You know, there is a barn about twenty-three miles from here."

I thought it might not be a bad idea.

"Don't do it today if you don't have to. There is a bridge before it and three years ago a hiker thought he could make it from here and he didn't have to and died."

"Oh, well, I don't think I was planning on going thirty miles today anyways." I ate quickly because I was so hungry. The burger was finished, and it had some mayo, lettuce and a tomato on it. It was delicious. It wasn't huge but it was a sustainable lunch and I was extremely grateful for the little flavor of home. All the granola and ramen was driving my taste buds crazy.

"Do you think I'll be able to make it into Damascus if I hitchhike?" I asked Jimmy looking at the remnants of my plate.

"Oh yeah, there is a highway that is coming up and you can probably get a ride, here, I'll give you some cardboard for you to write on."

Frog ripped the old cardboard into a square.

"They won't pick you up if you don't look like hiker trash," he said with assurance.

I guess I could understand what he was referring to. Some of the people I had seen, people who (especially the ones I was with at the moment) had money and could very easily maneuver their ways through the woods, but I began to realize that everyone was on the same team and trying to get each other along to the next point regardless. There were people I had seen who hadn't bathed in months, who were only skin and bones. There was a rule I had personally picked up by experienced up by this point: the less you had, the more people were willing to give. I was very grateful.

I looked on the table. There were some chopsticks along with some forks in a holder. I was trying to deny to myself that I wasn't still very hungry.

"Is there a Chinese restaurant nearby?" I asked pointlessly.

Charlotte laughed out loud.

"Cheerio, you say the funniest, most random things." She said.

It was a confidence booster. I took the compliment without explaining why the thought popped into my mind.

Jimmy answered, "Not for forty miles."

Charlotte looked at me and shrugged, "Eh, that's an easy two day."

I chuckled. “Alright, I think I’m gonna get going.” The last thing I had to do was pop my blister.

“Charlotte, do you have a knife?”

“Yeah, I do. It’s outside.”

“Cool, goodbye everybody.”

Raccoon didn’t really look up, “G’bye, Cheerio.”

Ghost was a little more sentimental. “Good luck,” and gave me a small salute.

“Hope your knee gets better,” I said to him.

Gonzo all of a sudden got up from his chair very abruptly. “I’m leaving as well.”

It was odd but not that strange, just in the way that it seemed like the idea dawned on him. I felt as though it came from some sort of competitively. He walked out very quickly and didn’t really say goodbye to anyone.

“Before you go, Cheerio, do you think that you could put a pin in our map on the wall of where you come from?” Jimmy asked.

“Oh sure.”

I walked over into the living room area. There was a big map. Most of the pins were from people along the trail anyways, who must’ve gotten sick of their boring lives and just decided to walk through the whole entire mountain range. I put mine in. Jimmy had an old camera, and I smiled. Raccoon leaned into the picture with me and we probably looked great. It was strange. As I began to walk out of the room, I felt a connection with almost everyone in it. It really would have been nice to spend the night, relax with them for another night. I went out through the backdoor with Charlotte. She went through her bag and pulled out the knife for me. She decided to sit with me.

“This might be gross,” I said.

“I like gross stuff. Trust me, this is going to be nothing.”

“I was just prepping.”

I looked on my feet and there was a blister I hadn’t noticed on my other foot. The worst one was on my big toe and it looked like another toe coming off of it. It really was disgusting. I took my foot-long knife and began to pierce through the skin. It took a few tries. I punctured the first one by pressing a little too deep and out came light creamy red pus mixed with my blood.

“That *is* disgusting,” she said.

The other one was simple. Pop, clear liquid and it was done.

Chapter 16

The walk back to the Appalachian Trail was uphill as expected. Although walking is what most of this journey consisted of, it may be the most boring part to explain. The entire trail began to melt together besides a few gorgeous views and awful uphill mountain climbs. I love nature, but just like anything there is a law of moderation and when you are over exposed your mind begins to think a different way. I would never know how long I would go without seeing another person. Sometimes I would get spurts of energy and just start dancing. Since I was so deep into the woods, I didn't have any internet, I would just sing to myself.

It was like I was going crazy, but really I was just allowing myself to feel the freedom which the constraints of the real world hold against other people. I would talk out loud to myself. Sometimes I would just mutter ideas, and other times I would have full on conversations between different parts of my head and its consciousness. Really, I was just confused and unsure of what I was going to do in New York once I got there.

I didn't have a place to stay. Staying in a city is much different than being in the woods and I had heard it was an extremely dangerous city. I tried not to focus on these parts and to think about the things that I had going for me. It wasn't about what I had done, it was about who I thought I was and what I could do. Who knew? I knew. I knew I could do things that I wanted to regardless of what anybody thought. I lived in my own world. I am someone who deeply believes in the idea that if you think it, it can happen, or at least something will come of it. I have been put in extraordinary situations just by allowing my brain to have the assurance that everything is going to be alright.

I felt so trapped before as if college was the only option that I was given after high school. Things were different. I saw a young man, with a long blonde ponytail and a baby face with peach fuzz coming out of it where a beard should be. He was sitting on a tree.

"You mind if I sit down next to you?" I needed a break.

"Not at all man."

"Where you coming from?" I asked.

"I'm Southbound, I'm from Virginia. How about you?"

"I'm coming from North Carolina."

"I just spent a few days in Asheville."

"You did?" I asked.

"Yeah, man cool place. Great people."

"Yeah, it's a pretty hip town."

"So... College eh?" He winked an eyebrow.

"Haha, yup." I said ashamed.

"I assumed you didn't go?" He asked.

"It's worthwhile."

"Yeah, well I'm not going. It sucks." He crossed his arms.

"Well, technically you can't really say that." I waved my finger.

"Technically I can, man."

"Well. Yeah. It sucks. I might not go back." I said.

"How long have you been enrolled?" He asked.

"Two years."

"Why would you not go back?" He switched tones as if he was now concerned for my well-being.

"Why do you care? I thought college sucked."

"Well, it does. But that's just because it takes four years. If you're already halfway there why don't you just finish. You're done with all the core classes anyways."

"See this is what I meant. You think college sucks for a completely different reason than why it does."

"Probably, I haven't been." He responded.

"Well, don't just visit." I offered.

"We should get stoned." He grinned.

"Yeah, man. We should."

"No worries man. I've got you."

He reached in and packed a small orange bowl and we began smoking it. To be honest I don't really remember what we talked about after that. I'm sure it was nothing important but all the same the most sincere things to talk about with someone. He was only eighteen and was lonely since he didn't see anybody going the same way as him. I told him how unprepared I was.

"How heavy is your pack?" I asked him.

"I think, after food supply about twenty pounds."

"Wait, What?"

"Why? How much is yours?"

"I don't know. I got it down to around to fifty."

"Ah shit man. That's rough."

"Eh, I'll power through. How does it look up ahead? Is it uphill?"

"Yeah, mainly, do you not have a trail book?" He asked.

"No, I don't, but I'll probably be ok."

"Here, I have some old sheets from mine, since I'm going the opposite direction as you, you can have them."

I began to read through them. It seemed I had a ways to go until there was the barn. I wasn't worried though, there was a shelter about eight miles from where I was.

"Listen man, there isn't water for a while after this, so fill up here." I took his advice and when I was done, we both went on our own ways.

As I walked, I began to see a short dirt road. The sun was still up, and the day was mystical. I was glad to be in the forest and felt freer than ever. That's when I made the horrible decision to call Don since I had a little service.

"Hello." He yelled quietly.

"Hi dad, how are you?"

"I'm good. Are you ready to come home? I think it's been long enough." I could tell in his voice that his initial rage had worn off, but he was still hurt.

"No, I was just calling to let you know, everything is alright, and I'm happy out here."

"Well call your grandmother. She is worried sick."

"Good to hear from *you*. I'm glad you are happy. I'm happy."

"Alright, Goodbye."

I tried calling my grandmother, but she didn't pick up. So, I tried my sister who was probably fondling her cats when I called her. She was worried, but only slightly, it seemed she had something to get back to. After we hung up, a gigantic car with a horse on the back in a stall rolled up.

Horses are such gracious animals. However, they can be quite large. Immersed in the beautiful golden bronze thick mane, I was in awe of the horse's grace. I heard from behind me, a girl and the gallop of a much smaller animal followed by her brother.

"Oh, hey." I hugged Kendal.

"Hey Cheerio." The puppy hopped on my knees.

"What took you guys so long?"

"We got caught up behind a bear. Apparently, there are more walking around at the moment, so we have to be careful if we are going to progress."

"I ain't afraid. I have my sword with me and I know a brutal way to kill one if it attacks."

"We're saved." She lowered her eyelids.

I got down on my knees playing with the adorable thing, and we all took a moment to witness the animals. We decided to progress together, but very slowly. Her brother stared and made strange observations looking out for wild bears.

"After seeing that mama, we're gonna have to call home."

I guess if you were on the road for a month, you'd miss your mama too. I wasn't afraid of getting mauled, and I never saw the bear. We came across a long uphill, which is just as scary. The sun was beginning to set on the day. I passed a campsite, and then another one where Kendal and her brother decided stay for the night. I wanted to get to the next shelter, but it was beginning to get dark. I kept walking until I just couldn't anymore, but it kept getting steeper and steeper. I had had it for the day, but when you've had it and where there is a good spot for you to rest does not always match up. I came across a man who was tenting with his wife in his underwear.

"Do you know where the next shelter is?" I asked trying not to affront anyone.

"It's about two miles more, but there is a campsite in about a half mile."

I'm sure they intended to be away from people and that's why they were camping in the spot they were. I wanted to make it, to go as far as I could, but all the same, it had been another long day, after long day, after long day and my body craved rest. I thought I would be able to make it the two miles but once I got to a flat campsite, I was so angsty and sticky from the humidity that in no way was I in the mood to go any further.

However, when you get to camp, that is not as far as you go for the day, you have to set up your tent, and make dinner and build a fire which I guess are close to the same things adults have to do after a long day of work. They make dinner, clean up and wash the dishes. I looked around and there weren't that many people at the campsite, but there was what appeared to be a large fire. I was thankful that I didn't have to make one myself tonight. I setup my tent as usual but the ground was very unsteady. Nobody was really close by to me but only because the size of the campsite ranged very large on top of this small mountain, and I was distant from all of the other occupants. The tent was on slightly slanted ground, but I didn't care by the time I was done setting up. I stuffed everything inside lazily and proceeded over to the fire.

There was a huge log roasting over the pit, and three men drinking from all different types of bottles of what appeared to be whiskey.

"Howdy men." I nodded as I approached.

"Helluva evening for a fire ain't it." The alpha older male called back.

"Glad it's already been built by the time I got here."

"Go ahead." The youngest of the three said.

I began to boil my water.

"You're not gonna make it." The alpha eyed me sipping his drink.

"I'm not really a hiker. I'm just going to New York."

"New York is a long way from here friend. " The beta said.

"Are you running away?" The alpha asked.

"Not really."

"Cause if you're running away, you're not going to make it. Hahaha."

They all took deep sips of their whiskey.

"I like to think of it as walking home."

"Hey, I like that. You might make it after all." He tipped his hat. "We've seen people coming from the North and boy do they look awful. Faces all torn up, looking' like skeletons."

The imagery in my head got to me

"It's because they don't eat right." The beta said.

I was concerned about my own diet. I was so hungry I was munching on the last few of my granola bars. I really had lost a substantial amount of weight in a shockingly short amount of time. The water had come to a boil and I poured in the potato mixture and stirred it.

"I remember seeing these punk ass kids, who were carrying lawn chairs on their backs. Like, *Yeah, we're just gonna walk to Maine with this on our backs*. Yeah right." The young one said.

"They had coca cola 12 packs. That kinda weight ain't making it far." The beta said.

"Yeah that's wild." I said with a mouth full of food.

"I threw out my back a few years ago carrying too much weight, had trouble walking for two years after that." The alpha said.

I sorta liked these guys, but they were just new faces somewhere new. I finished up my dehydrated mashed potatoes and filled up again for some ramen. They began to pull out cigarillos and smoked them. It was peaceful, and it all had a nice aesthetic in the woods, smoking and all, but I had had a long day of smoking. I wasn't interested after they had been so doubtful of my quest.

"Well, Goodnight." I said.

"Night."

My ramen wasn't done, but I wasn't waiting. I've learned to love the taste of crunchy noodles. I went and hung my bear bag in the dark and I slipped into my tent to fall asleep. This was the coldest night I had experienced thus far. My blanket did not begin to cover up the frosty air. My legs were moaning the entire time I was trying to fall asleep. There was too much pain running up and down my legs, I couldn't go to bed. It felt like a knife was cutting at my sides.

I laid in the fetal position for eight long hours unable to drift away from the discomfort. I got out of my tent to a pink sunrise because of my grumbling stomach. The beginning of the day began to tint light blue around it the pink sunny side up egg in the sky. I hugged a tree for dear life and out came a foul smelling chunky liquid goo.

For fifteen minutes in the cold bare morning air I stood freezing, able to see my breath at the break of dawn, covered in goosebumps. When it was finally over, and I pulled everything over me, I went back into my tent. Luckily the day was just beginning, and the sun was rising along with the temperature. I closed my eyes for as long as I could and gave myself the rest. I needed it. If muscles were tearing quicker than I was allowing them to repair, this was the time to let them do what they needed. I slept in until around ten o'clock which is dismally late in the woods, but it did wonders for my legs.

The rest of my body on the other hand was still in a critical condition and needed to move slowly. I was not happy. I knew that these crossroads were expected when you put yourself in a situation, miles from any medical help or even just a warm bed. Chrissake, I took my luck as it came, and I was only becoming stronger because of what I had allowed my body to go through. The worse it got, the easier it would become I told myself.

By the time I broke down my tent I realized I was basically out of water, which is not a good thing when all of your hydration had just gone out the back end. I sat and ate the rest of my Cheerios that I had saved. Someone told me that they were not very good for energy, but the way I saw it, carbs were carbs, they were going to get me going for the day. I sat back as everything slowly found its way into my backpack organized, as it should be. I didn't know where any nearby water source was, but I had heard there was one close to the campsite.

A woman with tremendously muscular legs walked up to the camp as I ate my cereal in pain.

"Do you know where the water source is?" She asked.

"No."

"Alright, well I'm going to take a piss."

"Nice." She began to walk over to where I had left my lovely art piece this morning. I hoped she wouldn't see it.

She came back after about ten minutes.

"I found the water source," she smiled at me.

"Which way is it?"

"Just down that path, about a quarter mile down and you'll find a stream."

"Great. I was running low on water."

"Well fill up, I don't think there is another water source for ten miles."

I got up and thanked her and went down the hill with my two water bottles. I filled up quickly since I left my backpack at the campsite. I got on the road as fast as I could after I got water. I was surprised that it was so downhill. I was making good time. I passed a man and his wife and smiled gracefully as I did. It wasn't until I got to the bottom of the hill, three miles down that I realized I was going in the wrong direction.

I had just spent half of my morning thinking I was making great time when in fact I was just going the wrong way. It was like I was being told to quit. I knew that wasn't going to happen that easy. I didn't have a choice at the end of the day. I went up the hill again, which was not as beautiful the third time seeing it. I was obviously not in a good mood, so once I caught up with the married couple that I had seen me pass them the night before in their underwear, going North, I had a stiff little word with them.

"Next time you see someone going the opposite direction, let them know before they end up in Georgia." I said to them.

"Oh yeah, Honey." She tapped her husband's belly. "We were laughing to ourselves about that."

"Well, next time, I guess. Just make sure they know." I wasn't really mad at them, it wasn't their fault.

"Alright, will do. You can pass us." The husband said.

This was followed by a different kind of climb, almost like a giant staircase made out of boulders. It was steep and beautiful now that I was getting somewhere, I began to marvel in the beauty of nature and how much more alluring walking to New York was than I had originally imagined it would be, just chain restaurants and along highways. Eventually there was a large overlook. I saw two overweight gentleman smoking cigarettes.

"Do you have an extra? I've had a wonderful morning." I said out of breath.

One gave me the cigarette and the other lit it.

"I just went three miles in the wrong direction." I bragged.

"Hehe. Damn now that's stupid. Didn't you recognize what you were looking at?" One of them asked.

"All this forest starts to kinda mix together like a bad drink." I was obviously being bashful.

"At least it's easy on the eyes." The other one said.

I looked out over farmland combined with roads, and the trees. The houses of nice wealth and open land were sprawled out on the country. I thought about getting off the trail and taking the road, asking to stay in the wealthy homes of people I didn't know just off of the pure inspiration my story would give them. Ah, how nice it is to dream. I knew the forest was my only assured way to NYC whether I liked it or not. I just also knew it would take me well over two months if I stayed on it.

I thanked the gentlemen for the needed cigarette and walked off with it only half burnt. I enjoyed myself with the rest and the forest took on a new meaning with the gracefulness and lavish that a young man with a cigarette allows. I remembered I was free. No rules. If I wanted to I could just as well go to Cuba. Of course, I was getting a little ahead of myself as anyone does when they lust for adventure.

It was not much of an adventurous day in the ways of many things happening. It was relatively straightforward; however, it was similar to reeling in a fish the way Hemingway wrote of in *The Old Man and the Sea*. Days in and days out I was pushing myself to the limit. There was no breaking if I wanted to get where I wanted to go. I barely knew where that was or what it looked like and it was hard to gauge exactly how far you *should* travel opposed to how far you could travel.

As the days went by and thanks to the nice rejuvenation of sleeping in, I was beginning to be able to take on more miles, however this was my first long stride. There was the well-known barn that Jimmy had mentioned that I was trying to get to.

"Everyone has a good time at the Barn." He said to Gonzo just before he abruptly decided to leave. Muscles were constantly being pulled in all directions and all of them were being used. I took maybe thirty minutes for a peanut butter tortilla and jelly break, and I was out of granola bars. I would break the ramen into little crackers and pour the chicken flavoring in the packaging and shake it up. If I closed my eyes and believed, it sort of tasted like crunchy chicken and I was thankful.

Any time I took off the pack, I'd have to maneuver it back on and it would pull down on my shoulders like hell. There was a strap that went around my waist and it would displace some of the weight onto my hips, but there was another strap that would displace that to my pectorals. It was a full body workout, all the time. I had gone sixteen miles so far and everything was beginning to wear and tear on me. I was sore. Something started to feel wrong on my toe. Every step just felt like a numb pain. I just figured I would adjust to the pain like I had with all the other things that hurt.

It is usually better to go all in or try harder for something of greater reward than it is to accept one's work as finished by midday. It was past midday, but that only meant that it was going to begin to cool down. I felt every tiny molecule in my legs using all of the force it could. I caught up with the woman who found the water this morning with the thick calves. I passed her, and then took a piss and she passed me, and then I was walking quickly to get to the barn and saw her again and passed her for the second time. I felt awkward mainly because of the size of my knife and how it hung from my chest as though I could have been likely to murder her.

By the end of the trail there was a spoon in the road. The road split off into three directions. When two roads diverged in the woods there is a right or a wrong way to go and we all love to die of frostbite by going the less travelled. However, a spoon in the road allows for infinite directions and possibilities none of which are necessarily right or wrong but all lead to different outcomes.

"I think it's this way." The woman said coming up behind me.

"Your guess is probably better than mine." So, I followed.

"Glad you made it here. I'm Raven." She had jet black hair.

"Cheerio, what made you want to hike the AT?"

"Well, I finished grad school to become an architect and I had a job and then I felt like I was stuck there, and I quit and decided to do something completely different, since I wasn't reaching my potential."

She was someone you could tell was very self-invested for better or for worse. I avoided my age. My shabby beard spoke for itself anyways. We could see the barn and there were a lot of people. As we walked up, I saw Gonzo next to the three men drinking whisky and the barn. The overlook into the mountains was the most beautiful I had seen yet. The sun was setting with a peachy glow in the sky. You could see for miles as the reaching pines hugged the wavy mountains like a sound wave or a heartbeat on a monitor. Across the eyes in all ways looked like a bed for God himself.

The barn was very interesting to me. You could tell there was years of probably foul activities that had happened in the old building over the years. The first floor had a dirt floor and what basically came out to three little rooms, one of which were people could eat or write at a table. If you turned down the main hall and made a left, you would be standing over a cliff where there was a fire pit and a front porch. The porch was filled to the brim with a middle-aged looking hiker group and the fire pit was surrounded by younger hippy looking kin.

I went upstairs where there was enough room for twenty or more hikers to all lay out but there was only me and another fellow off by the window. I was starving as usual but more than that I was almost too tired to eat. I got the strength to eat those dehydrated mashed potatoes. Downstairs over to the fire there were two guys, one with a shabby beard and a bandana and the other with darker long dreadlocks. Whenever I got to a camp, I realized that I needed time to decompress before I did much. It can be similar for when you go to a party. It takes time before you really want to talk to someone, but once you've been there for an hour everybody is your friend.

I wasn't talkative at first, but they were. I wasn't really listening either. I just used the fire to my advantage until my water boiled and threw in some dehydrated mashed potatoes. I was really beginning to enjoy this routine of the same food every day for all my meals. There was something ritualistic about it. I knew exactly how much pleasure I would get from each meal and although it wasn't enough for the amount of work I was doing, it filled me up.

I looked over at the guys and noticed they were smoking a bong. I laughed. Did people out here really have no care in the world? Smoking pot is part of what people do today. I just imagined that in a state of constant travel people would want to be cautious. It began to dawn on me that hiking was really meant to be sort of a fun thing people did. Not a gritty tortuous way of travel that I had been treating it like.

"Have you guys been carrying that this whole way?" I looked at their glass.

"Oh yeah." They said with pride. "Wanna hit?"

"Nah man, I'm good."

"You sure?"

"Yeah, I'm fine." I was already pretty high from some residual amount of cannabinoids coming out of my sweat glands throughout the day, that I was just happy to be there. I didn't need to add anything on top of it. The mashed potatoes had a cheesy taste that only the most deprived taste buds could begin to taste.

"Dinner smells great." The one with dreadlocks joked sarcastically to the middle-aged clan about the smell.

The older clan looked very young for old people. They were all in their late fifties. With one tough crew cut woman, along with a few husbands and wives.

I heard a familiar voice come from behind us.

"Hello everybody." A very chipper Raccoon said to everyone.

"Good evening." The younger crowd said.

"I just had my first eighteen-mile day." He said proudly.

"Well tip of the hat to you good sir." I said happy to see my old friend.

"Hey Cheerio." He smiled back.

"I'm am going to make some dinner and go to bed." He said.

"Hopefully not where I can hear you." I laughed. "Want to go get water?" I asked him. "I don't have enough for another round of ramen."

"Yeah sure. Lemme just put my pack down." He put it on the last slab of the porch next to the older crowd.

"Have a good walk?" I asked as we walked off.

"Oh yeah. I don't think I would have made it without my medicine though."

"Oh?" I assumed some painkiller or anxiety medication.

"All *natural.*" He winked.

Motherfucker. Was everyone on this damn trail getting high?

"Hey Cheerio, I've gotta ask you something?"

"What?"

"Well, I was walking today, and I walked right past some shit in the middle of a campsite."

"What are you saying?"

"Well, you were in the bathroom for a pretty long time at Greasy Creek."

I'll admit, I was a little bit offended by his accusation.

"Obviously you are not supposed to shit at a campsite!" I said as we began to fill up our water.

"I'm just wondering...It's just that you are still new to the trail and I don't know if you *knew* you're not supposed to shit at a campsite."

"Well...It was me. Yeah, I know. I made a mistake, but my body was being very aggressive this morning."

"Ok. I just wanted to know. In the future make sure you do it at least six hundred feet off the trail."

"Sounds good." I supposed I was putting everyone at risk of cross contamination.

"I'll see you at the bonfire." I walked off.

I went up to Gonzo. I was thinking about how my knife was not only excess weight, but it came off as very aggressive when I had it out.

"Hey man, I'll reconsider your offer when we get to Trail Days."

"Already got one. Bought this guy today for fifteen dollars."

"Damn. Well, how are you getting to Trail days anyways, it starts in two days and were like seventy miles away."

"I was thinking about getting to Hampton and the making a huge poster that says, "Damascus or Bust!" and I'd just stand in the street dancing like a lunatic until someone picks me up."

"That sounds like a good plan, actually. Do you mind if I travel with you until Hampton?"

"No problem."

"Sweet, let's say we leave here around nine tomorrow morning?" I said.

"Sure thing."

The barn was something special. There was a long stretch of grass, which is where so many people camped looking out along the gorgeous view. It was just a nice collection of people and an estranged place in the middle of the forest that was obviously a landmark of the trail.

People rolled in until late into the night, and some people cowboy camped. I wrote in my journal that night as I was getting ready for bed.

Day 7

To think of the thoughts racing through my head one week ago as I laid on my friend's floor disturbed by the thoughts of risking my life to get away from one I no longer felt any meaning in. I wondered what this trip would be like. I had fear in my heart, tears in my eyes, and longed for lost love. I am beginning to find peace where there were shadows and my scars are beginning to heal from the grace of the wind and sun. I am still in pain though, do not let me deceive you as I deceive myself that I am not. I look like a mud bath and would welcome a mudslide as a shower. I am beaten in every way possible but at least my heart is beating.

My initial tears and rips of muscles along my legs are beginning to heal but I don't have smooth long legs of a model I'll tell you that. Each day I am a little freer. Less concerned with the ways I look and more interested in things other than myself. This journey will be paved with great memories I have shared with the folks I have met. I am beginning to loosen up a little bit and am more interested in the world than I was locked in my dorm of depression. Days come with long ranges of silence filled with copious noise of people. I have been in and out of people's homes, and barns, sleeping in the woods, shelters and whatever else is available. I am somewhat well fed.

Peace is the main feeling along the path and the trees. And I am allowing myself to be in control as I let go of it. There may be better options of travel and choices of who to go with each day, but different challenges give me a new strength within myself I did not contain the day before. To say I am happy is a lie, but I have not been defeated and that is worthy. Life is hard, but beauty is only found through the harshest and ugliest of conditions. The worse it gets the easier it is to find joy within and without. I hope if anything I become less shallow and impatient through this journey. But I have also stabbed and killed some wildlife. Trees mainly.

Before I went to sleep, I got a call from my dad.

"Hello?" I was glad to hear his voice even though I knew he would be mad at me.

"Where are you? Keep your phone on." He was missing that tone of anger.

"I'm in a barn. I'm safe. I'm with a lot of people."

"Alright well, you are still only about an hour from Asheville. Call up one of your buddies and go home."

I tried to sound strong. The idea of giving up had long past, but the possibility of seeing one of my friends and hiking with them for a day would have been nice.

"I am home."

"Alright. Well, I've told all my friends about what you did to me and they all think what you did was atrocious. They told me I should just throw out *all* of your things."

"Dad if you didn't save my favorite sweater, I swear to god I am never coming back."

"Gone."

"And all my books?"

"All gone."

"Well you put this on yourself."

"It was a long pause until I realized he wasn't being serious

"Good to hear from you."

I was feeling so homesick and he could tell.

"Alright, well. You should probably think about coming home soon. Goodnight."

"Goodnight Dad. Oh, and expect a package coming to you soon."

It wasn't a cold night, but it wasn't warm either. I could hear the wind hitting against the barn. I made the mistake of thinking there were too many people around to hang a bear bag. In the middle of the night big rats, which would run past me and nibble on my toes, terrorized me and one licked my face. I was very alarmed. After that, I had trouble falling asleep. I rested up and, in the morning, even though a long journey laid before me I was very motivated and felt as though my first day of my second week had endless opportunities.

Chapter 17

The free spirited seasonally aged group left early. I could hear them through the floorboards getting ready. I had caught the gloriousness of the sunrise from the day before and I thought I would look out the window for a glimpse at this morning's sun. I had never seen such a paramount vastness of beauty day in and day out. The skill to appreciate our earth in the way it was meant to be each morning, and listened to during the night, was being reread.

I had some time to spare, too much time. I realized that I was always going to feel good in the mornings and that I should take advantage of that. I did yoga.

I did sun salutations, warrior poses, crow, camel, fish, tree and bridge pose. Ouch. I hadn't taken my socks off the night before and twenty-three miles was far enough to give me a brand-new blister on my feet. My socks were crusty, and disgusting. I decided it was time for a fresh pair. I only had two. When I checked my other foot, the other blister I popped had filled back up again and was starting to get hard.

I asked the other man who shared the large vacant upstairs of the barn if he had a small pocketknife. No luck. I was forced to use my own again. I went out by a window in the morning sun. At first, I thought quick force would work. I pushed in quickly, but no tear. I decided that a prolonged amount of force would eventually make the bubbles on my feet pop. It stung and hurt, and god did I push hard into my skin, but it just wouldn't rip the skin. The knife was too thick. Finally, the knife had little pointed blades that came off the side of it, I decided to rub it against my feet until it ripped open the blister. It was bloody painful but worked.

It was around 8 o' clock. I thought about asking some people for assistance, but I just cracked open my last ramen instead. The crunchy chicken was an interesting breakfast, but I drank a lot of water and knew I was going to have to refill before I left. I was ready. I thought I would go check on Gonzo so we could blow this popsicle stand. I walked across the range and all of the hikers were getting ready, breaking down their tents, but Gonzo hadn't left his yet. I knocked on his tent door, which had some burnt roaches next to it.

"Are you up?"

"I'm about to get up." His voice was full of morning fatigue.

"Well, listen man I'm ready to go. I'll just meet you in Hampton if that's alright."

"Go ahead. I'll see you there."

"Sounds good."

I had already begun to develop the ability to work on my own terms instead of relying on another person or group to be safe and efficient, but this was the beginning of feeling like I was possibly going ahead of some of the other hikers I had become so comfortable with. I got my bag and went to fill it up with water. Two beautiful dogs came up to me. It reminded me of Kendal and her puppy, but these dogs were huge.

"Howdy" a tough but cute looking woman with a huge backpack called out to me in an authoritative voice.

"Hey."

"I'm Manhandler." She gave off the vibe that she was a raver at some point in her life. She was wearing scanty clothing that was aesthetically pleasing, new but bright and colorful, and she had a lip piercing.

"Cheerio."

"You going to Trail Days?" She asked in a deep Californian accent.

"I was planning on it."

"Me too, bud."

We began to go up the mountain and she was a few paces in front of me moving her butt in that way that makes it sway and hard to take your eyes off it. She was going at a quick pace, which my hormones wanted to keep up with, but my legs just couldn't. The world around us was mesmerizing. I had never imagined America to be so beautiful. The hills were much more than hills, two miles up, half a mile down, another mile up.

However, walking through the tall grass there were

multiple snakes. At first, I just saw baby snakes that looked like big slithery worms, but then I saw mama, and then papa. These snakes were not huge, but I definitely don't feel comfortable around them at all. I had warmed up to disgusting creatures in the wild, I had seen over a hundred centipedes, and other creepy spiders. Snakes were just part of the deal. The way I saw it, the quicker I could get out of the vicinity of where the snakes where, the safer I would be. I started to run because I was scared and uncomfortable. I ran for about a minute and then I was tired, and I saw someone finishing up packing up their campsite. It was a red headed chap with a pointy nose.

"Teddy?!" I called out.

"Cheerio, what's good?" We gave each other hugs.

"Damn, a lot of snakes this morning." I said.

"Oh, I haven't been on the trail yet."

"Well look out." I began to walk away.

"Hold up, I'm about to leave." He threw on his backpack and we started walking together.

I had been walking for a half an hour or so, so I was awake, I could tell he was still tired since he was yawning like eighteen-year old's do in the morning. I could see hikers the size of ants climbing up the mountain in the far distance. There was no getting around it. The only thing that surrounded the mountains was deep forest that nobody could know their way out of. The only way out was up and over.

We began our ascension. Teddy seemed interested in me, as I was with him. I told him about my food situation, and he let me know that he was getting off the trail for a short moment to visit his grandmother who lived in Virginia and that he could probably assist me by giving me the rest of his food since he was going to restock anyways. Once we got to the top and sat down, the assorted husbands and wives were sitting there too, all eating and taking pictures. Teddy and I took a break and talked about the facts of life, how I was in college and how he didn't plan to go. I called over to the middle-aged crowd.

"How many of you went to college?" I asked.

Five of the six raised their hands.

"How many of you regret it." Two hands were left up.

A tough woman with blazer shades, and the most authoritative of the group was the one who didn't go to college. "Why didn't you go?" I asked her.

"I just didn't know what I wanted to do once I went to college and I felt like I was wasting my time. Here's the thing. It also goes the other way, if you know what you want to do, you don't need a bunch of wannabe teachers telling you how to do it. You're smart, figure it out."

"She makes the most money of all us now," One of the husbands said.

"It's not all about money, Todd," she said with an extra exhale. "I'm doing what I love, and I happen to get paid a lot for it."

"What do you do?" Teddy asked.

"I run a very successful photography blog. All black and white of these mountains, I've also written a few books."

"She's very highly regarded." A blonde wife said.

"And what do you guys do?" I asked the rest of the crowd.

"Well, I'm a housewife." A wife with ponytails said with a smile and a hug of her husband who shrugged with a smile.

"Insurance marketing." He said.

"Sales," The two other men said.

"I work for the city of Atlanta," The blonde woman said.

"And she makes the most money out of all of you?" I asked them all.

They were silent.

"You're the one who's going to college, aren't you?" The woman with shades asked.

"Yeah." I said.

"Wanna know how I know?"

"How?" I asked.

"Because you care about the money. Do you hear him," She said pointing to Teddy, "Asking how much money we all make?"

"No" I said.

"That's because he didn't go to college. He knows there's enough money. Listen, I was extremely lucky. Not going to college is not easy." She looked at Teddy and pointed. "But going to college, you're more likely to end up somewhere you won't want to be."

I looked at Teddy. "Goddamnit, I wish I never enrolled in college."

"I don't think I'm going man. Barely finished high school, but out here, opportunity is endless every day." He took out ramen, a big bag of raisins, Oreos, a nice meal to go, a few cliff bars, and some tea mix and gave it all to me. I was silent. The gratitude I felt for his generosity was beyond words. Mathematically, the miles compared to dollars I had, was irrational but this new food made me know I could get at least a little bit further along.

Raven rolled up. "Is this really the top?" she exclaimed.

Everyone was pretty much getting ready to go by that point. The hill or small mountain took a lot of energy out of everyone, but we all knew it was the morning and had a long way to go.

"I might just move on if you aren't going fast enough. My grandma is waiting for me." Teddy let me know.

"Well, that hurts my feelings," I said as a joke with some honesty in it. "If I get too tired it'll be so long forever, I guess."

"Goodbye," he feigned waving with a smile.

I like that people younger than you really cut to the chase.

"So, are you religious?" He asked.

"Umm. Yes, sort of. I am a Unitarian."

"I just ask because of that cross you wear around your neck. Are you a Christian?"

"Yes, but I would say that spiritually I feel most closely connected to Hinduism, due to the Ramayana, a gorgeous epic poem that has a thousand pages that just explains Sita's beauty. Any religion that holds that high of regard towards women, I believe in. What are you?"

"I'm an Atheist, but I believe in Astrology. There are two types, but I don't remember which one is newer. Western and Vedic. One of them is complete bullshit, like the horoscope shit is bullshit. However, the constellations were based off of the Hindus and then the Egyptians got a hold of it and assigned a birth chart to have Gods symbolize people's lives based on where the stars were when they were born."

"That's beautiful, any and all form of understanding oneself and the universe are forms of religion and spirituality. I'm an Aries."

"Yeah, but that is only one of your signs. I'm a rising Virgo."

"I know my rising moon signs and all that. I've got to recheck all of that stuff. What does Virgo mean?"

"It means I'm sort of a go getter. I work really hard. What about Aires?"

"Umm, I think has something to do with being stubborn or dominant. I can get sort of aggressive in arguments." I said.

"I feel that. When I was in high school everybody made fun of me because I wanted to do something that nobody else was doing. I graduated early so that I could go on this trip." He said.

"Oh really? I guess that makes sense."

"Yeah, only thing was I didn't get to walk the stage."

"Dude, walking the stage is the biggest amount of bullshit I have ever been through."

"Oh, I know."

"I literally took my pants and underwear off before the ceremony started and graduated with nothing on under my robe."

"Haha, I literally hate all of those kids anyway, they are stuck in some auditorium and I am hiking the Appalachian Trail."

"I wish I still had legs like you, boys." One of the middle-aged men interjected.

As we passed him, I said, "It isn't easy for me either."

"I can imagine." He looked at my pack.

"Like my family isn't well off or anything." We continued walking. "I had to work for all of my gear, and my grandparents gave me *some* money for me to do it."

"I believe you."

"I have been preparing for this for six months."

"It took me three days of preparation, and then I left." I said.

"Damn."

"The only person I remotely am going to miss is Abigail." He said.

"Who's she?"

"Just some girl." He said.

"Is that so? *Just* some girl."

"Alright she's *that* girl. You know that girl?

"Hell, I know three of them." I said.

"What? You believe in polygamy?"

"Haha, not anymore. When I was your age I did. I believed in buying a big farm, many of them actually, all over the world and just having many husbands and wives and thousands of children all over the world."

"That's kind of weird for a Christian."

"Unitarian, thank you very much."

"That doesn't make any sense. All these people are just going to marry you and let you marry other people and then go travelling around the world marrying more people, having babies with more people."

"One big happy family," I said with restored belief.

"There is no part of me that is polyamorous. I could never share someone with someone else."

"Capitalist." I joked. "We are so caught up in the ideal of legal marriage and property that we can begin to solidify the real importance of - Alright forget it, tell me about Abigail?"

"Well, it's a long story."

"We've got plenty of miles ahead of us." I said.

"I guess I'll just start freshman year when I started smoking pot."

"Ah so we're hearing the full story, I was twelve myself."

"Good, so you know all about it. I started smoking and I loved it. Nothing was as wonderful when I discovered weed."

Oh, the *discovery* of weed is a whole other story than the ability to handle it once you have matured. My older stepbrother was the one who introduced it to me under a bridge. The next time after that I ran into my little stepsister who had just tried it for the first time. She was also the first person I ever got drunk with. I remember things getting out of hand very quickly after that. Those were some of my favorite summers of my life, building forts off of the canal on the golf courses. I was spending time with these particularly notorious stoners, and everyone in my family told to stay away from my stepsister and even my mom's house.

"I feel you," I said

"No, I mean, after I found out about weed that was all I did, for basically the rest of high school."

"I feel you man."

"Quarters every weekend started to turn into a half ounce. and then an ounce. I just smoked so much until I hated myself."

"Yup. Sophomore year was when it got bad for me. Dabs."

"Oh, so you know about Dabs. Dude, I would do dabs every day before school. I had no control over myself, but what was worse, I didn't have control over what other people were doing. I would get so depressed, but everybody was doing it that I felt like didn't really have an option."

"Well, how did you know Abigail?"

"Abigail was my best friend's girlfriend."

"Ahhh, Teddy!" I smiled disapprovingly.

"We have been best friends since freshman year. He is like the Yin to my Yang. I am all literature and he is all science. We do everything together and it's almost like slightly a competitive relationship, but I love him to death."

"Haha. I feel you."

"I began to withdraw from my friends. She began texting me. She's the kind of girl everybody wants. Truly the most beautiful girl in our grade. Her eyes are so soft and sweet. Gorgeous cheeks."

"I got the picture."

"Well we started texting and then we went out on what you would imagine is a date, but we didn't refer to it as a date."

"Yeah, I know the kind."

"Then I started *building castles in my head.*" I loved how he said that because I knew exactly what he meant. Maybe you do too. It's like you live in the old times and you are a knight and she is a princess. Sounds corny as hell, but I've been there. It's like your dreams and reality merge and the cannon of everything you've ever been exposed to become more important than any form of discernment.

"I suppose scientology isn't accurate to what most people would believe but if someone believes in it, I don't suppose the illogical is necessarily harmful."

"She and I would text all night, but not really talk about my best friend. Finally, they broke up, and she began to pursue me. I felt bad, but I had such strong feelings toward her that it really didn't matter."

"There are no rules with love and war. Listen, I am listening, but we are moving rather quickly." I said.

"Do you want to switch backpacks with me?"

"You don't mind?"

I took off my backpack and put on his.

"Are you serious? This feels like a feather. Literally, I feel like I've forgotten all of my books for class. This is so light."

He was struggling on the other hand. "Oh god man. You've been carrying all of this?"

"It was a lot heavier when I left."

"Dude, this is too much to be carrying." He said, struggling.

"Physically yes. Mentally no. Carry on with your story."

"Well, I guess, she got morally conflicted. Like she was getting in the way of our friendship and didn't want to, so she stopped talking to me."

"I guess that's noble of her."

"Yeah, but that sucked for me. I got so close to having the girl of my dreams, but she bailed because of moral reasons."

"At least you even got close to the girl of your dreams. I can't barely talk to mine."

"Trust me, it's much worse to get close to something like that and then to have it taken from you."

"Possibly.

"When I finally decide to get a girlfriend, she is going to be something else."

"Oh really?" Surprised by his confidence that some perfect girl would just come along and be by his side for eternity. "You better have the maturity to look back at someone and recognize that the objective truth only exists to us alone."

"I mean, I've never had sex or anything, but I'd rather save it for someone special."

"You do that."

"So, after she stopped talking to me. I decided to say fuck it. I quit smoking pot and decided go on this trip. Next thing you know she decides she wants to talk with me again."

"So, did you meet up with her?"

"Yeah, we did, but I could tell that she was just doing it because she was worried about me. There wasn't anything real there, plus I've decided to be sober. Almost four months."

"Nice dude."

"I'm going to go a year."

"That's how long I want to go someday."

"My friends that I was hiking with, who are a little ahead of me, are apparently at some shuttle stop where they are giving out free beer."

"How many miles ahead are they?"

"They are about 30 miles ahead of us."

"Oh, do you wanna catch up to them?"

"No, I'm avoiding Trail Days so that I can stay sober."

"Listen man, you don't have to blow off Trail Days just because you are staying sober. If you come, I'll stay sober with you."

"Nah, man, that's why I'm going to stay with my grandma for the weekend. That sort of ambience sort of makes me want to do drugs, which I don't want to do."

"I respect that."

"Can we switch backpacks again?" he asked.

"Sure. It was nice to have the weight off my shoulders."

"Yeah, I've carried some heavy packs, but that one felt the worst of all of them."

"Cheerio, don't mention any of this drugs stuff around my grandma when she pulls up."

"Hey grandma, wanna dab?" I joked. "Of course, I'm not going to mention anything."

"I really hope you make it to New York." We came up to a road and his Grandma pulled up and next thing I knew I was alone again.

The road diverted in a way that I didn't know where the trail got back on. I waited for a minute and checked my phone, which didn't have much service. A truck pulled up on the scene.

A man wearing big black stitched leather boots hopped out of the vehicle.

"Want a coke?"

"I'll take a coke, thank you."

"Take your bag off, relax. You're close to town. I run the 42nd oldest hostel on the Appalachian trail."

"Wow."

Raven came out of the trees to witness our encounter.

I sat back and took a deep drink of my coke. I wasn't particularly excited about drinking the caffeine, but I needed the energy.

"Our hostel is doing shuttles into Trail Days. Only 50 dollars."

"I think I'll try to get as far in as I can," Raven nodded to me.

"I think I'll be fine too." I said.

"Well, I'm from New York and I'm a real snob about pizza. Our town has a pizzeria that puts Manhattan to shame."

I wanted to spit out his coke for defiling the good name of New York. I also wanted pizza. Raven did too.

"I'll go get a slice. You coming Cheerio?

I wanted to. To compliment the sweet flavor of my brisk ice-cold drink with some scalding hot pizza would turn this journey into a vacation, but I didn't have the funds to frivolously throw around like that.

"I'm sorry, I wish I could."

"Well, there is a hostel down the road, and they have food trucks that are giving away food." The man in the boots said. "Just follow the big road for about a mile down and you'll run into it on your left side."

Raven got into the car with him and they drove off onto the busy road. Cars were flying by every ten seconds and I was standing on the wrong side. I found a quick gap and ran across. The quick pace of things was exciting. It was nothing more than a small town in the deep South, but to me, after a week in the woods, it felt like a big city. I began to revel in the beauty of the quaint cuteness of nowhere towns caught in the middle of nothing other than a young man's fantasy.

I began to feel like Kerouac. Without a plan, ready to just jump to the next town or believe in the next idea that came my way. Trail Days was a thought of the past, the highway was the only thing on my mind now. It was only a short romance that lasted as long as a usual late-night lust. The glistening sun was hot as hell, and the coke wasn't sitting in my stomach well. I felt the humidity stick to my skin.

I went off the road into a rabbit hole that I assumed was the hostel. The grounds were filled with scrap metal and old motorcycles. There was an old mobile home that hadn't been moved in decades and a tin Winnebago that came straight out of a science fiction movie. I decided to knock. What I saw open the door was nothing less than an alien hiding out on our planet. Its skin was peeling from every direction. It made sure I couldn't see into the door, but I could hear many caged animals screaming for freedom. Birds mostly.

"Who is it?" a female voice called out from inside.

"Is this the hostel?" I asked confused.

"No." I peered through the open door to reveal he was in suspenders and pajama pants. A true lunatic living his life the in peace of the country and the cheap land it offers. "Go back up the hill and you'll see a sign for it."

I wanted to be friends and become a part of this unopened book so badly, but I assumed staying on the premise would end me up dead. I found the road again after being lost in this stranger's head for what felt like a day's walk. The sign for the real hostel was grand and commercial. It was a homestyle paid for by generations of injustice.

As I walked onto the commercialized land, I realized I was in wonderland. This was much more than any old barn. This was Southern money. An old plantation trying to do good after its ancestors. It was one gigantic farm, and an old building on a hill. It was probably a hundred acres. There were waterfalls pouring down from the old building, which was covered in bridges and flowers. It streamed into a river one could follow into the hostel.

There was a small storefront selling rice, snickers, and tuna. Parked in the parking lot there were three food trucks all set up ready to sell. I innocently went and asked for a hot dog, which was apparently seven dollars, not free. No thank you. I went around back and saw the three whiskey drinkers sitting under an umbrella table. We waved, but I went upstairs to the hostel. There was nobody working the desk, so I let myself in. Two large dogs lay on the ground exhausted. There was a nice couch, beds, a shower, which I truly wanted to jump in and wash quickly without anyone knowing the better, but I was there for an outlet. I plugged in my phone and sat back on the couch.

I walked back into the foyer after a full inspection and there were three new gentlemen eating at a table. One spoke French.

"Bonjour." I spoke to him. "Comment ca va?" My French is not perfect, but I am close to fluent apart from punctuation.

"Bonjour, ca va bien." (I am well) "Et vous?" (And you?)

"Oh la vache, cette un difficile de promener de Nord Caroline au New York." (Oh my god, it's hard to walk from North Carolina to New York.)

"Combien Miles?" (How many miles")
"Mille." (a thousand)
"Hey man, did you say you are walking to New York?" The other guy asked.
"Yeah."
"I'm an engineer. I work, well worked in New York. Upper West Side."
"No shit. Well, I'm going there to be an artist."
"What do you do?"
"Well, primarily, I sing, secondarily, I can dance."
"Can you act?" He asked.
"Anyone can act."
"Oh, so a little bit of everything."
"That's the trade." I smiled one of those million-dollar smiles.
"Where are you gonna stay?" the third one asked. "New York is expensive."
"Yeah, I also have like no money. I was just planning on staying on the streets really. It's not me I'm worried about, it's my backpack, which I hope I can stash at my friend's place."
"The streets get rough man. I mean, you're gonna need to eat. Dumplings in Chinatown are cheap."
"And one-dollar pizza." I said with hope.
They laughed. "You want some of this? I'm not eating any more of it." It was a creamy Philly cheese steak that I indeed wanted, along with all the fries, which were all finished in less than a minute.
"I think there are some Artist community living spaces in Brooklyn," the engineer said.
"Yeah, that's really the only part of New York I care about. What did you think? I'd be homeless in Manhattan?"
"I don't know what I think about you. Here take this." It was a ten-dollar bill. "Hey good luck to ya." And they left.
Manhandler who owns the two big dogs lying on the foreground and who was flaunting in front of me from this morning came in the room. She was petite, but you could feel the force around her.
"You wanna get out of here?" She asked me in a

seductive manner.

"Where we going?" Thinking it was rhetorical but up for the challenge.

"I'm getting a ride to Hampton, you want in?"

"I do. Yes, that's perfect for me."

"Alright, but one thing first."

"What?"

"I need you to help me put this piercing in my lip, and screw it in."

"What?"

She pulled out a small little ring. "Don't be shy, come here." I went over to her, and she took me into a bedroom where she laid back. I began to work my ways of pushing this piercing in and trying to screw it closed.

"You're kinda cute."

"Thanks." My hands got a little shaky, she began to laugh at me. It took about eleven minutes before I closed it, and we looked at each other face to face. She grabbed the back of the hair on my head and bit the metallic in her lip.

"Thanks sweetie, just making sure it's in there tight, too bad I've got a boyfriend."

This was my best hope to getting to Trail Days.

"There's a girl with a truck and we are leaving for a resort in Hampton, in five. If you're lucky, she'll give you a ride." She left the room.

What the hell just happened? Sex crazed animals.

I quickly put my shoes on, went out the door and down the stairs. I saw a girl in black tank top.

"You're going to Hampton?"

"Yup," she said throwing her backpack into the backseat."

"Do you have any room?"

"Ehhh, it might be a little tight."

"I don't mind sitting on the back of the truck."

"Alright, that shouldn't be a problem then. Just, you know, throw me a little money for the gas."

I decided not to mention that my funds were not pretty. I didn't know how much she was expecting; all the shuttles were fifty dollars and up.

"You coming or what?" Manhandler came up from

behind me.

"Yeah, I think so." The back of the trunk lowered, and her two dogs hopped up.

"Are you riding in back then?" The one in the tank top asked me.

"I think that's the only place there's room."

"Alright well, watch out for my dogs. Just make sure they don't jump over the edge or anything like that." Manhandler said.

I love when people make you responsible for things you didn't plan for.

"Eh, ok."

There were five or six other backpacks all lined in the back leaving me enough space to sit next to the dogs. They were not comfortable or calm. As the car started, the bigger dog of the two instantly stood up and it seemed like it was not enjoying the idea of moving. The truck swung around a sharp turn and the dog barked. I tried to comfort it but the more I held onto the dog, the more it resisted against me.

I felt like the dog and I were having a battle of the egos. The other dog was a smaller female and a doll, who sat the whole ride. I decided I would mimic the only rational one and just let the bigger dog create its own fears. Only I would get in such a petty disagreement with a dog. I'm very insecure. As I relaxed so did the big dog. It sat down for a few minutes, but once we reached the open road it stood back up. Its ears flapped in the wind and it transformed from being a dog, to the self-ruling fierceness of a horse. It was beautiful to watch. Dogs love the car. I decided this would be a good time to take a nap.

It was a special kind of nap. One where your eyes are closed, and you drift away but the adrenaline around the situation is the dream you'd wished for. I felt so alive sleeping in the back of a stranger's truck, not knowing where I was heading other than believing it was North, and hopefully East. My eyes were closed for what felt like twenty minutes, a perfect amount of time to recharge and have my muscles scream. I picked up my head and we were in the center of some town. You have no idea how wonderful it looked. Porcelain porches and WWII concrete homes. Lost in the middle of America, and I knew if I were to come up to any of these stranger's house with the load I had on my back, I would have been home for the night. We pulled into a bank.

"Do you want to get out here?" Manhandler asked as she got out of the car. "I'm going to get some money for Trail Days. We can take you back to the trail if you want?"

"I just don't really know where this is, or how far we are from Damascus. If I stay on the trail will I go right through the town?"

"Yeah, it does?"

"What's the scoop?" the girl who owned the truck asked.

"We're gonna take him back to the trail."

"You know the trail is back a few miles."

"That's fine, if you don't mind taking me there."

"Fine with me, give us a minute to take out some cash."

I waited with the dogs and used them as therapy for the loneliness the road bestowed upon me day in and day out. I learned to love loneliness, it was all I knew would keep on giving, but I'll admit it gave too much. Once they got back in the truck I felt the engine roar under me. I wanted to take another nap, but I new the forest would be close. I laid back and looked up at the blue sky and watched it fade into green as the trees began to reach out above us. Green is my favorite color. I had spiritual meanings for all colors, but I always have identified with green. It means learning, growth and new energy to me.

Chapter 18

I lifted my head up off the lap of the dogs and witnessed old country homes hidden from the world. The old wood was beginning to crumble. I thought of how lucky one would have to be to live in one of them, to have the means to never engage with other humans for a lifetime. We hopped out, and there was a scruffy looking man, short but hefty. He was wearing a black shirt with cut off sleeves and was carrying a walking stick. He recognized the girl driving and they hugged. I was grateful to be with somebody new, but I thought about how I might not see some of the people I had been lucky enough to meet on my journey so far. That was the way it was, you meet people, but you never really got to know anybody. Whenever you are dropped off somewhere you don't really know, it's very frightening at first. They talked and Manhandler gave me a pat on the back, and I asked the gentleman if I could walk with him.

"It's better with company." he said.

"Are you going to Trail Days?"

"I'm trying to make it on time." He answered.

"Let's get going then." We waved goodbye and I gave the girl who drove eight quarters.

"I hope this is enough for gas."

"Eh, sometimes, you have a lot to give, and some days it ain't much." She said.

Although I was only away from the Trail for a short time, it was refreshing to be back. I began to crave the wilderness. It was the only thing that made sense. When you are travelling, especially alone, your mind begins to wander into places that are unknown, and I was definitely going a little stir crazy.

"What's your name?" I asked the shaggy mate.

"I'm Sasquatch."

"Where you coming from?"

"Florida." The young bearded man said.

"Damn, so you've been walking a long ways."

"Yep."

"Why'd you do all this?" I asked

"Well, I ran out of money. I used to be a mechanic and the shop I worked for went out of business, so I thought I'd walk to a better life."

"Going anywhere in particular?"

"No, but I'm sure it will find me."

I was envious of his hope. It was something that was beginning to escape me the closer I got to New York. I wasn't down and out. The first round was over though, and I had had a few blows to the chest and face. We walked but the trail was especially confusing. He didn't have a map either, but I had the few pages that had been ripped out a few miles back.

"We are supposed to go past a footbridge," I said.

Sure enough it came and we arrived at a crossroads. One trail lead one way, and the other led far down a hill. Far down, big rocks that took a long time to get down off of each of them. I dropped my backpack off because I knew if we were going the wrong way, I was not going to carry all that weight back up. We got to the bottom and there was a beautiful pond looking out on a gigantic waterfall. Although I had only known the man for a short time, we were comfortable with each other.

"Listen man, I smell disgusting. Do you mind if I hop in this pond for a moment?" I asked.

"We've got a little time, go ahead."

"I'm gonna get naked."

"Ain't nothing I've never seen before."

There was a long collection of shallow rocks before the pond began to get deeper to the point where I couldn't stand. I walked in bare naked and slowly, nearly walking on all fours found my way to the deeper section. The second I couldn't stand I put all of my energy into my stroke and went out as far as I could into the waterfall. The pond was grotesque but still water. I had never felt so cleansed in the whole trip. The mist of the waterfall hit the back of my head and I slowly submerged my whole body into the pool of water. I enjoyed it, swam around while cleaning not only my body but my soul. Once I got back on land in the nude, I quickly threw my clothes back on before a family walked by.

I was sure that we should go back the way we came, but he said that he could see that the trail continued along the shallow rocks onto the other side and we should go deeper into the unknown. I trusted him as he had trusted me to not die in the water. There was a small memorial by the water where a father and his son had lost their lives a year before. The danger of swimming by waterfalls is that the fall creates a high current, which you must swim against in order to tread in the same spot. I thought of the dead molecules, which had rotted in the lake now on my skin. I thought it was beautiful like I was gathering new information from reincarnation in its physical form.

I climbed up the rocks and grabbed my backpack which was still hidden under a few leaves. I put it back on with a new freshness I hadn't felt in like forever and we plunged further in. It wasn't long before we came across a bonfire. Two men looked like they had been living in the woods. One was definitely a distant relative of one of my friends who is currently a rapper in Miami, I could see it the structure of his size.

"Good to see you, Squatch." There was a rough intimidation in his voice but the kind that had been through cold winters alone and was grateful to see a friend. "We're camping out here, but up ahead there are free shuttles that are going into Trail Days. Riff Raff is there."

Riff Raff the rapper came to my head.

"You are going to go along this thin rocky path, and you should see them in about four miles."

"Are you going?" I asked the rough husky man.

"No, we just caught this trout from the river." He revealed a fish with its head cut off. "We are going to walk into Trail Days on Saturday, but do y'all have weed? Here." He took off his necklace, which was a small bowl and packed it with light neon green marijuana. He forced it into my hand along with a lighter.

"Smoke up, good things are ahead."

I inhaled deeply into the bowl, and he packed another. Soon the movements of the forest were alive, and my adrenaline was racing with what lay ahead.

"Do you have a bag?" Grizzly asked me.

"I do."

I pulled out my zip lock of marijuana and he put about a gram into it.

"It'll keep you safe. Now Go!" All of sudden there was urgency to the situation, which was not to be negotiated with. "There has been a bear sighting." He said, as we left.

I was more worried that my heavy thick backpack wasn't going to make it along the thin cliff that ran across the river. It had a deep fall into it, especially while feeling the way I was. I wanted to see a bear at this point. I had my knife ready. We went along the thin route and climbed over a small rock. I got a little ahead of myself the way marijuana often makes people. Four miles is a long walk and I sped walked for the first two, until I lost my breath.

Sasquatch took his idle time. He was obviously a more skilled hiker than I was. We came across some wildlife, including a large snake and a gecko. Amphibians are quite interesting under the gentle dreamlike aura of weed. All of sudden there were houses emerging from the woods, but we were still in the deep forest. I wasn't sure where we were anymore. It didn't seem like the Appalachian Trail, it felt like a lived-in forest with emerging houses. Next thing, I knew we came across a road with a small sign that read.

Trail Magic
Riff Raff
Call this number

"I suppose we should call the number." Sasquatch recommended. "They might give us a ride."

I turned my phone on. "I'll call...just in case." The phone rang.

"Hello?"

"Where are you?" A hick Southern voice answered.

"We're off of a road."

"Alright we will be there in a few."

We waited for a few minutes and a huge SUV pulled up. Two men both with beards, and ponytails hopped out.

"You here for Riff Raff?"

"Yep!" I exclaimed.

They opened up the trunk and threw our bags in the back.

"Is my bag going to be safe?"

"It's all safe man." He looked at me as though I hadn't understood some code yet.

"So, is Riff Raff actually there, like around, just with the people."

He looked at me confused.

"Yeah." I grew up with musicians, so being backstage with The Grateful Dead and smoking a square with Mac Demarco didn't leave me star struck. It wasn't out of the atmosphere that if Riff Raff the rapper might be causally around, and I'd get to smoke a fat blunt with him.

"Not Riff Raff the rapper." The ponytailed man corrected. "Riff Raff the crew."

"Oh," It made sense, but at the same time it didn't. I didn't really know what a crew was.

"Well what should I do with this knife? Won't they not like that at a festival?"

"Just put it in your bag, man. C'mon."

If you have ever been to Lollapalooza, or Bonnaroo they'll check your shit like you are a terrorist, unless you are VIP, press or sneak in I've heard.

We got into the car and they blasted heavy music, but boy it felt great. I felt like I was being escorted. They dropped us off and the property extended from a wide driveway and modern wooden house which had open geometrical windows, to a extensive back yard filled with cars. There was a longhaired ripped man playing with his children, and his young beautiful wife. The SUV pulled into the driveway and then off into the gravel walkway. There were about two hundred people scrambling around. It wasn't gigantic, but there was a lot of commotion compared to the silence of miles alone in the woods. I was instantly very happy.

I checked the license plates of the parked cars. They were from New Jersey, Georgia, and then I saw one from New York! All my worries drifted away. It was like receiving an A. I could literally see the progress of my time of travelling and I could feel myself achieving my goal. I walked into the party, and a nice unshaven earthy lady said, "We're glad you're here, get some food."

"If you need any for the road," Her husband turned over, "we've got plenty. More than anyone could ever eat." I looked over her shoulder and I saw a gigantic pile of name brand foods just stacked on top of each other. Chips, pretzels, cookies, and it was all free. It was like winning the lottery.

"Hey man this is great! I'mma go find a beer." Sasquatch turned to me and disappeared into the party.

I was excited and the world was spinning around in my wonderfully baked brain. I thought I should still be somewhat responsible before I indulge in the goodness that waited. I went deep into the back yard, which stretched at least forty acres long. I found myself a beautiful camping spot and set everything up. Although most of these people were rough Southern folk, none of them would have hurt a fly or stolen a shoe. I went back and boy was I hungry. I had not eaten anything, but Ramen and granola and they were serving up good ol' chili, for meat-lovers and for vegans. I had myself a chili hotdog, then a vegan Sriracha salad, and then another round of both. I dove into the pile of cookies and found some lemon meringue sugar cookies. I would have eaten the whole line of food in my intoxication, but I thought I would put them out for everyone. I felt something I hadn't felt in almost a hundred miles. FULL. Sasquatch threw me a beer.

"Were finishing this one straight away my friend!" I love excess when it arrives on time.

We swallowed our beer and instantly grabbed another. We drank into the evening around a roaring fire. I spoke with immigrants, people from New York, lesbians, and then I had something I didn't expect to find on the road. I had neighbors.

I went back to my tent and a young man and his wife had set up next to me.

"Evening." He said politely Southern.

"Howdy." His sweet redheaded wife waved.

"Guess we're neighbors." I shrugged.

"Guess we are."

"Sam, and this my wife Louise." They introduced themselves.

"Lovely to meet you guys, let's go get some more food."

"Where you guys from?"

"Asheville."

"That's where I go to College."

"Nice town," There was a sorrow to his voice.

"Well, we *were* from Asheville. We got evicted." Louise said.

"Oh shit."

"Yeah, the woman we were renting our apartment from didn't like us so we were out of a home and we decided to do this," Sam said.

That was crazy. There were people doing this not because it was some grandiose idea in their head, but because they basically had to.

"What are you guys gonna do when it's over?" I asked

"We haven't decided yet, maybe hike the PCT. We're trying to not think about that, we are just trying to enjoy what we have while we have it."

"Amen."

"We will have to make it work." Louise chimed in.

"How many beers have you had?" I asked trying to lighten the mood.

Sam was on his fifth and I was on my third.

"Zero." Louise made an O with her hands.

"Well would you guys want to smoke some weed later?" I took a shot in the dark.

She nodded her head and shrugged. "Sure, that sounds nice."

"Alright before bed, we can all smoke," I declared with a smile and Sam and I cheered our beers. Mine was out. I went to go get some water to clear my head and I realized that there was *only* beer in the cooler. That was it. There weren't any kids at the party except babies and one preteen. Eh, what the hell I thought, I don't have to be up for work in the morning.

Riff Raff was an organized hiking troop. They all had matching tee shirts and were as tough as they come. One of them had a tattoo on his face, the men were well built, and the women all wore scandalous shorts or skirts. It wasn't long before I recognized who their leader was. He wore a nice cowboy hat with flowers emerging from it and carried around a book. His name was Disney. Everybody would be constantly calling him over to drink with them, and he had the best seat at the fire. He spoke with wisdom and always had something on his mind.

"Whatever the young is interested in, is the future," He said openly.

I wondered how many of these people were trying to escape their realities walking through mountains for half a year. The concept of hiking is a healthy one and an unhealthy one. There is nothing more cleaning and spiritually grounding than being with nature. It takes you away from the world we all know, but wanting to re-accustom yourself out of society can reveal a basis of being unhappy with one you're living in. The way we all talk with each other drunk and stoned is an ancient tradition. Friends were like family, families you get to keep for one or two days before you really get sick of them. I looked around and although I liked these people, I wondered what their places were in the real world. I have a few scholarly friends, but I've always preferred the rougher crowd personally. I've always felt like I never was good enough for the smart kids, and perhaps smarter than the beatniks. I looked at Disney. I related to the man. He was the best of the worst, and that's all I've ever been.

I was in the back washing my hands and a woman who was clearly tripping on LSD came up to me.

"What are you?" she asked with her eyes somewhere else.

"I am three women in one body? What are you?"

"We are all the same atoms slowly disintegrating

and reviving as we each die and are reborn…" She looked up. "That sounds crowded." She laughed.

I nodded my head. People on acid make me smile because I know how to handle them, they are usually looking for something just outside of what you would do on any casual day. God, I've had some beautiful memories just sitting on benches at the park.

"Here, take your hands and fill them up with water." I said and she did.

We enjoyed being human fountains for a few minutes until I felt like I had something much more practicable to be doing. What a shame, I wish I had wasted more time doing the extravagant.

I asked the woman who owned the property if I could use the Wi-Fi.

"Of course." She was so sweet, interested in where I came from and what I was doing, like any mother.

"Al!" She yelled at her drunken husband. "This boy needs our help! Go get the laptop. He is an artist." I looked at him with a little bit of remorse to trouble him, but we were in agreement. I went back over, and the owner of the house had returned with a laptop in his hand. So, I began to log on to social media. There were over 100 pictures and videos I had taken. I sat back and began to enjoy the show. I just watched as it slowly downloaded and drank beer. It was a simple joy but one that takes patience to learn to love. All of a sudden, I looked over and I saw a man covered in sweat. His dark beard was masking the night air. It was Bear.

"Holy shit man, did you walk here?"

He nodded his head.

"Damn. You are a true hiker. I have no worth compared to what you can do."

"Ahh, don't say it like that, but I need to put my shit down." He went out into the dark night area of where the tents were. I was so impressed. The car ride to where I got dropped off was only about 20 minutes, but still it seemed like a far distance that I would not have imagined seeing anyone from the previous days. I checked my phone and thought that with a connection to wifi perhaps Spotify would download. It worked. I logged in and for the first time in what felt like a lifetime I could see my music again.

There was a large speaker and people were beginning to wind down. These people never really wound down, but there were less people awake, and the people who were awake, the alcohol in their system was depressing them. Only a few of the really rowdy were still making obnoxious noise. Disney went up to the speaker and played his very own song, which was a cover of Lorde. It was a parody with references to the group of Riff Raff. It was one of a kind, exceptional. After he played his song no music was going into the aux cord through the speaker, so I stood up. I went right over, and I began to play my music.

Chai music is songs or a vibe that will carry a crowd to have a good time but allow them to speak to each other. They enjoyed every one of my songs except the one by the Alabama Shakes which I think proved that they had a little bit of racism in them. The South has some things that are great about it and some things that I just don't understand. People really seemed to enjoy my music, which made me feel good. However, I was still focusing on downloading the images, and anytime there was a song I didn't want to play, I was running back and forth all over the camp like a drunken buffoon.

"Hey man, try to enjoy yourself." Sasquatch said.

"I swear to god, sometimes I am the most stress-free person alive, but another part of me just wants to try so hard at whatever I am doing. It doesn't even matter what it is."

"Try harder to let go man. Everyone's having a great time."

"Yeah, maybe. I don't know man. How can everybody be so carefree when most of them don't have any other place to go."

"That's because this is home to them. They don't need anywhere else to go."

The way he said it made me have a realization. It was so stuck in my head that I had to get somewhere the way people tell say you have to go to college. I was stressing so much on getting to my destination that I was forgetting to enjoy the journey. I didn't just mean New York either. We all want to be successful in whatever we do, reach a goal, people don't recognize the beauty of the different ways to achieve things because although we are born into the land of opportunity, we are bred into a life of consistency. It's like finishing college with straight A's but nobody to celebrate with.

I resorted to my favorite kind of celebratory indulgence. There was a pack of cigarettes on the table unclaimed. If you've never smoked a cigarette while drunk you haven't lived. A cigarette is a delightful pleasure. It leaves you wanting more. The true tone of a late night began to rise over the scene. Everyone who was still drinking (which was everyone) was either surrounding the fire or the table next to the counter where the laptop was. I had been sitting there for hours, slowly sipping beers and sneaking cigarettes in between the time I was choosing songs, so I gave back the owner of the house his computer.

Bear came up to me with a handful of weed. "You wanna roll this for me?"

"Sure, I just am going to need a few rolling papers."

Out of the dark a few hands offered me papers. The people around the table were talking about random crap that gets on drunken people's mind. As I rolled, I heard a woman's voice say, "I'm trying to see how far into debt I can actually go." Which was responded by, "I can actually show you exactly how far you can go into debt."

I really don't know much about money, or at least that side of it. The extendo joint was finished and I knew I had to smoke it quickly so I could get back to my neighbors and have another smoking circle with them. The joint burned for about 7 minutes. It was pretty fat and by the end everybody was talking about old Black-Eyed Peas songs.

"Where is the love guys?" I asked open endedly.

"What's your deal man? How old are you?" A muscular Hispanic man with a cleft chin asked me. He was playing rough and was obviously very intoxicated.

"Man, chill out." I hit the weed and passed it and took another sip of beer to avoid the term trail baby being acknowledged.

"I hate that question," A muddy guy scruffy looking deadhead said.

"Which one?" I asked

"How old are you?"

"Why?" I asked.

"Well because then everybody wants to know how old everybody is and then it always comes back to me."

"How old are you?"

"I'm seventeen."

I would not have guessed it. He looked a lot older than seventeen.

"You didn't finish High school?"

"Who needs a GED?" he smiled sarcastically showing some green teeth.

I didn't really know. Most people I knew had got one, but anyone could get a job if they *know* someone. There is a skill to knowing how to finish something you start. He could definitely clean up, cut his hair, take a bath, brush his teeth and you'd never know the better that he was "uneducated." He seemed intelligent.

Patience is a difficult thing to reconcile with. We wonder if we will miss out on opportunities if we wait too long. To me it made no difference. Not all of us share the same slice of life. I went over to the bonfire where my music was still playing and some guy who was from Philadelphia said he liked my sound and that I should come visit him sometime. We exchanged numbers. I was ready for bed, but I let the music play on as I sat down with my neighbors.

"Hey guys." It was Louise and Sam and a new fellow, Tentpole.

"Oh, how'd you get that name?" I asked, thinking Tentpole was a very strange name.

"On my first night I got hit in the head with my Tentpole and it stuck. I dunno, I don't really like it but it's the one I was given."

"Why don't you change it?"

"I mean, a trail name isn't something you can just

change or make for yourself. If it was, I'd go by 12 inches."

I went into my bag and got weed out. Tentpole had a pipe. I was just smoking for the hell of it now. Marijuana doesn't really work like alcohol. You can indeed get too high, but after a certain point you start to plateau, and you have to smoke a LOT more to feel much of a difference. We all just chilled out and talked about things that are not important but felt like they were. We laughed about how we would probably hear Tentpole beating off. We joked about how much smarter it is to smoke weed than it is to drink, and then, Sam and I got another beer. Sam and Louise were going to take acid on Friday, and Tentpole was waiting until Saturday. I hadn't decided yet if I was going to or not, I didn't really have the money.

"What's the difference between a homeless person and a hiker?" Sam asked.

"What?"

"Trekking poles." We all burst out laughing. We were drunk but that made us lifelong friends.

"This party is *very* Tennessee," Louise spoke up.

"Yes. Very Tennessee," Sam said, almost to himself.

"When you're from the North, it's all just The South."

All of a sudden out of the bushes we heard, "Where is it!" A dark shadow emerged. "Ahhh Fuck, I can't find my bag!"

It was yelling. I got a closer look at it. I was drunk but I was sure that it was just a homeless person trying to fit in, under the assumption he was a hiker. His face was covered in pockmarks and overgrown shag.

"FUUUUCKKK. Have you guys seen my bag?" He was nearly incoherent, and he seemed dangerous."

"No, I'm sorry man." He went over to my tent. "I swear I left it right here."

The idea of sleeping with all these people being safe turned into a drunken nightmare. I imagined the Riff Raff clan picking out my tent in the middle of the night to terrorize. He kept repeating himself that he had lost his bag and that it was left right next to my tent. I was getting anxious and the weed was no longer helping but throwing me deeper into a state of panic. I wanted to say something, but I was afraid what this drunken animal might do.

After about 10 minutes of everyone being uncomfortable, someone from the fire had said they had found his bag. He began to drunkenly apologize to all of us, but the more he apologized the more hysterical he got.

"SORRRY DISNEY." Now I was interested. I followed him over to the bonfire, telling my neighbors goodnight. I wanted to get my phone before it was stolen from the speakers.

Disney handled himself calmly, "That's alright Bad Wolf."

"I KNOW YOU WANNA KEEP IT FAMILY FRIENDLLY."

"It's fine. Bad Wolf," Disney said surrounded by the fire.

"I'MF SORWY I ROOINED THE NIGHT."

"THAT'S ENOUGH BAD WOLF, NOW GO TO SLEEP."

"SOWRRRRY. I'MMM SOOWRRYY EVVERRYBODY"

All this Tennessee was starting to get to me. The last thing to do was to grab some food before bed from the giant stack. I found food I only dreamed of the night before. I took some white popcorn, and chocolate covered pretzels. I truly had a luxury all to myself in the middle of nowhere with nothing. I went back in my tent. The world spun around me. When you are scared everything is hypersensitive. I indeed heard Tentpole beat off, and then Sam and Louise having sex. You could tell they were trying to be quiet about it, but you could almost feel that last good pump. Once again, although people surrounded me, I felt alone.

Chapter 19

I was still a little tipsy when I woke up around 8 o'clock. Most people were already getting packed up. Anyone who knows pot understands what it's like the morning after you smoke a lump sum of it. It's like a hangover of too much goodness. The only reason I didn't sleep in later was because I needed a ride out to Trail Days and was worried I wouldn't get one. It was still about twenty miles away.

There were beer cans all over the place and the morning dew made everything a little moist. The last thing I wanted to do was drink more or feel the taste of smoke down my dry throat. All of a sudden you wouldn't guess who was up and ready to go with a big smile in his face, drinking a pint of whiskey in one hand with a cigarette hanging from their lip. It was Bad Wolf.

There was no way that he didn't feel dead inside; he was a drunken hyena howling into the night. I just thought about the damage being done to one's body and I couldn't stomach it, I wanted no part of him. I looked around the bar and found an orange for breakfast. I packed everything up, went out to the curb and began to write out on my piece of cardboard on a white Volvo.

T-R-A-I-L D-A I scribbled

"Alright who's coming with me?" I turned around. The scratchy rough voice rung through my head. Bad Wolf was packing up his things and getting into the car I was writing on.

"You got room for one more?" I asked humbled.

"Sure, come on." In the light he still looked like a guy that had done way too many drugs, no education, and was probably the person your parents warned you about getting into a car with. None of that matters when someone has a car, it's early in the morning, you've had a long night of drinking, and need to get somewhere, none of that matters. People began to swarm the car, everybody looking for a ride. The trunk was full. I got into the car with my backpack on my lap and the guy to the left of me also had his pack on his lap. Bad Wolf was in the front and the seventeen-year-old was on the other window seat. Bad Wolf was being loud as hell, he was so excited about this weekend as if he had waited all year for the good times to finally come. He was one scary guy.

He pulled out a bunch of styrofoam cups and began to pour out some whisky in each and offered us all cigarettes. There was no refusing.

"TRAIL DAYS HERE WE COME."

I was all in. The radio was turned up to full volume and we drove off like rebels of society.

"You know I got this car for free? Let's hope she makes it there," Bad Wolf barked.

"Has she broke down before?" I asked with the taste of whisky and a freshly peeled orange on my tongue with a slight tone of concern.

"Yeah, but you can't turn down a free car." The image of all of us getting arrested and caught for the array of drugs that were surely stowed away in the car along with the drunk owner of the vehicle flashed by me.

Everyone shared drug experiences, times they'd been too drunk to remember and women they'd regretted sleeping with. Bad Wolf would out do each story told by getting nastier and nastier. Hookers, running from the police, jail fights. The end of his adventures honored me. I'd read the hell out of *that* book. However, seven hours of sleep and eleven overdue beers, mixed with a little tropical morning whiskey was beginning to get to me. I've never had a hangover before, but this was touching upon a little too much to deal with. I closed my eyes. I expected that if I were to fall asleep that I would wake up with sharpie on my face. After about a minute I opened my eyes to see Bad Wolf shushing and turning down the radio like a gentleman. His respect for others surprised me and everyone in the back seat was content. It was very odd, but as we often do, I misjudged the compassion of this bizarre creature. I woke up to stretch my legs at a side of the road gas station.

"This place has great bacon, cheese and sausage English muffin sandwiches. Anybody want one?" I raised my hand along with the other occupants. He went in and came out with his hands full of them, along with Mountain Dew.

Along the road a familiar moustache appeared. We must've been close to Trail Days.

"Hey you made it." It was the YouTube star from the first shelter.

"Yeah, did you walk in?" I asked trying to hide the circus I was travelling with.

"Yeah, I'm about to go to a coffee shop with Wi-Fi so I can edit some videos, just picked up my computer from the post office." He said holding up a box.

"Nice dude, that's a clever way to have your computer on the road without having to carry it." I said.

"Yeah, man. Hope to see you in Tent City."

"See ya around."

We waved each other off.

I turned back around at the mess I was travelling with. A tye dye hippie, a coke head, a runaway and one designated driver. We all shimmied back into the car.

"They have a parking lot where we can park for the next three days, but it's five dollars." Bad Wolf asked if anybody could assist. I pulled out a crumpled one-dollar bill to help.

We took a turn down into the main drive of town. It was nothing special, I didn't really know what to think of it. Some of the buildings were boarded up, some of them looked like nice old-time stores, a few looked fresh. I just didn't really have any attachment to the town at the time since I was in a new place. I thought it was an odd place to have a festival, that's for sure. The only festival I had been to was Pitchfork. Pretty large scale compared to this this town that looked like it had a capacity of five hundred people maximum. We went down another turn, past a baseball field, and into a parking lot and parked up.

"I gotta go get a parking pass, stay here." Bad Wolf got out of the car.

We waited for a few minutes and he came back with more crap in his hands than he had left with, which included, stickers, muffins and coffee. He was holding the parking pass between his ring finger and his index. He put everything down and slapped the sticker on the vehicle.

There were policemen by the gate. Lovely.

"By the way, don't smoke in the forest during the day. The cops patrol it." He whispered loudly.

"Five dollars please." A nice gruff Southern woman asked me.

I nudged him on his shoulder.

"You didn't say this was going to cost anything. I thought it was a free festival."

"It's five dollars. Just, that is very cheap for what you will get for five dollars."

"Alright." I took out the ten that had been given to me at the last hostel and was given change of another five. The way I saw it, it was rent for the next three days. The walk into the forest was about two hundred feet from the gate. It was magnificent as if it was leading up to some great covenant hidden away from society. We got in and there were tents beginning to be set up. The festival technically commenced on Friday and went until Sunday, but you could arrive on Thursday. We went in, over a little drive that was paved with rocks and into the Riff Raff area.

"All of this is ours." Bad Wolf exclaimed with wonder in his eyes and extending his arms as if to give the whole place a big hug. "Just find a place to tent, off to the side works well."

Disney was already there. Bad Wolf was explaining how excited he was, and all that, and Disney beginning to get annoyed calling Bad Wolf just some punk kid, not worthy of the name of Riff Raff. I just ignored the background noise and I found a little crevice to park my tent for the next few days in a place that looked somewhat out of the way of traffic. I liked my spot, it was surrounded by bushes and in the far back of this little area. I set everything up, threw my backpack inside and fell right back asleep. My body was more than exhausted.

I had walked an average of seventeen miles every single day up until this point, and the night before I did not get the sleep that was needed for that. I was tired. After about two hours of rejoicing in the first sense of what it meant to "relax", I popped my head out of my tent, which I now noticed was surrounded by a few more tents. I got up and had a deep stretch that hurt my body.

"Howdy," I said to a guy setting up his tent near mine. "I'm glad to be your neighbor for the next three days."

A handsome boney man with long hair in a red shirt smiled.

"Hey man, we're neighbors. I like that."

"Gimme a hug," I added a little bit more energy to the situation.

"Alright forsure."

"I'm Cheerio."

"I'm Mantis." I could see where he had gotten the name. His legs and bones were lanky and long. His facial structure was that of the insect.

"Did you just get in?"

"Yep."

"You walk in?" I asked.

"Nah, I took a shuttle from Erwin."

Oh nice, Erwin is sweet."

"Well I'm going into town, you need anything, Butter? Flour?" He joked.

"Hahaha, nah, but let's grab a beer sometime tonight."

"You betcha."

I shuffled back in and grabbed my vaporizer and thought I would go explore the town myself. I threw on my Jansport and forged my way through the festival. It was such an odd feeling to only be carrying only some weed, quarters and a water bottle on my back. I recognized the thought process behind Dr. Fix-it's method, the less you carry the freer you are. Without all that shit I had in my tent I could go anywhere. It was sort of like having a little house on my back. It's something I someday hope I can do, just go anywhere without anything.

I left the premises of the festival and looked at the world around me. It was a gorgeous sight; a bunch of people were coming in from the trail. When you see a group of hikers you can't help but envy them. Everybody was dirty and had everything on their backs, I felt like I was part of a special club. I began to walk into town, or where I guessed town was, and I found the baseball field.

A young guy with long curly blonde hair on a Penny board came up to me He didn't seem like he actually listened to Slayer, which was on his t-shirt.

"You just get in?" he asked in a voice that could have only come from childhood of surfing.

"Yep. You a hiker?"

"Haha, sorta, I'm more of just a traveler."

"I respect that, I'm sorta doing the same thing."

"Yeah, but I'm looking for a little bit of weed this morning."

"I figured. I got some, might as well get the day started," I smiled.

"Let's go to somewhere less crowded, I've heard that the cops are a nuisance out here."

"Aren't they everywhere." He said briskly.

We went to the baseball field. I began to climb to the top of the bleachers. I looked through the window of the announcer's seat and realized that it could be moved. I opened one, climbed through an unlocked the door. I rolled us a joint and looked out at the empty baseball field. It was like looking out at the real American pastime. Nothing. What a game.

I may have quite the millennial mentality in full throttle. Kids believing that things will be given to them their whole lives no matter where they go, but life can't really be as hard as everyone keeps telling me it is. I just wanna have fun and get paid while doing it. There is a way that you can do that. If you get enough people interested in whatever the hell you are doing online or in Social Media, companies will just pay you to produce content or sponsor their products. It's very strange. It's all out West I've been told.

Anyway, we got to talking and this guy had 10,000 followers on Instagram while I had about three hundred.

We did a follow for a follow so we each gained one person in our repertoire. We snuck out of the baseball announcer seats and climbed back down to the street level. We split and I directed him towards Tent City. I followed the grass lines, which were roped off with celebratory flags and went further, closer into the town. I saw another familiar face, which was glad to see me.

"Hey! It's *you,*" he pointed at me.

It was iPod, the British lad from my first night in a shelter. He was wearing these strange Lennon glasses that covered the corner of his eyelids with leather. I gave him a high five.

"I'm glad you made it here, this far. I was a bit worried with all those clothes you had," he sounded ecstatic to see me.

"I'm down to two pairs of everything. It's still a bit heavy though."

"Eh, if you made it this far, I'm sure you'll get along. I'll see you in the forest then? We'll share a beer or something?"

"Yeah, I'm ready to have a good time." And we simply walked off from each other.

I didn't really know what I was looking for in town, but I just couldn't relax like I was supposed to. My body was wired to the expectation of working as hard as I could for as long as I could. I walked in and there was a bar, "Hey Joe." There was a nice guy outside who was meant to check Ids.

"Are you twenty-one?" He asked, piercing his sunglasses at me, while laying back in a sun chair.

"Uh, yeah..."

"Really?"

"No. I forgot my ID. I'm not twenty-one."

"Oh, yah know. Thanks for being honest. You can just go in. Nobody's watching."

I went in. The atmosphere was great. It was a checkered tile floor with some tables and a big bar in the middle.

"Hello."

"You want a table? Or the bar."

"Err, uh I'll take a table."

I was pressured by the ambiance of the place to sit down. I longed for the bar from my table, but it was too late. I didn't really want to do this anymore. What if I *was* carded and then I would have to be obnoxiously told to leave. I cracked under the pressure when she came back.

"What'll ya have?" The waitress asked me.

"I'll take a fish taco, thanks."

"Anything to drink?"

"No water is fine."

Damnit, why the hell did I order a fucking fish taco? I don't have the money for that. I have at most ten dollars, in change. It had nothing to do with not being old enough to order a beer, it just had to do with the fact that I didn't have enough money to buy a beer, but I ended up buying something more expensive. At least I used this time to recharge my phone for a little bit. My dad called while I was waiting for my food.

"Hello?" I was happy to hear from him but didn't want to show it.

"Oh, Hello." He was solemn.

"Yes?"

"It looks like you're in Damascus, Virginia."

"Yep."

"You must be running low on money."

"Yep."

"I'm not sending you any money." He assured.

"Please Dad, it is a matter of life and death. I don't have enough for a meal." Referencing the tacos I just ordered.

"Alright, well I have a birthday card from your Aunt but that's it. I'll send to Damascus, overnight and *hopefully* there is some money in it. Do you need anything else?"

"No. How's Everything?"

"I'm fine." He said. "We all miss you."

I'm sure. The small remote amount of contact with my family was two texts. One - to my stepmother, apologizing for what I did to my dad. Two - to my brother, congratulating him about graduating college. *I* was missing the hell out of everyone. The best advice my father ever gave me was how I shouldn't follow my dreams. What kind of home is that? I wanted to go home, but the attitude that my family has towards me makes me feel like a nuisance.

The conversation ended when the fish tacos came out and I thanked the waitress. In front of me on the table were two tiny ass tacos with three pieces of shrimp and some chopped lettuce, spicy chipotle sauce, tomatoes and cilantro all wrapped up in an itty-bitty tortilla. It was beautiful. I looked at the check and it was no way in hell worth eight dollars. I looked around the bar. Everyone was with each other and laughing and enjoying the good things to come on this weekend, and I sat alone with my phone plugged into the wall.

Two individuals walked in, one pale blonde with a pixie cut and a quirky girl with straight hair and oversized glasses, both had tattoos and piercings. I paid the eight dollars with a four-quarter tip and walked up to the bar over by the unorthodox couple. I saw a guitar off to the corner and asked blonde if she played.

"It's his." He pointed to a man with an off the beaten path about him. The man was sitting a seat over closer to the guitar, and the door.

"You mind playing a song?" I asked.

"Yeah, sure but let's go outside. I'm leaving town in about five minutes."

"Where you going?"

"New Orleans." When he said that I was ready to let everything I had imagined up in my head to just let it all go. I was looking for the American dream. A place to live, and a reason to do it. I thought I would find that in New York, but really a place as alive as New Orleans would do just as well. We went outside and he played a song only a passing traveler could play. One with heart and soul and rhythm. It rang through the crowd and matched the air filled with livelihood. The moment of tenderness mimicked itself in a dance against the blue sky. He deserved eight dollars more than that taco. A man on the road with nothing on his back but his songs. A man dying for freedom only found in an empty wallet.

“Is there a place to go swimming here in town?” The tall blonde asked.

“We got about a Dollar General,” said the bouncer under a yellow umbrella. “It takes nine minutes to go from one end of town to the other. Nine minutes. Do you have any idea how many times I’ve walked through this whole town in ten minutes in my life? I’m almost thirty.”

I thought of wasted hours. I’ve done an obscene amount of walking through my town, though.

“The pool’s closed, but if you go up that road there is a swimming hole about fourteen feet deep, people love to go to there. Hell, last year I told these people about it and they said, man, that swimming hole was a great time.”

“Alright thanks, I gotta go grab my swim suit.” The quirky one posed.

“Are you guys going back to the festival?” I asked.

“Yeah,” the pixie responded.

“Can, I walk with y’all. I just got in,” I said like the lonely traveler I was.

“Sure.”

I thanked the guitarist and wished him luck and began to walk back to the festival with the girls I’d just met. They were “who the fuck cares” old. They were both from Seattle. We crossed a bridge which I didn’t remember taking getting to town.

“Trix,” said the blonde.

“I’m Albern.” I shook their hand.

“Is this your first Trail Days?” The blonde asked in a chic nature.

“Haha, yeah first time on the road too.” I said warmly.

“We did the PCT last year and we had to come back for more,” Albern spoke.

“I feel you. I’ve never experienced such a thrill in my whole life. I definitely want to do something like this again.”

“You should.”

I realized I left my phone back at the bar like a dumbass. I thought about everything that would happen if I lost my phone. If it was stolen, I was probably not making it anywhere.

"Ah shit."

"What?"

"I left my phone back at the bar. Nice to meet y'all. Hope you have fun swimming," I said in a frantic blush. Leaving my phone unattended is something that would only occur because of smoking too much pot.

I ran back to the door.

"Do you have my phone?"

"You left it and he had to go."

I took a moment to catch my breath.

"Did he take it with him?" The world spun. How was I going to find a man going to New Orleans?

"Nah, I got it right here."

"Oh." I was envious of the man who can pick up everything and just leave it all behind, even another man's phone. I thanked him and thought I would explore the town just a little bit more. Why not? It was just a small quaint little town, and this was its biggest event of the year. A bunch of hiker trash coming through and god dammit did they take pride in it.

I saw some random guy waving at me from across the street.

I crossed. "Hey man it's me..." I didn't recognize him. "Your *Neighbor*."

"Oh Mantis. How you doing buddy?"

"I'm great man. I'm going to a friend's house."

All of a sudden, I realized he was surrounded by a group of supermen carrying cases of beers. You know, the type that knows how to laugh and drink really hard.

"Oh, sounds good man. I kinda gotta shit, do you mind If I come over?" I began to assert the situation.

"Ight, fuck it, Let's get things going." One of them yelled like they were in a b-line.

"Shit don't start til I take a shit." I said over to Mantis.

We began walking along one of the roads and they got louder and louder about something.

Hey Mantis, have you gotten lucky this trip?" I walked curtly.

He was a good-looking guy. Adult, probably over thirty, but as an attractive a man as they come.

"One time."

"What happened?"

"I was in a parking lot walking through alone, and this woman started yelling something across the ways at me. I was about to ignore her, but then something in my mind told me to listen to her. I went back and she was interested in two frogs having sex

"Weird."

"She asked me what I was doing, with the big backpack and all, and I said I was hiking the Appalachian Trail, and it looked like it was about to rain. Next thing we knew we got in her car and went to a bar and she said that she would spring for a hotel."

"Woah." The thought of a woman putting someone up like that, was peculiar to me, but at the same time it made sense. It wasn't a sexist thought, but I'd been around Southern gentleman's practice. Also, when you also live in an alt-left bubble long enough, new traditions are born.

"Did you?" Making love is a romantic term, which remains a mystery from society.

"We did." Once that night, twice in the morning."

My favorite playwright once said that they just didn't believe sex was as important to society as everyone makes it out to be. I have meditated on that thought for a long time. I didn't agree with them at the time. A healthy balance is important, but we have hormones. Part of a new generation with no morals. I still believe the world is becoming an over sexualized place. In the same way that the Sixties was a revolution, except just the opposite and twice as superficial. People today don't just run around naked and make love for no reason anymore. I suppose things are just changing and part of me is from the Fifties. Socially, sex isn't always the first thing we all talk about but is becoming the first thing we think about. I did not intake food with any balance the night before. I basically ate a full bag of white popcorn, thirty chocolate covered pretzels, three chilidogs, fifteen shortbread cookies, and a salad. I needed to poop pronto. We got to a place with a nice back porch filled up with old chairs and writing on the wall.

"The bathroom is in there and take a left."

I walked into what was a beautiful kitchen. Wooden, but had a feeling of an old cottage. I shuffled around into a dark back room where I saw some quiet looking man taking a nap on a couch. I went into the bathroom.

"What is this place?" I asked once outside.

"It's the Log." Mantis said. It seemed like a small hotel.

"I'd stick around, but I kinda wanna take care of a few things before I get hammered. It's not even noon."

"At trail days that's late to get getting started," a fashionable one of the crowd slyly remarked.

"I'll be back after dinner or something like that. Peace."

I walked back through the town with my head feeling light as a cloud. Anytime I'm in the South I can't help but think of peaches. I could use a good peach in my palm. A little marijuana helped me to look back at the town with objective love and just walk around instead of going somewhere in particular. I had more than nine minutes to spare. I had already figured out the whole layout of the town besides a few other bridges I hadn't wandered past, but once you get lost, you become more aware of your surroundings. The parking lot, which was empty this morning when we arrived, was now filled to the brim. I was excited about the energy in the air, which is really just the sound of motorcycles.

I saw a face, which made me smile. "Bear." I hugged them.

"How ye doin' Cheerio."

"Glad to be here. We made it. What are you doing?"

"Well. I don't know. I think this place has a shower truck of some sort that is run by a church."

"You know what sounds really nice?"

"What?" He asked.

"Taking a shower." I raised my head to the sun.

"Let's do it man. They have laundry, too."

“Alright after we grab yours, let's grab mine too.” I said making a plan.

We went into Tent City where the party was beginning to become alive, even though it was only noon on the day before it was officially supposed to begin. We took a hard left through some pine and I saw where Bear was camping. He was out on an island that seemed as though it would take some maneuvering to get across the river. He began hopping from rock to rock. I just took my shoes off and got my feet a little wet. A wonderful reminder that there are always different ways to achieve the same goal. We were out on the island and I saw a familiar tent next to his. Horizon was standing next to it.

Bear pulled out a joint.

“You wanna get in on this?” he asked Horizon.

“Hell yeah.” She smiled and seemed relaxed, already very high and trying to gather her thoughts which were a little all over the place it seemed. She walked over to us and gave me a one-armed hug.

“Good to see you.”

I was glad that the happiness in the atmosphere overruled any amount of awkwardness that could have been.

“Good to see you too,” I tried to say in a reserved enjoyment.

An older gentleman whose tent was set up on the small beach of the island turned around.

“I’ll get in on this.” He climbed up to our level.

“Is it supposed to rain?” Horizon asked us.

“I think so,” Bear said.

“It’s rained every year at Trail Days for the past three years,” the other tanned man said.

“Hey, it rained at Woodstock,” I said, and the joint was lit.

“Your tent looks like it’s kinda close to the river. If that rises, you're going to get flooded,” Horizon said to the dude, releasing a cough as she said it.

“Can’t have lakefront property without some sort of problem,” he smiled.

You could tell that he was older than all of us by a considerable amount of years. He wasn’t old old, but the kind of person who probably got lost somewhere along in their mid-thirties and never really found a home anywhere.

"Guess what my trail name is." He looked at me.

I was high so I was like, "Flower man, Man on the Moon, or Lazer."

"It's Long Dong."

"Are you serious? Did you give that name to yourself?" I replied a little unamused by the immaturity of the older gentleman.

"I didn't give this name to myself, it came to me."

"More like came out of you." Horizon laughed.

I rolled my eyes a little and they all looked at me as if my judgment was as apparent in these circles as a pink elephant. A trick, if you ever find yourself in these sorts of circles is you always want to be weirder than the people around you. Some people would argue it the other way, but those people usually buy their friendships. The joint sizzled down to its end.

"Wanna grab your laundry?" I asked Bear.

"Yeah, sure."

"I'll see y'all around," I said, mostly to Horizon.

We crossed the river and weaved through the woods all the way into my tent. I grabbed my bag, but I also wanted to wash what I was wearing. I took off my shirt and underwear. There was one pair of maroon shorts I hadn't worn yet that are a little tight. As we passed through The Riff Raff area and things were in motion. Everybody was digging a huge hole as wide as a grave around. Some were gathering huge rocks from the river.

"What's this for?" I asked

"Fire pit," a bearded man holding a beer said gruffly.

"Dear lord, that's the largest fire pit I've ever seen in my life. When's it gonna be finished?"

"Tonight."

"I'll be there." I said.

Nothing like a good fire pit. Especially when you can just sit back and relax with people who know how to have a good time. We went to the truck where the showers were. Lovely old women were running the place with their husbands, and food was laid out under a tented area with a place to charge your phone which I took advantage of. You could tell Jesus was present.

"Would you like us to wash your clothes?" You couldn't tell if these old women loved you or just wanted to save you.

"Yes please."

"You can borrow some of our clothes while you wait. I looked through them and there was a men's large red t-shirt that I grabbed. As I was about to get into the shower out came a man who was an XXL. I went into the shower and my head just touched the ceiling of the shower and it wasn't spacious either. I have no idea how that man fit inside.

There were three showers inside the truck. I was in the first one. As I was stoned enjoying my shower, possibly singing a silly shampoo song, an old man opened the door and said, "Yeah this one's available" and threw open my curtain exposing me to the world. I don't mind getting naked and all, but I like to know when I'm going to be showing off. The man was mortified and shut the shower curtain as quickly as he could. I just smiled and shook my head, nothing unusual on the road. I came out of that shower a changed man.

I'm actually extremely addicted to showers. They clear your head and you get to smell good, most good things just muddy you up and have a horrible after effect. I got to use soap and I wasn't covered in algae when I came out of it. I felt as fresh as a passing wind. Bear came out with a towel wrapped around his waist and a chiseled chestnut chest.

"I think you are supposed to get dressed in the truck." He swung off the towel and revealed a pair of shorts, and a grin.

"Ah, good one."

"How long is the laundry supposed to take?" I asked him.

"About two hours."

Nothing like time to kill.

"I think I'm gonna go into town." He said.

"I'm going to stick around here for just a little bit, charge my phone and eat a little."

"I'll see you soon man."

I began eating bananas, almonds, snickers, yogurt and goldfish. This was lunch since that fish taco was not nearly enough. As I sat back, I looked around me at the other hikers in this refuge, an old man from the gut of America and his wife filing her nails were surrounded by bearded dirty hikers. I turned to him.

"Where you from?"

"Damascus, Virginia." He had a thick accent.

"I hear it's nice there."

"Look around," he said. "It is exciting."

"I suppose so. Most people I know get very bored, but the older I'm getting and the harder I work the less you have time for that."

"You're so young?" he said, sounding confused, by me trying to sound wise.

"Not realistically."

He didn't understand what I said.

"Why ain't you young?"

"Kids these days man."

"Oh yeah." He nodded his head and I nodded mine in similar distaste.

"I'm growing a beard, so I won't be associated with them. How long have you been growing yours?"

"Almost twenty years. Are you going to finish the trail?"

"I want to." I shrugged. I didn't want to go home. There was never a dull moment on the road, and it accepted me more than my family was ever willing. I have a pretty short attention span. I also enjoy variety and talking to a lot of different people. I decided that I would go into town just to look around just a little bit more. I was also craving a beer.

I was about to leave but his wife grabbed my arm.

"They are having a dinner for everyone at the fire station, would you like a meal ticket."

"Yes please." Now this is what I'm talking about.

I hoped that I could get through the whole weekend without having to buy another meal. I skipped along the grassy plain towards town, which was now lined with tents for conservatories from New Jersey and churches in West Virginia. I was interested but didn't feel like stopping to engage in that conversation just yet. I waved at the baseball field, and tipped my hat to the bar, until I came across the fire station. Inside were two long empty tables for two hundred at least. All of the plates were out, and chairs lined up. I thought it was just gorgeous to look at, almost like a bizarre art piece. My meal ticket was for six o'clock and it was about five.

I decided I'd go stop by the Log. I walked up and I saw Gonzo sitting on the front porch with a case of beers.

"Hey man, Good to see you. When did y'all get in?

"Raccoon and I got here around two."

"Nice man, is he in Tent City?"

"Yeah, wanna beer?"

"Sure, it might be best to go around back." Mantis and I gave each other high fives as we entered. There were all sorts of dirty young people laying around. The smell of marijuana was potent. I didn't really know what to think of the place, it definitely was a safe haven of some sort, it's just hard to get comfortable when you don't know everyone the way they all seem to know each other.

"Hey, are you going to dinner at the firehouse?" Mantis asked me.

"Yeah, I think so."

"What time are you going?"

"My ticket is for six."

"Damn, mine's for five. I gotta get going but I don't have anyone to go with."

"I'm sure you'll find somebody." I said.

Gonzo and I went beyond the porch to where there was an Eno hammock hanging low to the ground next to a lawn chair. I mixed some tobacco with marijuana and rolled a thick spliff for us to ease into the night with.

"New York Eh?" He said as he passed the spliff back to me.

"Yep, New York City."

"You know it's not going to be like this, the city is very different than the Appalachian Trail."

"I'd bet. But I also believe that people are inherently good and that something, or somebody will come along, and I will be fine. There are 7 million people, somebody has got to have a heart."

"Man, people, nobody gives a shit about anybody but themselves there." He shook his head as though he knew too much.

We both nodded our heads as we watched the sun set and let the numbness in my bones take over what had been the first day without a rigorous workout. I felt at peace and wasn't worried about what was yet to come. I had gone this far.

As far as I was concerned, I was in no rush to be homeless.

Chapter 20

I was waiting in line for the food at the firehouse with a guy who looked like my dad if he was around my age named Seth. He had a mustache, peppered hair and was skinny. We got along well. The firehouse was having fried chicken, biscuits, and beans for dinner each night. Afterward, there was a table with a whole layout of pies and treats. The fried chicken was made from chickens that had never seen the light of day, and it was amazing. I kid you not I have never tasted anything so succulent in my entire life. The biscuits were warm as a bosom and the chocolate cake was heart stopping. I ended up sitting with Seth and his friends. He was a little further along on the trail than I was. I was feeling slightly homesick.

"Did you ever get homesick?" I asked him

"Yeah, I did, but it went away pretty quickly."

"When?" I asked.

"Around the second week, but now I don't want to go home."

"Have you seen the ponies?"

"Oh yeah, I've seen the ponies." He whipped out his phone and showed me his Instagram which had over a thousand followers as well.

"I think that is where I am going to try and go after this festival. I can't miss out on the ponies."

"Do not my friend."

We finished dinner and it wasn't dark, but the air was getting blue. There had been word of a wine and cheese meet and greet but I forgot to get the address, so I just wandered to the outskirts of town. I was homesick as hell. I wanted to go back to my old life. I missed waking up, and biking over to my girlfriends' house and going to the beach, but none of that was promised back at home so it wasn't an option.

I thought about my first love, Austin Rains. The last time I saw her was at a festival and boy did we dance together. We will always dance together. Rains taught me how to dance. She made me laugh when it was hard. She would also drop things all the time, so life had a dull

moment. The happiest I ever was, and I was a loser. And that girl taught me how to dance. I just wish the world had more excuses to dance in the rain together more often. I roamed the Southern town and looked at beautiful houses. Not big homes, but homes that had real families in them that laughed and ate dinner together.
I walked past the bar Hey Joe's and back to where the Dollar General was, but across the street from the festival there was *another* church. There was a small concert playing old fashioned rock and country hits that everybody enjoys singing along and dancing to. It was the first time I had heard a live band in the whole journey. There were people just dancing and enjoying life. I was one of them. I danced and felt my legs move and my hips hit the rhythms like a tambourine, soon I just let myself go the way that it is supposed to be when someone dances. I've written essays on how nervous people get when it comes to dancing, like we are all still in middle school. The truth is nobody cares about how you look, they are all much too concerned with how they look. I swear, bands should hire me just to attend their shows. If I want to, I can get a whole crowd dancing.

I really feel good when I am around any church. I think they promote positive vibes and there is so much grunge in the world that wants to make everything so edgy that it just gets old. It's a lot harder to be nice to people and believe in God than it is to say there isn't one and do whatever you want. I didn't really hang around too long, I decided I'd go into the forest of grunge. The night air had awoken the life in Tent City. People were all wandering around to the rhythm of a good time. No cops were in the city and everyone was letting loose. Hikers are scandalous hippie trash at its finest. I got back to around where my tent was placed, and Riff Raff was in full throttle. The fire roared and the sound system was set up. Heavy hip-hop forced everyone to get very congested. Hard dancing existed far and close from each other. Bodies rubbed with barely anything on and spirits were awoken in people you wouldn't dare to touch. I don't hold anything back while I dance, whether I'm with someone or not, it's the only thing that truly makes me feel alive.

I saw the odd couple from the bar, and they were grooving. We all started dancing together and they gave me a beer, which was finished in the duration of one song. Things were getting stranger and I liked it. Vision blurred, people yelled, and I took deep pleasure in each second of it. The fire boomed and got hotter on our skin. Sweat dripped from all of our bodies and got on one another. I went back to the tent to remove my shirt. I came back and I saw Raccoon was enjoying himself in a lawn chair. I ran over and gave that motherfucker a big hug. He was glad to see me and even got up to do a little jig. It was not a scene of any restraint, for any one.

Good men will always have trouble resisting anything they shouldn't do. I was not ashamed then and excuse me if I am now. I got people's attention by dancing wildly and then I left so as not to make a scene of myself. I found small groups of people smoking bowls of weed in the forest I sat down with. People from other countries, Germany, Spain, Asia, all with a hell of a lot of Tennessee. We laughed about the metric system and diets of other countries. There were so many girls. I'm talking about just real girls that make you laugh, ones that go to college or didn't go because they actually had something they liked to do, like art. Occasionally a young man can be an artist, but women are always made of art. Growing up all of my friends were girls and I used to get made fun of because of it. Men like to laugh, and women like to love. I made friends with people whose names I never heard. A lot of beer was everywhere, and drugs were encouraged.

I got a good group around one a.m. Two girls and one guy, all tripping. It felt really nice to dive into each of our life stories and really listen. The one girl who was Jewish with curly hair, was an orphan. She was never adopted and when she was eighteen, she decided to hike this trail. The guy was a musician, he had a strange looking guitar. It was very thin, and he had brought it on the trail. He had dark hair and the face of a dragonfly. He played his songs for us, I tried to play but I was a little rusty. The other girl had finished college but regretted ever going. I felt like was just a little bit of each of those people in different ways.

People often just talk about nothing. Sometimes that is nice, but it's so hard to get to know anyone when they can't expose anything real about themselves. Around three, I went to my tent, it was early compared to everyone else. There was a guy posted up.

"Sorry, is this your tent?" He asked me

"Yeah?"

"Uh, I put my tent next to yours, like almost right on top of yours."

"It's alright. We get to be closer this way."

"Blunt?"

Yes please, and then I fell asleep a foot away from the center of the commotion in my tent. It was around ten o'clock in the morning when I woke up dazed and confused. I yawned and laid back. I hadn't picked up my laundry yet, but I assumed it was still there. Eventually, I got out of my tent and the same guy from last night posted up right next to my tent.

"Wanna get in on this?" He was smoking another blunt which is a tobacco leaf wrap to roll marijuana with.

"Yeah, why not."

We smoked it down to a nub and everything was magnified with the morning air as the sun peered through the trees. I was kind of hungry. I walked around and sure enough people were already drinking beers and I was confused by their will to get drunk so early. I surely would need a nap at some point in the day if I was drinking beer for breakfast. There was a small tea tent that was set up towards the front of the forest. I went over to it because they were serving a better breakfast equivalent. A nice man and his wife and three daughters were sitting on wooden log benches.

"Would you like some tea?" He offered.

"Yes please."

"Hot or cold."

"Hot please."

Hot was the wrong choice. It burned my lips and I was not hydrated at all. I went over to the church across the street. Inside there was a large buffet of food. Warm muffins, orange juice, bacon, eggs. I was set. I ate like a horse and sat back trying to figure out what I was going to do for the day. I didn't know what my plans were. I was thinking possibly of never coming home again. Never seeing my parents or family until I had made something of myself somewhere else.

I left and outside on the porch of the church there was a row of guitars. When there's an option, if you play guitar or any instrument, you might understand when I say you've got to pick the right guitar to get the right sound or feeling you are looking for. There were glossy guitars, black guitars, but I took a smooth oak guitar and felt like playing some music. The strings hurt my fingers since it had been a little bit since I had last really played. I took the guitar out into a quiet field. I wrote a song. It's often hard to write a song that actually means something, but I had so much raw emotion and material I was working with, one sort of just flew out of me.

It wasn't anything profound, but it got the gears moving.

What Do You Hear?

```
 Em                          C                        G
I walk to the places and see all the faces, I breathe
      Em                          C                    G
I'm trying to find what this world can mean to me
          Em    C
And I'm so, scared
      G                          Em
Of finding this peace that is missing
              C                                              G
And your hands mend my heart it's goddamn heavenly
 Am      C          G
To be a part of something
```

A Em (interlude)

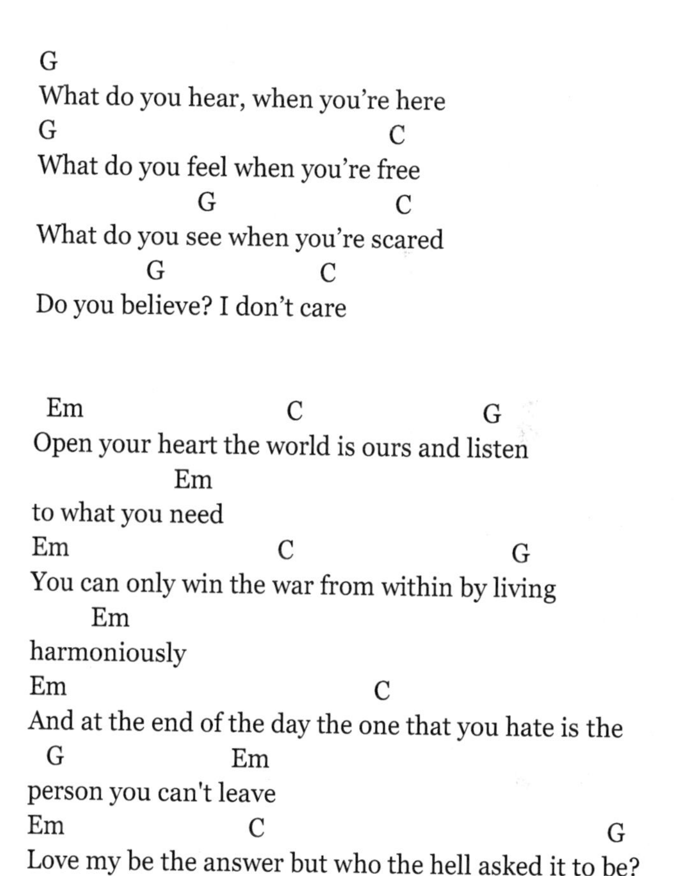
G
What do you hear, when you're here
G C
What do you feel when you're free
G C
What do you see when you're scared
G C
Do you believe? I don't care

Em C G
Open your heart the world is ours and listen
Em
to what you need
Em C G
You can only win the war from within by living
Em
harmoniously
Em C
And at the end of the day the one that you hate is the
G Em
person you can't leave
Em C G
Love my be the answer but who the hell asked it to be?

Before I'm a songwriter, I'm a poet. All poetry is, is telling the truth. I'm very ashamed of most of my work, especially when I first compose it. I will not feel the same about the world as I did when I walked through it alone for the first time, and all these words are just fleeting memories to capture how I felt. I've changed since I've walked, and I've changed since I've written this sentence.

Out there in a small field with a guitar I felt so far apart from everyone. I tried not to wander away from the church but you do need some silence when you write a song so you can hear your heart metronome. Plus, that blunt got me thinking. I tried to enjoy myself. I went back to Tent City. Things were really starting to get set up now. Tents that looked like small houses were going up. A huge dome that was hung from a tree fifteen feet up was being put together by a group of hikers. I hung around Riff Raff for a little bit.

They decided they were going to go tube sliding along the river. I thought I would join in. I just wore my shorts and we went to the far end of the forest. The river wasn't roaring, but it had a fun current, and I got to share a tube with a woman in her mid-forties. It was a giant flamingo. We cracked a beer together on the way down. It was a group activity and I knew all the people the least, so I was given some shit. I can laugh at myself pretty badly. We got to the end of the river down where Bear had set up his tent and I saw Horizon wave at me as we were coming up on the beach that Long Dong was tenting by.

"Hey what's up!" I called from the shallow river.

"I'm about to go into town. To the post office," Horizon told me.

"Really? I might have a package that is coming today. Do you mind if I come with you?"

"I don't mind."

I didn't have shoes on, but I wasn't really wet beyond my knees and I was wearing a t-shirt. Horizon and I walked out of the madness and started to head for the town. It was nice walking with her. We joked about our age differences, but you could tell at heart we were similar in age more than we were different. I asked her what kind of work she did, and she said that she did all kind of things. She got her masters, which I thought was impressive. I let her know that I was just going to become an internet sensation and become a millionaire the old-fashioned way. You could tell she believed in me, but not really. I think that was the majority of our age difference. The Internet.

Before we got to the post office, I suggested that I needed to get some sunglasses but didn't have any money to spare. I let her know I could just meet her at the post office, but she probably wouldn't recognize me under my new shades. I went into a sporting goods store. It was sort of smallish but getting good business on a weekend like this. There was one man behind the counter eying me. I went over to the sunglasses.

"Do you guys have backpacks for sale?" Horizon came in, distracting the shop owner.

"Um, yes, in the back."

I took a pair off the shelf, slipped it into my back pocket and left.

"Thank you, I'll come back tomorrow," she paid no attention to me as I left.

She tried on the sunglasses and we laughed on our way to the post office. She liked them. Once we go to the post office, and I kid you not, Louis C.K. himself worked there. His mannerisms, his cut to the chase eyebrows, bald red head, made him a close relative to say the least. Have you ever noticed that we are all just different relatives of ourselves somewhere else? When you meet someone who looks and acts exactly the same as someone you know and the genes are obviously the same, it's very odd. The postman told me he didn't have my letter, which sort of made me feel like a creeper. Horizon got hers and walked with it over her head like it was a pot of water as if she was from Egypt.

The town was lively. Old fashioned cars drove through, some of them with big Trump stickers on the back. When we got back closer to Tent City, we got caught in a frisbee circle. Again, it was the kind of guys who look like they belong in a frat but probably didn't even go to college. They all had beers in their hands and were attractive. I joined in on the frisbee passing. I talked with one of them with a sleeveless shirt and made fun with him at the rest of them. I had a beer that I was drinking and walked right past a few cops.

"Is that beer open?" The mustached cop asked me.

That open container could have really screwed me over.

"Oh no, this was just an empty bottle I picked up off the ground," I said, on my toes.

"Oh, well, throw it out." The deputy said.

Me, all the boys and even Horizon snickered as I slowly walked away. The crew went ahead, and Horizon was stopping off at the laundry truck. I grabbed my clean clothes off the table. They were in a nice trash bag. I said goodbye to her and went back to Tent City. Riff Raff's fire was roaring, and everyone was drinking heavily. I suppose open containers were legal in the forest. The day was unwinding but people were picking up the pace. It wasn't long before I thought I would go to the Log before I settled in for the night. I knew there was another dinner at the fire station again. These walks to and from town were not specifically short. About a mile and a half each way. Two, if you went all the way to the Log.

The couches were full on the back porch of the small hotel. There were two characters that stood out. One old man with a beard named Billie, who was much too old to be hanging around all these twenty-year olds, but cooler than all of them just the same. The other person, whose appearance stood out, was a ginormous guy in a purple shirt with a long ponytail. He was at least seven feet tall. His name was BFG and he was the owner of the place and also sold weed.

Gonzo was chilling back, and a few of the guys I saw at the barn with the shabby beards and dreadlocks. One was trying to read a book. People were all joking with each other, the way people do when they get relaxed around each other, usually at someone's expense. I hung around BFG and Billie while we rolled six or seven blunts and they all got shared with different people, and I ended up in the best spot. It was the perfect seat to get passed through and just observe everything. I got blitzed. There was one strange moment when the Blackalachian, the only black I hiker I ever met, came around the old hostel dog had a deep bark at the look of him. Almost like the dog was a racist. Everyone shushed the dog. Nobody there was racist or would have dared to even hint at it. Younger people aren't racist the way it was instilled into older generations and watchdogs.

BFG, Billie and the Blacklachian were the icons of people you just looked at and are like, damn, I bet they all smoke a lot of weed. The first time Billie had hiked the trail was in 1970, which was after he had kids. The Blacklachian had an enormous afro, guitar and was from Philly. BFG had a David Foster Wallace look about him but was gangster at heart. He was holding at least a fifty hundred-dollar bills in his hand. We were all silly, but we were real.

"BFG, Can I take a picture of you?" I thought he looked too badass holding all the money hanging a blunt from his lips.

"Not right now! Damn." He broke into laughter. "I mean shit, not right NOW." He flexed the money.

Time flew by and I missed the six o'clock dinner that I had the ticket for today and went to the seven o'clock one instead and they really didn't care. The line was filled with festival guys as well. I stunk up the place and was awkward with who I picked to sit next to. I ate with a family that was hiking, not the whole trail, but for the summer, just to see how far they could go together. The kids were ten and eleven and were very entertaining. I wasn't very talkative, but I was interested in them. A beautiful family is a rare thing to come by. Parents might disagree after years of comparing themselves to all the other school children and their parents, but once you get out of the suburbs and into the real world, a family that sticks together is becoming a very rare thing indeed.

The fried chicken sat in my stomach well. The ends of my fingers had been losing their nutrients and becoming dry and peeling at the ends of them but had now returned to a smooth state. I left the firehouse and bummed a cigarette in the back and headed back to Tent City since I knew that there would probably be something exciting going on, it was almost eight o'clock and people had been drinking for the last twelve hours.

I got in and the music was as electrifying as the night before. Riff Raff had a dominant nature about them, like they wanted to control the attitude of the festival. I hadn't been there for the years before, but you could tell they were intimidating. I have a very trusting nature about me, and I liked them on the basis that they were the first people I rolled into town with. The Riff Raff pit was less congested than the night before, and I wondered where everyone was. The members of the *elite* group were more intoxicated than the night before and trying harder to have a good time. There was still a lot of people all over the place, I thought I would explore a little bit more of the grounds. I went down a short path and found where the real party for the night was. I am not over exaggerating, a fire the size of a small home was burning surrounded by hundreds of hikers in an open field, mostly without clothes on.

Everyone was banging pots and pans, and someone had a trumpet they hiked with. Songs blew into the wind, which would shout and ignite rage in and out over the beat of drums and tambourines. Covered in mud, people were overpowering their emotion to the commotion of the revolution. It was more than just a sight to see. It was the music and raw energy of the forest dwellers. I love human beings, when we all let go of anything and reveal everything.

I kept dancing around, but the fire was hot. It nearly burned the skin, and everyone just kept throwing more and more wood on top of it. It wouldn't have been hard for it to get out of hand and the whole forest to burn down. Everyone was intoxicated, and even when the fire got too strong and people tried to throw water on it, the water became vapor before it touched the burning logs. I was covered in sweat in about five minutes. Everyone was topless, so I ran back to my tent and took off most of my clothes. When I came out Mantis was standing by our tents.

"Hey man. You gotta see this fire," I said to him.

"You gotta see *these* man." He revealed little crowns that looked like mints.

"Ooooh, fun. What are those?"

"El Diablo." His eyes burned.

"Could your *neighbor* borrow one?" I smiled. "I have no money for basically anything, some ecstasy would really do some wonders."

He was thinking. He looked at me and smiled and gave me a pill.

"Do I need to take it with water?"

"No, let it dissolve on your tongue," he said with his eyes now watering.

"Oh shit! Dude we gotta go to this gigantic fire man, everybody's naked!"

The pill tasted salty and bitter as I led him through the forest to the circle fire jam. I don't need drugs to have a good time, but I'm the sort of person that after my first drink I'm likely to finish off the bottle. We arrived and things were getting wilder and wilder. I saw Gonzo in a speedo running around asking people to draw all over him. He looked crazy but the kind of person you hoped to have a conversation with.

"What are you on?" I asked him once I got a hold of him.

"Five tabs of Acid."

For those of you who have never taken it, and it is all relative, but the best time to take LSD is five o'clock in the morning so it can kick in as the sun rises and you can enjoy your day tripping and have the end of the day to reflect on what you've learned and possibly get some work done in the evening. You should also have a safe place to go mentally and physically. It was the middle of the night, I had no home and was about to indulge on a drug that I could not foresee the effects of.

I got a little worried that my mind might go to a place that was dark and make me rethink everything. The mind can go to places and reflections you'd never dream imaginable sober, good or horrible. I was talking to a man covered in sharpie in a speedo.

"I might check back in with you in an hour."

I felt lightheaded but not ecstatic. Mantis was next to me and I saw Don't Be Impatient wearing a yellow sports bra and Kendal with her hair down casually over her shoulders sitting on a log sharing one of those bourbon bottles you can hold in your palm. Don't Be Impatient acted more excited to see me than Kendal.

"HEY!" She got up and gave me a hug.

"AHHH! What's up guys! This is my friend Mantis." I hugged Kendal and she hugged me with slight betrayal.

"When did you guys meet up?" I asked them.

"We drove in together," Don't Be Impatient said.

"Where's your dog?"

"He's in our tent, hopefully sleeping," Kendal smiled.

We all began to circle around the fire drinking and smoking weed. At events like this, you wouldn't even consider drinking and weed "drugs", it's just what everybody does. I'm usually a relatively fit guy, but since I hadn't been eating that much my muscles were pushing out of my skin and ecstasy makes me sweat. A lot. You could see my abs glisten with sweat against the fire. Slowly but surely, we were all dancing against each other fiercely.

Usually tall men get pretty territorial when they dance. Mantis was a gentleman. Kendal and I were slowly forming into one being. Touching human skin started to make me hard and she enjoyed it. The beat began to reach deep into my head, and I felt my whole body vibrate. Kendal would turn around and graze her fingers over me, which made me convulse. It was probably apparent I was on something, but everyone was.

Kendal reached around and grabbed my long hair and pulled me in. I was drunk and she wasn't that big, so I picked her up and we danced with her legs wrapped around me. I'm sure we were making a sight of ourselves, but again, everyone was. Charlotte and Mantis were having a great time with themselves. They weren't going all in, but they were gambling with each other. Eventually the fire felt like it was burning the hairs off of my arms. The drugs had truly taken ahold.

It wasn't pleasure that I was feeling, but pain due to the untamed flames. The chaos of everything spun around us as if I was transfixed with this girl, dissecting each touch. Colors magnified and the crevices in these road urchins became apparent. The stars were a light show of their own. It was too much for my brain to handle, I needed to get out of there. I took Kendal's hand and we went deeper into the field away from the crowd.

There were still people in small pockets as we went. There was a fire tamer. He would spin the fire and occasionally take a swig of some liquid and spit it out to explode. My mind couldn't process it all quick enough and it all moved in detailed fractals. I whispered in Kendal's ear, "Watch this."

I once watched a video of a man who could juggle to the sound of music. There is a small chance that I looked foolish as I mimicked the fire tamer, perhaps the way a drunken person believes they can sing karaoke. I stood my ground as not to territorialize the performance but to compliment it with my movement. As the fire spun quicker, I would jump high as if I held the fire in my own hand and was controlling it through my movements. It was very spiritual. At some parts I was laying on the ground turning into a somersault upwards reaching for the sky. I am a Fire sign.

Once I finished, the fire tamer shook my hand, and I bowed to him. Someone came up to me and said that they had never seen someone mirror flames that way before and thought it was a beautiful addition. I peered over to Kendal who was clapping her hands slowly. When I walked up to her, she grabbed me and kissed me. It felt like melted chocolate and alcohol.

I grabbed her smaller body closer and she bit my lip. "Ugh, dammit." she rolled her eyes.

"What?"

"Now, I wanna fuck you." She whispered.

"That doesn't have to be a problem," I said with humor in my voice. She kept kissing me and it got more intense, my whole body was having small spasms until I finally took her by the hand led her through the wild, quiet as a mouse, to my tent. As I said, my tent was nothing fancy, a small blanket and no pillow, but when you are in the intimacy of another person, surroundings don't always matter.

We kept kissing and got rough with each other and soon both of our pants were off. Her legs were prickly, but the ecstasy exaggerated each hair tickling my leg.

Soon we were reached into our underwear and I held my ground trying to stay in control, which was showing to be very difficult. She enjoyed that she had control over me but quickly I put her on her back.

I am no lesbian, but my tongue is a better dancer than I am. She didn't smell fresh but had probably showered in the past two or three days. She pulled my hair as I slowly maneuvered myself and then quickly tickled herself. She finished dramatically and quickly pulled me up to her eye level and asked if I had a condom. I heard somewhere that if you have sex on ecstasy that your brain will become overcome with excitement that you will never be as happy again. I was not willing to take that risk.

"I actually don't really want to have sex." I whispered to her. She looked at me confused.

"I'm sorry, I'm on ecstasy," she looked at me as though she was astonished.

"I would have sex with you, just not tonight."

She sat up and pushed me away from her.

"Why not?" she asked.

I was laughing. "Because, I'm on molly or ecstasy, or whatever."

"Why is that a problem? You literally just wanted to have sex with me. You just ate me out."

"Yeah, but I don't think it's a good idea. I don't want to sleep with you for emotional reasons. Would you wanna blow me?"

Now she looked pissed. "No! I will not blow you."

"What difference does it make?" I asked bewildered.

"Apparently it makes a difference to you whether or not *you* can sleep with someone."

Arguing with someone while you're on drugs is like trying to communicate with someone who only speaks Portuguese. I was sort of confused on where or how we got to this point in the conversation. It obviously was too late for anything and I wasn't being a gentleman. It was like a Freudian slip in my mind that was trying to justify why I wasn't a horrible person. She was searching around the tent for her underwear and pants.

"Listen, you have some interesting ideas when you talk. I was thinking about sticking around another day, but I think I'm going to leave the festival tomorrow morning."

She pulled her pants on. I don't know where that came from. It felt like she was trying to justify why I didn't sleep with her to protect her own ego.

"I hope you find what you're looking for in New York." It was a little harsh and dramatic, but alcohol and drugs make things have an essence of importance as though these moments will live on forever in our lives, when in reality we usually forget them by morning.

I laid back but I didn't sleep on my bundled-up clothes. I checked my phone, which looked like a little light show. I would go in and out of deep comfort where everything would fade and then I would feel wide awake as though I had never closed my eyes. I'd drift back off quickly before it was light out when you have the most realistic dreams. I was with my best friend's ex-girlfriend and we slowly knew what we were doing together was wrong, so we stopped. When we left their room, they asked if we had just had sex, and we looked to each other for an answer, which we couldn't find. I woke up from that dream covered in sweat to find myself in another dream, being consoled by his ex-girlfriend that she had had the same dream.

Chapter 21

My head swayed back and forth as I lifted it up. The aura of green radiated around me and I unzipped everything and walked to the post office. I enjoy a morning walk. It clears the head, but I had nothing on the mind, since it hurt a little too much to think about anything. I arrived at the post office and Louie was standing there looking depressed as usual. I told him my name in a way to perk up his mood, but he was unimpressed and just seemed annoyed. He gave me my package which came in a yellow envelope.

I opened it as I walked back. It had a Chipotle gift card, two twenty-dollar bills and a nice note. It wasn't much, but it made me feel safe. I waited around just standing there smoking a soft cigarette but the morning sun in my greasy hair made everything feel a little harsh. I went back to Tent City over by Bear and Horizon's camp.

"Good Morning." I said low enough for any nearby tent to overhear.

"Hey Cheerio." Bear said.

"Whatcha reading?"

"Walden."

Sure enough Horizon poked her head out.

"Wonderful. Listen, I'm going into town, if anybody wants to come with?"

"What are you doing in town?" Horizon asked.

"I'm going swimming." I said.

"Eh, I'll come. Lemme get my swimsuit on."

"I'll meet you at the entrance."

I threw on my swimsuit and grabbed some weed. When we met back up, I asked her how her night went.

"It went well you could say."

"Oooh, what does that mean?"

"I'm a very lucky woman," she taunted like a cat.

"I'm sure you are. And yet, you still spend time with me, just some young trail baby."

"Who knows, you might be famous someday." Our relationship had a sensual tension to it, but not on the surface. It was more like we both were searching for our conversation to point us to it. I told her about my experience from the night before and she hugged me lovingly and laughed.

"So, what did you really do before you came out here?" I finally asked her after we had gotten closer to town.

"It's really quite boring. You wouldn't care, or even understand it."

"That's not fair."

"It's simple really. I went to college in Middlebury, Vermont. Got a degree in business. Straight out of college I went to work at a firm. Hated it. I did that for 8 years. I was sick of going to work with the people I worked with and I decided to go somewhere else and do something different."

"What didn't you like?"

"It wasn't business, but at the same time it was. It's just competitiveness everywhere with everyone and ultimately yourself. If you find yourself caught in it, at any age, but especially when you get older, it drains you, it makes you feel worthless regardless of how much money you make. You don't have real friends, you have work friends. You can't live your whole life comparing yourself, I should have known better." She said.

"I sometimes compare myself to others, but I've heard there is enough space for success no matter where you go or what you do."

"Haha, not in money."

"Or anything else, apparently. There *is* enough success or money. It's just our belief in those things, expectations of more that is not enough, never satisfied. So, we work harder, eat less, and what we once dreamed of becomes a living nightmare."

"That's why I said fuck it. I became isolated in my own self-righteousness. It kept me from ever being happy. I sold my apartment, bought a backpack and gave everything up."

"Yeah, that's what I did too."

"Why would you want to give up college? Everything is given to you."

"I wanted more."

"Isn't that hypocritical of what you just said?" She asked.

"No, because you had something compared to what most people's standards is something in this world. I was just a kid in college."

"That's still a lot."

"But my life hadn't even begun, yet. You had a life. It wasn't making you happy and you were able to let go of *others'* perception of what you were doing to make you happy. You actually were brave enough to listen to yourself, to do something completely different, actually start over. And if you can do that at your age, that is a hell of a lot braver than someone who hasn't even started listening."

"I'm not that old you know, just compared to all you little fuckers who think they know everything about the world. We all go down a lot of roads in life kid, a lot of times you're going in the wrong direction, and before you know it, you're lost."

"That's why I'm walking home."

"It's never too late to start over, but I swear to god if you die out here. . ." She waved her finger.

"Please. I'm already dead inside." She hugged me with angry endearment.

We waited in line at the Dollar General, where I bought some cheap ramen so I could get cash out. It was sort of eerie to see the swimming pool empty with rust and chipped paint during what felt like summer. It had a dark sense to it. I assumed all of the schools were out for summer and pools would be open for season but that's when I realized it wasn't even June yet. Just a little further was a small path that had a huge drop down into a river.

"I suppose we just jump in?" I joked.

"Grab a few roots and let's climb down." She said.

I took my shirt off and she was wearing a black two piece. I was covered in mud by the time I got down to the swimming hole. I jumped in off a rock. I didn't dare see how deep it was. Horizon got in with a little bit more ease into it. I feel free in the water like I'm flying and dancing at once, light as a feather. I was a swimmer once.

After we both were in, it was quiet. We were the only people around, we treaded water and talked. We'd swim closer together, and then we distanced ourselves and just enjoyed the nature on our own. I floated looking up and noticed that the sky was looking a little grey.

"Do you think we should get going soon?"

"No, let it rain."

Soon enough the grey clouds overhead began to thunder, and we were rained on and watched the droplets of water make art out of the world. We got out, and there was another way back into town without having to climb up that drop. We grabbed our clothes but didn't put them on because we were already wet.

At Trail Days every year there is a parade that everybody can participate in. I didn't know about it, but I was happy once I had learned about it. The streets were flooded, and we were just in our swimsuits in the rain. It wasn't the first time I was in a parade, but it was the first time where I felt like I was standing with a group of people instead of just trying to showcase myself in front of others as a spectacle. We'd dance together, cheer in unity, we were felt by everyone around us. It was a good time and place to be alive. I saw a familiar face come up to me. He was wearing a blue Michigan hat. It was Sonic, the hiker I met on my first day on the trail.

"Hey man, are you still interested in getting a new backpack?"

"Well, I heard they were just giving them away here," I said with hope that ended as I finished the sentence.

"Haha, yeah well I won a raffle and I'm trying to sell my old backpack for fifty bucks."

"Oh, I don't have money like that man."

"I'd go down to forty, I just don't want it to go to waste."

"How much does it carry?"

"Sixty liters."

"Oh well, yeah I might be able to work something out. *MAYBE.*"

"You wanna go look at it?"

"Sure."

Horizon stayed at the parade while we walked back to camp. The frame was very light, I put it on, and it felt like a high-end luxury I could have only dreamt of. These backpacks go for around two hundred dollars. I asked if I could try to fill up the backpack with my stuff. Sonic threw me the empty pack. I went back into my tent and began to unload everything. By the time I went back to the camp, I found my tent in a puddle half underwater. My old backpack looked like crap. My brain and body were too exhausted to see the activity through and I laid back in defeat. I slept there with the job half done for about an hour and thought that the backpack was too small to fit everything I had.

Eventually I got out of the tent and the Riff Raff crowd were preparing some egg stew. They fed me like the good people they were at heart and I went back in my tent and finished the job. Everything just fit. I went back into the woods and asked Sonic if he would want weed in exchange for the backpack and he said he only wanted the money.

The rain settled down.

I broke down my tent and stuffed it into the new backpack. I was done with sleeping in the middle of a party in the forest. The Log up the street said that they would let you camp for free so I would just spend the night there. I told Sonic I would buy it and gave him the birthday money I'd been given.

I started walking towards the shower truck church and began shouting. "Backpack! 40 dollars! Who needs a backpack?"

Instantly a guy with his face covered in tattoos came up to me.

"We need a backpack." He said pointing at his girlfriend who had pigtails.

"Do you have anything to give me?" I asked

He pulled me over and whispered in my ear. "H?" Eyes Widening.

"Anything else?"

"Man listen we just really need the backpack."

I looked over at the girl who looked hostage. I was hesitant, but I more just wanted to get rid of it.

"How much do you got?"

"Listen, I don't have a lot," he said to me.

"Let's just see," I said observing. He had a small plastic bag with brown powder in it.

"What else?"

"About a gram of hash oil. It's a good deal. We really need the backpack." He handed me the oil and plastic bag. I was resistant but he knew I wanted it. "Don't say anything. The police are right here." I stopped cold and panicked. It was a dirty trick and I wasn't thinking clearly. I thought for sure I was about to be cuffed. I stuffed it in my pocket nonchalantly, exchanged the backpack and we walked away as though we had never met. I was not at fault. Drugs in this country are a problem. It felt like I was holding a gun. I was too scared to hold onto it, but too infatuated to throw it out.

Before I go any further, the only thing I will say is this. We so often neglect to respect that a proper drug fueled experience will leave one with a fresh new perspective on things and filled with deep thought that could never have been developed otherwise. What drugs *lead* to is what's dangerous, not the drug itself. I know people who have been to rehab multiple times for it all, but they were in rehab by the time they were abusing Advil. I've had enough adversity in my life to know that very sparse use of an infamous opioid wasn't going to do much damage anyways.

Thank God my heart is stoned sober. I needed Jesus, and a sandwich. I left the campground and walked down the road. First, I came across one church with a sun-tanned woman with short grey hair lady in a sundress was taking charge, dominating conversations, giving out hats, and coffee. I put on a red wool hat and drank a coffee on the hot Southern day now that the rain had dispersed and been replaced with the sun. It was fitting. I was taking new steps into the unknown, changing into something I had never been before, going places further and beyond. I left to be put in these positions, these moral conflicts which are meant to test character. I am only as good as the next man, and what he would do.

I decided to listen to the fat woman knitting on a church porch.

"Really Deirdre, you *must* volunteer on the road." She was a very authoritative person, even more so than me.

"It'll get you away from that husband of yours and you will get to see the country. Three weeks, that's all I'm asking."

The woman looked bullied and depressed and did not seem convinced.

"Where are you all from?" I finally got a word in.

"Virginia Beach Baptist Church."

"Are you on the ocean?" I sipped politely.

"Yes."

"Do you need any help or have any room? I wouldn't mind seeing her."

"We are leaving in an hour. We might have room if that is where you want to go." I thought about it but didn't really.

Part of me loved the idea of just walking along a shoreline for two months until I got to Long Island. I just wanted to romanticize that really, I was nowhere and really didn't care where I was going next. No one in the world was accountable for me, and the people who did know about where I was had no control over what I did next. It was a depressing exhilaration. I think it's called being an adult.

"I think I'm all right. I'll be sure to visit you next time I'm over there." I walked off.

It didn't really satisfy the spiritual renewal I was looking for. It was just a good way to look out the window. I kept walking towards the Log and there was another church promoting good spirits. They were washing hikers' feet. There is a story in the Bible that talks about how Jesus cleaned the feet of the Disciples. I sat and soaked my feet in the soapy water. There was dead skin all over them. A Christian began to wash and massage my swollen feet and asked if I was a believer and I am. He let me know that I was forgiven for all the wrong I had done. They told me I was loved. That they loved me, as a child of God and as any person. It was a very intimate foot massage. Right on time.

I got to the Log, which had become a prominent place to spend my time. The usual suspects were there. BFG, Billie, The Blackalachian and Gonzo. We had all seen each other around more or less. There was just one guy left that I hadn't really talked to. He was a heavy-built guy with a beard and an exceptional psychedelic shirt. I sat back for about a half hour before I engaged in any conversation but eventually we were talking, and it turned out he was from Brooklyn. He was about three hundred miles ahead of me and told me that I was welcome to go along with him on the trail, and to call him if he was in New York when I got there.

We all sat back as though we had nothing to hide, but this was sort of the place where people go to hide out. We had been kicking back and there wasn't any real urgency, but time passed, and more people came. It began to get dark and there was a holler for people to go down into Tent City. It was the last night I was going to be spending at the festival, so I still might as well go enjoy it. By now I had gotten the strong understanding that nobody looked through anybody's things. My backpack was locked away. I hid it in a dark back corner and emptied my pockets.

I took my shoes off since I wanted to be as light and unattached as I could be. Next thing I knew I was in the back of a pickup truck feeling the winds of freedom blow through my hair drinking a beer. Everyone was in a good mood. It was going to be a good night. There is a much different attitude people have when they flock together as opposed to arriving alone. I was ready to dance, and nothing was important. The grand fire in the field was being stoked. The Riff Raff were all together in their grimy swing as usual. People were cooking burgers.

A young man with a guitar stood around Riff Raff's fire singing out his noble aspirations. I joined him and trusted in the words of his songs. They gave me potency to well regard the world I was trying to escape and the allusion of connection. I was welcomed back into earth's nest, reminding me of the distance of my dreams. The only way to succeed is to believe that regardless of whatever happens, you have success. I suppose it was a fleeting belief into the night, but the sun also rises. I was more worried about getting to church in the morning than indulging in anything else for the weekend.

I sang with men and women, I smooshed my feet deep into the earth gooey mud. We are all just the same but different. There was an excuse of a class system regarding the three main tenting areas. Wonderland, Riff Raff and Billsville. In Wonderland there was a Giant old mattress that was *used* in the middle of the commotion. Nobody was thinking straight. And yet, it was chic, where people did blow but didn't want you to see; a lot of college dropouts making something of themselves. Billsville was just far enough across the woods that only Disney would be allowed under their tent dome, the rest of them were a little too dirty, and drunk. Billsville was just a bunch of youngsters singing songs and adults acting like they know what's going on.

I assume I am welcome anywhere. I was given a bag full of tobacco from a kind of a gentleman in Wonderland. It was very good Carolina tobacco, rich and dark in flavor. In between these hubs there were campsites that ranged from family friendly to hobos. I stopped off at one and smoked a few bowls with a dad, his son and his son's friends. They were from Ohio and were hiking the trail next year.

The dad's name was Gator and the boys hadn't gotten trail names yet. They said they were on their way back up to Michigan in the morning. I asked if it wouldn't be too far out of their way to take me to Grayson Highlands, where the ponies were. It was only about fifteen miles away. They were more than happy to help. Gator wanted to keep the sense of adventure going. We smoked together, enjoyed the beer and girls looking for love, and men filled with regret. People came and joined. People love to tell you about themselves. Talk about something else. I'm sick of it. Supposedly we are separated from one another by politics, wealth, and appearance. I think the only thing that separates people is their ability to laugh. Humor is the highest form of intelligence.

Goddamn, I love the country. For instance, everybody you saw probably had a knife or was carrying a gun with them. There was no protection or search as you entered this place. I felt safer there then I do at a festival in the North where everything is ransacked. The hostility of searching puts people in a threat mode and they become more aggressive. In the South nobody cared, for the most part, if you were there, you were family. This land, the forest, was everyone's land. It belongs to nobody, and no one was superior. Everybody talked shit about the Riff Raff clan, though.

There was one woman who stood above everybody else. I had heard about her a few times. A living legend. Her name was Ms. Janis. She was known for giving the best trail magic and had been collectively regarded as a witch and was very elusive to find on the trail. She was a plump sweet nice red headed woman, able to compose everyone's attention. The night got a little rowdy. Shirts were off, and there was a deep thick mud around the fire. Nobody cared, or at least I didn't. My whole legs were covered in mud. Mrs. Janis emerged to commemorate the festival, and everybody became quiet.

"Another year of Thru Hiking has gone by," She announced.

Everybody cheered.

"Y'all need to stay safe. Another great successful Trail Days. We want to make sure that everybody makes it to Katon."

"And Springer!" someone called out. The crowd broke into informal laughter.

Those are the two ends of the Appalachian Trail. It ends at Katon, Maine in the North, and Springer in Georgia in the South.

"Alrighty now. Calm down." The laughter broke. "We want to make it a safe year. Travel with people, and let's have another great year without any trouble now."

The crowd erupted into applause. "WE LOVE YOU, MISS JANIS!" She couldn't walk away from all that attention gracefully, but finally she got out of the spotlight. People returned to being rowdy as hell. I saw Jimmy and Elizabeth from Greasy Creek. I gave Jimmy a hug and thanked him for the help. Raccoon was there drinking bourbon and Don't Be Impatient was over with E.T. from Uncle Johnny's. They looked really happy. Raccoon made me finish off a bottle of whiskey, which I did in fashionable excitement while dancing around the screaming fire pit. I was dancing around the fire for a long time and it grew and grew, until it was at a dangerous level.

Ms. Janis emerged out of the forest, this time in a whole new pair of clothes and a vengeance.

"Y'all look like a bunch of hiker trash about to burn down this goddamn forest. Get some water on that fire." Everybody was scared as hell. "Y'all have been out here all night and this fire has been dehydrating all of you. You are gonna pass out if you don't drink water."

"Water break!" I called out and the crowd reacted by laughing and shuffling. She walked off and there was dispersed clapping. I walked through the field after her but heard a barking dog. It sounded like it was running towards me and sure enough out of the darkness a greyhound was running.

I was quick to react and grabbed its collar. "Where you going fella?" I hoped someone would claim the dog. I went back to the entrance, where I heard a low piercing yell. "EY! THAT'S MY FUCKING DOG." I looked over and it was Cyborg. I brought the dog over and handed it to him. He didn't acknowledge me or thank me. I was sick of the bullshit. Doesn't matter who you are or where you go, there are always assholes. I walked back through the town all the way to the hotel. It was a long walk, about two miles. I wanted to get ready for church tomorrow.

After a long trail of muddy footprints back to the hotel. I sat back in an old chair that probably had bugs and a raggedy old blanket that wasn't much better. Home. There was a father and son from Boone, NC. I recall being at a party there once and I was introduced to an old frat brother who now worked for the FBI. He told me that his job was to identify people at social events who seem to pose the most threat of being involved with crime. As I slowly began to drift off, another man with tattoos who called the sleeves on his shirt the "hiring line" said that was why he didn't have any tattoos beyond his sleeves. I thought it was an interesting way to go about it, somewhat respectable. He wanted more of them, one of Elvis, he said. He was sharing about how he had done a lot of outrageous things, I don't know, man *stuff*. Guns were involved, manly things I can't recall, and he claimed that the government showed up at his door one day and asked him to join their services for a mission.

He said that by the time they showed up, he already had a family had to respectfully decline. He said, "I told them, sorry, you're about fifteen years too late."

My friend once googled how to kill the president and ten minutes later the secret service was at his house, so don't assume they aren't aware of who you are and what's really going on. It made me wonder about the inner workings of the government and people who work for it without our knowledge.

Chapter 22

I woke up to the sound of rain, which was more soothing than an alarm on my phone, but a little discouraging. It didn't really matter all that much, I was excited to get to church, whatever God would tell me in a sermon would be all I would need. Religious ceremonies are the leading cause of happiness in the world.

Apparently, I had slept through a good amount of people coming by and crashing because there were tons of people sprawled out all over the place when I woke up. I pulled a garbage bag over my body so I wouldn't get wet and checked my phone for the nearest church, or the one with the most symbolic value. Sure enough there was one that was a little bit further but it was on the street with the name of Paris's mother.

Three people who were up all night pulled into the lot. They all looked like they hadn't slept. The first guy spoke, "Have you seen my phone?" he asked.

"Ugh, I'm sorry man, what kind was it?"

"It was an iPhone, I will pay forty dollars to anybody who can find my phone."

I needed the money, but I needed Jesus more.

"I'll let people know." I did not have time to deal with that.

He went inside.

"Hey, do you guys think you could give me a ride?"

"To where?"

"Um, I'm trying to go to the church with the most symbolic value in my life, and it's a little bit further, just past Tent City."

They both looked at each other. "What drugs are you on, and where can I get them?"

"Hahaha, I'm not on anything. Church is gonna be wild, though."

"Hahaha, communion?"

I shrugged. That wasn't what I meant. In the house of the Lord there is a high unlike anything.

"Yeah sure, we will take you." When we got in the car the scene was especially comical. I mean I was just in a trash bag, on my way to church with these two hung over people, lost in some other random part of the world.

I thanked them for the ride and said God bless like some Jesus freak. The church was quaint, dark wood on the inside. An old fart in an adorable yellow raincoat and I were the first people in there. I took off the garbage bag but kept it next to me for the walk back. Eventually the families rolled in, all two or three generations ahead of me. Until finally the pastor came in.

She spoke of a man travelling. It was about Jonah, and how he was travelling to Nineveh, but got scared and went somewhere else and ended up in a belly of a whale. We all sang and as soon as it had started it ended. Singing is one of my favorite parts of church. Sometimes the words to the songs are strange, and a little over the top about how great God is. To this day, I'm very thankful I believe in something. The absence of faith is a very cold life for me, but I've also flown too close to the sun. I thanked the preacher for the good word, she was very interested in where I was going, and I let her know that the service reminded me of where I wanted to go. I began to walk back to my things. I passed by Tent City and thought I would maybe say goodbye to Horizon. She would probably be up since it was early enough.

I went in, and looked at the wreckage of the forest, some people just openly lying in the dirt. I crossed the river and I saw Bear's tent up, but Horizon's was already gone. I wondered about how I would probably never see her again, but people weren't the reason why I came out here. They couldn't be. I made one last cross through town in the light rain and it was about finished by the time I made it all the way across. People were getting up about now. And soon enough everybody was awake getting ready for the day. Hikers wake up early. People were lounging, a young ethnic looking man coming out of a shower with a beautiful woman. Gator's car was coming at ten and it was about nine.

Two men that fit into the scene but at the same time didn't, came by. They looked too floral, preppy and Californian to be part of this crowd. They both had unique facial hair. One had a fedora on, and the other was holding a guitar. I thought of the two con men in *The Adventures Huckleberry Finn*. They spoke off beat, you could tell were trying to be funny, but they fell far from being suave about it at all. One of them remarked that everybody here was above average in attractiveness. Everyone seemed mutually agreeable, but I wondered if it was a shot at me. I don't know really, but insecurity strikes. I asked if I could fiddle with the guitar. I began fingerpicking. I just looked back and let go of that image I think everybody holds themselves standard to and let myself go. Slowly singing louder and louder. People seemed to enjoy it as morning music.

Every Time I See Your Face
*Fingerpicking

```
C                                          Am
Ain't it strange that everybody seems the same
                                    F
 and I don't have the time nor patience
                       C
 to figure out why I'm not
 C
And if there was someone to blame,
     Am
 I'd have to look at my own shame
          F                              C
 which makes me feel like I'm not good enough
       C                          Am
I probably smoke too much and I definitely don't give a
             F                        C
fuck, the whole world's seen me with all my clothes off
          C
But the lord knows I like to laugh,
 Am
taught me to write cause I couldn't act
      F                      C
so darling let me ask, can I please have this dance
```

Chorus

C Am
Cause I know where I'm going but I'm lost
F C
I know what I'm trying to say but every time
G
I see your face, I forget how to talk

"Did you write that?" The one with the fedora asked.

"Yeah."

"That's really good. Your voice has good range. I'm Bert and this is Vern."

I waved to them and was sure they were very successful or happy whatever they were up to. They just had a swindling tune to them. I wanted to be their friends but at the end of a long weekend everybody was my friend and they were just posturing to stand out. Nothing wrong with that, everybody wants to stand out in some way or another.

"Alright I'm going to get breakfast," BFG said, emerging from inside. "What does everybody want?" Everybody was up when he said that. He was like a grand wizard to us all, keeping us under his wing. Everybody swarmed around him placing their needs like helpless chicks, finally he looked at me.

"And you?"

"A bacon, egg and cheese English muffin please." I smiled like part of the family.

He winked one of those wise winks only a man of his supreme foundation would be able to so casually pass off. I closed my eyes embarrassed of his generosity. I went inside and looked around and the kid from Brooklyn was just getting up. All the beds were out in the open and another couple was sleeping in each other's arms. I had seen their faces around and they weren't together when I saw them separately, and I wondered if they had been sexual in such a public bedroom. I didn't want to wonder long enough to find out.

I went back outside, and an Asian girl was explaining how she had stayed three weeks in Hot Springs.

"I packed everything up and was on my way out and came across a river with a bunch of dirty hippies," she started, "just like y'all and they convinced me to stay the night and next thing I knew it was three weeks later."

The thought of it disgusted me and at the same time I was envious. I am a twenty-year-old young man, but I feel like I don't have a day to spare. I am much too concerned with the pace of life that living in a major city has bestowed upon me. I am competitive in the worst of ways. I am envious of people who can lay around for three weeks on an already not very productive calling of walking through the mountains, but I am much more jealous of people who have accomplished something with their lives.

I got a text from Gator. He said that he would be arriving in fifteen minutes, a perfect amount of time to eat breakfast. BFG arrived and everybody swarmed the table until I got my breakfast. I began to hug everybody goodbye. It was nice to meet all of them. This had been an easy weekend to replenish my energy, but it was time to accomplish what I had set out to do. I waited across the street and sure enough they pulled up in a dangerous looking truck. A big old one that probably came out of the 70's. I loved it, the country grime that keeps people good and together in times of need. They pulled over, I hopped in and we got gas.

Chapter 23

The car ride was bizarre. A bowl was packed, and a map was open. We couldn't get out of Damascus for our lives. It was like a ghost town you could never leave, filled with truehearted independents and lost generations. How couldn't you get lost, in the deep green sea and voluptuous mountains? Thick and stretching nature for miles and miles and miles. No one was making sense of the map either way. We thought we were going North and then South, East, West, upside down, the damn car was boxed. We threw out the map. Next, we were all on our phones trying to make sense of the winding roads.

"I don't have service," I said, expecting someone else to have it. "Do you have any?" I asked in desperation.

"Nope." Gator's son responded.

"Nope." The youngest in the car answered.

"And nope." Gator slapped his phone on the dashboard.

It was actually wonderful moment that is becoming unfairly rare. Nobody knew where to go, and we had nothing to rely on but ourselves. Some of my first memories were getting home at five in the morning after a night of endless driving, getting directions at toll booths and convenience stores with my mother.

"Let's take a right and follow it down." I said.

That was enough for them. We went down the straight road which would rise and fall. We would pass stores with wind wheels spinning and signs for small stores. One last time we reached our heads out the window asking for directions.

"Do ya know where the Grayson Highlands are?" I asked a man with a shepherd's beard.

"You are close, but you need to turn around. Follow that road and you will run into the Trail."

Their sweet kindness juxtaposed with the chaos of the whole situation was unusual. The world looked Irish. I felt like I was in a different country trying to interpret a land based in a different language. I was confident that this was the last time we were going to need to ask for directions. The reason I was confident was because it seemed like everybody in the car was getting annoyed with this detour and I might just be dropped off at the next gas station. Wide deep green fields and only a dirt road with a small bathroom stall standing out. The sky was beginning to take a greyer tint. We got out of the car at what seemed to be the Highlands.

"Yeh want any food?"

"You have already done so much."

"Oh, don't be silly. Do you like Beef Jerky?"

I wasn't going to pass it up.

"Yeah, sure. Seriously though you don't have to give me anything else."

"You like goldfish?"

"Yes."

"Get him one of those liquid flavor changers."

They gave me handfuls of food. Good food too. Food that I could snack on but would also get me a lot further. The amount of food I had was probably the majority of the weight I was carrying, which was a good thing. My backpack was still forcefully painful, but I was glad that it meant that I had enough of what I needed. It would only get lighter from here on out and this was a good excuse to eat while I was walking.

"Cheerio. I'm glad we could help. Can we take a picture?" Gator asked.

"Oh sure, let's get one of you and me, and then let's get one of everybody."

You could tell that he was glad to have extended his hand. He had done good and deserved the picture to remember his deed. I hugged his family and hoped to see them again before this beautiful mess we call life concludes, but just like that they drove off and I walked away.

I saw a new crew of hikers. They looked like pure red humans. Great genes, expensive clothing and gear. I felt much less like a homeless person because of my nicer backpack but longed for the South instead of pressing forward to the next best thing. I was about to get to trekking, but I saw a post box where hikers could sign in so other people could see where they were. I thought I would sign it. Friends from the past might be glad to see I made it this far.

It was a little premature to think this since I was only a few miles ahead in the first place. Instead of stopping for lunch, I just pulled out some trail mix and began to eat away at it as I walked. The dirt path was very level for a while, but eventually it led up into the deep mountainous woods.

I felt the drizzle of the day begin. I had a few trash bags, but I didn't want to have any of my clothes to get wet because if they did, I would just have to carry them, and they would get my other clothes wet and make the whole pile heavier. I stopped and began to take everything off besides my basketball shorts. I was sporting being in the open and I thought that I would be able to take on anything.

The first half of my morning wasn't so bad but that was because I was travelling from wide pines up into the mountains. The trees cut the wind as the elevation rose. The puddles soaked my feet by the time that I made it to the first shelter. It was evidently much newer than the shelters I'd stayed at. Those had darkened wood from years of wear and tear of just existing in the woods. This one looked like it was built in the late 80's or early 90's. The wood was fresh and there was no graffiti besides some fine sketches of names in the walls.

As I pulled up, I was glad to see the last person I saw from my original family on the road. It was iPod in a corner, pulling a cigarette out of a zip lock bag."

"Ey mate."

"Glad to see you."

"You want one? It's an American Spirit."

"Haha, nah, even though those are healthier, I need some time to relax from all that noise."

"Fair enough. When did you leave?" He went on smoking.

"This morning. I got a ride this morning only about five miles back."

I was quiet as usual, back on the road felt unusual again after the break, and my body wasn't readjusted.

"Are you done for the day then?"

"It's only noon, I can't stop here. I just think I should eat something. How far is the next shelter?" I asked.

"Eight miles."

"That's not so bad." I pulled out dry Ramen and began to chomp on it. iPod was not impressed. He looked like he was even going to gag. I really don't understand, it tastes great.

A few other hikers showed up and rain truly began.

"I should get going before it gets too bad out there." iPod got his stuff and was off. "I'll see you mate." By the way he took off it seemed like he never wanted to see me again on this trail. He was the type to be very competitive with himself you could tell. I lounged around for about five minutes. I climbed up a ladder inside of the shelter and there was an upstairs. There was plenty of room in the warm roofed-in attic space. A cozy night sounded nice, but I had just had three comfortable days and this trip wasn't about relaxing.

I stood as the rain seemed like it was beginning to get better, lighter, but I nodded at the hikers who were done for the day, taking out food and unrolling their backpacks and gave them a small wave as I went into the wild, wearing no shirt. At first, I believed I could handle the weather, but that was only because I was shielded by the forest.

By the time that I got towards open views looking out along the mountains, the rain had picked up and was frigid. The worst part was the wind. Raindrops would pierce against my skin, feeling like little shards of glass. I tried to find a place of peace. To ignore the outside world and be calm within.

That was when I saw two of the biggest snakes come out and onto the trail blocking it. I couldn't walk past them, they were at least 4-5 feet long each. They seemed like two parents. I was stone cold frozen. One was still and the other slithered closer. I began to back up but that only made both of them wind towards me. I jumped off the path and through the thick of the woods to avoid them but everywhere I stepped felt like a python was about to bite me apart from the feeling of all the sticks cutting my skin.

I swatted the trees and picked up my knees pushing onward. Not too soon getting back onto the path, another tall grassed area revealed itself in the wide open. I didn't know which way to go. A sign read "Horses" So I went down that one, and after about a half a mile I realized that the path was meant for people who were riding horses, not to imply that there were horses up ahead. In chilling defeat, I turned back around.

What a wonderful welcome back to the trail after being pampered for the last weekend. Part of me wanted to go back to the first shelter, at least I knew there would be room and it would get me out of this situation. Part of me thought maybe God was mad at me. Maybe I wasn't going where I needed to go.

I chose a path out of spite and prayed that it would take me out of whatever hell I was lost in. I went down it, and still it looked like a path that had two wheels that had been driven over it, but surely it was too narrow for a car. I continued along, wary of snakes and other predatory animals due to adrenaline. The wind, that awful wind would just not let up. Eventually, the path began to look more familiar and I became more comfortable, as soon as I was at ease the rest of my body went straight back into painful horror. The rain soaked through the entirety of my skin, which was wrinkling. Discomfort was not the word to express the pain and disappointment of my return to the unknown, it was an unknown.

Little did I know, this was one of the roughest parts of the trail. All of it can be awful with the wrong attitude. The rocks just became gigantic. They were stretching over me, sharp and jagged. On top of a mountain, there were little mountains to be overcome. This was not easy, lakefront climbing of rocks, these were giant unforgiving rocks you had to pull yourself up and hopefully stretch your way back down to the ground if your legs reached. I wasn't so lucky. I slipped. Falling forward, roughly scrapping my hands, I slammed into the stone and had cut myself in my abdomen. I screamed out undisciplined anger.

My blood mixed with rain looked poetic like the tears my body longed to give. I screamed out for a long dry moment. I screamed at all the failures I had had in my life, and I screamed because I was not going to let them be my legacy. Even our darkest times can be laughed at to ease the pain. Even my loudest screams were unaccounted for and left me alone in the intensity of this storm. Part of me just wanted to take a nap in the middle of the rain, bleed out to death, and wake up a raisin. Each step I took hurt, and pushed blood out, and my backpack was pressing against that area as well.

I began to go a little crazy, muttering to myself odd words, and odd thoughts, laughing deeply and then being close to tears. Explaining myself to no one and being glad I had no one to explain myself to. I couldn't tell you all the strange things my mind thinks up. Usually it's nothing really, completely random, but other times very overarching in some sense. There is a system of numbers in my head that mean a variety of things. I used to be very interested in what it all meant, but at the end of the day they are all just numbers.

People enjoy simpler answers to the world, but they deserve the truth. Violence is never the answer. Aggression of reason can be harmful. When you must think one way and impose that over others, is a dangerous motive. I am a pacifist, but a good honest fight between two men is one of the most ingrained parts of our being. That's not violence, that's art. It could be positive competition to ingrain work ethic, not based on anything other than collective betterment and health. The Imagination Olympics for everybody. There should be pride in a sense of pristine health. Control and will is the way. There is always a question to be answered somewhere in my head or heart anyway. I think that is what was hardest about this trip. Accepting how very hard it is to see the world so romantically any more.

"You know that girl that you're in love with?" A sly serpent asked me.

I nodded my head.

"Well, I'm fucking her in the ass right now." He preyed on me.

It was a little depressing I guess because these girls I thought about probably rarely thought of me. If they thought I was caught in a rainstorm, surrounded by snakes, freezing cold with nothing on, I'd've probably deserved it. I just hoped wherever they were, they were happy.

Another big rock that needed climbing stood before me. I wasn't going to get over it by staring at it, and that certainly wouldn't warm me up either. I thought about ironically giving it a hug, but at the same time fuck that stupid rock. I was just as likely to break my neck than to give it a hug. I grabbed a good grip of the rock with my bare hand and squeezed it more tightly than was needed to let out the pent-up aggression that was cycling through my bloodstream, kicked my feet up high like the dancer I am at heart and pulled myself over the natural structure.

What I saw next is ingrained in my head as one of those mesmerizing sights that bewilder you to your core at first glance, like the first time you see your father's penis in a urinal when you are a six-year-old. I kid you not, forty wild ponies nonchalantly going about their business in the middle of this rainy day. My heart calmed and I began to take a deeper breath of the fresh smooth rich air I had been missing. The best part were the young ponies that stood behind their mothers, those I did not approach. I didn't approach any of them really or take my phone out because of the rain and because you can't capture all of life.

I looked but it is important not to disturb nature. It was very gentle. Every sound that had been suffocating me evaporated. I think they heard me. I suppose there are gentler souls who can touch the graceful beasts without harming them. I didn't linger either. My second wind came on, but I did not have enough hair to protect my body from the wind and just aching cold rain. I walked for five sappy miles after that until I came up to a gated structure. It was hard to see that the shelter was completely full. About seven people, with no room.

There were two lanky hippies both with dreadlocks to their butts, two upset looking Italians with a strong female lead, an old man next to a young man no older than me, as well one man, who looked like he was ready to piss himself in the corner. And there was a table bench that the roof *just* extended over. It was all for me. I wanted to cry a little bit, but I just looked around at people who were tenting in this messy weather and knew it would have been unwise to do so. I spoke to no one. It was an hour before the old man rose to eat dinner and I was frozen still with my bare skin exposed, but at least I was drying under the foot of roof that went over the table seat. What I had imagined as being a visit of beauty turned out to be a cold night. I sat and sulked in the depression that was this scene. The longer I sat the worse I felt, I needed to get some clothing on me, or I was going to catch pneumonia. The old man began to take out a stove and cook for himself on the table where I was sleeping tonight.

"Ye all right?"

"A bit cold."

"You need to put a sweater or something on."

"I'm s-sorry I'm just h-hungry." I said through my chattering teeth. Luckily my clothes were dry, and I threw on every layer I could. I felt better after that. I looked through my food and ate some goldfish and finished the bag.

"Do you think I could use your stove?" I asked.

"When I'm done you can use it."

Two minutes of boiling water later he handed it to me. I began to light the bottom of it. I was about to fill it up with water.

"Dammit! You don't know how to use it." He grabbed it out of my hand. He then realized that he was being a little terse with me. There was a layer of crusted over food that existed on the bottom of my pan from multiple usages of cooking. He didn't say anything but handed it back to me. I cooked on low and the food did me well. Everyone was tired and the old man went back to rest quickly after he ate. There was nothing to do but sleep.

It was already darkish because of the clouds but the sky was quickly turned off. I was sore after just one day of walking. I pulled out my clothing pillow and draped my blanket over me to make sure it didn't touch the ground. Then I tucked it under me like I was a burrito. I wasn't warm by any means.

Years of meditation prepared me for this moment. There are many practices of sensing each part of your body until complete projection. I did just the opposite of that. I was trying to feel no sensation at all. I wanted to ignore it all. I wanted to forget about this stupid idea. I think the only thing that kept me warm was actually being glad I had gone through with trying something for once.

I woke up four or five times. I couldn't stay warm since there was physically just not enough blanket or width of the bench. My feet were cold. They had two socks over them but didn't stay warm either. Instead, the absence of everything I just felt as one radiant ache. Surely enough my mind wandered into short random events with people that have never happened. Of all the random things I think about and see, and digress into, and enjoy understanding, and over explaining, a wandering old friend visited me that morning to wake me up. Nobody was up, and the crumbs of my ramen was out on the table I was sleeping on. I heard something approaching before I saw it, but I was so lost I probably imagined what I was hearing was part of a dream.

I opened my eyes and standing at my feet in the cooling blue light of the morning was a dark black spotted pony. It was almost as if it knew it was out of place in the world. I was never so humbled than to see a wild beast approach me. Of course it only wanted food, and acted unafraid. The pony welcomed my presence and came close enough that if it knew how it would have just taken a seat at the bench and lit a cigarette to catch up over. I rolled my eyes into the back of my head in disbelief.

"Hungry eh?" I asked.

"Nay, some of the other hikers have already fed me this morning. I'm actually just lost. Do you think you could help me?" The pony remarked.

"Where are you trying to go?" I asked sitting up.

"I really don't think it matters, I just want to get there."

"What's there?"

"Nothing, just something a little more special that what's here. Are you going there?" It nearly shook its head as if to brush off a fly.

"Probably." I said.

"Oh, so *you're* gonna go nowhere," It neighed.

"No. I'll have you know I've come a very long way to get here."

"Here? Are you anywhere you expected?"

"Not exactly." I grabbed the ramen off the table to offer her.

"Then what are you doing near here?" The pony ate from my hand.

"I should be sleeping."

"I'm sure you are."

"Am I?"

"You don't see?"

"What?" I asked.

"Somewhere else is always nowhere. Here is the best we can ever be."

I was unable to stay sitting upright. The small horse lingered after I had fed it but galloped slowly drifting away from me. Soon enough the sun was rising, and the old man and his companion were ready to ship off. Another man got up quite quickly and left the campsite around six am. Followed by the Italian couple around seven.

Finally, there was room in the shelter. I took advantage of the space available. I rolled out my thermal pad and shut my eyes. I was exhausted but grateful the long night was over. I was going to try and get as much out of a morning nap as I could. I laid there for a good two hours, and it was that type of sleep where two hours feels like a really long time, so my body felt awake in the morning and I welcomed the new day ahead of me.

A poor chap walked up to the shelter holding his soaking tent. He couldn't stop complaining. The girl with the dreadlocks made a face of being annoyed, which made me smile since, finally, I wasn't the one doing the complaining. She had one of those faces that was too pretty for her own good, and probably didn't know what to do with it. Her and her boyfriend still seemed like a sweet runaway couple.

"Hey, a guy from last night gave up and left all this food. You can grab some if you want," she snickered.

I looked into the bag and there were plenty of ramen noodles, rice meals, and PB&J granola bars from Trader Joe's. I slowly engaged with the hippies throughout the morning over breakfast.

"So where did you guys meet?" I asked.

"Two days ago."

"Oh wow, well good luck to ya. That's awesome to find what you were looking for – if that's what you're looking for out here."

Their smiles gave away they were keeping something from me.

"We are actually from Madison, Wisconsin. We've been on the whole trail together," the man said.

"Oh yeah? Were you guys at Trail Days?"

"Yeah, Friday and Saturday."

"Did you have fun?"

"If you consider rolling in the mud on molly fun," she laughed.

"Haha, I did the same thing."

"This one was gone," she smiled naively.

"You were a mess," he said back a little less sweetly.

"I wasn't the one who got drunk and fell asleep all Saturday." She took a shot back at him, a little aggressively.

"I'm coming from North Carolina," I butted in.

"Oh, the Carolina's were beautiful and nice, his son visited us in the Smokies actually." She said.

They had already forgotten whatever had just happened. They looked at each other smiling with the revealing information to a stranger. I looked him in the eyes, and realized he was older than her by a few years. I mean he was sort of conventionally attractive, but not much more so than me. And she was well out of my league. It really made me wonder what we compromise in our lives for beauty, and whether aestheticism is essential. Maybe I was missing something.

Water was somewhat close to the campsite and a few big gulps woke me up for the day.

"How many miles a day do you usually go?" she asked me, packing up.

"About twenty." My muscles had grown in my legs since my journey began, and I knew I could put on more miles if needed. "I'm probably just going to the third shelter from here."

"Yeah, then we will see you," she said.

It was one of those odd places where people are just ominously older than me, and I still am not exactly sure what my mid to late twenties have in store for me. I was intrigued by them somewhat, but it may have just been the afterglow of the festival.

Chapter 24

There was a feeling of just getting away from that campsite that impended a good day. Sometimes just the way you hear good morning will decide how you will feel for the day. Down the mountains and into the open fields again, the pastures were very green, but the skies were still somewhat grey. The path began to turn into a stream. A very deep stream that went above my ankles and splashed my shorts. I never stopped. I kept going and I was glad for the stamina that had come to me from a long time in the wilderness. Snakes were present, often. I never seemed to get out of a snake pit, it felt like. Every mile I would go I would see two or more. Black ones, light speckled green ones, camouflage colored one, I was comfortable in the rush. I would look over my shoulder every five minutes thinking one was right behind me.

There was one last gap to get over for the day and I saw the old man who yelled at me at the last shelter with his young prodigy posting up a tent in a puddle under a tree. I thought I would stop, and I did, but I knew I couldn't rest. One night of unbearable sleep is one thing, but two nights and you will more than likely experience hallucinations.

"It's about four more miles up to the top." The old man said.

"I've got to make it," I said over the rain.

"Last night really surprised me."

"Why?"

"Just people, so unwilling to give up their space."

"Oh, well you know. It was pretty crowded." I said.

"I had to do a lot of work to get a space myself," the old man bargained. "You looked like you were about to freeze to death. Nobody helped. Those people were nasty."

"Well, we've made it this far. Where are y'all coming from?"

"Pennsylvania," the younger man replied.

"How do you two know each other?"

"He was my student, many years ago, in college."

"Interesting. Well, I better get ahead. You know, see you up the trail."

I left them and quickly tried to make my way up to the top where a shelter was, and it was a mistake. I slipped and was half drenched and the other half of me felt that I had overused my muscles accordingly. I was disappointed in such a foolish mistake that could have easily resulted in injury, but I also understood I needed to get out of the rain pronto. I picked myself up slow and steady and it took another two hours in the pouring rain to go only four miles uphill. Those awful snakes stuck in my head the whole time. I didn't have time to get bit.

I saw one other man and got a very serious drawn-out intensity from him that gave me the shudders. Bleak and depressing as hell. When I finally reached the cabin, it came with a warm welcome from a few fellows, and there was space. This structure was the nicest I had seen yet. Built after 2000. You would just want to stay there with someone for a few days in the woods.

All men, good men. Striving or doing their best to succeed but failing in their own right. There were two alphas. A tall bearded man named Yin and some chic unnamed fellow who stayed in the cabin most of the night. They were hiking 36 miles tomorrow, getting up at five am. An old greying stoner, who was young at heart but only in the absence of maturity. Two meatheads. All enjoying beer, fire and food. Everyone cooked so lovely.

It was as if food was the only reason they came out to this barren forest. They made Mexican cuisine, and cooked canned meals over the fire, some of them had preserved meats. I was enticed, and they were generous. After dinner the weed came out, and I brushed my teeth. Yin was going through his things and I noticed he had a copy of *On the Road* by Jack Kerouac.

"Nice, I love Kerouac," I said to him

"Oh, you've read the book?"

"No, but I tell people I have. I enjoy more of Ginsberg's work. His poetry. What part are you in the book?"

"Oh, I don't know. Kerouac is just hitchhiking, and

then him and his friend get in a fight over some girl and then he's back out travelling. The usual."

"Ah, people often critique his work that he was merely vomiting his every thought on the page instead of writing." I said.

"I suppose, but I don't really know a lot about writing."

"A lot of people don't," I shrugged.

I slept in comfortable quarters with the gentlemen. Before I slept, I eavesdropped on them all gossiping like little girls about husbands whose wives had been hunting them down and checking up on them making sure they were keeping their noses clean. Apparently not all of them had been. It wasn't comfortable, but it was at least warm inside the cabin with everyone's body warmth somewhat radiating off of each other.

Five am came and the two men left. Then the sun rose, then the rest did. It is horrible feeling like you are going to forget something when you are travelling. It's sort of hard to keep everything straight. Phone, tarp, tent, clothes, food, water, filter, hats, all of it. Compared to the first day it didn't have its spark of "life or death" necessarily. We all left minutes apart. I had myself a morning smoke which is important sometimes. I knew it was going to be another rainy day. The woods were standing in solidarity with the earth and sky. A beautiful complexion of cool colors that warmed my soul but left me with an empty feeling. Some of the path had man-made structures like bridges and stairs, as if the nature had asked for it.

I came across a road. A long stretching dark concrete road. There was a stray dog down it going due North. It raised a pause for concern in my mind. For the dog and my own ambitious integrity. Had I found myself too dependent on the woods, missing out on the chase of life in small towns and cities? I thought again and I understood thoughts like that are likely to get me killed, but I decided to follow the dog.

It was light brown, wet, with stringy overgrown hair that hung in shag. It looked at me as I approached and then continued at its pace as if it had wanted me to follow. I caught up with it after about a minute, it seemed trained, very odd. I didn't really care much anymore. A good dog is as much of a reason for everything these days. Sure enough a big dark green truck pulled up.

"Bessie!" The man called after the animal. He was calm as if he had just let her roam aimlessly through the roads of the hills. The driver got out of the car and was a lot bigger than me, but not much taller. He had the Southern cut body of a man who ate too much meat and fished for long days.

"Heller." He said to me as only a passing kindness more occupied with getting Bessie into the truck, who was taunting around his presence in a playful manner rather than an unbehaved sense.

"Are you one of 'em hikers?" He looked at me after his dance had concluded with Bessie smiling with her tongue licking the moist air.

"Sorta. I'm just trying to get to New York. Where does this road lead?"

"Ah well, you gonna go right through Sugar Grove. I can take you up along the way if you need a lift."

"Why not."

The dog hopped in the backseat and I hopped into the front. The car ride was not unlike the other hitchhiking experiences I had undergone. All oldish gruff men who thrived in the outdoors. He had some fishing poles and surely guns in the back. We started off with small talk. I asked if he was married. He met his wife when he was twenty and never looked back. He had three sons and daughters. One of his sons was doing well for himself in some other part of the country, one had committed suicide, and his youngest son was the priest of the town. His daughter was having a tough time since her husband had been diagnosed with leukemia.

"These are hard times in this country." We agreed.

He spoke with truth in his words rather than understanding. He was not pitiful or spiteful of anything, though the car ride showed this man had experienced quite a lot of loss but was at peace with what he was given and what he had earned. First, we stopped at the local school where his wife worked. He called her up.

"How you doing, darling?"

"Wwwmwmwm"

"Well, I'm right outside with a young man who's walking to New York City and I thought I'd say hello."

"Wwwmwmwm"

"I ain't got nothin' to do. That's why I'm driving around right now."

"Wmwmwmw"

"Alright, well I'll see you at home in two hours." He hung up.

Next, we went to the local church where his son, the priest, was out in the parking lot.

"Hello good sir," he greeted me as if I had already become talk of the town. It sincerely looked like a town that nothing happened there at all times.

"I'mma take this man up the road here a ways, I'll see you at dinner." We drove off.

"God bless!" I called out to the priest.

Then he gave me a little history lesson by touring the town. We drove up through the high hills and down through the dumps.

"Up there, that used to be my two hundred acres," he pointed to a beautiful cabin, overlooking a gorgeous field.

"Built it myself."

The land and the property looked like freedom itself. We all have the right to be justly free within our own means, it doesn't matter where we live.

"Then my boy died. I got depressed and we lost it."

We continued along the road. He was telling me all sorts of names of men and women he knew, all of them were tragedies.

"Bill Brett. Married for twenty years. Suicide. Horrible, left the children with that woman. She got cancer now." And that was just one of them

"Janet Kingsley, Cancer." He said blatantly "Josh Findley, Suicide." He pointed at another house. "Cancer." It felt like there was unmistakably a high rate of death, however perhaps a town of this size was better at recognizing when a tragedy struck than bigger and quicker ones where people are so caught up with themselves.

"Do a lot of people have a cancer here?"

"It's untypically high. We're not too off from a nuclear plant and it plays with our soil. The cows eat it, and it cycles."

"Aren't you afraid?" I asked.

"What can you do? The medical bills are too much to leave this place." Again, he wasn't upset, he just spoke with soft defeated truth.

"You know there is a real bad drug problem in these parts."

"Where?"

"Oh, right along here. In these trailers. Meth is real bad."

"Any heroin?" I croaked as I said with slight anxiety resurfacing.

"Oh, I'm sure, but meth is the killer."

We went through the trash town. It was splendid. Beautiful among the pines, but gross between the Southern alleyways. What life existed here? And who was willing to find out about it all? Nobody. He dropped me off at a gas station after about a ten-minute drive. It was a corner to be left off at as good as any other. Across the ways was a restaurant, some other small store off another ways.

"Now, be careful. Here's my phone number. I want you to call me if you make it to New York."

"I'll letcha know."

Although the place he left me off at was livelier than Sugar Grove, it was still rather bleak. A light rain let down on the scene. I walked into the gas station and asked if I could charge my phone. The storeowner told me that there was a charger outside around the back. I went around and there was an outlet jutting out of the wall next to a bowl of cat food. I felt like an animal, but still I charged my phone because I knew that I didn't know the next time I was going to be able to.

A cat rolled around the corner. A tabby cat, not very gracious, a rough one that had been expected to live outdoors in the small structure that the shop owner had set up. The storeowner and his kids came out around back and the children were as full of life as ever. As if growing up at a gas station was one wonderful field trip that never ended. The storeowner vaped as he watched me and they all went inside.

A large white van rolled up and out came a very curious looking man with glasses and suspenders who was overweight with curly hair hanging down from his bald top.

"How you doing sir?" I said trying to hide the fact that I looked like the utter scum of the earth.

He nodded his head. "Good to see you." He said with a little pep in his step. He went inside for about fifteen minutes while the car was running. I took that time to feel as though I was ready to give up. I wanted an out. Days on days on days of rain. Gas station cat food, I know what comes next and I was not in the mood to suck any dick. I did the suburban equivalent and called my father. Who of course told me to call it in, that my mother's new husband's sister lived about two hours away. None of that was going to work. I would end up in the belly of a whale.

The strange salesman came out. I took the opportunity to ask where he was going.

"Where are you trying to go," he asked me.

"New York City."

"NEW YORK. Jesus, I lived there for eight years."

"Why did you leave?"

"Because *variety* is the spice of life... Ain't that true?"

"I suppose. I'm sure I would get bored of it like anything after too long."

"You better find some artists. Which you will."

"Where are you going?" I asked.

"Nowhere. You ever seen one of these?" He pulled out a fidget spinner.

"No, I have not."

"You ain't never seen one of these before?" He was surprised.

"No what does it do?"

He didn't respond.

“Listen man I have way too much weight I am carrying. And it’s all from just little stuff that I shouldn’t really be carrying. It all adds up, so one more stupid thing isn’t going to help.” I said.

“Everyone is gonna know what these are kid. Everyone’s got em.”

“Well, not me.” Every year there is always some stupid trend that everyone gets into almost like a fashion statement. Often, they are clothes or just useless things everyone is interested in for some reason and then nobody cares.

He drove off and I was alone again, and I was getting cold since I wasn’t moving. I saw a man wearing thick cowboy boots, a strong build and bushy face. A true Southern man getting into a nice SUV. How I was only one step off into his world. He got into the car and I had missed my chance.

I looked out into the empty field of old scrap metals such as an old shopping cart. I supposed that snakes and rain were my only option. I pulled everything on and began for the trail again. Once I turned the corner, I realized that that nice Chrysler SUV was still parked up. I walked up to the automobile with the most amount of confidence I could muster up from the bottom of the world.

“Hello.” I said formally.

“Nice to meet you, good sir.” He sounded like a good ol’ Texan.

“Where are you going?” I asked.

“Well, I’m going all the way to D.C if that’s what you're looking for.”

At that moment, uh that glorious stupendous tear-jerking explorational feeling of all opportunity seeped back into my life as though the sun had risen from my chest and up into the sky. I knew then I needed to get the hell out of this jungle.

“Pleasure to meet you. My name is Jack Wright.”

“Blake Gordon, Special Force Operative.” He shook my hand.

He emulated success of political gain and freedom of a living legend.

“Listen, I’ll take you anywhere North if that’s where you're going.”

“I am not just going North. D.C is where I’d like to go.”

We agreed without words, he was not a man to be reasoned with because he done enough of it.

Chapter 25

I enjoy big cars. They just exude excitement. I wasn't too quick to do anything with any sudden movement that might be off putting. He'd probably snap my neck. He was robust and muscular, perhaps balding in the slightest, but his sunglasses shone through it all. What had this man seen? I don't know why I'm interested in some people, but I just am. There are always calculations we can do with one another's social standings to look at the thick of a human being beyond all that is important, the soul of a man. When you are going to be in the car with someone for an hour it's important to get small talk out of the way.

"I got my wife and my son," he spoke as if he was married but he wasn't wearing a ring.

"Why don't you wear a ring?"

"Well, I'm still in denial of the whole thing." He brushed off.

"What happened?" I asked.

"I travelled too much."

"When did you meet?"

"While I was in the army." He said firmly.

"Do you have a picture?"

"Yeah, you do Instagram?" He raised an eyebrow.

Not bad. "Yeah I got one." I pulled out my phone.

"I do alright for myself."

"I'm sure you do." I really did.

"Here is the mother of my child, and that's my boy next to her." He showed me a picture.

It was sweet. Even though he wasn't structurally part of them, he had a life with these people. He loved them dearly. His wife looked a little bit like Austin with aged beautifully auburn hair.

"What did you do while you were in the army?"

"Hell, you know I don't really like to talk much about it, but I must've done something right."

A brief pause.

"I do the sorta stuff you know happens, but you think you don't."

"You work for the government?"

"Special Ops."

"You know that the government killed a Black Panther leader. Snuck right into his bedroom and murdered him." I said.

"They do it all the time."

"Kennedy?"

"You bet." He answered.

"Where have you been?" I asked.

"Where ain't I been? Middle East, Japan, Brazil, the Caribbean, China, Russia. All sorts."

"Did you go there with the army?"

"I started travelling with them, but you catch on to a few things overseas." He shook his head.

I just thought of capitalist foul play and exploitation of cultures.

"I prefer The States more these days." He compromised.

We sat in silence for a while.

"You know what the worst thing in the world is..." He asked me.

I had a few thoughts on my mind.

"Arabic Extremists." It was apparent then that he was a right winged man, it was obvious before, but this sealed our fate that we had many differences in our view of the world.

"What about extremists on the other side, American Extremists." I said.

"Americans don't preach harming others for self-gain."

"What are you talking about? The entirety of Christianity was just people killing each other for the hell of it, and capitalism is the exploitation of the less fortunate." I tried not to start an argument like every Social Justice Warrior.

"When children are taught to kill for the greater good. I just can't stand for it," he shook his head. "When I was in Afghanistan, when nobody was around, that meant something was about to go off. So, they all knew, even the kids." He said.

"Well that's because we were trying to control a situation that didn't necessarily need to include us. Extremists usually only make up a small portion of the entirety of the Middle East."

He didn't say anything, I assumed he had seen more on that topic in the Middle East than me.

"There is nothing worse than Arab Extremists. Period. Their religion teaches them to kill us," he said firmly.

I wanted to change his mind, but I could tell this was an old dog not willing to learn new tricks. We broke into lighter political issues, such as a recent presidential election.

"Not my president." I crossed my arms prepared to be kicked out.

"Business is cruel, and that is what our country needs to change, a businessman." He responded.

"You're not supposed to have feelings in business, and that is not what our world needs. A politician should be a good man. You're looking for a tyrant."

We were at a checkmate as a time of silence passed.

To be honest, he didn't seem too happy with whatever the president was doing at the time either. American basically sold out for what is right, thinking they might earn an extra buck and got conned by a great con artist. He knows how to run a good campaign but that's it. It's not that hard when you have a budget. That's the reason he won, free press.

I thought now was as good of a time as any to let Paul, my old school mate at Georgetown who texted me, know that I was going to be in D.C. It felt like a real adventure was on the horizon of every day and every moment. I was exhilarated when I called. I left him a one of a kind message.

"Oh yes, Paul? Hope you are doing well old friend. It seems that I will be in America's capital sooner than I thought. I hope this isn't an inconvenience to you. I'd much rather just see you than be a burden in any case, sleeping on a couch. Call me back when you get this message. Love ya."

What fullness! What fun. I was a vagabond on the road without a plan but never the less getting somewhere indeed. It was like I was trying really hard a lot of the time, but always for necessities sake that would leave me sleeping in mud. When things got good, I wouldn't have to work for the rest of the week. I wasn't exactly sure what my plan was in D.C though. I mean it was a city and I had not been urban camping yet.

Blake's phone rang. He picked up.

"Hello. Oh Nothing. With this boy here from Carolina... Hey do you want to work?" he eyed me.

"What sort of work?"

"Confidential." He raised his eyebrow.

The purity of the American Dream at its finest. A young man with aspirations and an obvious capacity to work. This was enough to intrigue this fine gentleman, why in the hell would I need a degree? I had no money and I wasn't sure if I was going to make any of it either, but still I had nowhere I needed to be anytime soon. If you could live like that forever you could do anything.

"For how long?" I asked.

"About a week, maybe a month."

"How much?

He paused when he looked at me and continued on with his conversation as if he was talking to a brother of his. There was money in his voice, laughing every few moments or so.

"Alright. I'll call you back tomorrow." He hung up. "We might just have a job for you if you're looking. I know a guy working on a project."

"What sort of project."

"Nothing too exciting. Paperwork."

"Paperwork?"

"What is it?"

"Corporal legal. There's just some people who we want to understand a little better."

"Who?" I asked.

"In Washington it don't matter if you're in the government, business, their all criminals. See I came out of one of the best times in the world. The eighties." He gripped the wheel of his car with force and drove faster.

“Uh, I hate the eighties.”

“Why you would say something like that?”

“The eighties is full of capitalist greed, and is just iconicized as a kinda imprudent time in America that I think people are kinda getting back to.”

“Boy, helluva lot of it happened, but no worse than the sixties.”

“Don’t get me started.” I said.

“So yer a Flower child?” he asked me.

“No *Sir*.”

“Your hair's long enough.”

“That’s because I have hair. If I could go back to one point in all of history, I would go to Woodstock, but that doesn’t mean I’m not educated.”

“We had some good music in the eighties.”

“Hair metal and disco?” I said sarcastically.

“You ain’t even know.”

“What Fleetwood Mac? ZZ top?” I dug a little further.

“I saw both of them.”

“Not bad. Any hair metal?”

“Aerosmith.”

I grinned, “Alright.”

“Michael Jackson?” He winked.

“Alright brother,” I grinned wide. “You know I play music.” I said.

“You do? What do ye play?”

“Acoustic singer song writer, I’m looking for a drummer.”

I plugged my phone in to the aux and put it on. My senior year in high school flashed back for a moment. I’m such a weird person. I’ve always been weird. I remember hiding in the hallways with a guitar singing to myself because I couldn’t sing in front of all my friends who were actually talented and in bands and shows. We listened to the music. He reached down onto his armrest, which had a XXL enchilada waiting for him. He took a generous bite.

“Well, I’m not opposed, to assist if you need my help.” I finally said. “I could really use the money.”

“You’ll be fine,” he said pulling me under his wing.

I anticipated what that could entail and at the same time I didn't want to get caught up in a city for no reason if I didn't have to. Politics, sheesh. We didn't discuss it further. I tried to show that he didn't need to do me any favors if he didn't want to. He said that If I wanted work, I had it, but I would have to be somewhere at six am tomorrow.

Even though at the moment I was very comfortable in an SUV, I needed a place to be at four o'clock *today*. I needed a place to be at seven o'clock *tonight*. I needed a place to be at *midnight*. I couldn't get caught up in a time loop, only focusing on being somewhere, especially not in a city I didn't know anything about, I tried not to be too worried. When he put on his music it was a combination of Soundgarden and Cash. A little rough around the edges, but this man was just that. He took another phone call.

"Babe." He said.

He put it on speakerphone.

"Hey baby. Why'd you call?" She responded.

"Why am I calling? I suppose I should just now and then shouldn't I?"

"Oh Baby." He smiled.

I thought it was his wife.

"I'm on my way up to D.C." He said to her.

"Are you gonna get right back here and into my pussy."

"Yeeahp." We held in giggles like schoolboys.

"Good cause that's where I want you to be." The car got a little hotter.

"What are you doing?" he said nonchalantly and with power in his voice.

"Oh, I just went shopping. I got a scarf, and a sweater. Did you like that massage last night baby?"

"Yeeaph."

"And you liked wearing panties last night baby?"

The laughter took a halt, and there was a brief embarrassing tense pause.

"Well I'll be back soon. Just wanted to call you to tell you, I love you."

"I love you too baby."

When he hung up he gave me a winking turn.

"Not bad," I said to him.

"Ain't is it?" he said.

It wasn't long before he dialed another number.

"Hello?" A female voice answered.

"How is my favorite sweetheart doing?"

"Oh, you are just the kindest thing." She said.

"You know I can't go all day without thinking boutcha." He snarked.

"Oh please, what have you done this time?"

"Nothing, what're you doing?"

"Oh... you know, nothing really."

"What'ya mean?" He said a little sweeter.

"Well, I'm drinking some tea, but not all that much. Actually, I'm glad you called."

"Why's that?"

"Well, I need to take care of some of these car payments. 14,000."

How much of it have you paid off?" He asked, now ignoring me.

"Seven."

"Well, we will talk about it when I get home, but I'm sure we can figure it out. Your little girl doing alright?"

"Yeah, I'm gonna pick her up from school soon. She misses her daddy."

"Well, take good care of her."

"Well, it was nice of you to call," she said with a deep exhale as if she didn't know what she was doing with her life since she had listened too much to people, men in particular.

"I'll talk with you soon honey." He was ready to press end.

"Bye."

"Bye now."

"So that was number two?" I asked when the phone call ended.

"Nah that's number one."

"Oh?"

"And how old are these women?"

"The first one is twenty-nine." He looked about fifty.

"What about the second one?"

"She's almost forty."

He pulled out his phone and showcased me the two women. Both blondes. One with a button face and the other showing off her backside. They looked good as any but were by no means the elegant beauty of the picture he showed me of his first aged wife.

"That little girl of hers is the sweetest thing this earth has ever seen."

"I'd bet," I nodded confused if the child was his.

"This little thing couldn't touch a fly."

"I don't know if that's true. I don't trust children that much." I said.

"Harmless, and my baby gets damn mad at her, drunk of course."

"I can imagine." I tried not to get quieter.

"I had to take her a few weeks back after she had yelled at that child for doing basically nothing."

"What did she do?" I asked.

"Oh, I suppose she wasn't going where her mama told her to go. And she starts yelling and hollering at this poor child. Tears. And I grab my girl and say if you ever touch that soul again there won't be no hesitating."

This man was fucked up. We all are. I mean, the world is fucked up, but fuck. I could commentate about his adulterous injustice towards women, or his flawed intention to help children, not to mention his political beliefs aside. There are millions of situations worse than this, but dynamics are complicated by human nature. Still as this man stood, he had done no injustice on my behalf, and I still treated him as a good man.

We pulled up to a gas station. It was a Wawa, but I didn't know what that was at the time. A Wawa is one of the most wonderful creations of humans. Basically, a gas station restaurant that has all the fun foods you could ever want. I didn't have money to spend but I needed to use the bathroom. I had never been to the East Coast before, but it was apparent the second I stepped out of that car, I wasn't in Kansas anymore.

Chapter 26

The East coast gets a lot of shit, not as much as the West Coast, but still. I was a little worried to say the least. I had heard they were all very uptight assholes. I mean yeah, they can be persnickety but no worse than any stereotype is true. You could tell people cared much more about their appearance. Very suit and tie even on a Tuesday afternoon at a gas station. I was encapsulated by my surroundings, I could feel myself changing as the social geography altered as well.

I felt like I was on speed. Everything was just a little too amplified for my personal preference. I couldn't really think straight. I was getting close to a city, far away from any trail, I was low on money, and I had to shit. I called my dad.

"Hello?"

"Hi dad."

"Oh, hi." He didn't seem all that concerned anymore.

"I'm in D.C." I pleaded proud of myself.

"WHAT?! That is a major city, what are you going to do?"

"I'm working on that."

"You have no money. I know you've had your fun, but I really think it is time to come home."

"No, I've been doing some thinking and I think that I can make it to New York and stay a few weeks."

"Uh huh."

"I mean, it's really my call anyway however long I want to stay out here."

"I don't like the idea of you in a city without a place to stay." He said.

"I will be fine."

"If you want you can use some of your money from your bank account." He finally folded.

"I could really use some spare money right about now, but I'll be alright."

"You have to, you can't just be in Washington DC with no money."

"I have done fine this whole time, I think I can handle a few days in a different atmosphere."

"You have not been to DC and you do *not* know what you are talking about." He said trying to domesticate the situation.

"Well where should I avoid?" I said casually.

"Well, it's set up in quadrants."

"Which is the nicest?"

"The North West Quadrant."

"Where should I avoid?"

"The South East one."

"Then it's simple, it's just about getting in the right circle."

"You are a sociopath."

"Thank you."

"Alright anything *else*." He asked rolling his eyes behind the line. "Oh actually, your computer is fucked."

"No, it's not, just take it to a shop."

"You sent it with a bunch of wet clothes! The hard drive is smooshed, and it doesn't even turn on." He yelled.

"Put it in rice."

"I will have you committed to a hospital do you hear me?!" He tried to pull back his authority.

"I've heard it all before."

"I am not joking."

"Anything else?"

"Call your grandparents."

We hung up.

Finally, a man walked out of the bathroom and I used it. When I was finished, I walked out to Blake finishing his enchilada.

"Ready?" He said. "We're about 20 minutes away." I hadn't heard from Paul, my friend from high school. A suspicion came that he had heard the news but was not sure what to do with the information I had left him. He's smart, he'll figure it out. More importantly I could figure something out. We had one last stretch on a highway that led into D.C. The streets were beginning to get wild and curvy as we entered the capital of this country. Polished marble looking buildings didn't tower as much as emerge from the middle of nowhere, combined with a mess of a few chain restaurants. It was commercial from the get-go. I was overstimulated, but I didn't want to showcase any emotion.

Sure enough we pulled into a Hilton hotel, with a white arc entrance, a pool, and a gate. We were in the parking lot. I made sure not to make any sudden movements. I was casual as I could be, being that I had nowhere to go.

"Well, are ye coming?" Blake asked me.

"I'll come in for a brief moment, but I won't stay long." I said, humbly, without any expectation.

"Alright." He nodded his head to his luggage and picked up his suitcase, but I left my bag in the car.

I followed him. I was uncomfortable. Everything was too much in the direct vicinity of me. The dim orange light of the deep red lounge was soothing, but I wasn't sure how out of place I really was. I had hitchhiked twice today. I suppose I looked like some sort of athletic type, with all my mesh wears, but was probably very stinky. I stayed in the lobby while he went over to the desk. He grabbed some cookies and brought them to me. I was still on the, "eat everything you can" mentality and those cookies were a blessing. I ate them one by one until they were gone. He was still discussing the room with the authoritative bearded black man behind the counter. I pulled out my cell phone and dialed the number to the other gentleman who was kind enough to take me to a gas station earlier today.

"Room 110." Blake walked over and whispered in my ear and kept moving. I stood in the lobby for as long as I could've. I really was opposed from barging in somewhere uninvited. He sort of did invite me. I just couldn't be so sure. Maybe he was just getting something and then we would be ready to leave. After about ten minutes I thought it was pretty apparent I should let myself in. The room was very nice. A suite, that had a kitchen and a little living space and a double white bed. Blake was sprawled out, shoes off with a beer in his hand with the TV on.

"Sit down. Stay a while." He barely looked up.

I softly let myself through the door. It was one of those situations where I knew I should be confident, but that attitude wasn't entirely what I was feeling. It's really not every day you are in this situation.

"You want something to drink?" he asked.

"Sure."

"Look in the fridge there, pick out something you like."

I opened up and it was filled with rows of Heinekens and Corona's, and a Guinness. I took a Corona. A beer was exactly what I wanted, but I needed to stay a least a little bit on my feet. A cold fresh beer went down sweetly, and I felt that I had earned it. Although it was only a Tuesday, it felt like Friday afternoon had arrived. I took a seat on the couch and we listened to the news. Nothing too interesting, just what you would imagine from local D.C broadcasting.

I got my first sense of East Coast pride. People care about the Carolina news as well, but it's not being broadcasted 24/7 live all the time. We sat in each other's company like men. Not saying a word if not needed. I can't explain what my first feeling of Washington D.C was like. A great deal of emotion was pouring over me, as you would expect. I could tell there was a great deal of power in this city. Men without borders. It was filthy. It consumed my inner calm and made me dance like a puppet.

"You know there is a dinner here, if you'd like?" he smiled.

"Honestly sir, you have done more than enough for me." I almost stood up ready to go.

"Nonsense, you like veggie burgers?"

"Yes. I do," I said, polite beyond words.

"Well, you're gonna help yourself, and then we can go."

We went down into the lounge where there was a restaurant space. There was a buffet and hard plates. A relatively open bar, but I would not be drinking publicly in this city tonight. I took two veggie burgers and a chicken sub off the plate. There were green beans and potatoes, and fresh fruit. I drank lemonade, and boy was it sweet. I discussed his service over dinner. He had done some Air Force work and his son had followed in his footsteps. The manager walked over.

"Is everything going well, Mr. Gordon?"

"Everything's fine, Adrian."

"And you are?" Adrian eyed me.

"This is my son," Blake said patting me on the back.

"Oh yes, are you the one in the Air Force?"

"Like father like son." Blake grabbed my shoulder.

"Well enjoy your stay. Mr. Gordon is a very well regarded here. Are you sure you are fine?" He pointed to my drink.

"Yes. We've got to be up in the morning," Blake ended the conversation.

He smiled and walked off.

"A lot of fuss for you." I said, a little impressed.

"Kid, this ain't nothing."

I went back for thirds and we went back to the room. It was getting dark. This was it. I was on the edge of asking him about staying the night at some point, I really wanted to, but this man had a delicate complexity to him. I didn't know if I would get kicked out just for asking. The situation was just too improbable to have this much luck.

"If your gonna go best go now-"

"-I should probably go."

We spoke over each other.

"You don't have to youn-" he raised his hands a little.

"I don't have to?"

"You can stay-"

"-Stay?" I chirped.

"Listen, if you need a place to stay, this place is yours." It was a simplistic enough gesture, but it rung through me like church bells. He threw me the keys to the car, and I brought my backpack in. It wasn't long before I was collecting my dirty laundry and fluffing a pillow on the couch and preparing to shower. It had been a long day. Every day was a long day. They always are. It was my first shower in almost a week, and I stunk like shit. Not anymore. I rubbed soapy shampoo all up and down and sang a few tunes in the shower.

I came out and Blake was looking ready to nod off. I quickly did some laundry, which cost me a few quarters. I was clammy as a pearl. I called my grandparents and they were proud of me. They were worried, but probably knew I knew best. The TV lingered on through the night. I lied down on a green couch and had my small knit wool blanket and a hotel pillow. I couldn't fall asleep. I thought all about things like family and marriage, but you don't want to hear about that.

Chapter 27

Blake rose about 5:45, turned the TV up right as he got up. I rolled over. He showered but sprung up as soon as he was ready.

"Am I coming with?" I asked, disheveled.

"Yeah, let's get breakfast."

I was ready in a flash but by no means had anything formal on.

Breakfast was classic eggs and sausage, bacon, two muffins, fruit, coffee and orange juice. We peeled out pretty early. Blake sipped his morning coffee. I was too suspicious to ask questions. We parked up in a parking lot and walked across the street into some windowed blue building close to The Capitol.

There was a wooden interior. It had black tiled floors and a tall structure with a big round clock. Down a hallway and up the elevator lead to the interior of narrow passages with private rooms and offices. We opened one door at the end of the hall. I looked around and there was a woman sitting at another desk.

"Stay here." He walked right past the woman.

The waiting room was nothing shy of lounge material but very bare. Leather chairs, but no magazines or coffee tables. To say I felt uncomfortable is an understatement. I felt exposed, and I had no idea what my role was in this. A bell rang at the woman's desk.

"Mr. Carter will see you now." The dark brunette eyed me.

I opened the maroon wooden door into a spectacle of an array of hunted animals mixed with old leather volumes of books. An office unlike any that I had seen before, except for in Hemingway documentaries. Very elite, Harvardesque. I walked in but couldn't even approach the man behind a desk.

"I'd like you to meet my friend Tanner." Blake finally said, almost embarrassed.

"Pleasure sir," I postured myself in the most formal way I could, in my wool sweater and button up flannel.

"This young man here is *walking* to New York City." Blake lightly shook his head with a smile.

"Is that right?" There was a taste of expensive salmon bagels with capers on his lips.

"Well, I've gotten a few lifts." I tried to not shake.

"Blake tells me you want work." Tanner turned.

"If there is any available."

"There is always work to be done." He wasn't mean, but the words weren't nice.

"What sort of work."

"For an artist?" I felt like they knew more about me than I had known, or I was a dead giveaway. "It's an infamous industry of the aristocrat." Tanner said.

"He seems capable, why not construction?" Blake said menacingly.

"Listen. Do you need any money?" Tanner said as if asking the question was already a waste.

I didn't know what to say or understand.

"You're here for a week. Why not enjoy yourself?" Blake raised his shoulders.

"Like fifty bucks?" I said.

They both burst out in hysterics without making a sound.

"Why not a hundred?" Tanner snarled.

"I don't think I could just accept that, it's too much."

"I would be offended if you didn't," Tanner said with a smile waltzing over to his desk and pulled out a big green bill.

"On the house." He handed it to me, and my eyes widened, it was like Charlie's golden ticket. A big fat Benjamin. "You've got Blake's number. If you decide to finish school you should call him, he's a good man, and there may be some potential to involve yourself up here," he finished standing above me. "It is nice to meet you, young man. We will be keeping an eye out for you."

We shook hands and he threw me out with the same handshake. "Welcome to the Capital of the United States." The door slammed.

This is what I'm talking about. A little respect. Alright. I'll take it. Yes, welcome. Welcome to the machine. I probably should've been more concerned, but I was unmistakably overpowered and couldn't have questioned their almost probe like attitude towards me.

"Now you're going to want to know your way around this city," Blake said with a little bit of authority in his voice once we got back into the car. "I have a meeting, where do you want me to drop you off?"

"I don't know. Where are the bars and the art life in this city?"

"You're probably looking for Dupont Circle."

"What Quadrant is that in?"

He looked at me for a moment seemingly surprised that I knew about the quadrant system.

"The upper West."

"What do you have to do for the rest of the day?" I asked.

"I could tell you...but then I'd have to kill ya." He said innocently.

"Right, right." I rolled my eyes and smiled.

"Call, if you want. I can pick you up around six for dinner, unless you wanna stay out. I'm going to drop you off by the Capitol. Just head North."

We both knew I wouldn't have a problem getting around and enjoying myself. I hopped out of the car.

"Just see the monuments and don't go beyond any roped off areas," he yelled from the window.

"Which way is the White House?"

He looked around for a moment.

"That way," he said, pointing down some brick street.

"Thank you, for everything."

He drove off.

Washington is not like New York. It's very modern. All the buildings are fresh, and the streets are clean and wide. I took my time to enjoy it. I was probably the slowest moving thing in that whole city. I had nowhere to be. I had nothing but time. I went through the parks, which ranged in and out within the city. The cobblestone streets felt interesting on my boots.

I am against all of what our country stands for and basically everything that it touches, and no longer feel represented by my political system. We all have a political obligation to stand for what we believe is right. There are so many ways to swing every story that I might as well get my own straight before I start speaking for other people.

Democracy doesn't work the way it should. It should be that everyone has a voice, instead it is one loud voice yelling over one another. Twitter, what a pathetic way to run a country. I went over to the White House. I knew nobody was home. First, I thought of all the great men who had once stood for something in this country, followed by the generational corruption I am sure still lingered in the bedrooms. I just gave it the middle finger. I miss Obama. He was such a rational person. Always spoke with such composed common interest. I don't know if he would have saved our country, but he sure as hell didn't ruin it.

Nothing in D.C is particularly close to each other. I did as much walking in that city as I would have on the Appalachian Trail. It's at least a mile from the Capitol to the Lincoln Monument. I just strutted around with my headphones in, flashing people that walked by with a big smile and a wave. Hopefully it brightened a few days. I wanted to get out of the tourist area as soon as possible.

On my way up Connecticut Avenue, I came across an old-time apartment that had been turned into a business. In the window in deep painted purple letters the word, "DANCE" shimmered through the window. If you are a dancer, you are inherently obliged to be part of the community. It is not always a common thing to find such dedication in the field. I walked into a room that was filled with incense and an elevator. The elevator lead to another door. With a schedule that said, "Work for classes." and a phone number. I texted them that I wanted to work for them. It wasn't long before they let me know that this weekend, I could come by in the morning to exchange work for classes.

I went back out into the street. I walked past a few churches, the streets were all white. The concrete was so white. I felt so strange. So free, so aligned with what I set out to do in the first place. Go somewhere where big things happened. I didn't care if I was a part of it, it was just good to know about it. If I told everything that happened, it would change it, almost devalue it by taking my experience and making it completely someone else's.

I hate being a man. A good man anyway. It takes a lot of work. Anyone can be a horrible person, but it takes true grit and character to act with dignity and nobility. I have never found a man I cannot conquer, but women often brush me off. Anyway, I looked up and found the kind of guys that probably aren't brushed off often. I size them up to their peripherals and eventually was walking in their conversation. They were talking about something stupid, like sex or weed. And one of them briefly talked about how he was going to order weed legally from a website that drops off baked goods.

"Is weed really legal here?" I chimed in.

"Sure is."

"No way." I was in awe, excitement.

"This website Red Eye Bakery." He said pulling out his phone. "They will give you a free gift (an 8th of weed) if you ordered fifty dollars' worth of cookies."

Never mind that. I know how to buy weed. It's not very hard. I guessed a suitor would be in Dupont Circle. Washington just had such a business on the mind all the time vibe. I wanted to relax. I found a park where people were smoking. I already had some sorts of smokable herbs and spices. I was so impressed and dumbfounded by the ability to smoke marijuana freely. I openly took out my weed and rolled a spliff, which is weed mixed with tobacco.

The crowd surrounding me was tough. Inner-city people. Just people that would look out of place anywhere.

"Can you believe it?" I said to a man in a curious workingman's outfit.

"What's that?" he asked with yellow in his eyes.

"This harmless plant can be enjoyed freely in the nation's capital. What a time."

"That's marijuana?" he asked as I handed it to him, and he took a sniff.

"Indeed, have some."

“Oh, no thank you.” He kindly declined.

“Suit yourself, I’m trying to get more.”

“That right?” he asked sullen.

“Watch this.”

I stood up and casually rolled over to some rough don’t-fuck-with-me impoverished people.

“Yo, Where the loud at?” I said.

Two men looked up.

“Man! Get the fuck up outta here!”

“NAH,” The taller of the two answered standing up. “Nah. He good, he good.”

“He lookin’ to bust us.” The kingpin said.

“Brah, I gotchu.” he stood up and mosied over. “Whatchu need?”

“How much can I get for a hunid?”

“A hunid? Oh *sheet*. A lot.”

“Word, like a quarter?” I asked.

“Quarter Pound?” He asked.

“Nah, quarter ounce.”

“‘Ight forsure, wait here. Give me the money.”

“Nah bro.”

“I *need* the money.” He said.

“Nah, bring it here and I’ll give you the cash.”

“Ight, bet.”

I sat back and the gentleman in suspenders watched me.

“You enjoy that?” I asked sarcastically.

He laughed from his chest once, “Ha.”

Eleven minutes went by. He came back cupping loose weed in both of his hands.

“You forreal?” I asked him, displeased.

“Yeah, it’s good bud.”

“I’m not saying it ain’t kush, but you’re just carrying open it like that?”

“Yeah bro.”

“Neva.” I said as I pulled out my bag very openly and put the weed in it. I paid the motherfucker, thanked him and dug in rolling a fat joint and facing it.

“That is my first legal time smoking in my whole life.” I said blazed.

“Is that right?” The odd fellow still sitting there winced.

It really made me glad. There is no reason why such an honestly harmless plant should be so villainized. I didn’t know at the time it wasn’t in fact legal to smoke publicly, but possession of the plant is permitted in our nation’s capital. I breathed deep and enjoyed the urban setting with a fresh mindset. The pace I was moving at slowed and I was able to take in life for a moment. With the time to slow down, I realized that there was a tear along the strap on my Jansport.

“Do you know anyone who can sew with a needle and thread?” I pondered aloud.

“Oh sure, I can do that.” The mysterious gentleman said.

“Do you have a needle and thread?” I asked.

“Oh sure.”

“You want to go?” He offered.

“Works for me.”

We got up and I followed him through the streets. He pulled out a pack of Marlboro reds and shared them with me.

“You live here?” I asked him

“Yes,” he said, seemingly distant. He felt like someone who was only pretending to fit in with society. He did an all right job, but you could tell the clothes he was wearing were stale. We went down into the train.

“Do you have a MetroCard?” he asked me.

“Nope,” I said with a sense of pride. I’d been walking.

He began to play with the machine and out popped a credit card looking train pass. He slid it across the machine, which blinked for a moment. He began putting money on it. A lot of money, upwards of forty dollars I suppose, I was set for transportation in this city. We got on the train. I’ve been obsessed with trains ever since I was younger.

The trains in Washington were wide, but full.

“It’s rush hour right now,” he assured me. “The train costs more at this time.”

He told me his name. He seemed screwed on enough. He had lived all along the east coast all his life. He began to delve into some of the history of Washington and its political presence in the city.

"Every four years a whole new flood of people come through to the city, so everyone's always on the move."

"What quadrant do you live in?" I asked the stranger.

"The South West Quadrant."

"Oh."

"We were the next stop," we got off.

When we got out, it was definitely lower class than downtown. The buildings were browner. A young girl, who was the tiniest of a group, apparently saw someone she didn't like.

"Ah hell nah! Don't even start," she said louder above the rest of them.

Some other girl approached. "Get the fuck outta here!"

"Bitch do you know who you are talking to? Get out my face," she said, aligning her words with clapping.

"GET OUT MY FACE. GET OUT MA FACE!" Her voice turned into a screech and the public was beginning to become aware. The other girl pushed the tiny one and she came back with an open hand slap.

The gentleman I was with sort of shrugged like, well, this is it.

"Will you wait right here?" he asked.

"Yes."

He left and I just stood back idly watching the world spin around me. It wasn't long before the police showed. I watched, trying not to be involved or make too much of a spectacle of myself filming the incident. The police were very well intentioned. They were not looking to arrest these girls. They were just attempting to calm it down. It lasted about three minutes in total and then everyone was back to their normal business as though nothing had happened at all in the first place.

It seemed like everything was involved with the next. I was intrigued by the dynamic of the city. It was very desegregated. The city had people from all walks of life going by. It was also a very secure city. One building or parkway terrace connected to the next and it was as though this corner of the city was its own tight knit community. Mr. Cronkite (as he referred to himself on the train) returned not a moment too soon with a needle and thread in his hand. We walked about two or three blocks, which I realized was South. We came into a very odd-looking structured building. It felt as though it had been made post WWII and was nothing more than a holding cell for the inmates of the city.

"Is this a mental facility?" I asked him.

"No, why?"

"It just seems like this place is meant for a certain type of person. I can't really place my finger on it."

He got his mail and we went in an elevator and rose up six floors. It was a casual apartment hallway, and I went further into the box and then into his apartment. The decor was strange and close to that of a hoarder. He had a huge television, but six others that laid beside a couch. This is a time when I probably should not have put such open faith into humanity. His bed was right in the doorway, next to large bookshelves filled with memorabilia and books. I'm a bit of a snoop in people's places, but I felt uncomfortable. I let go of the fear and took a seat at the end of the bed, which was in the middle of his living room. He laid out on it.

"Do you want to sew it?" He asked me.

"I might know how, I guess I'll try it out."

He handed me a freshly unopened needle and thread.

"Did you just buy this?" I asked.

"Yes."

"Oh." And didn't think any more of it.

"Could you just tie the thread through the needle for me."

"Yes."

"Did you go to college?" I asked him.

"Yes."

"Where?"

"Pennsylvania."

"You went to Penn?"

"For undergraduate."

I was a little shocked by the state of his living and apartment that this was the squalor that can await from a degree of that elitism.

"My friend out here goes to Georgetown."

"Penn is better than Georgetown." He said for the millionth time in his life.

"No, it's not."

"In rankings."

A cat ran past us.

"You have a cat?"

"I have two cats."

"Will I get to see them?" I asked.

"That all depends if they feel safe around you."

I began to weave the thread through the backpack, but it was more frayed than I expected.

"Do you think you could do this?" I asked him, again.

I handed him the backpack and needle. He placed the needle in his mouth and put on some glasses. I began to snoop around a little bit more. There really wasn't much. A kitchen in back which had some old food, jelly and bread. It was such a dark room. A dark state of living, his existence screamed emptiness. I looked on his bookshelf. Nothing recognizable but not even Hemingway would be in this man's catalog. I saw a cardboard box that had *Porno* scribbled on it in sharpie.

"Is that porn?" I said.

"Probably."

"Girls or guys?"

"Both I presume." He remotely acknowledged.

"Can I look at it?"

"If you'd like."

I reached for the box and used my upper body strength to lift the damn heavy thing. The bookshelf was not as stable as I had assumed, and it made a lot of commotion as I moved it. I opened the box and saw young Californian looking boys no older than sixteen on the cover of some naughty magazine. I was inherently initially taken aback but looked deeper.

This box was filled with the world's gruel. It was all probably covered with this man's cum, but I couldn't stop. He just went on sewing. What were this man's sexual fantasies? The longer I looked the more I realized that there was no straight porn in the box. Instead there was very obscure fetish porn of all young men. The pictures were enticing but what really made me *throb* was a yellow booklet that looked like it was from the forties with an illustration of a Nazi in leather forcing his dick into another Nazi's mouth.

"You use this stuff?" My voice clapped.

"Some of it." He pulled another string through.

"Can I have this one?" Referring to the one with the Nazi's on it.

"It's yours."

The room was briefly tense.

"Can I smoke in here?" I asked.

"What do you think?" He handed me an ashtray that was next to his bedside. I uneasily rolled a spliff. I lit it standing up one last time for final inspections before I made a run for it. I looked at a pill bottle.

"What are these for?" I said a little damp.

"What do you think?"

"Schizophrenia?" I answered.

"No."

"Bipolar."

"No. It's the most common disease in the world."

"Heart failure?"

"Bingo."

How prophetic.

"Were you ever married?"

"Yes."

"What happened?"

"...Women just always try to improve you."

"And you'd rather..." I wasn't going to say it. "...Live like this"

"I wouldn't say that I chose this."

"Do you think porn is a worse addiction than smoking?"

"Yes."

The conversation stopped cold. The backpack was finished being sewn but we were at a stalemate.

"Do you want to fuck me?" I asked scared.

"Yes."

"Men find me much more attractive than women." I said.

"Only if you would want to do that sort of thing," he finished.

"Do you want to?" I asked again.

"Yes."

I looked around for that bloody cat. Apparently, I'm not trustworthy.

"Is this like a common thing? You just bring fashionable boys into your room and fuck them?"

"No."

I had nowhere to go. I reflected for as long as I could, but more than I was scared, I felt very sorry for this man. Hundreds of ashed cigarettes laid by his bedside. What a horrible place to call home. It was so draining to be on the road, so unknown whether you'd receive love. Although I had help, I was still alone on this journey and it made me lonely. But I thought about how alone this poor man was. Years of filth stuck on porn unable to get anywhere or do anything but smoke. If I was feeling lonely, I can only imagine what this untouched soul felt like just to get out of bed in the morning. I looked at his crumbling structure and collapsed. He reached for me. I could see how delicate he wanted to be with my light frame.

"Come, just for a moment." He brushed away a blanket that revealed more porn laying on his bed which he covered back up again.

"You get ten minutes." I said like a cheap whore.

I climbed into bed with him as he reached me into his arms. He began to nibble at my neck. His five o'clock shadow was rough against my own light hairs on my face. He quickly took his opportunity and began to kiss me. His breath was that of old tobaccos and just old stench.

"Please, no kissing."

He acted as though he didn't hear me. He may have moved from my lips but became more open mouthed around the rest of me, sucking on my ear. I got the chills and sat up.

"I'm sorry. I'm really not much fun." I said embarrassed.

He reached for me again, this time truly chilling my bones. I felt bad, guilted into a situation I should not have been a part of. I was on the other side of an aggressor who was intent on being sexual when there wasn't an aroused limb or thought lingering in my whole body. I have been on the other end of this situation loads of times, disturbingly unaware. Men are always wanting to boink anything they can get their hands on, but to have the tables turned was very revealing. I am regretful of anytime I have ever pressured someone sexually.

I just wanted to leave but I felt like I couldn't go. I gazed down at the man so cocooned into his bed. It was so deeply slept in that my mind mirrored the lethargy and gave up back into his arms. He continued to slowly explore and massage areas that I felt violated. I continued to press him off of me.

"Please let's just lay. You can hold me." I said, uncomfortably trying to comfort him.

I readjusted and he put his arms around me and honestly, I was back to being thankful anything on this earth appreciated me. It didn't last forever and this time he went with intention to unbutton my pants.

"Please," he squealed.

"I'm sorry but no."

"Can I just touch your ass?"

"I just don't really feel like taking my pants off right now."

"Then let me play with your bellybutton."

"Why?"

"I just like that sort of thing."

"That sort of *thing*?" I asked.

"Forget it, just comeback."

There wasn't no in this situation. If I denied him, he wouldn't let it go. I just was sucked into being stuck. I succumbed to a place I hoped didn't exist but knew did.

And for one last godforsaken time I rolled the eyes in my head back into a dwelling that was no nobler than that of my heroin den in college. I was all out of resistance. I let him run his hand up through my shirt and rub my nipples and grope my cock and all that shit. He looked deep into my eyes. There was an old neighbor when I was growing up who once asked me to show him my penis, but that was fear of clowns and this was lying next to one.

No cat was going to show its nose. This whole thing felt dangerous. I had had enough. I felt the awful feeling of only being wanted as a physical means. It was the worst human experience that I could think of. I felt like a poor girl. Someone who wasn't even looked at. Just sex. An end.

Like a black hole in the universe time ceased to exist. Like a never-ending ride which I couldn't tell when I was going to get off. I might have spent years in that bed. You can't understand the depth and potency of an old gentleman's emotions and it was very painful, almost humiliating. I wanted to please him, but I was disgusted. I was disgusting. His stained lips and teeth. His wasted intellect. The addiction in his life. All just a part of who I am. We can't escape things happening to us. We can avoid them if we are lucky, but to undo something is rarely ever possible. The end of a century took a turn and I picked up my head from his rough two hundred count sheet pillow and hoped I would see a cat who could explain what just happened to me.

I would have killed that animal at that moment. I gathered my things, which were not all intact. I had left everything everywhere. The lie of comfortability contained me in this man's capsule. He handed me a pack of cigarettes and kissed me goodbye. I rode the elevator down back to the street and the world looked like an aquarium from the glass floor out of ground structure. I felt like a fish out of water. The air was hard to breathe in and I didn't last very long without a cigarette, which made things no easier.

Weed,
wallet,
phone,
please get me home

Chapter 28

Back into the center of town was not a kind commute. Everyone just looked so strange to me. Not in a first-time sort of way, but it was a reminder that we are all so unexamined by everyone but ourselves, and over examined by ourselves we are. We never change the way we look day to day, but I love seeing the miniscule difference in myself in photos from a year ago. Luckily, nobody really notices. Some days we are confident and can talk to anyone or be anything. Somedays the only people who will take you is the homeless. I wasn't looking for them, but one found me.

"Hey. You gotta cig?" The mess who lived on the street asked me.

"Yeah, here it's yours." I gave him the pack after I took two or three out.

"Do you gotta phone?" He asked.

"Yeah."

"Like a smartphone?" He asked, again.

"Yeah."

"Tell me this. If you pay for that phone you can look at porn on that?"

"Yeah." I answered.

"You serious? You can just watch porn? Anywhere? For real?"

"Really, man." I assured, worried.

"Damn I gotta get me one of those."

"Enjoy yourself." I walked off complacent. I've caught men masturbating in public before. It's quite a shock at first but it almost fits right in. We think about sex an awful lot, but having restraint is what separates socialites from savages. Downtown was probably three or four train stops away, so probably four or five miles. The worldly order began to take back its place and I was consumed in society and myself.

It's best to just move forward in these instances. I know it sounds cliché, but I had to brush it off as though nothing had happened. There is really no need to access these memories. They don't define me as a person. I will be the only one kept awake by its horror. Society had a lot of other stuff to deal with. I had gotten out of the South West quadrant and everyone just seemed so preppy again. As if everyone had Ivy League parents to brag about or were hiding that they didn't.

Then I saw someone who did not belong. Someone who looked like me. A scruffy equivalent was passing by. His shaven head had only just begun to grow back hair, but his beard was one that could not hide the face of a man I recognized.

Mark Thompson blinked his eyes in disbelief and recognized me from college. A strange man Mark is. You'd imagine I'd be shocked to see him, but he was such an inconsistency in the world that it made sense I would run into him. Mark had spent, to my knowledge, the better half of the year at my college unenrolled but inferring to people that he was.

He was homeless and lived under a stairwell on campus back in North Carolina. There were many rumors about him that varied from him being a creeper to being the next Steve Jobs. I didn't imagine he was in a much better place than I was when I ran into him. He had lived all over the country out of his car and had been to seminary. Last I heard he was on his way to Boston.

"Mark?" I asked in disbelief.

"Yeah."

"Are you still on your way to Boston?" I asked, confused to see him here.

He looked around as though people were looking for him, but it changed into a deep exhale.

"Yeeeah. Currently I'm just staying here in town though."

"Washington D.C?"

"Yep."

"What are you doing here?"

"I'm currently telling people that I'm studying at the University of Georgetown."

"In the summer?" I asked.

"Yeahp."

"Wild. Is it a good space for your research?" He was

deep in research in spiritual health.

"It's a little different." He shrugged inconspicuously.

"How so?"

"People look a little different."

"I suppose, do you think they know any more?"

"Not really, maybe a little more math."

I laughed a little. "Where is Georgetown?" I asked.

He pointed off in the distance... It had gotten dark.

"Maybe I will check it out tomorrow. What are you doing tonight?"

"There is a standup bar I've been hanging out at." He said.

"Standup? Where?"

"The place is called The Beer Garden."

"Is it a real bar?" I asked.

"Yep."

"Well, that isn't unachievable, I can just say I'm *filming* the event. Show me where this place is."

"Alright, but the thing is I actually stole this beer from there, so I don't know if I am going to go back in."

"Nonsense. What happened?"

"Well, I stole this beer from behind the bar." He revealed a capped bottle.

"Oh?"

"And the bartender asked me why the cap was still on the bottle, and I said I brought it from somewhere else, and he told me I couldn't do that, and I left a few minutes after that."

"Is it an open mic?" I wondered.

"Yeah."

"Can you show me where it is?"

"Sure."

We walked along the now darkened streets of Washington DC. He wasn't that interested in my journey, he's more of the type to be very invested with himself, rightly so, he's almost thirty and hasn't done anything with his life. He expects books to be written about his life. The concrete curbs weren't very lively, but it was a city nonetheless. People were out, doing their best to look good. We took a few cuts closer towards big streets filled with lighted clothing stores but eventually were off the main drive to where a quaint bar like The Beer Garden lived.

It had a pub feeling on the outside and there was a staircase up to the door.

"Well, this is it." He said. "I'm going to wait out here." He finished.

"If I get in, I'm going to do a set, but I might be back in a few minutes if it doesn't work out."

We didn't exchange information because I don't think either of us really thought I was going to make it through the door. I pulled open the light wooden door and a little plump woman with short hair and a high voice was manning the door.

"Gotcha ID?"

"Oh, I'm just here to film the show, I won't be drinking anything tonight."

"Alright, you go through honey."

"Sweet."

And easy as that, you're able to get past that stupid law. I've done it many times before, and if I'm tripping, I could maneuver myself into the VIP room at the Walnut Room. It's a little bit of an unfair advantage. It can be about quick slips as much as being with the right person at the right time. Money helps. The bar was filled and there was an array of old pictures of comedians along a mirrored wall and a stage with someone talking about something supposedly funny. The room was dark lit and wooden with an accent of green.

A big guy who I thought was the bouncer came up to me. I thought I was busted but he pulled out a signup sheet for the open mic and I put my name down casually. I could really focus on the first comedian once the adrenaline had subsided.

"Ight, so how many of y'all are actually from D.C?" He opened strongly.

About half of the bar raised their hands.

"Word. Then for the rest of you here, you can get the fuck out."

The crowd laughed.

"Listen up. If you ain't from Washington, you gotta

go, if you wanna keep your life tonight."

More laughter.

"I'm serious, in Washington anyone can just pull you off the street if they don't like you. Throw you in their car, cut you up, roll you in a carpet, throw you in the Potomac River and NO ONE WOULD EVER NOTICE."

Roaring laughter.

"We are cut throat in Washington, man. I once saw a guy cut off a dude's finger for drinking his beer."

Loud laughter and suddenly I felt a little less comfortable,

"I'm serious. I'll probably end up killing one of y'all right now."

I started thinking up jokes.

The next comedian with dreads, fresh Nike jean jacket, looked about twenty-seven.

"I don't smoke weed, but everybody thinks I do." I grinned since I had been smoking that day.

"You think it'd be awesome, but not really. I mean there is a good thing to everybody thinking you're a fun guy until you don't have weed... or smoke it."

The crowd was in good humor, laughing, drinking.

"It's kinda good sometimes though. Like when I don't wanna smoke and people are smoking and they don't want me to smoke with them because I didn't *throw in*."

Laughter that only a select few truly rejoiced in, myself included.

"It's like, not having to smoke without denying anybody."

After that was an old dude with curly hair. He was lanky and reminded me of my tallest friend if his prunes dried up and he got married. He opened with, "So Mother's Day was this week, let's have a round of applause for that."

He was a complainer, a good one. He cut the shit, but I couldn't tell if this was his first time on stage or not. It ended with him trying physical humor of lifting up his shirt and revealing that some ungodly looking thing was attached to his stomach. He was funny but mainly memorable because of his height.

I had buttloads of raw material to just yell at these people. Usually, I have a full sheet of notes, pages of jokes I can just pull up and use, but they were all erased when my phone got wiped and nothing was all that memorable or had earned me a standing ovation, so I thought I'd go out on my feet. I'll just be excited and explain I'm walking across the country. Listen to my heart and what is the deal with porn in this city? Yeah, that's good.

After him was a woman. She was dope. She had dyed white hair and glasses and right when she started talking, she reminded me of my friend who is a writer.

"Yeeeeeaaaaah. Tuesday Night Eh? Open mike? Ehhhh?" She raised her shoulders.

I was on my knees. Couldn't hold it together for a second and was embarrassed for the both of us.

"I'm not a cat lady. I have two cats. That's chill right?"

I was holding it together.

"I AM a Feminist."

Pause.

"Yeah. Men.... Mennnn." She started to act like a monkey and just kept saying the word "Man." It was Genius.

"I'm 33 and divorced. Yeah, been down that road, not going back. I had a twenty-one-year-old hit on me the other night. What does that even mean? I took him home, Lord knows what I was thinking, and he didn't know what the Nintendo 64 was, so I had to send him home. I'm sorry."

The guy who was running the show came up behind me. He told me that I was almost on deck."

"You'll be up after her," he said, and gave me a nudge of reassurance." I went behind a curtain, and I could still hear through the red sheet, but my mind was calm before I went on stage. The woman finished and got off stage into the back.

"That was great," I mustered up with a little prep in my voice.

"Thanks, I heard you laughing."

I looked like an asshole when she said it to me. I often hate myself.

"Good luck." She cooled me off with a cold shoulder. This was my last chance to solidify something to say on stage while also concealing my light boner. I tell ya man, older women, over thirty, forget it. I was really trying to prep up as much confidence as possible.

The host leapt back on stage and caught back everyone's attention.

"Let's give a warm welcome to our last act of the night."

The crowd had mainly dispersed but there was still life in the room.

I walked on. "Hello, Washington. Thank you very much. It's nice to be here, ya damn crooks and capitalists...and apparently murderers."

Light chuckles.

"I'm actually walking to New York City."

The crowd acknowledged the statement.

"I've seen plenty of snakes, and bugs but I think I'm realizing I've had a irrational fear of Alligators...probably my whole life."

Noises which felt like reciprocation

"I actually got a foot-long knife that I could cut an arm off with. I guess if I thought I was going to get murdered it would probably be in a city. But not D.C, probably like Philly or something. Plus, if anybody's gonna kill me out here, it's gonna be the government. I'm coming for you, pumpkin head!"

It felt like it landed with a slap.

"Speaking of privacy, is there a porn problem in this country today?"

Dead silence.

"No? Well good...I'm exploring this beautiful country trying get some good poetry out of our political and social culture. And let me tell you something about this country." I began to get a little louder. "No piece of ass is half as gorgeous as America! Sorry Feminists."

Applause.

"I suppose though...if I was gonna travel for like a few years it might be nice to bring a girl with me." I composed the room softly. "Like, I would bring a bad bitch to mars. You feel me?" I apparently thought to myself aloud.

Laughter erupted.

"I'm also just 21, but I think I might have more luck than the guy who didn't know what the Nintendo 64 was. Atari, Nintendo, Instagram, those games were my childhood."

Less laughter, but not bad

"Anyways, Thank you all very much Washington. Goodnight."

There were groups of separated applause, but I felt alive.

The night finished strong and with a loose collectivity in the atmosphere. I looked around as a few of the comics headed back to the bar. I look no younger than Mark Thompson and I was inside anyways, I might as well get a drink. I casually, coolly, calmly and charismatically approached the bench. Two down was the female performer's white hair streaked in the light. One closer to me was the first comic who talked about murder in the city, he was a collected black dude.

The bar tender eyed me.

"What'll have? We are closing up." I'm not very seasoned in this game. Someday I will have a definite answer roll off my tongue, a nice IPA, but right now I just don't want to say anything that will end me up with a kitty cocktail.

"I'll take a Corona if you've got one."

"Sure thing buddy, that's 4 dollars."

I had a five. It was splendid. I looked down the bar. Everyone was doing after show catch up. I was very attracted to the performer, but I bet she was a cat person and I wouldn't want a young fox to just directly walk up to her. Instead I humored myself, and just turned to who was next me, the groovy dude on his phone chilling and a young kid talking with the tall comic behind him.

"What's up man, you did pretty good tonight." The guy next to me looked up from his phone just to be polite.

"Nah. Not me, You guys were honestly really the

true talent up there." I said.

"So, you walking to New York?" the bartender asked me, handing my beer. I sipped my drink, started to wash it all down.

"Yeah."

The first comic, who was sitting next to me put his phone down.

"Walking," he said it as an answer to his own question.

"Yep."

"Bro... you're *walking*?!" beginning to get the attention of the rest of the bar.

"Yeah."

"Dawg, dawg, dawg. You WALKIN'?"

"A thousand miles."

"From where?"

"North Carolina."

"D-Damn d-dude that is a l-long w-way," the kid who looked my age revealed a stutter.

"Oh man, I know I did something wrong to meet you man. Here I go, years of my life thinking I'm just fine and here comes young Christian Bale walking across the damn country. You don't need to always be doing all that." The comic sitting at the bar said.

"I couldn't give you an answer why I'm doing it."

"Alright, well at least he ain't crazy. You gotta website or something?" The tall comic asked me.

"I actually am on Instagram."

"Word." He gave me his, which had 2598 followers.

"I'll look out for you," he said with endearment.

"W-where are you s-staying in Washington?" the young guy asked.

"In Vienna. Do you have an Instagram?"

"Sure."

I looked at his credentials. He had 987 followers. Definitely killing it.

"How old are you man?" I asked the kid. He was wearing a Snoopy shirt.

"Twenty-two." he said,

"Yeah, Noah has been around these parts way beyond here. This is just an open mic," The tall comic said.

"Are there other shows?" I asked.

"Yeah just go to dcstandup.com" Noah pointed to my phone, seemingly having had a little bit to drink.

"Sweet. So, you guys are all from here, born and raised?" I inquired.

The two older men laughed.

"For the most part, I've been playing this city for a minute." The black guy sipped his beer.

"Yeah, I've been married and living just outside the city for almost eighteen years," the tall guy explained, relatively happily.

"I'm from Baltimore." The divorced comic invited herself into our conversation. "Where you say you were coming from again? North Carolina?" she raised her eyebrows.

"Well, I go to college in North Carolina."

They all nodded in what seemed like unison.

"How long have you been here?" I asked her.

"Two years."

Well, I was at a dead end. I probably actually wasn't but you know when women are just so bloody gorgeous you forget everything you were going to say. She wasn't like orthodoxly stunning, but she just had such a law of attraction about her. She seemed like the type of person who liked to talk. Marriage hadn't crossed my mind, but I dug a little deeper.

"Do you like it here?" I gestured.

She looked over at the other men in the room.

"It has its comforts - You wanna go outside for a smoke?" she asked the black guy sitting at the bar.

"Yeah sure."

"D-Do you have a ride home?" The young guy with the stutter asked.

"No." I said, more interested in going outside.

"Good luck in New York kid," the tall guy said to me finishing his last drink.

"You ever been?" I asked

"Ha, yeah. You'll grow up quick there."

"I'm already dead."

"Good. You'll need to be." The divorcee had been

delaying her departure.

The rest of the comics left on that note. We walked out of the bar onto an umbrellaed stairway. It had started to rain, and the air smelled moist mixed with smoke. The two aspiring aged actors stood somewhat engaged in a deep conversation smoking. I pulled out one of the cigarettes that I had been given by the old man and lit it. I looked into my backpack and pulled out the old Nazi book that had the cartoon of the two men fornicating.

The other conversations seemed to have settled.

"Take a look at this masterpiece," I chuckled exhaling the smoke.

"What is it?" She asked me.

"It's old pornographic literature," I read aloud. "'General Johnson grabbed the Kernel by his cock and began to stroke it and he began to moan aggressively.'"

"No way!" She seemed interested.

"I think it's somewhat authentic, trying to show off a little bit of my publication knowledge." She began to really become intrigued with the small book. I continued to smoke and tried to look occupied. It obviously failed since all I began to think about was the relationship between the black comic and her.

It probably wasn't, but I assumed it was sexual, people can just be friends, especially older people, but they had a pull between them. It was distant yet potent. She didn't look up from the little book, but I began to feel that her interest was beginning to return to the man. He and I locked eyes for a brief moment.

"Are you guys getting on anything tonight?" I asked.

He sort of gave me a look of disinterest, but she looked up as though she might be willing to take on some loose responsibilities for the evening.

The young comic pulled me aside, "D-Do you have a ride home?"

"No." I peeked my head out at the downpour.

"W-Where are y-you staying?"

"Just outside of the city."

"What t-train d-do you take?"

"The grey line, is there a train nearby?"

"Yeash."

"Could you give me a ride?" I realigned my priorities.

"Sure."

"We should get going if I-I'm gonna give you a lift to the train station."

This made the woman look up from the book, realize how she had fallen into a light trance, mainly due to the erotic cover or mesmerizing humorous language. She looked back at the offensive imagery and was repulsed by her own arousal. She placed it in my hand, finished her cigarette, and ashed it in the concrete ashtray.

"Alright are you ready to go?" I asked the young comic.

"Sure." I moved ahead of the pace of the late-night conversation, which was exhausting in the first place, and left before anyone could leave before me. I lightly grazed my eyes past the late-night cultured woman, shook her partner's hand and jumped into the rain with my new companion. The rain picked up the second that we got out from under the umbrella. It was bad in the first place but added to the ambiance. Pretty quickly the rain seeped into our clothing and were uncomfortable. His car wasn't far.

I swung into the seat. It was fur and to be honest it didn't take much to rejoice in the simple pleasure of a comfortable car seat. We buckled up. Always important. The rain was heavy, fogging our view. I felt a little trapped, but he pulled out of his parking space quickly and we shot out onto the street. He'd been drinking, but not much.

"Listen if you ever want to got-to another sh-show, there is one this Thursday, DM me and they'll-ll hook y-you up."

"Thanks man."

The drive was quick. He pulled up to the curb by a train station.

"This is you, Ch-Cheers." He said.

"God bless."

I walked down the long stairwell to the train station.

The floor was a brown old laminated brick. I scanned my card and sat down at the bench and waited for the train. The station wasn't empty. There was a woman who looked like she had been out on the town, and another mother on the phone. I just wanted it all to end. It'd been a long day. My phone was getting low on battery.

My mother has always been quite absent in my life, and this trip was no different. Although our sporadic encounters have always been rather extravagant, she has left longing with a distance for a substantial relationship after her second marriage. I'm not sure if my idea of a mom is human, just an assortment of things like old jewelry, cordovan heels and Norah Jones concerts I was taken to when I was younger. I waited for about 15 minutes until the train came and got on. The ride wasn't much better, a good forty minutes. The hotel was a few blocks from the station.

Before I snuck in the back door, I lit a cigarette in the parking lot stairwell and began to sing the song Iris to myself. There wasn't anything funny about it at all. I just sang to myself in an empty parking lot and cried the songs of a missed elusive childhood we all barely can remember.

I came in and the TV was on, his shoes were off, and Blake laid there on the bed. I didn't want to turn on a light, but my phone had died. In the pitch black I shuffled off my pants, laid out my backpack, and cuddled into the couch with my small blanket. With a loud snore he awoke.

"Oh, yer here."

"Yeah, I had a fantastic night."

"You did? Glad to hear."

"I did a stand-up show."

"Hehe, course ya did."

"You mind if I turn on the bathroom light."

"Not at all."

I admired the effects this trip had had on my body. No longer a place of scarce food and losing weight, but an intense transformation into muscle on my body. I brushed my teeth as the nightly routine it was.

Chapter 29

The morning came on much brighter than I expected. As usual I was exhausted. I had had a long day and night, and urban settings can be very draining. There seemed to be a lot of commotion coming from Blake. He was packing up, fully dressed, so I sat up.

"Listen," I said in the equivalent of drunken haze from my slumber hangover, "I just want to thank you again, what you are doing is one of the most generous things that has ever happened to me."

"Don't worry about it," he seemed a little tense, like he wanted to get out of the room.

"No, I'm serious, I wanna give you a hug."

"That'll be fine," he stopped me. "Well, I'm not gonna be staying here, but my company is paying for the room, you can stay."

"You're off?" I asked, a little curious about his character.

"Yeah, I'm leaving. You got extra keys?" he asked.

"Yep."

"Well, I hope to hear from you once you get famous or whatever."

"Haha, thank you, but probably not going to happen."

"All the same, I remember what it's like to be a young man searching for something, and I wish the best to you."

"Alright."

He grabbed his bags, and like that he was gone.

I waited a generous 3 minutes after he left to jump in that grand old bed. Ugh.

Good Lord you cherish materialistic things a little bit more after you've been away from them for a while. Breakfast was next. I got everything again and then back to bed with everything off. While I was naked, I decided I might as well take a shower. Freshen up for the day.

Even though I'd probably tell you I was only going to lightly spark a head high in my shower, I reached deep into my bag of green. Opening the bathroom window, I would describe this feeling very close to freedom. No pants. A view. Something somewhat alarming goes off in man's head when it's been that long since a touch of home. My balls are sort of like the weather. If they're hanging low, let it snow, let it snow, let it snow. I was somewhere in the hacky sack range.

I was much too open, I didn't have to do anything all day if I didn't feel like it. Deep down I did feel like doing something, but my head was in the mood for relaxation. As much as this was a pilgrimage, it was a vacation. I popped my sunglasses on, and I felt like part of something bigger than me, even though I didn't think that this city was the true leader in our democracy or even knew I was in town visiting.

You can only read in bed for so long, an hour is a good marker for me. I wanted to be tired, but I felt quite light. I rolled my head into the sheets and made sweet love to them, but there was no denying that it was time to get up. The effects of solitude started to settle in. Although I was in the midst of city, I felt more alone now than ever. Like I was searching for it. This loneliness. An ache in me wanted to stay, but I still felt jaded about the whole experience.

I had to let go of my blind state, no matter how hard I tried to picture something in my head, I just didn't have *anyone* to speak to. I was becoming isolated from society, and it had only been a half hour. Time is one of the greatest concepts we have in this world. Sometimes a minute never ends. Once I was out, I rolled a fresh morning cigarette. It was very calming. I remembered that I was not just looking for something but that I should let things find me. I was set on the thought of going to Georgetown. It wasn't in the center of the city, but just North.

The streets were wide and weaved all around and I always felt a little too close to a byway. You had to cross a bridge to get out to Georgetown. As I was crossing over the water, I saw a pier that edged off under it with graffiti and people. It seemed close enough to something that could lead me to some culture, something non-tourist like. I jutted off and down where I saw the collection of rouge young people all congregating.

I was intimidated by the young people who looked a little too introspective for my tastes and slowly surrounded me. I pulled out my pouch and within seconds someone wanted to roll with me. As much as I lie to myself, I have spent countless hours in circles just as these. Aimless smoking culture. Starlight was the only spectacle that stood out, an evidently homeless black trans. They were talking with a couple from Vermont, but quickly we became more interested in each other's conceit. The couple was really just two parasites, and we separated relatively quickly, whether they left on their own accord or Starlight and I created exclusivity around our conversation I don't recall. It all looked heavy, figuratively and literally. A large cardboard box filled with clothes, old newspapers, rocks and other miscellaneous meaningful objects sat on the side, which was Starlight's living condition.

"Has it been raining lately?" I asked

"A little bit."

"How long have you been here?"

"Three months."

"Damn."

"It's not that long. I've lived in other cities for longer, with less. "

"Where?"

"Philly."

"What is like there?

"The scene is good. Good dick."

"What's the gay scene like out here?"

It became apparent that Starlight was discouraged by the term gay. I personally believe it had to do with black cultural stereotypes towards homosexuality.

"It's not so much that we are gay, as much as that we go out looking for a good time and we have to decide whether or not we are going to give into our pleasures, which we always tend to."

They began to change, taking off their shirt, revealing what seemed to be estrogen induced breasted and a yellow sports bra, and the rest was a makeshift raincoat outfit, which continued to become more and more elaborate. We sat and smoked for an hour, both just lost and free, feeling the harsh smoke age our skin and clean our lungs. The thing is, I, for the most part, can walk away from that culture undetected. If I want, I can throw on a Ralph Lauren shirt, comb my hair, shave and hide in the promise of suburbia. When my face smiles wide people are usually rather trusting of a good hardworking *conventional* gentleman.

I could have followed Starlight to a bar, but it was barely noon and I was in no mood for a drink. The whole day would go out the window, and I had to be wary of getting back to the hotel. I waved Starlight goodbye, as well to the whole culture, which I know some cannot escape and made my way towards higher education. Little townhouses back to back to back, and once you go up a long road that winds up a hill, the campus greets you with a kind gothic aesthetic. I felt very welcomed instantly.

It was sort of cute, but felt further from any city, like you were out in a field. I just cut through the buildings, which I knew would be open. It reminded me of my own college to be honest. God they were beautiful. You couldn't have a bad mindset in that atmosphere. I walked up a long staircase that had awards all along the wall. It wasn't long before I was in the library, which I walked into as though I had something really important that I needed to be working on.

I'm sure there was a slight odor under my lip but my recently trimmed facial hair might've made me look more mature. I opened a big maple door and entered where the books lived. However, there was a wise old lady at a front desk who caught me before I entered. I gave her a knowing nod and my ID. Down three flights to a much more modern spaced lab. The mind can capture such awe-inspiring images, which leave us breathless. For one to imagine professionally has all my respect in the world. I opened the door to it and inconspicuously took a seat. There was a gentleman nearby and we whispered to one another about each other's dreams.

Back outside, I peered through some bushes and saw some steps that lead into a secret garden. The slightly overgrown grass was mixed with a few natural daisies and violets, even a few small statues, a bench, and an array of birds in a small bath. A river ran through it. It was blindly human just getting a taste for the earth, in a garden. A few children wandered in. They seemed at least platonically interested.

My ego got the better of me, and I waved them off and they were the last humans I engaged with the next few days. I roamed the city until it got dark again and recluded back into my dwelling. My room. Every night the sun would go down and I would be alone, but it was enough to support all my needs and affairs. I was nowhere really. I had just been getting from one point to the next. Fixed, unable to enjoy any moment of it.

I'd gone this far. To the edge and off. There is nothing groundbreaking about smoking marijuana, but it is reaching a little deeper into that black bag which might just let me loosen up a little bit. I thought I should call up an old friend instead. To be honest death seemed like a sweet release. I've never been able to do what's right. Or chivalric, or honest. No one knew who I was, and nobody cared. I kept all the lights off. My soul had dilapidated, and solitude resided to an opiate cigar and brown lines quickly sniffed. I was drenched in a deluge of thick tar that filled the void.

Once it smiled a silent dell
Where the people did not dwell;
They had gone unto the wars,
Trusting to the mild-eyed stars,
Nightly, from their azure towers,
To keep watch above the flowers,
In the midst of which all day
The red sun-light lazily lay.
Now each visitor shall confess
The sad valley's restlessness.

-Edgar Allen Poe

Chapter 30

Sure enough I arose, the mess of breakfast having been spilled all along my sheets. Jelly in the pillows, mustard in my hair but breathlessly breathing. I probably missed a day of eating, but I was up for coffee. I walked away from it and locked it all away in my head, like the rest of the weekends of my life. By the time I crawled into the shower and slapped myself in the face hard enough to remember I was someone and hoped to forget this horrible part of who I was. I only had one outfit so I cannot stress how easy it was to look reputable. I took an early train out to the Dance Studio. Any source of light hurts my eyes. Paul my old Ivy Leaguer friend had let me know that he was free and that we should get together. After class, I replied. I was excited but I had been quite worried about the letter I sent to him about a year prior.

I waited outside aching for a cigarette, which I avoided as to not look unprofessional. A woman walked up pulling keys out of her purse.

"You here to work?" The established woman asked me.

"Yep." I swallowed.

"Great. We will get you set up upstairs."

"Thanks so much. I'm glad to be able to dance with y'all today."

"Oh no problem, I like that attitude."

Once we got upstairs, she laid her purse on the front desk, flipped on a lamp and opened up two sliding doors to the studio. I no longer rejected the light but was willing to let it fill me up once again. Where one can dance, expression can roam free like a wildfire. I jumped onto the open wooden floor and began to lightly improvise intending not to bring much attention to myself.

"There is a list in the back closet that will tell you everything you need to do before people start showing up," she said. "Also, let me know what you want for lunch."

"I'm sorry, I don't really have any money to spare." I lowered my head.

"Oh, you're good. We get it for you. We could get pizza or sandwiches. I think there is another girl coming in to do work as well."

"She can decide, I'm just honored to be given this opportunity."

"Thanks. Again, I like that."

I went back to where there were two bathrooms. It was nothing glamorous, but it felt like a breath of fresh air. I read the list. It was custodial work. Mop the floors, clean the bathrooms, wipe down the mirrors, lay out the mats. There is something very meditative about janitorial work especially in a dance studio. I cleaned the place like I was painting.

It wasn't long before people started showing up. I was going to be assisting for demonstrations of movement for the first class. I had the option to go to as many classes as I wanted. There is a lot of technique to self-defense in dance. During the school year an enraged intoxicated student attacked me, but because of my technique, I was able to use his weight that he leaned forward onto me against him, and he fell forward. The first class was Jujitsu.

Jujitsu is all about getting on your back and defending yourself from that angle. Everyone in the studio had skintight mesh wear and were wearing colors you would expect people preparing to fight aliens would wear. They looked good. Fit. I think the instructor was very credible in his craft, he spoke with a Brazilian accent.

"Ok everybody. Let's warm up with twenty-five Pooshups."

There was loud Zumba sounding music blasting and everybody got pumped up, including me.

"Today, I will not hurt you, my friend." He said to me in front of the class. "But I must remind you to relax,"

Since I am limber, my body was easily manipulated into the positions without feeling any sense of pain. He was quick. One second I would be standing, the next I'd be on my back or on top of him. I was so glad to feel any sense of human contact even if its foundation came from a form of fighting. It made me sentimental for the idea of how hard it is to work together. How we can often resort to violence just to solve our problems.

When the first class ended people thanked me. In reality, I was so thankful. After I moved all the mats from one room, I moved them into another room where yoga was being taught. This was the warm up I was looking for. There is a lot of controversy around hot yoga, and I agree that it is too powerful a form for Americans. It can be more intense than cocaine, but because of it I am very flexible. My consciousness of my breath is very articulate, and I was able to take my mind very far away from any rushing city during the yoga class.

I don't want to digress how lovely it is to work with beautiful women when I dance, but one of the women we were working with didn't have an arm. It was not the first time I had done yoga with someone who was missing a limb. Yoga is all about intrinsic balance, but when someone is missing a key component of their physicality, the individual transcends to new form of balance, or strengthens the other body parts to be able to hold advanced positions without extra assistance. I did not lose my focus in admiration for her, but respectfully noted it.

I wiped the wooden floor for the next class, which was basically a cardio Zumba class with a few splashes of technique mixed into it. The teacher was so energetic, and the whole class really went for it. I can imagine these classes were not cheap and it meant a lot to the people who were attending them. I thought about how they probably had jobs they were more focused on and dance was a break from it all.

Lunch came around and I changed back into my street clothes and left. I thought about how I should avoid smoking if possible. How it would reflect poorly on me, the dance community and I'm sure that Mr. Ivy League wouldn't really like it either. I didn't care. I sat at a bench and smoked. It didn't feel good. It didn't feel bad. It just was what it was and I'm nonchalantly that much closer to death. I brushed myself off and came back. The other girl who was helping for the day was finishing up her pizza.

"Hey, what's up? Could you show Amy how to wipe down these yoga mats?" Lisa, the owner asked me.

"Sure."

"You can eat more pizza if you'd like."

"Oh no problem. I'm not very hungry." I said, partially since I had just smoked.

I sat down with the other volunteer and we began wiping down yoga mats. I assisted, and then changed into my dance clothes. When I went back to the bathroom to change, there was a very handsome muscular man talking with a seemingly reputable woman. I was changing, trying to not bring any attention to myself while listening in on their conversation.

They were discussing grad school, and the instructor was explaining how he minored in dance before he went on to get a master's in public relations, and this was one of the ways he was paying for it. It's amazing what you can hear through a bathroom door.

I got out and asked if he was the instructor for the pole dancing classes.

"Yes, my name is Armando."

Caliente.

Armando took all of his clothes off except for his underwear which was relatively tight. He was very fond of himself, but not in that awful of a way. He seemed like he worked hard, but probably couldn't focus long enough on what was important to him so now he teaches pole dancing. Not a bad gig.

The class consisted mainly of women, Armando and me. For some, it seemed like their first class and others seemed to have had some experience. The thing is, Dance is Dance. I don't care if it is a striptease or the waltz, it is about expressing yourself through movement of the body. I took the class very seriously even though many of the women in the room didn't take me seriously.

For those of you who have never tried it, pole dancing is very hard. It takes a lot of abdominal strength, upper arm strength, and leg strength. You have to be able to hold your weight with other parts of your body besides your arms. And that was just the intro class. When the second class began, the room had diversified into women who probably danced professionally. They could do things that amazed me. The could swing their whole bodies upside down and grab onto the pole with their legs, hold it there and slowly rotate down holding themselves in between their chest and their upper thighs. It was beautiful. It made me want to work harder and achieve more.

Letting loose on the pole is not what you want to do; it will end up with you up lying on your back on the floor. Armando was something else. This man could hold his entire body weight in between his thighs, and this was a man with a lot of upper body strength. He, like me, truly stood for the discipline of the art itself and was not there to parade himself in self pride. Each time that I unsuccessfully did something he would be there standing over me with his bare sweaty pecs demonstrating on the pole how to properly execute the move on my pole which was now beginning to get a little bit sweaty.

Lisa, who ran the show, let me know that if I wanted to do anything in the future, she enjoyed working with me and I was welcomed back anytime. There was one dance class that was left for the day. "The Art of Seduction." I had ten minutes to spare before it started. As I was idly waiting in the dance room, showing off for myself, three young women walked into the room. They all wore skin tight clothing, had yoga bags and seemed in their mid-twenties. I tried hard to not pay any attention to them, and although the description I just gave of them probably makes them sound basic, these were 1 in 1000 type of women. Possibly highly professional, beautiful but with little to no display of narcissism, and not out of my league.

I just tried to look up at the ceiling and keep dancing, but pretty quickly one of them approached me.

"Are you in the right class?" One of them asked me.

I smirked out of embarrassment.

"Yes, I'm very passionate about dance." I answered.

She turned, and they didn't giggle, but they might as

well have like little girls. I am formally trained in Modern, Ballet and Contemporary Jazz so I doubted that I couldn't handle this. More people arrived from all walks of life. A Russian looking mother, an uptight lady, a curved redhead wearing lipstick. Finally, the real star showed up.

She drifted into the room like floating fire. Her skin was dark, but her hair was bright blue. She had long fingernails that were painted and hot damn she walked with power.

"Is this everybody?" She spoke with such dominance that put heat under all of our feet.

This was our instructor. Mystique.

The three young women and I tried to not look at each other. I'm serious, especially the first time a dance teacher reveals themselves, you ought to show them your utmost respect in the rare chance that you may be able to connect on a deeper level of mutual movement. The last thing I wanted to think about was sex in a class about seduction. This movement could be very useful for Jazz, plus I was wearing basketball shorts.

"I am going to instruct ourselves today. We are going to learn how to become comfortable with our bodies and ourselves. The first thing we are going to do is get in row and touch ourselves."

We all lined up in front of the mirror. Mystique, with pride began to rub her fingers all along herself, from her shoulders down in between her legs. We all were staring. She was definitely from a different planet, probably Venus. One of the rarest creatures of them all, someone not only not scared to be empowered by themselves, but not hindered by others. I felt comfortable as ever. I began to rub my fingers through each crevice of my muscles and feel the sweat of the day. I felt the fat cells boil with my blood with the rising pressure.

She picked on me since I was the only boy.

"Oh, don't be afraid sweety. Really get in there," she said, wrapping her arms around me as if she we were about to reenact the pottery scene from *Ghost*. I was doing my best to not be performing for anyone in the room, just myself. I just closed my eyes and thought about Paris. She gets irritated at me when I tell her that other women remind me of her, but it's true. That pulse of desire that can't be fixed which only made me reach deeply into the only thing I know as love.

"Now I want all of you to show me what a sexy walk looks like. You first," she eyed one of the girls who looked like she needed a good night out on the town.

The woman rolled her eyes as if she hadn't hoped for this spotlight. She took it with stride as we all turned around to face the mirror on the other side of the room and she slowly and smoothly slid her legs and hips across the floor trying to put emphasis on each of her steps and curves. The next girl followed and did similar slow movement, followed by the Russian mother who did the same only stiffer and then it was my turn.

For a man, sex appeal comes from power, intellect, and even authority. I did the opposite of these women and straightened my legs and walked with my chest in the air making eye contact straight ahead. The whole room seemed amused with my spin. We finished this exercise and continued with each of our separate energies of sex appeal by expressing ourselves to one of the sexiest artists alive. Frank Ocean.

Hips flew, I would stretch tall and yet come close enough within my own intimacy to kindle a flame. Some insects rip off the male's head after sex. I offered my two cents that maybe we shouldn't isolate each of us to show off what sex appeal looks like in a walk, but instead allow each of us to find our own voice of what sex appeal felt like, so we all merged.

And just as it usually starts with the fire of seduction, suddenly the class was over. We all stayed for talkback.

I kept on listening until through the door came a fresh blonde buzz cut that I hadn't seen in far too long. I really wanted to stay but I couldn't hold back running up to him and giving him a bear hug. Good ol' Paul was instantly laughing about how funny we looked to each other after having known each other since the first day of second grade. I revealed everything about my life to him on the playground, glad I did. We were boys together, loved and hated one another for as long as I've ever lived. If I had known where that leap of faith with friendship would have taken me, I'd tell everybody all about my life.

"You just came here and they gave you dance classes?" was his first question.

"Yeah. Hahaha. I just saw a sign in the window and that was enough to come up." I answered.

The artist atmosphere was of course a little shabby for the Ivy Leaguer and I was getting stale. I changed, thanked everyone at the studio and we rode the elevator out the building.

Chapter 31

"Haha, What's up?" He always utters and my imagination grows bigger than the both of us can halt.

"All we need is some sunglasses and we can find some music and run this town."

"Bro." He laughed up to a higher pitch. "I'm down."

"I have some really dope sunglasses, I think." I pulled out my stolen spectacles.

"Oh yeah, I actually have some shades myself. Hahaha." He pulled out a pair himself.

It's wonderful when you see someone that you knew before you knew yourself since you both know each other just as well, if not better than you know yourself.

"Even when you are walking across the country you pack shades." He laughed.

"Gotta look fresh."

We were letting the situation be in control of itself, but it's only for so long you can blindly be strutting in sunglasses before you should find something to do.

"So, what are you trying to do?" I could tell that both us wanted to catch up.

"Let's get a really good meal." The sound of coins dropping to the floor was in his voice. A rumor surfaced that he and John, my neighbor who now lived out in New York City now, had gotten quite stoned and gone to a classy steak dinner even though John is a vegetarian.

"I just ate, so I'm not that hungry right now, but what are you hungry for?"

"I am looking for something *really nice*." He answered.

"I think there is some good Chinese food out here."

"Not Chinese, but..." He looked up at the sky with his shades, "Sushi."

"I could go for some tashiki," I shrugged

We stopped in our tracks and there was a nice stone table.

"Or we could just sit down and talk for a little." I was actually nervous. I hadn't seen him since I sent him that letter.

"Do you know what I'm doing?" He asked me importantly.

"Something to do with Law?"

"Yes. I'm interning at the Public Defense Office, I just didn't know if you know what that is."

"I do."

"It's just some people at Georgetown didn't."

"Le crème de la *crème*. I took Business Law thank you very much," I said, offended for no reason.

He then went on to talk all about a bunch of crap I didn't understand.

"I think that is incredible, Paul. There is a lot that needs to be done for the impoverished in this country, but you aren't going home over summer?" I asked.

"Maybe for a weekend," he barely answered.

"Are you going to see anyone?"

"Probably just my parents." He said.

I thought briefly how his mother had caught me smoking in public.

"How's Georgetown?"

"Good. I'm in a band."

"Oh cool, what's it called?

"Brightside."

He pulled out his phone and I watched him and three other boys make melodic music, probably thinking he was the best looking of them all. He was, too.

"Nice, dude."

"How's North Carolina?"

"I'm definitely in a bubble down South."

"But that's so interesting."

"Well, I suppose. I went there for the mountains." I continued.

His eyes widen. "Oh my god, gorgeous."

"You already know. There is an intellectual culture there too." I rolled my eyes.

"I'm sick of Ivy culture myself," he uttered.

"Is that so?"

"Everyone is just so deep in the *game*. There's no time to even think of anything. I'm so happy, proud even, that you are travelling. There is no education like seeing the world and meeting people." He said. "I want to fall in love." He finished.

"The first time you fall in love is like feeling rain for the first time." I said looking up.

"You. You *fall* in love," he said to me.

"Have you ever been *in* love?" I asked, "Are you a virgin?" We didn't really talk all that much senior year.

"No."

"Who did you lose your virginity to?"

"Annie Crust."

"Annie Crust? You mean Ann Christ?"

"Yeah."

"Don't call her that." I said, "Did you love her?"

"I said I did."

"What was it like?" I asked.

"We hooked up and then she looked up at me and said I love you."

I could hear the emptiness in his words and feeling for the situation.

"I told her 'I love you,' but I don't think I've ever meant it," he ended.

"That's very similar to the first time Paris told me she loved me." I said, "She just quietly muttered it to me, and I could only feel the distance of where we were in our lives right next to each other that night. You're smart, every single infinitesimal thought manifests itself in a direction toward building a home with that creature. You've never felt that for someone?" I asked surprised.

"We..." He put his hand out like he was holding a dead fish, "had sex."

"Yes, but what kind of sex? Was it ya know... sensual sex or bang bang?"

"It was somewhat rough sex." He answered.

"Felt good?" I grinned.

"YEAH." We both broke out into boyhood laughter.

"When did it happen?"

"Junior year. You?"

"Much too young, nothing special." I said, "but what was losing *your* virginity like?" I reached further. "What happened?"

"Well. Ya know...I suppose. I don't really want to

share *how* I lost my virginity."

"I apologize." I said.

"I've told the story before," he said with tinted shame in his cheeks. "It was just different."

"I've actually been meaning to talk to you about something different," I said accidently changing the topic.

He looked up from a not too distant place in his mind.

"What?"

"The letter I sent you," I said potently.

"What letter?"

"You never got a letter from me revealing some liable details?"

"A letter?" He asked, apparently taken aback.

"Are you serious, Paul?" I asked. I had a sobering thought he was probably playing some trick on me.

"Yes, I'm serious, what was it about?" he asked.

"Someone." I said.

"Who?"

"Take a guess." I answered.

"Who?"

"Think of a girl."

"Paris?"

"A girl you dated." I retorted.

"Beth?"

When he said her name, I closed my eyes, which was the best I could do.

"What about her?" He asked.

"Were you two, *together* recently?" I suggested.

"What? No. What does she have to do with all this?"

"Oh. Nothing." I said a little pale.

For better or worse, I sort of symbolically reached out in the form of letters to a few friends in the name of the woman I planned to court. Beth and I had done theater with all of them in high school before I tragically got kicked out. One was Red, an older actor who once reminded me of the importance of innocence backstage. One was to The Great Greg Leroy III, one of my oldest and wisest mates. I wrote him that I wanted to go a year sober. The other was Paul, who I wrote I would murder if he slept with the love of my life.

We locked eyes.

"What is your relationship with Paris like?" he asked.

"She really is quite wonderful, sometimes a little sad every so often, I suppose."

"Sad?"

"No just. . . She's childlike."

"Childlike?" He asked as though his complex mind hadn't touched on the solidity of peace that comes from whispering in another person's ear goodnight.

"Yes, she makes me feel so young. She helped me a lot. You do believe in God, right?"

He didn't say anything.

"Well sort of. Like I believe that a lot of what happened in the Bible actually probably happened." He finally answered.

"Really?" Not really the same approach that I take to religion. "I meant like the force of god, and spiritual emotion."

One of those brief pauses waltzed through. We had revealed ourselves to one another after the years we'd been away, like old partners, but just really old friends. He tilted his head.

"Why?" he asked.

"Just some weird shit I did." I exhaled.

"What kind of weird shit?"

"Haven't you ever noticed the weird shit I do?" I asked as more of a reflection of my character.

"Well sort of." He acknowledged.

"I felt just like I never really fit in, I was an outsider. Have you been talking with the other people from that horrible show tune you all did without me?"

"A little bit yeah, but what does that have to do with *Beth*?"

"She just happens to mean the world to me. I should have realized sooner theater is just a vacant sense of glamour I'm not. I just thought you all thought I died or something."

"*You* died? I was more friends with the crowd that went to Ivy Leagues."

"No, I don't really care about them," I brushed off. "Why do you think about all *those* people?"

"They're my friends." He said. "But I just think they are the type of people to become very successful, move up on the Upper East Side, looking down on a lot of the world from their elitist view."

"I don't know about all that, I think they are trying to do the best they can." I responded.

"Like God complexes?" Paul asked.

"Well. No. Not *all* of them."

"How so?"

"Do you smoke?" I responded.

"Not really, but I once smoked this really nice cigarillo. It was very nice, very calming."

"You smoked a rillo?" I grinned. "Well, this is some very fine, North Carolinian Tobacco."

"I might take a puff," he compromised.

"It isn't God as much as it is Zen. How we treat the world, like a friend."

"But we were just talking about Christianity." He said.

"Sure, but I'm a Transcendentalist."

"What does that mean?"

"It means I seek out every form of God and religion on this earth."

"Oh yes, now that I can get on board with. I hate that I can be like, yeah, I know what people are like," he said.

"Do you like saying that?" I asked.

"No. I don't."

"Then shut up for once. God is just about living your best life in many ways, through devout reason of emotion and integrity. It is a constant balance between the good and evil that is within each other. The Yin and the Yang. Meditation. Yoga. Prayer. If you want to talk about a Christ complex, Jesus lived his life like a servant, yet within that holds the power of God and capability of anything. It is basically that within humans exists the complexity of Jesus and God in one. Jesus is the Servant, God is the Savior."

"And you deal with this?"

"When I was twelve, but faith is hard." I answered. "However, what is often misinterpreted is Mary. The Mother is actually the Holy *Spirit*. People create this complex within themselves, and get tied up into thinking they *are* Jesus Christ, or God when it is not a complexity between two forces, but three. Geometrically speaking this would create a strong shape, but in reality, creates an imbalance. In relation to *you know who*, in the midst of a serious personal enlightenment my heart took over my mind and I turned into a madman that terrorized Christmas. Pure, spiritual poetry only suicides could find feasible, all in tribal native ritual for a soulmate and to win the World Series."

"You were in love?" Paul asked.

"Do birds fly? I saw color for the first time, and for what it's worth now, I believed that the universe *is* on our side."

"Jack, I want to fall in love." He said to me like the smartest man in the world asking a question for the first time in his life.

"There were girls back there. Did you not see them?" I said ashing my cigarette.

"I want a real woman. There's girls everywhere." He said.

"Not for everyone." I said, admiring his stature. "We can't do a thing about who we love, it's something that happens to us. Problem is, I'm as likely to fall in love with a bird as I am with anyone."

"I just haven't found a girl that I, you know...I just haven't found that."

"You will. You'll find it. It'll find you." I promised.

"Do you have a book on you? I wouldn't mind reading for a bit." He said.

"I do." My heart sung.

Chapter 32

We discussed politics before we ordered our fish and were still talking about it once it arrived. I actually like to keep my political views private, but Paul was worried about the espionage that our president and his son-in-law were in. That it was likely that the president had some Russian intelligence and that was trying to be kept among the family. Really not my business. After that Paul explained how he was good on money. He won some competitions and his school granted him a lump sum in scholarship money. After these discussions and finishing a kinship meal, I asked one final question.

Listen, there is one last thing I want to mention before we get out of here."

"What's that?"

"Well a long time ago, John told me a story once, about how he climbed into bed with a spoon and was thankful for all he had."

"And?"

"And this spoon is not something that everybody is just given. It is a distinct difference between you and John, and George and I."

"Are you talking about money?"

"No. Money is exactly the thing I am not talking about," I appeased.

"Look at John, he's so happy. I'm happy for him, but he's never had to go through anything detrimental in his life which ultimately defines people growing up."

"I'm not sure I follow."

"The way you and John carry yourselves is not a mistake. It comes from a wholesome family, not just money. For example, do you think you would be at Georgetown if your parents were divorced? Or one of them died?"

He paused for a complacent moment, "Oh. All of this, it would be over. I would go home right away, but you know I worked really hard for where I am."

"Of course, you did better than any of us in school. That's what I'm saying. George and I have these adversities in our lives, that weren't our fault. These distractions we've dealt with when we were younger affected us in a way you and John don't always see."

"I think I see what you are talking about."

"Everyone has spoons in our hand, but some of them are rusted, bent or plastic instead of silver. It is not just money, though not all of us will always be fed or given food. My best judgment is the difference between my best friends. Just take it with a grain of salt. I hope nothing bad ever happens to you or John, but if the world was a different place, maybe George and I wouldn't have to had deal with what we did, and we'd maybe be in a different place. All I'm basically referring to is the first page of the Great Gatsby."

"I'm glad you brought this to my attention, I've not always acknowledged that with George losing a parent so young."

"What do you think about Power?" I asked.

He rolled his eyes.

"What do I think about power?" he asked.

"Yes." Looking at a young man wielding very much of it.

"You might as well ask what I think about Greed, or Death, History or Science."

"What? Why?"

"You are just asking such a broad question without any narrow answer."

"What about being *given* power?"

"I'm not sure I follow."

"What if the answer is the question itself?" I said.

"What do I think about power? I think that people want to have power, and too much power in one place creates corruption."

I could tell he was unimpressed.

"Excuse me," he said went to the bathroom. No words were exchanged from then on until we were outside of the restaurant. If either of us had spoken, that one would have lost. Power is what you apply to it. No, Power is what it applies itself to. It exists only in size of theory. I invited him to come to a stand-up show with me, but he said he wanted to get home early since he had work in the morning. I understood. I asked him for a ride to the show, though. In the car he put on his acoustic music, which was very modern and good and asked me about my latest music tastes.

I thought I would jazz things up and put on something groovy. I got too into it and while I was supposed to watch for the next turn, we missed it. The music built and I could tell Paul was getting tense, especially since the street we missed took us for quite the ride. Paul tried to back up and someone wasn't having it and still the music built. I just laughed feeling bad about how good I felt.

"That's it." He parked up.

"This is as far as you're taking me?"

"Yup."

I chuckled to myself.

"Alright then. I'll try to see you before I get out of this place." The car door shut. He drove off up to a red light. I waved as I walked past him. I was early for the show. About an hour early, which was good because then I could sign up to go first, but I had to wait. I signed up and walked around. I saw family units biking together, and couples holding hands. I then looked into a building and it looked old. Like *Mad Men* style, old clock and leather seats. It made me worried about how old America really was.

By the time the show actually came around I was not in the mood in the slightest. It had been too long since a dopamine rush. More than that, the way Paul left me made me feel a little sour about impressing anyone for the evening. Everyone is just going to care a whole lot about themselves and think they are doing you a favor if they talk to you. I went back and forth between the train and the venue about a hundred times, feeling like a failed artist if I didn't step on stage, and I got caught in a very interesting culture of Washington D.C.

I was outside of apparently a very club heavy area, and there were hundreds of what appeared to be gay African Americans. I was a little out of place, to be honest. It's not like I didn't stand out like a sore thumb, but I wasn't about to just go talk to anyone like I knew anything, however someone walked up to me.

"What are you doing here?" It was Starlight.

"I really don't know." I admitted to the universe.

"Here, just take my number so that while you are here you have someone to talk to."

I slowly walked back to the train looking at all the people sleeping on cardboard.

Chapter 33

The day of the Memorial Day Parade was the last of D.C. which stuck out. Everybody was downtown, people from all over the country. You felt like you couldn't move. Security was high but not intrusive. I felt a little more uneasy smoking in public than usual, but I had to look like the bad citizen I was. Nobody smokes nowadays anyway. The Botanical Garden's plants were incredible, dark green, tall and tropical, while others were dry and had the color and culture of Southwest lime.

There were multiple ceremonies happening all over the city at the same time, but it was apparent that the biggest one was the parade. As I was strolling down the drive, I realized I had been in the sun much too long and needed to put on some sunscreen. A nice family with a baby lent me some, and they were from Jersey, and reminded me why I was out there in the first place. For once, home was my country. I felt like a part of it. And to be honest it was really tiring. There are a lot of people doing things all the time in the name of American culture. Use your imagination. Families, dreamers, men and women, children and elders. Children no older than a month and people my age ready to die.

The Lincoln Memorial was a fitting center to this country's chaos. From there I walked all the way down to the park, finding more memorials than I had heard of. I discovered a war on my walk. Multiple generals were awarded. After each of these, veterans gave their speeches, there was a ceremony of wreaths valuing lieutenants who had fallen.

A woman in a yellow dress came out and she was the head of the foundation for the wives of fallen soldiers. So much life surrounded her, and I was heartbroken. This feeling continued as I watched the rest of the country rejoice. How hard it is to lose anyone, I couldn't imagine losing a lover, especially to war.

No one should have died for my vanity. The Vietnam Memorial and Korean Monument had old roses left. I saw people promoting their books and names written with charcoal. I came across a Bible and began to read it. Finally, I ended up around the Capitol Building and was getting depressed and dehydrated. I was beginning to feel like I was overstaying my welcome in this city. I wanted to say my goodbyes and get going. I texted Paul.

Me - You still wanna connect today?

Paul - I'm with my cousin now, we're going to a potluck, I'll text you around 6 and let you know what's up.

I had nothing better to do than just keep walking. All of sudden music started coming to me. It was a little bit whiny, but I had a whole song in my head. I pulled out my phone and began writing down lyrics. Literally just melodic poetry streaming from my blood. It was like I couldn't do anything but be honest with myself. I needed a guitar. I didn't think it would be too hard to find one.

I typed in guitar center into my phone, and it gave me a list of stores. I called a few of them but they weren't open, plus they were very far away. If you go a little North of the Capitol building it isn't all that glamorous. Old governmental buildings that are spread apart with little gaps that people congregate in. It just might not be everyone's favorite kind of person, the homeless. I was used to 'em, along the trail, trash is the best way to make company.

"Do any of you know where to find a guitar in this city?" I asked the small group.

They were all engaged in tense conversation and nobody looked up at first but when they did it seemed like they all looked at once.

"I'm sorry man, what do ya need?" One looked up from a tarnished looking woman. They all had dirt under their long fingernails and hadn't bathed in a while. You could see the years of stress in their skin of going days without food.

"I'm just wondering if any of you know where to find a guitar?" I asked.

"He's looking for a guitar!" Aggressively including me into the community.

"Drum city." One of em looked off uninterested but trying to get my attention at the same time.

"Where is that?" I addressed him.

"It's on 14th street."

"How do I get there?"

"The street numbers go up as you head East."

"Which way is East?"

Everybody looked up at the sun.

"It's that way."

"Once you get to 14th street, it's on Capitol street. Just look for Drum City."

"Once again, thank you all very much." You could tell they were sick of this city (and country) too.

I began to follow and count the streets up to eight. The higher and further away from the city it was apparent what was happening. Apart from the fact that every two years there are elections that bring a whole new assortment of people to the city of Washington, there are two majority groups of people in D.C. Young graduate students and the people that used to live in this city.

Gentrification doesn't always have to do with race, but when rich people basically raise the price of lower income areas and then the people who used to live there can't anymore. I was the only white person I saw past 6th street, and the change of what the streets felt like was eminent, older. It was a little dangerous, but it was aware of itself and not looking for trouble. I, like an idiot waved to everyone I saw like I was just visiting. Some of them who were out with their families, waved back, other lone men walking the streets did not acknowledge me.

Once I was on Capitol Street, I was in the midst of it. Some of the colors of the buildings had a New Orleanian feel, bright pink and orange, but were otherwise crumbling buildings. That is when I went into what all of these neighborhoods need. A good building where people can learn something and do something with their time. Drum City was one of the best establishments that I visited on my journey, bringing music to the streets.

The owner was a youngish guy, and he gave me a guitar and let me use a practice room. I instantly found music. The guitar was nearly broken, and the strings were probably from the late 90's, but it worked. In another practice room I could hear a drummer beating away. Just the pulse of the sound gave me life and I began to work. I had the lyrics out in front of me, I knew what chords I wanted to play, and I started recording on my phone.

In the midst of my creative endeavor Paul got back to me and asked me where I was. I sent him a picture of me in the studio with a guitar, slightly proud of my adaptability. He told me he would be there soon. I got as many rough cuts of the song as I could and the next thing I knew I was out the door with a brand new piece of art.

Before I'm Old

C   D
Let the story begin
                              G
Don't know where it starts
                              C
Don't know where it ends
                              D
My heart might be broken
              G   C
But I still, got all my friends
                           D
I still laugh in the wind
                        G
I still dance in the rain
                         C
I'm going my own way
C   D
Live not for tomorrow
C   G
Live For Today

Paul was parked across the street and when I rolled up, he was getting hassled by some guy who needed a ride.

After Paul declined to give the guy a ride, he looked at me.

"I would have given him a ride, I just don't know where he was trying to go."

"It's fine. He probably doesn't either." Paul picked up on my wittish mood pretty quick.

"How was your potluck?" I asked.

"It was good. I was with a lot of people in their mid-twenties, so that is an age where people's life decisions start to make a little more of a difference and it makes an apparent change."

"Hmm." I wondered.

"Like some people are still living off of their parents' money and others aren't." He said.

I thought about where I would be at that age. I doubt I would have any parents' money to life off of.

"But it was good."

"Yes." I could tell it was somewhat of an astute gathering, I probably would have ended up harassing someone. "So, you trying to do anything?" I asked.

"Well, I've got some time to spare, but I need to go grocery shopping."

I didn't say anything, I didn't want to be too presumptuous, but like an older brother I knew he wasn't about to leave me to starve.

"Let's find a Giant," he said.

"What's that?" I asked.

"It's a grocery store."

"Works for me."

I was done playing any tricks on him musically to get him riled up, so we just listened to his music. The car ride was like being at home a thousand miles away from it. It was just good to be with a friend. I often go long strenuous amounts of time forgetting I have any of friends in this world.

When we got out of the car, he opened the trunk and pulled out a skateboard.

"This summer, I want to learn how to get really

good at this."

"Just practice. I can only ollie on these things." I got excited.

He pushed himself along in the street and held his balance. A good way to spot a dancer in public is to just watch their feet. Balance is a key factor to skating that I have advantage over most people idly walking on eggshells. Sure enough right after he hopped on, he fell off. We were laughing like we were fourteen again. The grocery store was what you'd imagine. We laughed about brands and Paul was exceedingly generous. He really helped me out. A week's worth of Ramen, Cliff Bars, and Rice, it was enough to get me to New York.

"Paul, I'm going to be able to make it to New York with this."

He rolled his eyes, yeah right.

"No, I'm serious. I'll probably eat all this before I get there, but now it is possible. Like I *know* it is possible." It was like a whole structure of support underneath me, like a net that I could fall asleep on.

We got in the car once again, and I checked how far of a drive it was to my hotel, and it was like forty minutes both ways, so I wasn't about to ask for any more. We drove around and parked up close to a train station.

"Alright, this is my one moment of fatherly advice," he finally spit out.

He ought to wash out his mouth with soap for saying such a thing.

"When you get to New York...Don't stop there." He said.

I didn't let enough time for his words to sink in.

"I'm serious, people in New York think very highly of themselves. They have this attitude of it being all about themselves, and I really do think that about that place."

"Who do you think you are talking to?" I said opening the car door.

He tried to stop me.

I slammed it closed. "The sad fact is, I need to learn if I love myself more than everything that I was before all this. I need to see if I *could* fall in love with New York more than anyone else."

"I wish you luck."

"I'll see you soon old friend."

Chapter 34

During my last night in Washington, I swore off all drugs and my father called. He obviously felt guilty that something was going to happen to me, so he sent me fifty dollars. I ordered a train ticket to Harper's Ferry, West Virginia. It was only thirteen dollars. Right before you leave somewhere you always see stuff that makes you want to stay. After what now felt like a week of rest, I was still exhausted, and the second I stepped off in Harper's Ferry I was lost.

The town was beautiful. Something out of a movie. It looked like America's Greece. Hidden among the trees with a great bridge and flowing river and buildings from a colorful rustic time. It wasn't long before I started running into hikers. I had to ask which way North was. It was along some train tracks, into a tunnel, further into the wild and into Maryland.

The skies were grey and kept getting greyer until the downpour came. I was not ecstatic. I had dealt with rain in the past, but it was not a wonderful welcome back onto the road. It was too late to go home. I walked in the rain for about six hours and by the time it was getting dark I sought refuge at a hostel. I decided I wasn't going to pay to stay the night since there was a shack out back that I could sleep in for free. They let me stay in the common room for a while and I chatted with the other travelers. The person I liked the most like was an immigrant, who ordered pizza and shared it with me. He was a travel blogger and had photos of him all over the country. Also at the table was a woman hiking the trail who had just come from Colorado cutting the bud off of marijuana plants. Apparently, it is a business that is slowly getting harder to make as much profit off of.

She admitted that it was a hefty sum of about 1,400 dollars a week just cutting up a plant. An old couple joined us for the night. Although they said they weren't a couple, just old friends, but you could tell that they were travelling together, or had been living together or something. I found a guitar and the older woman stayed up with me since I was serenading her. The older woman loved every song I sang. She wasn't all there but when the man came in, you could tell she was the one with the power. To be honest I think it's unsettling that people of that age cannot be intimate with each other.

I went out back and pulled out my sleeping mat and slept to the sound of rain. I was cold, but I wasn't that wet. I lingered a little bit in the morning, ate breakfast even though it was meant for people who were staying there, but everyone seemed willing to share. It was confusing as hell to find the trail again after that. I ended up along a vast abyss of American homes in no man's land. I began to delve into all of my friends' playlists. I ended up following some trail, but I didn't know if it was the Appalachian Trail.

There was a parking lot with one of those cars that looked like it might've been parked there for days. A big old dark blue van with all of the shutter blinds closed. A feminine arm hung out the driver's window with a snake tattoo leading up to a cigarette in between her fingers.

"Hello. I don't mean to bother you." I waddled up.

"Bother you? I bet we bother you," she chuckled, her voice ragged.

"Oh, not at all, in fact I love your vehicle and whole aesthetic in general." The woman had thinning blond hair on her head, had done her make up this morning, was exceedingly thin and unnaturally perky and fierce at the same time.

"What can I help you with?" she said blowing out smoke.

"Well, I'm walking to New York and I seem to have lost the trail."

"Hang on baby, what are you doing?"

"I'm walking to New York." I said.

"Where you coming from?"

"I left from North Carolina."

"Yeah we were just in New York a couple of weeks ago." The man spoke up next to her.

"What were you doing there?" I asked.

"There's always something to do there. It's New York." The way she said it reminded me of how I had thought of the city. "I'm Denise by the way."

"Well, what can we help you with?" She got back to business.

"Oh, you know you've already helped really. I was just wondering if you could give me a lift a little bit up ahead, just so I can find the trail again."

"We can do that. Hop on in." I had started to love getting into stranger's cars, but this one especially had things lurking at every corner. Right when the door opened, I heard shuffling in the back and out popped a head.

"Don't mind that, it's just my son," the woman brushed off.

"S'up dude." A shaven skeleton boy awoke and looked into my soul.

He then pulled something out from under him and held it in his hand.

"Bed Bugs." There in his hand was a disgusting looking creature with far too many legs and pinchers.

"Burk come sit up front," his mother said.

He didn't say anything and although his body was much too slim, and his eyelids looked really heavy. He climbed over the seat and a dog woke up and climbed out of the back and onto my lap.

"Rufus. Don't be rowdy." She said.

"Oh, don't worry, I love dogs." I hugged it. Although I was in squalor I was in complete bliss.

"Do you mind if we run a quick errand before we take you where you need to be?"

"Oh sure, I'm not really in a hurry."

"Call back Leon," she looked at the man next to her up front briskly.

"I did call him!" He bucked back.

"Well call him again, we are going to stop by the store!"

"My partner, Fred," she said to me behind the wheel motioning to the man, "works at the liquor store and his stupid Indian boss didn't give him the key so he couldn't open up shop this morning."

Lovely.

"I don't mean to trouble you, but if we can make

money, we should." She lit another cigarette.

"What do you do?" I asked her.

"I'm a janitor," she said.

"Oh, custodial work can be very peaceful, plus you get the keys to all the fun spots."

"That's right." She looked over at her man, in control.

"How old are you?" I asked Burk.

"He's 20," she said.

This poor kid. I love him to death, but you could just tell that his mother had been drinking an awful lot when she was pregnant with him and it took him a while to formulate his thoughts when he ever had any.

"Yeah, we gotta get Burk a job, he dropped out of high school." She said.

"That's alright. I know a lot of people who formal education just isn't for them. What do you like?"

"He really good with technology," She said.

"If you can figure out how to work on computers, they will pay a buttload." I tried to stay positive.

We pulled up to the liquor store and nobody was there. They called the boss. I could hear him speak through the phone and both parties were being very nasty to each other. You could tell nobody respected anyone.

"Do you think you should stay here in case he shows up?" She asked him.

"He ain't coming. Let's go drop this kid off."

As we drove, the conversation never seemed to stop. They were the sweetest most horrible people I've ever met. They seemed genuinely interested in what I had to say, and I didn't realize it then, but they were all alt-right. Blind racists, who hate people just because of how they look. What do you do?

I let them know that it is foolish to treat someone wrongly, and they agreed. I don't want to say it, but I believe Denise was once raped, and had been hurt by someone of another culture. I hope I changed their hearts just a little bit. Love unconditionally. You cannot save people from themselves by telling them they are wrong, you must show them what is right. As if I have any answers.

"This is where they filmed the Blair Witch Project." Fred said.

"No way."

"Yeah, not a lot of people don't camp here anymore."

"I bet."

"This town is really creepy. It's extremely old and very small, and on the other side the speed limit is 50 miles per hour to let you know they want you to get the hell out." Denise said.

"Can we stop by it?"

"I don't see why not, but if you blink, you'll miss the whole thing.

Sure enough the city was one street and we drove slowly through it. We pulled into a graveyard and all got out. I looked at the gravestones and realized that a few of them were of children. Only three or ten-year-old lifespans. I'd never seen the Blair Witch Project before.

"Do you know the story of the Blair Witch or what everybody is so afraid of out here?"

"I think some kids died a couple years back in the forest," the man said.

A dark chill filled my body.

"Over there is the forest." It looked extremely ominous with only one path that lead up to the forest.

I don't know what compelled me, but I had a strange desire to spend the night. I walked back to the car conflicted. I looked out at a patrol cop who was parked up watching us. Everyone in the car was tense.

"Yeah, they've been watching us for about five minutes now. C'mon." Said Fred.

I couldn't explain what I was feeling. Either way I was putting myself in danger, but I wanted to put myself in *real* danger. The kind you can't hide from. I knew I would find what I was looking for in that forest. God or the Devil Himself. Or herself. I watched them exit the graveyard and peel out at 50 miles per hour just like everybody else that was afraid.

Chapter 35

It was the longest walk of my life into those deep woods. Everything in my mind was silent. I set up camp like it was any other campsite, but you could feel that there was something there that did not want to be disturbed. I finally started to sing and smoke to make the day pass but that didn't help my paranoia. I ate whatever I could stomach. The sunset came and passed through the pointed branches with the feeling of fall for some reason. It was colder than usual. I was detached. If you think I had any wireless connection, you must be joking. I don't think anybody in that town owned a car. This place didn't want to be seen. I built a nice fire, and just watched it dance. Sitting at the dinner table when I was younger, my family used to all to hold hands and could make the fire of the candles move depending on what we thought. The word Love would make the fire grow. Embers burned into a crumble and the dark glow of night found no comfort under the covers.

The earth knew what I was hiding. I regretted tormenting myself like this. In my tent I usually feel very safe from the outside world but tonight I was even more afraid. It wasn't before long that I heard an inexplicable noise. Must be the wind, but it sounded like a knocking. Surely, branches brushing up against each other, but then a light call reached out.

"*Ouch.*" I heard

"What?" I spoke up loudly trying to it scare off.

No response, but the knocking continued.

I tried to reassure myself that all of this was just in my head, but it was hopeless. I got out of my tent to take a quick look around. I couldn't see anything, but I kept hearing it.

"Go away." I demanded.

The knocking and scratching of the branches continued. I regretted letting the fire go out.

"I am not afraid." I said to myself.

The knocking stopped.

"That's right. There's nothing to be afraid of.

Goodnight."

But the way I said, "Goodnight" affirmed that there was indeed something or someone still there. I wished I had a Ouija board so at least I would know who or what I was dealing with. Most spirits are friendly, but not always.

"Who are you?"

A wind passed.

"Do you want me to leave?"

The knocking returned.

"Fuck." I got out of my tent, just to be sure.

In the dark, our minds know what we are afraid of which can create the visual image of fear in our heads better than we wish it could. Horrible demonic dead people, all visually looked like they were surrounding me. The sky looked like a dead cloud that had ghastly faces with black makeup lingering in it.

"This is stupid." I climbed back into my tent, more scared than ever.

"*Ouch.*"

"You're just the wind."

A minute passed.

Good lord get me the hell out of here.

"I'm sorry." I cried trying to rue all I had done. "Is that what you want to hear?" We both knew that was not the answer we were looking for.

"*OUCH.*"

Nearly in tears.

"I'm sorry. I hurt myself and I hurt others, and it's all because I think so much about myself. I want to stop. I want to go away. That's why I'm here. I'd rather be dead than face the real horror."

I was the monster.

I began to hear rustling in the distance, and it came closer very quickly all the way up to the tent and the whole thing shook. I got back out of the tent. I was delusional but not in the mood to just holler in a haunted forest. I was afraid to speak, but I was mad. Mad in the worst way. Impatient with the answers the world was giving me. One of the hardest things about being human is hearing the answers we don't want to accept or believe.

I couldn't fall back asleep and I started walking around three o' clock, losing two hats mysteriously in the dark. Once I got out, I just went along the road, and put my thumb up for anything that was passing that wasn't a cop.

"Where you going?" A greying man in an old Cadillac pulled up around five.

"Anywhere but here. New York?" I shrugged.

I don't really know where the hell he took me, I almost nodded off. He was a creepy fellow himself. He kept going on about how depressed he was, and how he wanted to commit suicide because his secretary had embezzled him and cost him his marriage and his business.

I just recycled the motions once I got on the trail. Walk, Walk, Walk. People should spend a lot more time in nature than they do, at least the parts that aren't haunted. It does all blend together just a little bit, but nature is such a unifying energy which leaves us basically breathless the entire time. I walked along and saw lone men in the early dawn seeping through as the sun came up. One looked like he was literally running the AT, another man was with his daughter.

I ate lunch by a stream, and accidently got turned around because of how similar everything looked. I saw a blond-haired gentleman walking with a limp and a walking stick.

"Is this North?" I asked.

"No."

"I knew it."

"Hello. I am Obi Wan Kenobi." He extended his hand.

"Nice to meet you Obi Wan, shall we walk?"

"Sure, I've only been out here about two weeks, so I haven't gotten my hiking legs yet," he said.

"What happened to your foot?" I pointed out that it was wrapped.

"Fungus."

"That's how Bob Marley died." I said.

"I don't think this is chronic or contagious."

"Why'd you come out here?"

“I’m actually trying to catch up with a friend from my childhood. He said he would wait for me before the Mason Dixon Line, at an upcoming park. You can come if you like. Are you good on water?” he asked.

“I just filled up.”

We arrived at one of the most American looking parks I’d ever seen. There were hundreds of benches along it, with multiple outdoor picnic areas for family gatherings. As we walked along it, it revealed a glorious view with a bright flag flying high.

“This is Young Giraffe, and Flannel,” Obi Wan introduced.

“Nice to meet you guys. I’m Cheerio.”

Both of them were somewhat scruffy. Young Giraffe’s beard wasn’t as filled in but he was taller.

“Should we get going? There is a Chinese buffet at the next town,” Flannel said.

My wallet blushed.

“I’m down,” I was just trying to move forward more than anything. Company was good, but I wasn’t invested. We all stopped for pictures at the Mason Dixon line though.

“Well, Southern hospitality is supposedly dead from this point on,” Young Giraffe said, smiling.

“They say that’s why there is less trail magic in the North,” Flannel agreed.

“How far is town?” I asked.

“Two miles,” Obi-Wan responded.

“Are we gonna walk or hitch?” I asked.

“I’m gonna wait for a ride.” Obi-Wan sat down.

We all lingered off to the side of a road for about a half hour just competing with each other. The real way men get to know one another. None of us really had any upper hand by the end of it.

“We might as well just start walking and if someone's coming, they’ll take us in to town.” I said.

“It’s more likely that they will stop if we are stopped, plus Obi Wan’s limp,” Flannel said.

“No don’t put this on me, I’m fine to walk,” Obi-wan said, getting up.

“Might as well.” Young Giraffe said.

I tried to fix my posture to lead as we walked so that they didn't feel like they were missing out on just sitting there for a ride that probably wouldn't have come for another hour.

"You wanna just ask someone if they'll give us a lift?" I asked.

"If you're offering," Flannel said.

I saw a woman working on her garden and blindly walked across the street. A giant pickup truck slammed on its brakes about a foot away from me, but I just kept walking to the woman as if I was expecting to have gotten hit.

"Hello," I waved to the nice woman.

"Cheerio!" Flannel ran across the street. "You were almost roadkill."

I looked back, "I suppose that was lucky. Hello, we are all young men hiking the Appalachian Trail and I was just wondering if you'd be able to stuff us four into your car and take us to town."

"Of course." The woman dropped her trowel. "What are all of your names?"

Slightly surprised, I replied. "I'm Cheerio and this is Flannel. Young Giraffe and Obi wan Kenobi are across the street."

"I helped a young woman get to town a few months ago. She actually stayed the night." She smiled.

"Really. Well, I'd be more than happy to help you with your garden for a place to stay for the night." I said, trying to save as much money as I could.

"I would, the only thing is my husband has surgery in the morning, but I'd be more than glad to give you all a ride."

"Are you sure? We all smell pretty ripe," Flannel chimed in.

"I've been in the garden all day, it's no problem."

She went into the house to grab her keys and her husband investigated the situation. He was kind, as good as a Southern gentleman, no better no worse. Young Giraffe made good talk with him, and we all were getting along like the relatives of this country we were.

"Cheerio take my number if you all need a ride

back," The woman's husband said.

"I think we might all split a hotel, Cheerio you are more than welcome to join," Young Giraffe offered.

"I don't know if I have money like that to spend."

"I think it's only seventy dollars, split four ways." Flannel explained.

"Five ways. Pear is gonna meet us at the hotel." Young Giraffe said.

"Sounds good, but I'll still take your number just in case."

We all stuffed in and I thought about Bad Wolves' car and wherever the hell on the trail he was.

"Are you sure you don't want me go to Walmart first?" the lady asked.

"We will go there later for resupply," Obi Wan said.

The hotel wasn't too shabby, but just your run of the mill hotel. We waited outside for thirty minutes and a genuine looking chap in a green shirt arrived.

"Hey guys."

"Pear." They all seemed happy.

"So, are we going to split this? Oh, hello, I'm Pear." He looked at me.

"Cheerio."

"Are you going to be joining?"

I was hesitant.

"It's literally like twenty bucks man," Flannel compromised.

"Yeah, I'm in. I could use a good rest up." In reality I was just getting comfortable on the road.

"Alright, maybe we shouldn't all go in at once."

"You go in and pay," Young Giraffe said to Pear.

We each handed Pear twenty dollars give or take. He went in and came out with a room card. "We're good."

We all grabbed our bags and headed upstairs. There were two master beds.

"We will pick straws for who sleeps on the floor later. Right now, I need a shower. We all do." Pear said.

We flipped on the television and one by one we all hopped in the shower and by the end of it, that room stunk and had mud all over it. Pear had some really good trail mix that he gave me. It was full of grains and seeds with dried apricots and cranberries, which reminded me of Paris' kitchen. Once we all spruced up and changed, we all grabbed our wallets and headed for the buffet.

The restaurant was a dream come true. It was a hidden gem Chinese restaurant. Every kind of fried meat in the world and I not only tried every single one, I got seconds, and thirds. We were competing for who could eat the most. I think we each shared five plates minimum, plus ice cream dessert. We talked about Tarantino films, *Stranger Things,* Stephen King. All the things I wanted to be talking about. We made jokes that cannot be captured. And compared all our beards, which Obi Wan had us all beat.

Pear was a writer. In writing, there is no need to be competitive with anyone (besides yourself) since no matter what, no two writers can say the same thing. Like the books they write, each individual writer belongs to a different genre, vocabulary and integrity. He'd written a novel, but a historical one about the Roman Empire. I was very interested until I started reading it. The last thing I will say about writing is that whenever you get a good idea, and you procrastinate on it, someone else will do it better.

We wobbled out of the restaurant and split up since Obi Wan had to go to Walmart for his fungus. I went with him since I didn't have anything better to do. I just looked at the vastness of Walmart and walked around a few paces behind. He went to the pharmaceutical section, which is always pleasant. I could never imagine all the problems that can go wrong with us. On the walk back to the hotel he revealed that he wasn't going to be able to keep up with all of us because of his foot. I felt sort of bad, because you could tell that he wanted to.

We lounged in the hotel room for a few hours after that. All of us were sprawled out on the beds and Obi Wan was soaking his foot. We were basically snoozing after our feast. Jeopardy was on, and Flannel challenged us all to see who could get the most answers. I'm not bad at these games, I just know what I know, and I don't really know much else.

Flannel knew all this very specific information about wars and scientists who'd discovered things. It turned out he was a big fan of the show and tried to never miss it if he could. I think the reason he knew so much was because he had been told all the answers before on the reruns. The answers to our problems are not always found out the same way.

After that some comic show came on, and it was about these four comedians based in New York. I watched as they terrorized the city and how the city terrorized them right back. One of their games was to see if they could get a hug from someone on the street. One of the comedians tried and literally a man just quietly responded, "Get the fuck away from me."

I laughed, because that will probably be me someday and nobody will want to give me a hug.

It felt so good to laugh. We all had our little inside jokes with each other. By that point it was time take a dip in the pool. The joy of feeling weightless as I plummeted to the bottom of the water was calming. I repeatedly kept jumping into the pool trying to make bigger waves than the next and pretty soon we were all doing it.

The hot tub really soaked in all the muscles I had been overusing, and I took the time to go back and forth between the cool and hot to sooth my bones. Whenever I get too comfortable with anyone or anything for that matter, I am prone to act out just a little bit. I'm not always aware of it, but this was one of those times I realized I was getting a little too comfortable.

We all were, we talked about our lives, who we were. The consensus was that if we were going to stick together, which was very unlikely, we were going to be moving fast. The instinctual Aries pissed the pool, and I thought about how far ahead of them I could probably get if I booked it. Then again, I didn't have my hiker legs either really. I could realistically do twenty every day, which I could not have done at the beginning of this journey.

Pear had actually started dating a girl that he met on the trail. When he pulled up her Instagram, I understood why he said he'd fallen in love with her. I'm not saying she was gorgeous, but whenever someone is in love with someone else, it's like you can look at them from all sides and see why everyone deserves to be loved so much. She apparently had gotten sick and was going to try and catch up in a few weeks.

It was dark by the time we got out, and Flannel brought up the interest of smoking some weed. I had a little bit. I swore all of it off and had to remind myself that drugs hurt. They do. It's in their healing nature. I don't see any problem with drugs or alcohol as long as I don't harm anyone but hurting myself is another story.

Back in the room I rolled two spliffs and there was one last run to Walmart for the night, so I went along.

"You smoke?" I asked Young Giraffe.

"No, it makes me paranoid."

"Understandable."

"I sure like it," Flannel chimed in.

"Me too," I said sharing the mixed spices.

Some other hikers recognized Flannel and Young Giraffe. A young couple, that was on the verge of marriage if I ever saw one. They partook. This time we entered Walmart like a band of thieves. These guys were about to buy all they needed for probably the next week. I was already set. We all separated, and I've been to a million Walmarts, and they are all the same, but I've never been bored in one.

I got lost in the arts and crafts section just thinking about all that could be created. Young Giraffe got all of his things and let me know that Flannel had gone back to the room.

"Bummer, I rolled two. One for the walk back." After we left, I reached into my pocket and the other spliff was gone.

"Or, I thought I did..." I kept looking but it was nowhere to be found. "Oh well. So why are you out here?" I asked Young Giraffe.

"My dad is sick," he said, solemnly.

"I would say I'm sorry, but that would imply that he isn't going to get better."

"Well, at least he isn't getting any worse. He is on

bedrest and he is sort of living his life vicariously through me. If that makes sense?"

"Of course, that's incredible. You are living your whole life *for* someone else, that's very noble," I said.

"I just hope it makes him happy."

"What were you likc in high school?"

"I cared a lot about sports."

"Ha. How was that?"

"It sucked."

"Really?" I was unsurprised.

"Not really." He seemed like he was being forced to say what he thought.

"What did you play?"

"Basketball."

"Were you any good?"

"Yeah, I was pretty good. I just didn't like the politics of it."

"What? Everybody sleeping with the same girl?" I poked.

"Haha, no. There was just this one kid who was really good, and he always got priority."

"Like they would always put him in games?" I asked.

"Yeah, and he got special clothing and it was just because his dad was friends with the coach, and he would give the team a lot of money, so it was always about him."

"Yeah, see, I hung out with stoners," I said and then caught myself. "Some of them were pretty bad actually. Social politics exists in every circle. Was he mean?"

"No, but he definitely saw himself above everyone."

"Relatable." I didn't want to relate. "And you left after high school to do the AT?"

"I went to college for a semester, but that was worse than high school."

"Tell me about it."

"Are you in college?" He asked.

"Currently, yes, I go to college, which is a rarer thing out here than I expected."

"It just-"

"Wasn't for you?" I finished his thought.

"It's not that it's not for me, I just like people out here a lot more."

"I respect that."

"Even though I played ball, I never really was like any of those kids and by the end I just started to resent it all." He said.

"I played one sport in high school and it was to impress a girl. " My face turned red. "God I was so awful."

"I'm sure you weren't that bad."

"No, literally, I once was in a game, and I threw the ball to her from the field and she was in the bleachers and wasn't even looking and it gave her a bloody nose."

"Haha, I'm sure it wasn't that bad."

I don't know what the hell I was doing in high school thinking I could play a sport, be in a play and take up smoking to look cooler all at once, but I would get up at five am and listen to Bright Eyes in the dead of winter before anyone was up and leave school at around seven at night. I was such an asshole. To everyone.

"Trust me, it was that bad."

Chapter 36

The rest of the night was spent deciding who was going to sleep on the floor. None of us really cared, a hotel floor was cozier than the dirt. I came up with a system that we would all play rock paper scissors, but whoever won the tournament would spend the night on the floor. Young Giraffe won so he slept on the floor. I stepped outside before everyone shut their eyes with a few loose cigarettes I had held onto. I was hoping that the woman who was working the desk would come out and join me. She did. I tried my hardest to just talk with her. I didn't want anything from anyone, I just needed a place to sit.

"You know. I wouldn't mind just staying right here," I said.

"What do you mean?"

"I mean this place has everything that I'd ever want. A nice play to sleep, Walmart right next door."

"I'm sure you want more than that."

"Sure I do, but I don't need anything else. No one does."

"I thought all you need is love." She answered.

"Do you have that?"

"No. No one does. Love isn't something you have, it's something you give."

"I just wonder if I'll ever see a place and think to myself, this it is. I'm home. I've found it."

"Looks like you have." She said sarcastically.

She was done with her job for the night and talking with me probably felt like overtime. I climbed into bed next to Pear all rusty from stale cigarette smoke and a new day arrived. Nobody on the trail sleeps in. Especially when there is free breakfast at stake. We had all eaten and by ten were discussing our next move.

"They have a bowling alley here!" Obi-Wan said excited.

The thought of bowling crossed my mind for a millisecond only because of how much fun I'd been having.

"It opens at noon and then we could always stay another night," Young Giraffe said appealing to Obi-Wan since he wanted to stick around with his childhood friend.

"I think I might hit the trail, guys. Get a head start in. I'll probably see you all up the ways." I finished breakfast.

There was mutual understanding in the room, and when one hiker is ready to leave, more are bound to follow. I hugged them all, hoping it wouldn't be the last time I saw them, and headed to Walmart where apparently you could easily hitch a ride back to the trail. I stood in the parking lot looking a little lost for about five minutes before someone came to the rescue.

A tall woman who was pushing a cart full of groceries was coming out of the store.

"Hey there." She smiled. "Need a ride?"

"I do need a ride actually," I smiled back.

"Which way are you heading?"

"North."

"Follow me."

She unloaded everything and I put away the shopping cart and threw my pack in the back.

"What's your name?" I asked her.

"Beth."

"Oh really? Are you married?"

"I spoil my husband." She answered grinning.

"Do you? Sounds lovely." The world could be so small and simple.

I got along just fine with Beth. I enjoyed her company. She'd tell a story and I'd talked about my music. We didn't have to talk, but when we did we would laugh a bit. She played some of my songs. She made me feel proud to be who I was.

"I've got to be honest with you."

"What?"

"I know I've only known you fifteen minutes, but I think I'm in love with you. No." I shook my head and she giggled. "Nothing." I laughed.

"C'mon now you can't do that."

"What? Why not? I don't know, it's not important, I

just don't think my old friend likes me anymore. You just have the same name as her." I said.

"Well, it's her loss."

"No, it's not."

"It's a little more complicated than that." She raised her eyebrow. "Were you two romantic?"

"Basically, just not really."

"It wouldn't matter." She shrugged. "I mean it would. But it doesn't."

"We grew up together. I still see so much of her in myself."

"Is that bad?"

"No, it isn't, but it probably scares her. I want to make sure I know who I am, or she knows who she is, or at least she knows who I am before we get to the bottom of this." I said.

She parked up where the trail began and hugged me goodbye.

My head was filled with dopamine and the bright morning made the day look promising. High in the woods, nothing like it. For some reason I kept getting the urge to go off trail, but it wasn't until I didn't know where to go that I actually ended up off of it. It was extremely daunting to not be following the trail and I kept telling myself that it was still early in the morning, so I could always find my way back if I needed to. I just used my compass and followed it North. I went through some very strange building structures. Huge mammoth buildings and hundreds of cars parked outside of them. Not just big buildings, they looked like modern castles almost, like a lab where research was being done, and great thinkers came in and out of. It was obviously some private property I was cutting through. Next, I came to a particularly Philadelphian old-style mental institution.

The structure was ominous, and I didn't want to go anywhere near it. I didn't want my past brushing up against it. Nightmares. I kept along the road, and sure enough, there was a post office no bigger than a bunk bed and a little town attached to it. As I looked from the outskirts, there was one building in the middle of the little town, which strangely stood out. I walked up to one of the doors and an Asian man in a kitchen was standing there started yelling at me.

"Use the other door!" He shut it immediately. I walked around the front and walked into the dim lit bar. It looked like a bar, but not a bar I'd ever seen before. It was like a coven for witches and dark outcasts.

"Who are you? Are you a hiker?" The guy from the kitchen asked me came to the front.

"Yeah, I'm sort of a hybrid."

"You look like a hiker to me. Put your bag down."

Behind him was a sign that read FAT TIRE.

"What do you want?" he asked.

"Do you have New Belgium Fat Tire?"

"Yeah, we do, you want a Fat Tire?"

"Sure."

"No problem."

The thing is, when a man walks into a bar with everything he owns on his back, you give that man a beer.

"Which way you heading?" he asked.

"North. I'm trying to make it to New York."

"Good route. What's your trail name?"

"Samurai Jack." I said, slyly putting the beer down on the bar. "Can I smoke in here?"

"Sure," he said, handing me an ashtray, and I lit up. I felt cool. I'd drunk at bars before, but I've never walked into one and ordered a beer, not to mention gotten to smoke. I wondered if my beard was beginning to make me look older.

"Just promise me that you'll sign this." He pulled out a big booklet. "It's all the hikers who have been through here."

"Do a lot come through?" I asked.

"A good handful. Someone also left this map, I don't know if it's any help to you, but you can take a look if you want."

"Thanks. How far are we from the trail now?" I asked.

"If you just follow that road and turn at the post office you can get back on."

"Hmm." I sipped my beer.

I don't remember how but we started talking about college, but I played it off as though I had graduated already.

"Used to do a lot of drinking back in those days, I'm sure you did too," I laughed.

"The good ol' days," he reminisced a little suspiciously.

He also gave me a little history lesson of the hotel. He apparently inherited it from his parents and runs the place now. Not too shabby. I was a little drunk and I used the bathroom and felt guilty about taking water from the sink. I don't know why. I gathered up some sense of a plan, bought a pack of cigarettes and walked back out into the open world.

Looking at the map, it seemed that if I went along a byway, I could make it into the next trail town and get back on there. It was an 8 mile stretch alongside racing cars but sure enough, I made it to where I needed to be, which was not where I wanted to go, but just somewhere to get me to the next place I was supposed to be. I sat down at some 50's looking diner outside at a picnic table and made a peanut butter and jelly tortilla, stuffed with the trail mix Pear gave me. Once I was full, I thought I might as well keep walking. As I left, a peculiar looking man with a grand ol' mustache arrived. It was good to see hikers to remind me that I wasn't crazy.

It was pretty brutal while climbing uphill. A woman stopped me.

"Are you a thru hiker?"

"Pretty much," I shrugged.

"Not with all that weight." She shook her head smiling.

"You get used to it," I shrugged.

"If you could, I'd let go of some of it."

"I've let go of a good deal, I don't even have a pillow."

"I hope you make it." We walked away.

The sun was beginning to set, and I didn't know where the next shelter was going to be, so I started to get a little tense. Of course I could pitch a tent, but jeez. I was really feeling the pain of endless walking. It had been over a twenty-mile day. Sure enough I came up to a nice shelter. One of the nicest I'd seen. There were two separate rooms for hikers, both pretty big. There were solid flat foundations where people could perch their tents up on and the shelter was surrounded by rhododendron. There were people, but I was too exhausted to talk.

I rolled out my sleeping pad and just listened for a good hour or two. This guy was pulling this poor woman's ear off all in the name of manhood. I was initially very turned off by him. The woman was a Park Ranger, or something along those lines. She went from shelter to shelter to make sure everything was in order. I just wanted to eat and go to bed. When I woke up, I started building a fire, and once I got some food in me, I started to feel a little better and made light conversation with them. She'd apparently done the whole AT the year before, and this was her way of giving back. He was a veteran of some sort, and bragged about how courageous he was, but had to get back to the wife since she only lets him out for a month at a time.

Flannel and Pear showed up next.

"Cheerio!"

"What's up guys?"

"Damn you must've been booking it." They said.

"I took a scenic route." I said under my breath. "Glad to see you guys, are Obi Wan and Young Giraffe behind you?"

"Yeah, they are a ways back. Young Giraffe wanted to spend some time with Obi Wan before they parted ways."

"I feel that."

The vet apparently had some hash and the Park Ranger didn't really mind but told us to be wary of nearby families. Young Giraffe arrived with a big smile since we had been reunited, and it became apparent that the chamber I had slept in was going to get a little bit cozier. In the morning, I watched the Park Ranger leave at five, and was grateful to sleep for a few more hours. Apparently, we all were grateful, because we didn't get up until ten.

We all had a relaxed breakfast that was supplied by the vet. Instant eggs, so I was filled up and ready to get some miles in hopefully. I wondered if I was going to be able to keep up with these guys. They'd been on the trail since Georgia, so if I was going to move with them, I was going to have to go quick.

Honestly, the one of us with the longest legs was the slowest. I don't think there is anything wrong with that. It is important to slow down and look at your surroundings. We kept a solid pace but when the pastures opened up, we all stopped and looked and rejoiced together. None of us were afraid to be weird around each other. At one point, Flannel, Pear and I got far enough ahead of Young Giraffe that we staged an ambush. We all hid and fought to the death.

By lunch we started to formulate a little bigger of a plan, a few days' worth of hiking that we could do together, and all stay together. Twenty-five-mile days minimum. I was up for the challenge. I think I was trying to just not be the runt of the pack, and I don't think I was. When I was with these mates, I forgot a lot about life. I forgot about all the reasons I was out there, and I wasn't looking forward to anything.

Still, girls came up in our conversation. Flannel was apparently going to stay with a girl from his college over the upcoming weekend. Pear was still worried about his sick girlfriend he'd met from the trail, and I just treaded lightly on the subject of my own romance. I think they could all tell I was hurting pretty bad. On that day, we crossed past the halfway point of the Appalachian Trail 1,050 miles. We stopped for pictures. I didn't really feel any reason to be in any of them, but I was anyway.

Another group of hikers stopped to take pictures at the halfway mark. They were wild. Well, one of them was crazy. You could tell he was a little sex deprived or something. He took his ass out for the pictures. The man with the extremely wonderful mustache at the last town was with that troop too, and as our group of four started to feel like eight. Mustacho Manny introduced himself and was the first to make sure we weren't lingering, so we all walked together.

As I said, I knew I was going to have to work to keep up with them. We were about fifteen miles deep and had six more to go. When you are tired, six miles can feel like an extremely long distance. It was beautiful though. Music helped. Some parts were tropical, other parts almost residential. A man called out from his porch.

"You're two weeks ahead of schedule!" He called to us.

There was too much pride and testosterone for us all to not cheer back at the man in excitement. I thought we were done once we came across a road, but there was still another mile walk into the campsite. The place reminded me of some rich suburban country club. Apparently, there was a challenge to eat a half gallon of ice cream and these men wasted no time buying a half gallon of ice cream each. I was not about to be the only one who didn't get one. Everybody got chocolate, and Neapolitan, but for some reason I went for banana marshmallow.

I don't know, I was craving all sorts of weird foods. They started the timer, and everyone began to dig in as fast as they could. Not me. I know for a fact I can perfectly consume a pint of ice cream, so a half gallon was pretty much out of the question.

Ten, fifteen, twenty minutes passed, and everybody was slowing his roll besides Mustacho. He finished the first quart of ice cream in about 25 minutes, followed by Young Giraffe at thirty. I made some impressive headway, but I began to feel like I had a rock in my stomach and was shoving a handful of peanut butter into my mouth.

"And Done. Forty-one minutes. Half Gallon Challenge Mustacho Manny style."

He looked so proud and fun. "That last spoonful was brutal." He said.

More than half of us realized we were not going to be finishing the half gallon challenge. Young Giraffe followed next and that was it. Nobody else finished. Nothing like a group of grown men competing to eat a half gallon of ice cream to make you feel like a bitch. If I ever eat banana marshmallow ice cream again it will be too soon. I decided to order an enchilada afterwards though and ended up having more of my ice cream for dessert. It didn't make things any worse, but it certainly didn't make it any better.

For some reason after that everyone thought it would be a great idea to go swimming. We all picked up our things and headed over to a small beach that was near a campsite. It was a very public area, so we all hid our packs behind the bathroom structure. The extreme tiredness of walking over twenty miles hadn't worn off and I was not very talkative in the group. The water in the lake was butt-ass cold, but once you get your head under everything just goes numb and you forget about it.

"I'd love to swim across this whole pond," I said to Mustached Manny.

"Oh yeah. Why don't you?" he smiled back.

"I don't really see a reason why not." I walked over to the rope that was separating the swimming section and began to head right into the center of the murky water. When I was past the middle of the very wide pond, I saw a strange looking head poking out of the surface of the water. It was a snake slithering across the top of the lake coming right at me. I literally forced every single muscle in my body with as much force as I could against that pond and was on the shore in 10 seconds or less.

"Well, that's enough of the beach for me," I said to him who was sprawled out on a towel.

"I think they have warm showers here," he said like he was trying to excite me back up.

"Yeah, that's where I'm going." I said out of breath.

Ugh, showers, the real grace of god. There was already shampoo in the stall and I took a good hour to myself in there, receiving as much natural dopamine that my body would give me. I went around the back of the bathroom building wearing nothing but a towel, got into some more comfortable attire, and once I was in long pants and a sweater, I lit up a cigarette.

Mustached Manny was sitting there, freshly showered as well.

“Hey man, you mind if I bum one?” he asked, “I’ll give you whatever is left of this beer.”

“It’s alright, you can have one, not really a fan of PBR.” I responded.

“Ah c’mon man.”

“Alright, it’s not that bad.” I took a generous chug.

“Is this your first thru hike?” he asked me.

“Sort of. I kinda just finished finals, got a backpack and decided to head out to New York.”

“New York eh? I’m just a hiker, but I lived out in New York for nine years as a chef.”

“You didn’t want to stay?”

“No. I just didn’t need to be there. That’s when I started to do all of this. I hiked the Pacific Coast Trail last year.”

“Impressive.”

“Not really.” He was humble for how enticing he was.

“No, really. Incredible. Doing this takes a shit load of discipline. I’m not very good at it.”

“We’re all learning. So, what, you got any money? You thinking about staying in the city?” he asked.

“Brooklyn if anything. I have about a hundred dollars right now, but technically I have enough to start over if I can get to it.”

“Alright.”

“How much would you suggest for someone who might be looking to stay out there.” I asked.

“Eh, you could probably get a long way with around 800.”

“Do you have 700 dollars to spare?”

“Ha, next time.” He finished his beer.

The troop came through with the crazy one from the other party talking loudly, taking control of everyone’s attention.

“I think I’m going to go 40 miles tomorrow!” He yelled.

“You better get some sleep,” Manny said instinctively.

“Not if I leave at 2 am.” He called back.

"Then you really better get some sleep." Manny responded.

"Well, we're not supposed to camp here," he retorted.

"We can *stealth* camp." Manny said, unperturbed.

"Obviously." He said.

"Let me know where you guys are gonna stealth camp," I said.

"Will do, Cheerio."

Stealth camping is where you camp near the bushes or wherever you won't be found and leave early enough in the morning so nobody sees you. Around the front of the bathroom Flannel and Pear and another bearded man were all talking about their own personal rigorous amounts of hiking.

"Yeah, we were doing something like a hundred twenty miles a week," the bearded man explained. "Not anymore. I just wanted to get here as soon as I could so I could be with my wife."

"You're married?" I asked him.

"Yes. We actually live in Spain." I could see the realm of being in love that was within him.

"I've been gone for about two months now, so I can take this last one easy since we're this far. Probably only do around sixty."

"I mean just sixty miles in itself is a very long distance," I reasoned.

"Oh, you're telling me man. We were in this bar. And we were talking about how we were heading to Maine and this guy looked up and was like, 'To Maine, like, *Canada* Maine?' and we were like, 'Yes.' He couldn't believe it. He just was hysterical."

We all laughed, but I was still a little distant from the long day. I just walked around the grounds getting ready for bed and by now it had gotten dark so I knew I should be on the lookout for where everybody was going to stealth camp. Young Giraffe was talking to some hipster-looking cat and looked intrigued. I don't know what they were talking about before I walked up, but the guy introduced himself.

“Are you a thru hiker as well?” the mysterious guy asked me.

“Pretty much,” I responded.

“Yo, I gotta question. Do people smoke weed on the trail?” he asked.

“They sure do.” I exhaled.

“Do you think it would be hard to sell along the AT?”

I shook my head. “Good sir, there is no place in this country more distant from the ties of the law than on that trail.” I answered.

“Nice man. Yeah, I was just thinking it might be a cool thing to do. Get in my car, camp along it, drive to hikers who are up ahead and need some bud.”

“Yeah, that’s not bad.” I shrugged.

“I recently just got divorced.” He looked at the girl he was with. “So, I’m just looking for a good culture of people man, and I think you guys might be it.”

“You wouldn’t be wrong.

“Be good to one another man,” he said

He gave us hugs since you could tell he needed it and then I looked at Young Giraffe, like “stealth camp?” Young Giraffe and I went around the back of the bathroom where our bags were and carried them to the designated spot where we were all sleeping for the night. Flannel was on a park bench and to be honest I was too tired to pitch a tent so I just got on a different picnic table and wrapped my little blanket around me as tight as I could. I was fearful that I wasn’t going to get up early enough with them. I had been texting my cousin about plans to visit her since where she lived went right past the AT in Pennsylvania, so I thought it would be a good idea to see her. I also wanted to see if I could make it to church.

Chapter 37

Stealth camping does not make for a good night's sleep. I was watching Flannel and in one second he was sleeping and the next he was ready to go. It wasn't even five o' clock. Luckily, I didn't have to break down my tent, so I was up and out pretty quickly. We all congregated by the bathroom where there was an overhead light. I opened up a fresh pack of Ramen and started to crunch on it.

"If the madman starts now, leaves at five and goes at a three mile an hour pace, no breaks, he will get there by nine o'clock tonight." Mustacho Manny said.

Godspeed for that wild animal.

They were all glorifying major hiking days, but none of them were in any rush to get a move on themselves it seemed like. I took the initiative. I didn't know where Young Giraffe and Pear were, so I said goodbye to Manny and Flannel and started making headway. The best time to hike is before the sunrise. I was trying to get a move on, but even after two hours of peace in the morning, it was only seven o' clock. I might just make it to church after all. Around the third hour Manny caught up to me and we talked for a little. I explained that I was just trying to *get* to New York rather than hike the whole way.

With that in mind, I took the first major-looking road off the trail, to see if I could get closer to Hershey. It was so early in the morning I wasn't worried. Days felt longer than you can even imagine. Every hour counted and you had to make every minute count. The wooded road opened up a little bit and soon I was along a railroad track. I didn't want my cousin Leslee to go too far out of her way to come get me, but I was about 20 miles away.

I just kept my head held high and had that thumb up. Many cars passed, but when they did, I felt even more alive, free. I didn't need any handout, I could have gotten anywhere I wanted. Gone 40 miles on foot. It just would have taken a lot of time so when a nice homely woman opened up her car door for me, I got in.

Her car had old neglected leather seats and a few broken wine glasses in the back.

"Where you trying to get to?"

"Hershey"

"I can't take you that far, but there is a Menard's which is about halfway."

"That'll do."

This woman reminded me of a lot of people. I have no idea how old her soul was, but it could have been a newborn or really really old. Her life story was interesting, but a tad condescending. She apparently worked for NASA. I thanked her for the lift, but I still had a few more miles if I was going to make it to Hershey. I called Les to let her know the situation. I was about ten miles away or something like that, not too bad. I told her that I was going to see if I could catch a service before we got together, and she said she would pick me up from the church if I found one that was having a sermon.

The sun was up by now, and I walked along a wide road with cars zooming by. I crossed the road, which seemed to make the sidewalk smaller and rush closer. Outside of a small condominium a well-dressed family posed with the grace of god.

"Are y'all going to church?" I asked in my musk.

The gentleman was helping his elder mother into the black vehicle. "Yes? You want to come?"

"If you would be so kind, I do." I hopped in the middle seat and my backpack fit in the trunk.

Ok, well I've been to a lot of churches in my day but this one was quite the one to see. The whole place had a big grand red carpet that lead up to the podium. Everyone was very elitist. It was communion so everyone was doubling down with red. It was by no means a bad church, a little phony, I wasn't completely spiritually engaged, but they got the message across. Blood of Christ, welts and cuts, the more it hurts the more god loves you. I ate the bread, but they made me feel undeserving of the blood. When it ended, I went out to the parking lot where my cousin was parked up. She got out of the car when she saw me and gave me a big hug.

"How are you?!" She said excited.

"I'm so happy to see you!" I said.

"What's this about you hiking the AT?"

"I'll tell you more about it in the car." I let go of her.

"You can put your backpack in the back."

I opened the car door up and stuffed it in and sat in the front.

"How was church?" she asked.

"It was alright. I suppose." It was not my kind of church.

"I want to hear all about what you're doing."

"I just decided that it was time to travel, I suppose."

"Ok, I understand that."

"It was just time."

"Did it have to do with school?" She asked.

"A little bit. Just that whole culture of college sometimes makes me feel a little bit worthless, but I do have friends, if that's what you're asking."

"Yeah, undergrad can be rough."

"Well, you know then. It just makes me feel a little claustrophobic. I just had to walk away, or at least feel like I was letting all that nonsense go for a while."

"Do you think you'll go back?"

"I don't know yet."

"How many years have you done?"

"Two. What about you? How much longer are you gonna be in med-school?"

"Forever," she said honestly but then corrected herself, "I have two years left, and then I can start residency."

"Is it hard?" I asked.

She took a deep breath. "It's what I signed up for." I've always felt like she and I have had a mutual understanding or respect for rigor, which stands out from most of my family.

"But I want to hear about your trip! What has been the craziest thing you have seen so far?"

I thought for a moment, but nothing came to mind, I had been through hell and my head felt like it had been smashed against pavement. "I dunno." I thought longer.

"I saw a weird veteran who was sort of an asshole, a little bit like your dad."

"Ok. Well, when did you start?"

"Um, I think almost four weeks ago."

"And how have you gotten food?"

"Well, I've lost a lot of weight, it hasn't been easy, but people have been kind. I stayed with a Special Ops agent in D.C. That was bizarre."

"So, people have just been giving to you?" she asked.

"The way I see it is, you know how it is in college? Everybody sort of competes with each other, not directly, but just with that sort of swing to things."

"Yeah." She understood.

"Well, when you have nothing. When you're not a part of that world, people are much more willing to help people who they see have less than them. They don't see them as a threat."

"Interesting."

"It really is. There has been a lot of deep thought throughout this journey."

"Like what else?"

"We will talk about it over lunch, but damn this place is incredible." I looked out the window.

Hershey looked like Miami after it had sunken under the ocean and was recovered. There were tall condominiums that reached high which overlooked, if I remember correctly, a lake. It was classic deep green and blue mixed to make the still rising sun complement the city.

"I really don't want to be a bother, but it would be nice to come inside and maybe just, ya know sit on a couch or something." I said when we parked up.

"I can imagine you're tired." You could tell she had to think about letting me in a little. It's not that she didn't trust me, though she may have had a reason not to, just collegiate roommate politics.

"We can see. My roommates are a little iffy, and I don't want to just barge in and say my cousin is visiting."

That was exactly what we did. We got onto a crowded street with small apartments that looked straight out of the seventies. I assume many old couples came there to die peacefully. Her house was what you would expect of a med student. It was almost overbearing how comfortable it was, but it was worn. I was in Pennsylvania now, and I never had been before. Everything was delicate, yet you felt like you could touch it or move it all around. There were open windows, little pictures, and other details, which indicated that people who were probably very good at math lived there. The couch was sunken into by my cousin's roommate knitting to occupy her time.

Their conversations were very interesting. They would go on about a patient they had or sick children with worried mothers.

"This one woman has come back three times with her baby, just because it has a little bit of a fever. I told her exactly what it was, but she definitely has the newborn sickness." Her roommate said.

I tried to be as inconspicuous as I could. I was already a slight intruder in the house, but still, I knew I was at home. I checked my phone and was sad to still see no response from Paris, so I took this time to text some of my mates on the trail. Pear said that he was at a bar and headed on to that resort, which looked like a nice place. It sounded wonderful and I felt a strange longing to go back to them, like I knew something more was happening with the world there, but I had places to be and was about twenty miles ahead of them.

We didn't stay long the first visit. I left my bag in the car. I did get a tour though. I think three girls were staying there and one was just married to a military man. Each of them had their own rooms. Les was on the top floor. I even saw the basement, which was a little spooky. I offered to sleep down there if it was a place to stay. Leslee said we could talk about it after lunch.

Just down the road we went to an art space that doubled as a restaurant. First off, I was overcome by the glorious art in the room. Usually these places are the ones to go to for good big canvas wall art. There were works of colorful women, Bob Marley and Pop-Art. I was still a little power drunk from being offered that beer a few days back, so when the woman behind the counter asked me if I would like anything to drink the first thing I did was eye the bar.

I do not smoke in front of my cousin, and I certainly was not about to push my luck ordering anything underage.

"Have anything you'd like." She looked at me.

I was looking at everything but a good ol' fashioned black bean burger with onion rings was what was going to hit the spot. We sat outside, and I watched other couples and wondered how below par I was societally. It didn't really matter since what is best about family is they accept you no matter what, and that was what I needed for what I was about to bring up.

Food relaxes us. I think when you are going to have an important discussion, having it over food never hurts, at least then something is enjoyable. When we sat down, she wanted me to explain as much as I could about the journey. I told her all the facts, people and places I'd been. The festival, hiker culture, and Washington D.C. I finally started to inch towards what was on my mind.

"So, are you dating anyone?" I asked.

"His name is Danny."

"Oh. How did you guys meet?"

"It's actually a funny story. Sort of embarrassing, but all of my friends told me that I should get this dating app and I did not want to, so one of my friends downloaded it for me, and the next day I came across Danny. And the next day we went out."

"What does he do?"

"He works at an animal shelter. He's really good with animals and is going to school to become a veterinarian."

"Respectable." I said.

"What about you? I remember there was that one girl?"

"Oh, yeah."

"Yeah, did anything ever happen with that?"

"Still working on it, sort of, not really."

"Why not?"

"I'm pretty sure she hates me. I once accidently

posted that I was in love with her, when I'm pretty sure she had a boyfriend. I just came to the conclusion that it would be best to give her as much space as possible."

"Oh my."

"I'm actually sort of hung up over another girl to be honest."

"Really? Which one is that?"

"Well, it's sort of a combination of three girls."

"That's no good, Jack." She shook her head, unapprovingly with a small smirk.

"Tell me about it. None of them are any better than the other. I love them all the same, just in such different ways. One was the *first* love of my life, one is my life, and one is the love of my life."

"That's a lot of love."

"I've actually been meaning to ask you about something for a while now."

"What is it?"

"I dunno, I might not like the answer."

"Just ask."

"Do you remember your boyfriend from high school? With the long hair?"

"Zac? Yes, what about him?" she asked.

"What was the reason you two never worked out?"

"Oh. Well, one day he came over and we were in the middle of making out and I just stopped and said, 'I can't do this anymore.' And it really sort of sucked because I didn't get any clothes back."

"Really?" I had thought for a long time it was him who left her. I was shocked she would dump someone, she's so polite. The truth was, I had been worried about this whole idea in my head. I fell in love so young and never fell out of it, just with different women. I was worried that I hadn't found out enough about who I was, and that being with someone is not the answer to finding that out, quite the opposite. As much as this trip was about how much I felt, it really was meant for how much I could let go of.

"I'm sorry." I said.

"Don't be sorry, it's nothing." You could tell that it wasn't exactly *nothing*.

The term *I love you* is just a metaphorical error, which can never properly express what we mean when we say it since it is so universal therefore so obsolete.

I felt bad for delving into the topic. Nothing was resolved, but everything changed. I thought of myself as the one who was leaving Paris, but I still lost her. Neither of us really left the other, we just left. At the end I did tell her to stop playing with my heart with all the back and forth we had been doing, but I think when you tell someone to leave, you really just hope they are going to turn around and want to stay. What happens when the right thing to do feels so wrong?

Lunch didn't end on that note, but it did put a combination of a damper and pep into the rest of the time I spent with Les. We both were comfortable and weren't, or at least I wasn't holding up any walls so I could just be myself. She could too but being herself was doing homework. We went back to her apartment for about forty-five minutes and I found a guitar stashed away behind a piano.

"Do you mind if I play this?" I asked the roommate. "I can go outside, or play quietly, I'm just trying to write a song every time I find a guitar, and I think this counts."

"Is it tuned?" Leslee's roommate asked.

"I can tune it." I said.

"Then go ahead. Also, I'm going to be making cookies later so if you want any you can have some." Her roommate offered.

"Thank you so much."

"So, you are walking to New York?" The roommate finally asked.

"Yeah."

"Do you know how many more miles you have to go?" She asked.

"No, but I don't think it is much more than 100."

"I know somebody who made it there from here in three days."

"Who?" Les chimed in.

"Michael."

"That's a pretty good pace," I shook my head.

I was hesitant since it still hadn't been decided if I was staying, but things were looking good. I went up to Les's room and started working on a song. Sometimes the chords come first, sometime the lyrics. This time, the lyrics started flowing, and they were honestly exactly what I was trying to say. To this day I think it is the best song I have ever written. It would not have happened without being reminded of the comforts of a home, and the life that I was trying to avoid on my journey.

I didn't finish the song in that first sitting, but I made good headway until it was time to go to a nearby coffee shop so Les could work on some homework, and I could read and write a little. I used my leatherback book to write a few ideas down from the journey and about the state of my well-being.

All that insecurity of comparing myself to others melted away. I don't know if it was just being with my cousin or the fact that I am truly proud of who I am around her. She was quiet, working, with headphones in. My mind was anything but quiet. I think the adrenaline of getting so close to New York that I could smell the bagels was starting to get to me.

After about an hour of reaching out to Austin, old mentors, and writing silly thoughts down, the cappuccino was getting to me and I was antsy. I just watched everyone who came through the door and I will admit they were all above average. I certainly wasn't too far below any of them, so the thought of really making it out here was becoming more and more of a possibility. I've never made any friends by being mean to people. We are all alone and lost in this world and sometimes all we need is someone to share our coffee with.

On the walk home, I was interested in what Les was working on.

"Neurosurgery."

"Brain surgery?" I asked.

"Yep."

"Is that what you want to do?"

"It isn't particularly what I want to do. I don't really know. We just have to know everything about everything in order to become a doctor." She answered.

"I would be horrible at it. I have much too shaky hands when I get nervous, and I can't imagine anything making me more unsteady than operating on someone's brain."

"They teach us how to keep our hands steady. You actually hold the arm you are operating with, with your good arm, to keep it steady."

"Well, next time I'm performing brain surgery I will remember that."

"I was gonna say," she smiled.

"You know, I've always said there are doctors and lawyers in this world."

"What does that mean?"

"You know, everyone can be broken down into a doctor or a lawyer, I think."

"In what ways?"

"Not much really, well, a lot actually. Usually math people are doctors and the people who read and write more are lawyers."

"I think I sort of get it."

"It's just the way people think. A good differentiation that I usually use is doctors usually have their life figured out, and lawyers are usually looking into questions for answers."

"Is that so? Why is that?"

"Lawyers are always trying to find the answer around something, to see it the way they see fit, to change the world around them. Doctors are all about facts, facts, expectations, so they usually arrive at an answer sooner, but just memorize theorems instead of learning anything. I don't know, it's just a theory."

"It's a pretty good one." She said.

When we got back to her place, we decided that she would ask if I could stay the night. There was about five minutes of uncertainty while she went and talked with her roommate. I took that time to take in a little more of the decor, which I realized was a little more worn than my first impression. It just seemed like a lot of time had passed in this building without anyone particularly paying any attention to it. On the surface it looked very well kept, but once you looked at the stale candy lying around next to the couch and the unvacuumed rug, you could tell that just as much went over these doctors' heads as they thought was going through them.

When Leslee returned she didn't look happy.

I didn't say anything.

"You can stay."

"YES!"

"But-" She silenced my excitement. "The thing is, we all get up very early in this house so If I am going to take you anywhere tomorrow, you are going to have to get up really early."

"I got up at five this morning."

"Alright. I just don't want to have to wake you up and then we are all running late."

"I promise, I can get up. Hikers get up before anyone."

"Good." I hugged her again. We went back outside to her car where we grabbed my backpack, and I brought it all the way up to her room on the third floor.

"Also, I am going to be Skyping with my parents tonight, so you are more than welcome to join."

"We are going to be talking with Aunt Jess and Uncle Arnold?"

"Yeah, I'll let you know before I call them."

"Please do, I would love to see them." Honestly, I did want to see them.

She left me alone in her room where I continued to work out this song. The lyrics came to me like poetry, and I had been very deprived of it, so whenever that happens something good is sure to come of it. All art is, is just being as honest as you possibly can, and I had no reason left to hide anything.

If I don't have Love

C   Em   Am   F
Soft sheets and apple pie I don't need you to remind me
C   Em   Am   F
why I left all of it behind
C   Em   Am
I've walked a thousand miles and I'll walk a thousand
F
more
C   Em   Am   F
no matter where it goes it still leads back to your door
C   Em   Am   F
And I'm just like the leaves on the trees in a breeze
C   Em   Am   F
clapping my hands at every little thing I see

C   Em   Am
But I'll take my time to realize that it's alright to live your
F   C   Em
life a little different from all those mathematicians
Am   F   C
with all their insights and inquisitions which make me
Em   Am   F
suspicious, if they are living with the convictions
C   Em
that keep them up at night

C   Em   Am   F
The sunrise keeps me alive don't think twice I'm still
blind
C   Em   Am
can read and write between the lines, I'll even make it
F
rhyme

C Em Am
But the birds are the only boss of me I wanna see on a
F
Monday morning
C Em Am
chirping bout how I should be working instead of
F
walking across the country
C Em Am
would if I get hungry, would if there's not a bed to share,
F C Em Am
Would if I don't comb my hair, would If I die tonight,
F C
would if I just don't care.

Em Am F

C Em Am
Would If I don't get an education, would If I can't fight
F C Em
for my nation, would if I don't ever get married, would if
Am F
I don't make a big enough salary
C Em
but if I stayed where I was
Am F
I would have never been enough
C Em Am F
so I'll say it right here on my knee praying to the lord
C Em Am F C
I'd rather have nothing If I don't have Love.

Chapter 38

"Sounds good." Les said to me as I came down for the Skype session.

"Yeah, I just haven't gotten it perfect yet."

"Still...sounds good."

"Alright, are we gonna do this?" I asked.

"Yeah, they will be ready in three minutes. Do you want a cookie? My roommate made some."

"Sure, I'll take a cookie." I walked into the kitchen, which was filled with just wonderful baked goods. I grabbed four cookies, since I didn't know the next time I would get such a sweet delicacy.

"They're on!" She called to me from the other room.

"Where is he? I wanna see him." I could hear my Aunt Jess.

"I'm right here." I waved into the camera.

"Oh! *He looks good actually.*" As though I would have been tattered up and looking like a homeless artist.

"I probably smell much worse," I joked.

"He actually doesn't smell that bad," Les said probably just on my behalf.

"Hey Aunt Jess, Hey Uncle Arnold."

"HEY JACK!" My Uncle Arnold exclaimed. When I was growing up he was my favorite uncle, but as the years passed he started to get a little too rigorous and neurotic for my tastes, but I really shouldn't talk, he's pretty cool and insanely smart. There is nothing wrong with being serious, and it is a trait of mine which can be weak occasionally.

"Hey Arnold, Hey Jess. How you guys doing?"

"We're doing alright but what about you?! Are you safe?"

"At the moment," I said trying to not be the center of attention.

"You seen any snakes?" Uncle Arnold asked.

"Oh yeah, I've seen quite a few of them. I'm still keeping my eye out for a bear though."

"A bear. Oooooh. Do you have protection? Nobody's giving you a hard time are they?" Aunt Jess asked.

"Yeah, I actually packed too big of a knife. The thing weighs like three pounds and all I've used it for is spreading peanut butter."

"All he's used it for is peanut butter, you hear that!" Jess poked at her husband.

Uncle Arnold made some corny joke.

"And you're going to New York? Why? What's out there?" Aunt Jess pushed further.

"Well, you remember last summer when I said I might look into some art schools out there?"

"Yes."

"Well, I don't remember anybody standing up on my behalf for that little notion. Might as well just look at a few schools and see what there is to offer."

"Ok. Very interesting. You know we love you." My aunt said.

"I know. I love you guys too. This is bizarre seeing you guys on this trip." It was like being at home as far away from home as you could get. After that Les took the lead and discussed all the things that she was doing this week at school. I envied them. So in love with each other. I am blessed to be part of their family, but it wasn't *my* family. I wondered what my siblings and even what my step-siblings were up to, and how hard it would be to get all of us on the phone.

The Skype session lasted for a full hour. My attention span lasted about twenty minutes maximum. I was just happy just to sit there. I wish I had brought the guitar down once it had ended. We said our goodbyes and I knew they'd be praying for me, for their sake. It was time for bed. I was given the couch. Les got me some blankets and asked me if I needed any food. I thought it would be best to take care of all that before morning.

"It wouldn't be a bad idea to see what you got," I agreed.

She gave me some Luna bars, cookies and some drink flavoring. Whatever I could get helped. I stuffed all of it into my backpack and pulled out a fresh t-shirt. One day was not long enough to wear out a pair of underwear.

"Do you mind if I take a shower?" I asked.

"Go right ahead. It's upstairs and the last door down the hall."

The shower reminded me of the ones in Rome since the showerhead was confusing. I reaped the rewards, which were long overdue in the form of another hour-long shower. I cleaned out my ears with some q-tips, which was gruesome and brushed my teeth, then slowly creaked out the bathroom door into the dark house. Everyone was asleep since it was about ten. It felt unsettlingly late and I worried about how hard it was going to be to get up in the morning. I went down to the cozy looking bed for me and cuddled deep into it. Some people are turned off by worn in pieces of furniture, but I usually get my best sleep in those types of places. It reminds me of all the other time people waste.

My dreams were bizarre, but I don't remember them.

I overslept but not by too much. I didn't look at my phone the night before, but my dad texted me that he was going to be in Philadelphia, only about fifty miles away from a certain point on the AT. I didn't really think much of it at the time, but I wasn't particularly unhappy about it. There just could've still been something up his sleeve. I heard Les in the shower and got everything ready quickly, though most of it was prepared. I was smart enough to not lay back down because about five minutes later Les came down looking a little tense.

"Are we running late?" I asked.

"Not yet. Do you want breakfast?" She replied.

It had slipped my mind, but it was probably a good idea. I ate a quick bowl of cereal and we were out the door. The cool air of any morning is heaven. I wish I was an early riser so I could catch this rare feeling which only this natural extremity can provide. I threw everything in the trunk and Leslee nibbled on a Luna bar as she drove. She wasn't quite satisfied with all the details I had given her about the trip, but I really didn't know what she was looking for. So, I just talked to her about her life as we aimed for the closest point of the AT.

"So, your roommate is married?" I asked.

"Yes."

"Does she like him?"

"I should hope so," she affirmed.

"Do a lot of people get married at your age?"

"A few of them. There are some people that you look at and are like, wow, I don't think that person is ready to get married."

"I feel that."

We turned into smaller hiker towns and the mountainous land became more prevalent as the streets began to wind. We went down one long stretch that made me wonder where the hell anybody lived. It looked like the worst of Detroit in the middle of a forest. Still the homely feeling was overbearing, and I had no fear.

We parked up for a moment and Les was adamant about whether I needed any more help, but she had done more than enough.

We got out of the car and I hugged her one last time.

"Good luck, I know you can do it." She said.

"I think I'll be alright. I love you."

"I love you, too."

Chapter 39

I found a post that said GEORGIA TO MAINE, but the arrows were pointing straight up and down. I must've read it upside down because I thought it said MAINE TO GEORGIA and began following it backwards as I had done many times before. I really am no marksman. It wasn't until I was halfway across the bridge that we drove in on that I saw a hiker, loaded up, with wide calves and a goatee, walking towards me.

"This is North right?" I asked.

"Nope. You're going South."

"Goddamnit."

I turned around and walked with him back to where I had technically started walking for the day. I observed his bag. There were some Mountain Dew cans he was carrying which I thought was a lot of weight for a small gain. Then again, there is the twenty-four beers in twenty-four hours challenge on the trail, and I really wasn't one to talk, my pack was bigger than his.

"Thru hiker?" he asked, nonchalantly.

"I think of myself more as a Fri Hiker. Like every night is Friday night and I'm just making my way along the AT."

"A Fri Hiker eh? Yeah, I'm a little hungover myself." He said.

The thought of putting anything in my body like alcohol sounded so detrimental to health, it was just silly. Then again, I shouldn't be talking.

"Sounds fun?" I said.

"Yeah, but after this, the towns start getting real spread out apart. The next stop is Port Clinton." I thought of the tragedy of a recent election.

"How far away is it?"

"About 50 miles." He said.

"So, you're aiming for tomorrow I suppose?"

"That's the goal. There's two shelters really close to here but after that there isn't one for seventeen miles so I wanna get a move on."

"How is the landscape for the day?" I asked.

"Well, people actually train to hike the AT in this section we are on right now, so it's pretty steep." He said.

"Wonderful."

"It's very steep and then it plateaus for a while and then it's probably steep again." He put in his headphones. "I'll see ya if I see ya."

He did walk quicker than me, but his strength seemed like it came from horrible decalcified bones pushing whatever toxins out of his blood. I'd been sober for a full day, so even the cloudy weather couldn't bring me down. However, the land was very hard, very rocky. Most of the AT is marked so you can see where you are going and if you don't see a "white blaze" then you have gone astray. I went astray, but so did he. We both found ourselves climbing over small rocks about 200 feet up until we realized we weren't going anywhere. Climbing down is much easier, but also more dangerous. One small slip and you are fucked.

We hiked together after that until the next shelter. I put in my headphones and went a little quicker than I would have gone without them in. The thing was I was listening to my own music, the songs I'd written and recorded on my phone. It filled me up so much. We stopped at the first shelter. It was shabby. Plenty of cigarette butts and someone waking up for the morning just about to head off.

"I'm going to get water here, and then leave," The first guy said.

"Good idea." I said.

We both got out our water pouches, and just like last time it took me about ten minutes longer than him and he wasn't waiting around. I didn't blame him, it looked like it was about to rain. I left as quickly as I could. After that I didn't see anyone for a long time. I'm glad I didn't get too lost, because I am sure I walked into a few bushes here or there that weren't on the trail. I just waltz into stuff when my mind is on autopilot. Once I got to the shelter after that, which was a good six miles or so, I began to feel that sense of wild wonder that can be compelling. It wasn't. I didn't know what I felt. The next shelter was seventeen miles away and I had already done about ten. I sat at the bench and rolled a cigarette, which I then turned into a spliff. I felt so remotely far away from society and anyone. Nobody was coming my way, I could tell.

I used this time to check the weather, which turned into me rubbing one out. I came full force outwards into the woods like I was making love to mother nature. After that I had to reassess my life. I was in a state of fight or flight. I knew I would be safe in the shelter for the night, but what good would that do? I wouldn't be much further along, and it would only save me from getting wet.

With as much force as I could, I put one step in front of the other and thought I would go for it. Nobody was around, and this was advanced hiking. Pennsylvania is infamous in the AT community for being extraordinarily rocky. Not only big rocks that you have to climb over, of which there were quite a few, but little stupid rocks that you hit your toe on about a hundred times an hour.

I began to sing. It is probably one of the most natural things I can do. I sang along to the few songs I had written, and they traumatized me over and over again. As much as the forest is a place to bring one peace, it takes us out of our civilized standards, and we begin to act like monkeys sometimes. I gave out a YAWP since no one could hear me. I feel like in the hours of those days I was further away from anyone than I had ever been in my whole life. I was very happy in my solitude.

When I did finally see someone, I was very skeptical and slightly threatened by them. This guy had a few of the red flags that hikers warn about on the AT. First off, his face was skeletal and marked with deep smoking trenches. His beard was longer than anyone would ever find acceptable and his pack was suspiciously light. I didn't approach him as I saw him sitting along the trail, but I did slow down since any human felt worthy of some form of communication.

"What's up man?" he asked as I slowed.

"Nothing much, been a long day. Which way are you coming from?"

"South."

"Oh, good, do you know how many more miles it is until the next shelter?"

"About four, or five, maybe six. Not undoable."

"I hope not man, it's been quite the day. I'm about to clock in at twenty-seven miles."

"Impressive. You coming from Georgia?"

"North Carolina. Where you coming from?"

"All over man, I've been out here nine months now."

"Good lord." I will attest to this now, that when you are hiking, and away from basic society and people, it does put a strain on your mental health. You begin to find yourself becoming very comfortable with the way you see things and it can be very good in many ways, but there is a reason for pause of concern. Nine months would be ridiculously outrageous.

"Any particular reason?" I asked.

"I just feel like I'm more home than I can handle."

"I think I understand. You wanna smoke some weed?"

"Yeah, I would be willing to smoke some herb." He said.

Of all the things that we carried with us, weed was light enough for us both to carry. We rolled a big joint and just talked about where we were from. He helped me find a closer sense of where I was going, which was primarily just away from him. When I got up to leave, he began to follow me.

"I thought you were going South?" I said.

"No. North?"

I didn't question it, but I did question my safety. He didn't say much as we talked, but still I made light conversation, trying to give him the benefit of the doubt that he wasn't going to murder me. The quieter it got, the worse my thoughts became.

"I think that the shelter is this way," he said.

I looked down a long road, which looked like it was leading off the trail, surely there was some structure beyond the pines, but I was just so hesitant to follow him anywhere that was not on the main trail. I knew my knife was accessible in my backpack, so I ventured with him further into the woods steadily and with caution. The road to the shelter was about half a mile and towards the end of it, I really became worried. Right before the shelter was a small campsite, and my legs were aching so horribly that it almost took my mind off being in the woods alone with this stranger. I nearly stopped and set up camp there, but my better instinct told me to keep walking.

The second I saw my first sign of other life all of my reservations were released. I saw the two guys that I had seen at the first shelter of the day.

"You made it? We were wondering if you were gonna show." The goateed one said.

I didn't say anything. The complete exhaustion of walking twenty-seven miles in one day set in and I was starving. Both of the other hikers had their cooking ware out.

"Do you mind if I could use your stove? I could pay you a little for it."

"Uh, when you say it like that. No problem man, you can use my stove when I'm done with it for free." The first hiker from this morning said.

"Thanks dude." I ate a lot that night. Two handfuls of rice, the last of the instant potatoes and a ramen, plus I nibbled on whatever other foods I had, but if I could reach it, it was eaten. I laid out my sleeping pad and layed down next to an elderly gentleman who was resting after his day. I tried not to invade his space, but the shelter was not very wide, and the two other hikers already had their stuff laid out as well.

I literally just had to lay down and embrace the pain of muscle being torn in my legs. I laid there for about twenty minutes until the last member of the night showed up. He was a tall, talkative, trim, dark haired gentleman.

"Oh damn, there's not space in here left. Do you guys just mind if I put this guitar under here, so it isn't left out it the rain." He said.

I didn't sit up but acknowledged him.

"You have a guitar?" I said breathing heavily.

"Yeah."

"Does it work?" I sat up.

"Of course."

"I don't mind it resting at my feet for the night if I can play it." I offered.

"I would be insulted if you didn't."

"I'm just trying to write a song every time I find a guitar on the road."

"Wow, that's cool. I just do it to make company. I'm going to camp back at that campsite back a little way, but you are more than welcome to join."

"Give me five minutes to wake up and I'll meetcha over there."

I layed back down and listened to the other hikers share their stories.

One of them said, "I was outside of a 7-11 and it was about three miles back to the trail, and I put my thumb up and I got in this guy's truck. He seemed like a normal dude, you know, we were talking about normal stuff, and then he asked if I could masturbate in front of him."

I lifted my head in suspicion of what I was hearing, but at the same time I wasn't surprised.

"Did you do it?" The other hiker lying next to him asked.

"No, I didn't do it. He said he was willing to pay me thirty bucks."

"There are some creeps out there."

I thought about being lost in that psychological state of wanting to watch strangers masturbate in front of you. It really can become an addiction just like any drug. I left the shelter and walked over to the campsite and the gentleman already had his guitar out. He was pretty good but did nothing memorable. I asked if I could play. I performed *if I don't have Love* for him and he seemed to really enjoy it.

"Wrote that last night," I finished.

"You wrote that last night?"

"Yup." I started to fiddle on the guitar looking for chords this time instead of lyrics to make a song.

"Damian" He reach out his hand.

"Jack. What do you do?" I asked him.

"Well, I'm twenty-five and I went to college but I'm

taking a little break from that for now."

"Did you not like college?"

"No, I did like college, there was just some stuff that happened while I was there."

"Oh, so you got kicked out of college."

"Yeah, but I'm going back next year."

"Why did you get kicked out?"

"Emails."

"Emails?"

"Yeah, I was emailing this girl and she didn't really enjoy them."

"Oh, one of *those* situations."

I didn't know this man well enough at the time, but during our company I found that he was a hindered soul. Damian's social skills were not dead, but they were not always accurately designated. I personally have some controversy around my life with that topic. Sometimes it's really hard when you think what you are doing is right, but there really is no clear answer. Even if your intentions are in the right place people may not always see it that way. I could tell that this guy was struggling deeply with thinking of himself and wondering if he'd ever be able to fall in love again in his life. Not that it wasn't within him, some of us just can't help but fall in love the way we do.

Slow Down
2nd Capo

```
C  E  Am F x 2

C       E                    Am      F
Slow down where you going?
C         E            Am              F
Come here I got something to show you
C           E                   Am        F
 I don't know what I'm talking about
              C        E               Am     F
I've been sitting here since happy hour
C                E      Am             F
And I don't even know your name
          C          E                  Am        F
but it doesn't matter because I'm not famous

So I sing

(Doo to the chords)
C E Am F x 2

 C       E                  Am     F
North bound on the road
C      E          Am      F
I got nowhere I need to go
     C             E                Am       F
And I don't know what I'm looking for
       C           E    Am      F
but I see that now less is more
     C               E         Am             F
And my heart still beats to these chords
            C           E       Am F
cause you're the girl that I adore

So I sing

(Doo to the chords)
C E Am F x 2
```

Chapter 40

I got better sleep than any of the other hikers I was sharing the shelter with. I couldn't get myself up and it had nothing to do with how much we were smoking last night. I was extremely sore, but I knew I had a long day of walking ahead of me, so I let the bird's chirping pick my head up and began to get ready. I lingered around a little bit with Damian.

I was trying to get a rough recording of the song I had written in the morning, and it's one of my favorites because you can hear the birds in the background when it starts. Damian let me know that he knew of a guy who ran a shelter in NYC, and he gave me his number. He really wasn't half bad.

You always feel so good about yourself after you've created something. I recorded the songs on my phone, and I was listening to them on repeat throughout my day. The songs carried me. I'm sure many of my musician friends feel the same way about hearing themselves. It wasn't just because I had created something, it was because I believed in what I had created.

The trails were just so bloody confusing, and I fell off the trail before noon. I was walking along what seemed like a road that cars had gone down, and sure enough, a man and a woman riding two enormous horses galloped up next to me.

"You know where the AT is?" I looked up.

"You just follow this path about five miles, and you'll come across a road. If you go down that road you'll get to Minersville, but the AT is along it."

"Thanks." My surroundings didn't look like any other part of the trail that I had been on. I went along the tall grass with the two beaten down horse paths for about an hour and a half until I came to the road the rider had spoken about. It was getting close to lunch, and I was running low on power so I thought it might not be a bad idea to stop by Minersville.

Minersville was just as interesting of an American

spectacle as the next. There was one nice restaurant that stood out. It had a pink front and caricature of a nice old grandma holding a pie. I made sure to avoid it since I probably couldn't afford it. However, all the other stores were nothing useful. Bars, tattoo parlors, head shops. I walked all the way to one end, before I turned back around and went into the pink restaurant. I was greeted at the door.

"Howdy partner? Can we help you?" A husky fellow greeted me.

"Um yes, do you think I could just plug in my phone and sit for a while."

"Of course. Are you hungry?"

"Yes. I don't have any money to spare though."

"Don't worry about it, you like grilled cheese?"

"Yes."

"Darling, get this man a grilled cheese and some fries." He said to a woman behind the counter.

"No. Please you are being too generous." I said.

"The lord says to help those in need." He responded.

"God bless."

The food came out.

"What do you want to drink?" he asked.

"Water is fine."

"Here, have one of these."

"What is it?"

"It's locally brewed green tea."

I took a sip.

"Wow that actually really hits the spot." It tasted like there was milk in the bottle since it came in a carton, but the liquid was clear. We chatted over the meal. He was a sweet man. A man of God. He was apparently running for mayor and said that he had invested a lot into the town. His restaurant had the Corinthians Verse 13:13, "And now these three remain: faith, hope and love. But the greatest of these is love."

"That's me and my wife's passage." He winked to me.

"You're married?"

"My wife is in the back right now. We run the store

together."

"What is your name?" I asked.

"Scott."

"I've always wanted to name my son Scott. Where are you from?"

"Carolina."

"North or South?"

"North." He said.

"Good, that's where I'm coming from."

"Well there you go."

"It was meant to be," I said, finishing up my lunch smiling.

"You got a Bible with you?"

"You know that is the one thing I have been looking for this whole trip to be honest, but I can't carry much more weight." He reached below the counter.

"I've been saving this one for ten years." It was a brown leather handheld New Testament, about the size of a deck of cards.

"I really don't know if I am worthy."

"Of course you are." He placed it in hands and fit perfectly in my palm.

"Scott, I'll never forget you."

"Before you go, let me grab my wife."

Out came a beautifully aged woman, and a chubby fourteen-year-old. It was like looking at all that I ever wanted to become in my hearts of heart.

"This is my wife Ann, and my son started working for us for the past six months."

I shook both of their hands, but I wanted to cry I was so grateful for the character in front of me.

"You ordered the grilled cheese?" She asked me.

"Yeah."

"Thanks, you were easy."

I looked up at him with a wink in his eye about the fact that he had ordered it for me since he didn't want to make his wife work any harder. I patted the kid on the shoulder. "Keep working man. You'll get to do anything you want."

They all came in for a group hug and I didn't know if they were blessing me or I was blessing them, but it was a moment of grace, and honestly the whole restaurant went silent in peace of the Lord. I shook the man's hand and it felt as though we were looking at each other from different points of our lives.

"Do any of you guys know which way the AT is?" I said, feeling a little unprepared but not worried.

"Just go down this road here and you'll get to the next gas station and you'll turn and it's right along there." Minersville was a little bit out of the way compared to most hiker towns, so I was a little surprised that he knew that.

"Thanks again. For everything."

The second walk through of the town was a little less appealing than the first. The niceties of the upscale suburban restaurant juxtaposed with the streets lined with drugs was eye opening. Once I got to the end, I stopped in the Dollar General to take a shit. I was sitting on the toilet and started thinking about Elvis and how he died.

Any nature looked mutilated from the offset houses' overgrown gardens contradicting that notion of being alone in a broken home. There were obvious homeless dens lurking beyond some tall trees. I investigated one and it was sad. Torn couches and bundles of clothing for comfort. After I went under a bridge, I noted not hearing anything about that. I think I went around three miles. Not bad, but not just a distance you want to turn around and spend an hour getting to nowhere. Right after the bridge there was this shack. It reminded me of one of my old friend's house. Outside, a man sat. He looked like a fat wart.

"Hello. You doing?" I chattered with a nod.

"I'm doing just well."

"I'm trying to find the AT."

"Well you're a little way off."

"Oh, I imagine."

"Where you coming from?" He asked.

"Came through *Minersville.*" I replied.

"Oh well, it's about fourteen miles up ahead to Port Clinton." He pointed.

"Thanks."

"I'll give ya a lift, but do you think you could move these two rugs to the back yard?"

"No problem." I went around the side of the house where there was all sorts of trash lying around. Not exactly worthless garbage but trash, just big wooden slats that had aged a long time in the rain, an old trap and some metallic sculptures. After I moved them, I went back to the front door. An older woman who looked seventy but was probably fifty opened it up halfway. The man came up behind her.

"We should be doing that, look at us." She said, self-aware.

It was hard to see around their wide frames but as I peeked through the door, it was apparent they were hoarders.

"Pleasure to meet you." I said to the man as I got into his rusty van. "You married to her?"

"No, we are just old old friends." He started the vehicle.

"Shame." I didn't say out loud.

"But I do have a son." He continued.

"I have a dad. He just texted me actually."

"Oh, ok, now I'm starting to get to know a little bit about you."

"A lot to know."

"Cocky. I like that. So, does anybody know you are out here?" He pulled out of the driveway.

"I hope not."

"Sorry. Your dad's cool with it, though?"

"He wants to see me, he's in Philadelphia."

"Is that a good thing?"

"Sort of, it wouldn't be bad to see him. We sort of left off at a rough place."

"What happened?"

"I didn't tell him I was going to do any of this." I said, apologetically.

"That's bad news, buddy. This whole trip is cursed. You're better off just going home right now if that's how you left it."

"We've been through much worse. He's a good man."

"I'm sure you have, but the actions of what you are doing are coming from a place that is hurting others and no good can come from that."

"This daddy day care?" I raised my head.

"Yes. Yes, it is. Today I am your dad and you are my son. I called my son today, it was his birthday and he is out in California, and I hate him!"

"Oh, then you must be who I've been looking for fatherly advice. Haven't you heard? It's all out in New York anyways."

"Those people are rough out there, and I'm sorry, based on what I've heard so far, I don't think you are going to make it."

"What? I've already made it. I followed my dream."

"What do you really want?" he asked.

"All sorts of things. Important things and some meaningless things." I said.

"Where you coming from? Where to where?"

"North Carolina to New York. I'm walking across America."

He looked like he was figuring out a math problem in his head.

Yeah but that is vertical, that isn't across the country." He shook his head.

"When was the last time you walked twenty miles?"

"I deserved that." He snapped.

"Deserved what? Buddy, I just don't need to be told everything I'm doing has no point to it, especially by you. What do you even do?" I asked.

"I'm a student."

I didn't even ask where because I am positive there was no Oxford comma.

"What are you studying?" I asked.

"I have years of files all about everything that I am going to formulate about a grand theory thesis that people will write about for generations to come."

So is everyone, but I wasn't the authority to tell this man his life's work was meaningless. Sounded like a lunatic. Lost in his head. I know the feeling. When you get working on something, or an idea starts working on you and you just believe so much that everything you are doing is leading to some solution.

"Trust me, there is a lot more to my story than that." I said.

"What? With you? Well, with what you are leading with, nobody is going to save you."

"I don't need anyone to *save* anything." I said.

"Oh yeah? How much money do you have right now?" He asked.

"On me? About a hundred dollars give or take some change in the bank."

"Well, making anything of yourself takes a lot of money."

"I don't need any money and if I did, I'd find *money*. I would do all of this even if nobody ever heard a single word of anything I ever had to say. Don't you dare tell me I need to go home. I am as close to home as far as *I'm* concerned, and it sure wasn't where I left things off with my father...or my mother for that matter. Home is where the heart is, and my idea of where I feel most loved may be a little broken, but don't tell me I'm wrong."

"Alright, that's what I want to hear, son." He shook his arm in exclamation.

"You're a little off, mate!" I wanted to grab hold of the wheel.

"No, I'm right on, everybody else is not doing anything."

"How can you account for so many people's lifestyles?" I asked.

"Research." He said.

"From what?"

"History."

"What history?" I asked.

He paused for a moment to think. "We are all slaves. No one even has any free thought and it is only an illusion forced on us by the Government." I was beginning to feel a little unsafe, although I knew this man could never harm anyone. It was a psychological unsafety. The net that we are indeed stuck into called security was still holding me like a hammock, and this man was cutting at the ropes.

"A little Nihilist, don't you think?" I asked.

"You'll get there someday." His dark grey eyes echoed.

"I hope not," I griped.

"So what? Are you gonna see your dad?" he asked.

"I don't know yet. If this is a predecessor of what it's going to be like, definitely not."

"Why do you say that?"

"He is very quick to condescend my dreams for his own vision, but to be honest I'm extremely tired. I get exhausted talking to him."

"You could be worse off, but nobody would ever really know...or care."

"You're starting to piss me off. I've been out here for a long time, doing some serious personal growth and you are kinda just shitting all over that."

"I just see things that you don't see."

"That's fine. Sure, I see that there were many things *wrong* with this journey from the beginning but that isn't A. a reason to not finish what I said I would do B. I don't need a second reason. There are some things you just don't say, but all that is to me is lying. I am going to say or see the things the way I believe in them."

"True, but nobody is going to listen to you."

"I really don't care."

"You will."

"Here is something a little nihilist. I care more about what I think of myself than what others think." I said stepping out of the car.

I love what I do more than any person could find solace to in New York. I was already flying away home. He said one last piece of advice when I left.

"Go home. You ain't worth it."

Chapter 41

I was left and driven off from like the last time I saw my father. The Coliseum of Port Clinton was an outdoor wooden tent-like structure that many hikers congregated at. There were a few tents posted up on the lawn in front of it, but I walked under the roof of the building and threw my shit in some corner and grabbed my pack of cigarettes. I was pissed. Of course I care about what other people think, everybody does. I lit one and then another and another. I wasn't paying much attention to the people around me, but there were quite a few of them.

This was usually the time of the day that I took to myself, but I quickly realized that all these people were intriguing. They were all in their mid to upper twenties for the most part and seemed to be travelling in some vibrant group. Some people arrived with wine and they were sharing. I really did not care about the world and I'm sure I was making a horrible first impression to everyone.

All I wanted to do was smoke and not talk with anyone so that maybe they would talk with me. I couldn't tell if I was out of place with these people, they were all far too comfortable with one another. One gorgeous man with a nice blonde beard was putting his hair in a bun and took his pants off and I took a peek. Not bad. There were the usual old men who were already getting ready for bed in the large structure, along with immigrants. Once it got to the point that there was a noticeable amount of cigarette butts all around me right up at the front of the walkway, I slowed my roll. The first man who reached out to me was a man wearing all red and had a very brownish greying long beard. He was older but you could tell still a young at heart.

"You mind if I join ya?" He sat next to me.

"Not at all."

"What's your name?"

"Cheerio. Yours?"

"Tonic and that one right there is my nephew

Xbox." He pointed inside.
"Nice to meet you.
"Long day?" he asked.
"Definitely. Are you all travelling together?"
"Most of us. We call ourselves the Fellowship."
"How many of there are you."
"I think something like fourteen of all of us together. We usually aren't all together though. We are all a few days apart from each other, give or take. That there is Feathers and he usually leads us on how many miles were going to go for the day." He pointed to the blonde man with a bun.
"How many miles do you guys usually go per day?" I asked.
"Twenty-five. Usually, right in that sweet spot."
"Ello. What are you going on about then?" A bald Englishman came over.
"Please come, sit," I mumbled.
"Thanks mate. Wild One,"
"Nice to meet you good sir. I'm Cheerio and headed to New York."
"You're taking the AT there then?" Wild One asked.
"Yeah."
"You know there is a lot quicker way to get there. It's only about a two-hour bus ride from here I bet," Tonic smiled from behind his sunglasses.
"I know, but what would be the point of that?" I asked.
"I suppose I agree with that," Tonic said, and Xbox came over.
"Where are you from?" I asked Wild One.
"England."
"Where in England."
"Southern England."
"Is it very green?"
"Yes. It's quite gorgeous actually." He said.
"It's good to take a little time for yourself every now and then, eh?" Xbox shrugged to Wild One.
Wild One held up his hand revealing a ring. "Yeah, got two little ones. A six and a ten-year-old now."
"Beautiful." I said.

"You got a light?" he asked, finishing rolling his cigarette.

"I gotcha."

Xbox muttered a few words to his uncle. He didn't really seem impressed enough with me to acknowledge my presence. I understood, in another situation I might've done the same to him. After that, two chaps pulled out of a car and started to walk up to our little discussion, which had now moved over to a bench in the middle of the Coliseum.

The energy of one of the men was a little overbearing. He had a wide smile and basically dreadlocked hair. He came stomping up to the campsite nearly yelling about the good prices of beer at the bar. It was a little overwhelming. I started to recluse back into my original silent distant behavior.

"We've got more wine," he said, "And tonight we are gonna go to the pub!"

Everybody was excited to hear about the good news and I wanted to join in as well, but I hoped that my age wouldn't be a problem. As the bottle of wine was shared among us, we loosened up and the conversation grew. I turned to the over welcoming one, and he smiled back at me.

"What's your name?" He asked.

"Cheerio, but when I'm in a bar, I go by Samurai Jack."

"Haha, alright I like that. When I first saw you I was like who was that sad guy?"

"Hahaha, yeah that's me sometimes. I might change my trail name to that."

"What?" He asked.

"sad guy." I said.

"Why'd you go by Cheerio?"

"I packed a full box of them when I left." I rolled my eyes.

"That's not so bad."

"What's your name?"

"I'm Ares."

"Pleasure to meet you." You could tell that this was a man who enjoyed life. I wanted to enjoy it as much as him.

“Feathers over there has been my best friend since high school.” He pointed to the blonde man who was now reading.

“Where are you from?” I asked.

“Connecticut, what about you?” He asked.

“North Carolina, Asheville.”

“Oh, I love Asheville. Great city.”

“I’m heading to New York.”

“Why?”

“It’s the city where dreams come alive, isn’t it?”

“I guess. Not really my cup of tea.” It was when he said that, a much-needed lift off of my shoulders that New York City might just not be everything that I was looking for occurred.

“And you are hiking there?” he said sipping the bottle, passing it to me.

“Planning on it.” I took a light sip.

“You gonna stay here for the night? Why don’t you come to the pub with us?”

“I was thinking about doing that.”

“C’mon join us. This is the Fellowship. We love to have people join us. I think there are thirteen of us now, you can be the fourteenth member.”

“It really sounds like a great group of people.”

“Oh, you’ll love us. Alright, you’re in.”

It wasn’t long after that that everyone started to get ready to go out for the night. I wasn’t sad anymore. Everyone looked at me like I was family. I probably was projecting a little bit, but I really do believe that when people get together in groups like this that they can treat one another much better. It was somewhat of a rainy night. Not downpour, but we were going to get wet. The only thing I had was a sweater and that is not a fabric that is favorable when wet. I asked around to see if I could use a jacket and sure enough, Feathers, the sexy peaceful dude was willing to help me out. He was reading and looking ready for bed and just asked that I try and keep everyone quiet when we get back and put it near his things.

About four or five us started walking into the town.

Right off the bat we were all cracking jokes at each other and talking about which ones of us were the biggest idiots. Bobcat seemed to be the one who was not carrying enough of his weight. I just kept my cool, hoping that there wouldn't be any problem at the bar. Ares told everybody that my new trail name was sad guy. Of all I ever was, a sad guy was enough.

The night was starting to creep up and just before it was too dark to see, a man in a car with a ten-gallon hat pulled up to us.

"Get outta town you filthy hikers!" We all looked a little surprised.

"I'm just messing with all of ya. I better see all of you tomorrow morning for donuts up at the barbershop."

Ares took the lead. "Ah yes, thank you!"

"Fare thee well." The man drove off.

Once we got closer to the bar there was a field that was in between the door and us. Bobcat walked across the field and nobody followed. We all took the road up to the porch and I prayed that there wasn't going to be anyone at the door checking ID's. If there was, I was just going to say I forgot it and push my way through. I was not in the mood. Nobody was standing there, and I inconspicuously walked in with all of them, matching their energy that we owned the place. However, this was a restaurant, not a bar. I was in the mood for some hard drinking and there were families sitting with their children all around.

"Table for five?" The diner waitress asked us.

"Yeah. Thanks." Ares said.

"Sounds good, seat yourself and I'll be right out to serve all of you."

We all sat around the table and I remembered that being around people usually means reaching into those lovely pockets I was being a scrooge about. Ya know what, I was happy, and it is important to be able to let yourself be grateful for the moments that are given to us. The waitress arrived at the end of the table.

"How we doing tonight, fellas?"

"Wonderful!" Ares pounded his fist on the table

childishly and there was an uproar reaction from the rest of us.

"Fantastic, what are we drinking tonight?" That question always gets me nervous whenever it is asked. I just haven't been asked it enough times.

"Coors" Bobcat said.

"Miller" Said Tonic

"Bud light." Said Xbox

"Can I have the Shandy special?" Wild One said.

"Sure thing honey."

"Corona" Ares said.

"I'll have a Corona," I said.

"Are you all twenty-one?"

"Yes." I said a little louder than everyone.

She closed one of her eyes as if to examine everyone.

"What about him?" She winked at me.

"I've already been carded." I said.

"By who?"

"Patsy."

"Who?" Ares said."

"I'm Patsy," she said a little more suspicious.

"It takes a man to travel the world..." I began.

"What's your birthday?" She asked.

"October 8th, 1994."

"That isn't 21," Ares said out loud.

"Yes, it is." I retorted.

"I'll kill ya. I swear to god, *I'll kill ya,"* she said waving her pen like it was knife.

"I swear."

"Alright, I'll be back with your drinks and be ready to take your orders. She left, but the tension about the question of my age stayed at the table.

"You're twenty-one, right?" Ares asked me.

"Yes." I shook my head no.

"Oh, why didn't you say that?"

"It doesn't matter."

"How old are all of you?"

Xbox was twenty-one, Bobcat was twenty-four, Tonic was forty-five, Ares was twenty-six, Wild One was thirty-seven and I was too young to buy a beer.

The beers came and I'll admit I was a little hasty to take a sip.

"Y'all know what you want?" Patsy asked the table.

"I'll get a Rueben."

Whenever there is a Rueben on the menu, I am sure to get it. I ate my Rueben in six seconds or less. I wasn't in the mood to smoke alone, so when Ares finished his food, I asked if he wanted to join me. He said he was up for it. We went out on the porch and I lit up. Ares was a real good man. He, in many ways, was what I was looking for in this trip. Someone to respect, that I could share my story with.

"You got a girl?" I asked.

"Yeah man. She's the best thing that ever happened to me. If it wasn't for her, I wouldn't be able to have made it on this trip. She sends me care packages along the way since I don't have that much money."

"Damn she sounds great."

"She really is. I love licking her clit with my mouth hole." He said, a little drunk.

"Hahaha. Lovely." I smiled.

"I'm actually going to see her next week. She's coming with my dad and we are all gonna stay in a hotel."

"My dad is in Philadelphia right now, and I'm debating whether or not I should go see him."

"I understand, that's rough."

"Tell me about it man. There is no single force in this world that doesn't want me to be myself more than him." I said.

"Who the fuck cares. You are on the Appalachian trail. You can do whatever you want out here." He said with valor in his words.

"Yeah, but what I want isn't really out here." I said.

"That's not the way to talk. This isn't about a girl, is it?" He asked.

"Yeah, I broke up with a girl who probably wasn't right for me."

"But that is good. I was in a relationship for three years that was extremely toxic to the both of us."

"That's a lot of what it felt like. I never felt like I was

actually a part of who she was or her life. That's not a bad thing, but it's hard when you want to get close to someone." I said.

"Listen, sometimes it is important to let go, it's probably the right thing to do."

"But I don't want that to be right."

"You will want to once you give it a try...Listen, the girl I'm with now, we sometimes see other people, it's not a bad thing. It's healthy." He said.

"How?"

"Because it makes us *fuller* people. Trust me, especially at your age you don't want to just build your life around some person."

"I already have, but it just happens to be around a different girl."

"Be a man! You can grow out that beard of yours and then when you return they will see how you've made something of yourself."

"Your beard isn't half bad," I admired. "What if *this* is the best beard I can grow?" I said, changing the tone a little bit more humorous.

"That? That's all you can let it grow out to be? Haha, well then that's the best damn beard you can grow, and you own it." He laughed.

"Hahaha, yeah. I'm sure none of it's as bad as I make it out to be. I'm just looking for an answer."

"And you will find it. Or it will come to you."

My own advice had come back around. Our cigarettes were out.

"Listen, I want to talk more about this later. Let's go back inside and get ready for the pub." He said.

"Yeah man, I was a little disappointed when we sat down at that restaurant, I was looking forward to drinking."

"Are you seriously not twenty-one?" He asked.

"Shhh."

"Really, I wouldn't have offered for you to drink if I knew you weren't."

"I assumed, but I wasn't worried that it wouldn't work."

"Eh, well I'm glad you came. Let's go to a real bar."

The conversation inside had obviously climaxed. Everyone was full and was otherwise getting ready to leave. I was a little upset that my meal was thirteen dollars, but when I looked in my wallet there was forty dollars folded with a note in it.

"Cheerio. You are a great guy and keep doing what you are doing." It was from Damian, the guy who had the guitar at last shelter. The thought about boundaries crossed my mind and I had to give him the benefit of the doubt that he didn't intentionally mean to cross those lines of going into my wallet. We all walked out a little buzzed and it was dark by now. The entrance to the place was not straightforward and we accidently all barged into an apartment that had three guys surrounding a beautiful bong.

"Oops, sorry, wrong place." I said.

"The bar door is around the back." One of the stoners said.

"Thanks."

The owner welcomed us into this town, and you could tell, everyone loved hikers.

"What'll it be, gentlemen?" the bartender asked. "We have two-dollar Sam Adams on tap."

"A round of those for everyone?" Ares called.

"Sounds like a plan," The bartender affirmed. "Alright let's just take care of the money upfront."

Everyone, myself included, took out our wallets and paid. They were tall glasses that I was sort of in the mood to finish easily. One in, we all went to play pool. I'm not bad at it. To my surprise, we won. It was a close game, down to the last ball. Luckily back at college I got a little bit of practice in. We were allowed to smoke in the bar and thank God. When I wasn't on the table I was really quite introverted. I wasn't particularly talkative just because all of these guys knew each other a little better, bars just aren't always my scene.

"You look like someone who has smoked a lot of cigarettes in his life," Bobcat said drunkenly to me.

I went on smoking and drinking my beer.

"Actually, you look like someone who would shoot up a school." I couldn't tell if he was just socially inept. I didn't acknowledge what he said and walked across the bar to Tonic and Xbox who were talking to some other guy who didn't look like good news and I was butting into a tense conversation.

"It's *good shit* man." The dark figure insisted.

"What-What is it?" Ares look calmed everyone down taking authority.

"He's saying that he's got a Percocet," Tonic stated.

"Can we look it up and find out?" Ares wondered with his whole body.

"I take these things man. They are good. I swear."

I wasn't really in the mood to get involved with all that, but you could tell that Ares was a little interested in it.

"Darts?" Xbox pulled me over.

"Never played before. I'm probably awful."

"Just throw the darts." He bought a game which was two quarters and no, I did not do fine. I don't really know the scoring of the game, but I got something around 128. I couldn't help but be a little distracted by the drug dealing that was going on. It seemed like tensions were starting to rise and the guy was getting unhappy.

"Who the fuck got 128 on Darts?" Ares asked, pushing people out of his way.

"I did. And I'm glad I've finally played that fucking game." When I said it, Ares turned from angry to delighted with me. You could tell that he did like me.

"Let's play another game!" He cheered again.

"I'll sit this one out," I sat down next to Tonic.

"So, you're in college?" Tonic asked me.

"Yeah, did you go?" I asked.

"Long time ago."

"What's up with that guy?" I pointed to the sketchy character with his hands in his pockets.

"He's just trying to sell fake drugs. Pay no attention to him. What are you studying?"

"I wrote my own major in Race."

"Yeah? Race. So, you what do you, like, focus on?"

"It's not particularly race, just the different standards of living. The radical change in thought behind

Black Lives Matter. The ecosystems of poverty in inner cities. Historical discrimination alive today. I could spend my whole life sitting here talking about any part of it, but you should look at the problem as a whole instead of just sects. How you relate with a person, and who that person is, can mean a lot more than who the world constructs us socially and economically. I am a little discouraged the focus of our country turned towards a wall."

"Well, how about this one? Why should I pay for illegal immigrants in this country?"

"Well, what about the ones with families? The little babies who can't help themselves?"

"That's fine if you were born in this country. Why am I paying for them to be here?"

"Do you have any idea how little those people make compared to you? We need Basic. Human. Rights. They don't know if they are going to be safe in their home country."

"It ain't easy for all of us."

"Well, I don't know if I have the solution off hand drunk at a bar, and I would love to talk more about this sober, but there is a long answer and a short answer. The long answer is, human beings are trying to get out of a place that possibly could kill them. What we need is a policy change. No, I suppose it shouldn't be on behalf of the American people to save them but what I would implement would be a tax, or create an optional tax for liberals, or any one who can afford living over a certain margin to save the lives of the less fortunate impacted. Or improve registration and visitation rights. America is founded on greed, lies and a false promise of freedom. As far as I'm concerned, immigrants should go somewhere else, but yes, I believe it is a human responsibility to help one another. It is a cultural problem on American's behalf to not support Socialism, or Communism, and how irresponsible it is for Capitalism to create such polar standards of life. Frankly, *we're* all out here probably because we got sick of how good our lives were.

"As long as they come through legally, I don't have a problem." Tonic appeased.

"Yeah, well our president sure isn't making that any easier. That is the worst form of racism in this world. He is isolating a specific group of people and trying to represent them as a threat, which is exactly what Hitler did to the Jews. He's done it more than once, to Mexico, North Korea and the countries of the Middle East."

"Not bad. I'm not changing my mind, but that was pretty good."

"Yeah, well, I'm saying it to you. Not just bystanders like you. The reason that racism is becoming more alive in this world than it ever has is because people don't respect and accept everyone diferent."

"Don't get mad at me."

"I'm not mad at you, I'm mad that problems like this exist in the world because of men like you."

"And you're gonna change that?" He asked.

"I'm gonna fucking try. A bigger change in this world can happen right here, one on one. Me to you."

He held out his hand and slipped me a small metallic container.

"Don't look at it now, but it's for the walk back." I was a little curious what he was handing me. "I'm calling it, anybody else joining me for the walk back?" Tonic called out.

"I'm staying for one more round and then we'll get some sleep." Ares said, as Xbox and Tonic thanked the bartender and walked out.

I was in the mood to stay. I am so back and forth with these social situations. I love them and I hate them. I'm glad I stayed though. I snuck out and rolled a small joint with what Tonic had given me and came back in nicely stoned. I ordered another beer and a pizza.

"500 Miles" by the Proclaimers came on. What a hell of a song. It was late enough so everyone was drunk enough to sing along. And boy did we sing. We were almost fighting each other we were so overjoyed with the energetic life that was filling the small space of the bar.

We all stumbled out of the bar and walked back to our tents. Luckily the rain had held off somewhat, so it wasn't half bad. I split the other joint I rolled with Ares. Laughter from men on top of the world. I tried especially hard to be quiet once we got back to the campsite, but it's always when you are trying to be extra cautious when you are drunk that you knock some crap over. Everybody was pretty bad compared what I was used to, but it was by no means festival commotion.

I placed Feather's jacket next to where he was sleeping though I couldn't see a damn thing. I just laid down. It was cold again. My blanket was not enough again, but I just hugged tightly onto the bundle of clothes I had as my pillow and waited for the sun to rise.

Chapter 42

I was glad that I didn't go back for a sixth beer. I watched Bobcat's posture change as he resisted from waking up and I wanted to make sure I wasn't the last one up, but this guy had definitely drank the most last night so I used him as a marker of a good time to rise. He fumbled around a few times, which would raise my adrenaline that it was time to sit up, but he just kept laying back down so again, my heart would settle.

I knew I had a few things I wanted to accomplish that morning, the first being those donuts at that barbershop. I might as well get a haircut while I'm in there. I liked my hair getting long, but I still wanted to be somewhat fresh cut. I also was running low on food and I knew there was a Walmart close by that I thought I should stop at since Feathers announced that they were going to be going three days without resupplying.

I thought it wouldn't be a bad idea to go along with the Fellowship if I could keep up. They were hitting the amount of miles I wanted to make and everybody just seemed so cool. Not to mention there was a bunch of women who were travelling with them, which it was getting safer and safer to say, they were a luxury to be found along the trail. They got up at five, so I knew I was going to have to get a move on if I was going to keep up. Whenever you don't have a tent, getting all of your belongings together is quite an easy task, even when you are hungover. I was walking out of the Coliseum by no means first, but by no means last. Even Ares was still waking up as I was leaving, his hair was a mess.

"Morning man." I said on my way onward.

"Hey hey, sad guy! What's up?"

"I've got to resupply and I'm going to get breakfast."

"Here, take my number. I live in Connecticut so if you are in New York and you ever need anything, my family is only a few hours away." I took down his number and gave him a hug.

"I'll see you up the trail." He said.

"We'll see."

I went into town which didn't have that four am feeling, but it was still somewhat early. The sun was rising beyond the small buildings and just past the town's post office there was the barbershop with a sign that read "Please Leave Bags Outside." I dropped my weight and went in and what did my eyes grace me with but another guitar.

Well, let's add that to the list of things I had to do that morning. The space was a hybrid of a barbershop and an antique shop. You could tell the owner smoked a lot of pot. There was great memorabilia of him on his wall and a few Willie Nelson posters hanging up. Xbox and Tonic were already in there along with a hiker couple.

"You getting a haircut?" I asked Tonic.

"No, just here for the donuts. You gotta let that hair grow man."

"I can't really grow much, as you can see."

Tonic pulled out his phone and showed me a picture of him with short hair and a trimmed beard. He was unrecognizable. I wasn't sure which state of living was more constraining.

"Do you mind if I play?" I asked the barber nodding my head to the guitar.

"Please do."

Writing a song doesn't sound that lovely. It's a lot of repetition and I was getting worried that it was annoying. After I got the first verse down, I decided to sing one of the songs I had already written. Everyone seemed receptive to it. However, after the brief period of sweet music, I went back to repeating the same chords and thinking twice about the words that were coming out. I was a little creatively drained if I'm being honest. The words didn't just come out like they had before.

One man was particularly interested in what I was doing. He had a small handheld camera and was filming me.

"You do YouTube?" he asked.

"Sometimes."

"You don't mind if I watch, do you?"

"Not at all." I said.

"Jerry, I'll go get the donuts, but don't let this kid leave," he appealed to the barber.

I worked on it for an hour and went out for a smoke break. I was sure it was too early for any cops to be staking out the barbershop. I thought a little bit of the green stuff wouldn't hurt but it was the last I had. I went back in with a fresh outlook and finished up the song. I needed a place to record. I asked if I could use the bathroom and Jerry, the bartender waved his hands in approval. It didn't take too many takes to get a good rough cut, however the bathroom amplified every single noise and you could hear the rest of the barbershop from under the door. It's what you get when you try to work with a hangover.

The donuts arrived and I was not shy. I probably ate three or four and downed a good cup of coffee. The man who brought them said he wanted to hear my song, so I performed it for everyone one last time. It was sort of a sad song, about saying goodbye which I was having trouble doing. The thing was, whenever I could grasp the idea that I could and or had let go of everything I was holding onto, I felt much more alive and my life had a lot more direction to it, but it just was a lot more pointless.

Nowhere

```
Bm                D     G            D
Picked out a flower in every state
  Bm         D          G                    D
Thought about you every hour of the day
  Bm        D     G            D
Sunday morning I go to church
Bm                D     G              D
My legs are broken my feet they hurt
Bm                D     G              D
But I'm still hoping to hear your words
Bm              D            G        D         Em       G
Take me or leave me, I'm still yours
```

Chorus

D G
Because I'd give up forever just to see you again
D G
And I can't live with us just being friends
D G
You're the only thing I've ever known
D G D G D
But now I'm nowhere and your, your gone

Bm D G D
Haven't slept in a week, but I'm still alive
Bm D G D
Sunburnt cheeks and tears in my eyes
Bm D G D
No matter where I go, no matter where I've gone
Bm D G D
There no forgiving me for things that I've done
Bm D G D
I'd give you what I have but it all just lies
Bm D G D Em G
I'd tell you what I know but I'm not wise

Repeat Chorus*

I looked over at the barber seat and there was a line, so it seemed that getting a haircut was not my forte.

"Is there anything else I can help you with?" The man with the camera said.

"Do you think you could give me a ride to the Walmart?" I asked.

"Sure thing."

I thanked the barbershop owner once again for his generosity and he waved back.

"I'll be right here," he smiled as I left.

Part of me would like to go back there and visit. Port Clinton was one hell of a gem in this country. Nothing fancy but good homely people that were all knit together you could tell. The photographer's car was parked on a gravel road and once we settled in, he got to talking.

"You know, I've written songs too," he said.

"You have? I really just do it as a hobby." I replied.

"Yeah, I took the lyrics of Black Magic Woman and wrote my own for this girl." He flipped on the radio.

He sounded like a love-struck teenager when he said that, though he was probably closer to sixty. The woman I imagined in my head was not very flattering, someone his age. I thought of big red hair and cheetah print clothing. His song was professionally produced, and the sound quality put whatever musical art I had made to shame. His voice was brilliant, good as one of the best tenor Southern singers I'd heard.

"She's eighteen now." He said once I was overwhelmed by the song.

The lyrics were very provocative to be about an eighteen-year-old.

Nimble finger tips.

"How'd you meet her?" I asked.

"She was a student at our Church, man. She has such this beautiful energy, she is so shy, and part of her is trying to get this expression out ." I had many mixed emotions as he described this to me.

I was heartbroken and torn. Love and its wonder. So many things to go wrong. So many things to be wrong with love. The timing, the distance, the age, the sex. Sometimes things are just unfair in the way that the world places them.

"What's her name?"

"Audrey."

"She sounds cool." I said.

"She's the love of my life man."

"I've got one of those," I whispered.

"Yeah, then you know."

I didn't know what I knew. I wanted him to be right.

I wanted the objective feeling that sometimes we feel about another person to be real. Regardless. His music overtook both of us, but I had the same question you're probably thinking right now.

"Have you ever?" I asked.

"No man- it's not like that. This love is pure. She's not really all there man, but it's just because she's so innocent." I questioned if he was all there.

"Are you attracted to her sexually?" I asked.

"I guess man, but these feeling are so far beyond that. I mean, don't get me wrong she's beautiful. She's just so talented."

"Are you guys friends?"

"We were, I helped her with the guitar. I gave her my old red Hummingbird one because she is so deserving of it. Light-years beyond anything I'd ever be capable of. And she was so humble. None of that ego that young people get today." He said.

"What happened?"

"Her mom, man. She didn't like that I bought her the guitar and thought we were spending too much time together. She ripped her away from me, just like that." You could see the pain tearing in every inch of his being as he said that last phrase.

"I'm sorry man, I don't know if you deserved that." I said honestly.

"It wasn't even about me man. It's what they did to her. They turned her against me. She said, *You're trying to hurt me! Get away from me*. It broke my heart." His eyes closed and revealed crevices of the tears he'd been crying.

Once we parked at the Walmart I asked if he knew where to get any weed, and he said he could take me to his brother's house to get some. The stop at the Walmart was quick, just tuna and rice and a little candy. I came back out and couldn't find his car right away. I didn't really remember the type of car he was driving. I was relieved once I identified it. He parked far away, and I wasn't sure if I could distinguish it until I saw his hunched over stature in the driver's seat.

"You get everything you need?" He asked as I got in.

"Yeah, now if we can just get some bud, I'll be ready to hit the road." I said.

"Alright my brother's house is about ten minutes away and then I'll drop you off at the trail. Just don't go telling anyone about this."

"Oh, who the hell am I going to tell? The barber looked like he smoked."

"Jerry, yeah he's a head man." As if the whole town knew about this secret.

It's just that the community here has a thing against us who all use pot." He said.

I worried if peer pressures never went away.

"It seems like a pretty laid-back town if I've ever seen one."

"No yeah, a lot of people try to make us look bad."

"Why?"

"Some of the wives think we're lazy. I don't get it man, we're good people."

"What the hell is there to do in Port Clinton?"

"I don't know man."

"Fall in love?" I asked.

"I guess."

He played his song on repeat. He kept talking about his love for this girl, and you could tell that it came from a place of such innocence that shouldn't exist in a man his age about someone hers. I felt bad because I knew there was nothing I could do. There isn't just a straightforward answer to so many of the problems in life. Love being at the forefront. As we drove to the outskirts, the small hidden town of Port Clinton no longer looked so small. It reached far around, and we drove on a highway. Maps confuse me, there is no way that the entirety of America is this small compared to the rest of the earth. There is far too much potent energy which exists in the lives of an endless sea of just lost individuals.

His brother's house was quaint and off to the side of some road. It had a little porch and a front door, but we went around back through the garage. A beautiful woman opened the door into the garage for us. I sometimes hate the English language, because when I say "beautiful" it had nothing to do with what she looked like. She was a little shorter than me, a face that looked kind when she smiled, but what was most beautiful about her was her ability to accept and her graciousness of whoever I, this stranger, was.

The garage didn't have a car in it, but it led to a wooden workspace area that reminded me of my grandfather's basement. The man sitting at the desk was unmistakably his brother although he had kept his facial hair and was much wider. He had a guitar on his lap as he sat at his desk.

"Is this yer friend?" The brother asked.

"Nice to meet you." I extended my hand.

"You have a lovely home and wife." I admired my surroundings. He had an assortment of pictures of him in the wild. One huge picture hung over his desk of him in an action shot pulling a bow and arrow with nothing but a small sling over his little hero.

"It's been a long time coming. This guitar in my hand is worth a thousand dollars." He showed it off to me.

"I actually wrote a song this morning." I said.

"I heard about that." He said.

"If I am really careful, would you mind if I played a song?" I asked. The thought of writing another song passed my mind but I didn't really have the time and I was getting a little drained having written three song in almost three days.

"If you promise to be real careful, we just restrung it." He handed it to me.

"Perfect."

I sang *If I don't have love* first and then we were all in agreement that I should keep going. It was good to practice these songs when I got the chance, at least then I'd have something to show up to New York with. There was an indescribable difference between the offhand guitars that I had been working with and this thousand-dollar one. The music rang through me, I sang with more emotion and I felt rich with soul.

I wanted to stay longer, I would've slept over had I not thought that I was missing out on whatever the

Fellowship was doing, although really there was no rush.

"Thank you so much. That was incredible." I said once I finished.

"She only plays as well as the one holding her." He said.

"Thank you, all of you."

"Do you still want that?" The brother asked pulling out a zip lock bag.

"Oh yeah I didn't think about it." I said.

"2 grams?"

"Yes please."

"That'll be twenty-five dollars."

A little steep but this was the road, and I could get into a deep digression about economics and supply, demand, and convenience, but it was worth whatever to just calm any other nerves that might arise. I gave him the money and told them I was running a little behind schedule so that I should get a move on. I gave everyone hugs and we headed out.

Once again, in the car ride, all I heard talk about was how in love he was.

"Even my own daughter is against me." He said.

"You're married?" I asked.

He shook his head yes.

"Well what about your *wife*? Wasn't she the love of your life at some time?"

"I don't know man. My wife has said things so hurtful to me, I could never forgive her."

"Don't you love her?"

"No man." Any lingering thought shut up after that.

"Listen." I said as we pulled up to where he was dropping me off. "I was held at gunpoint and the only thing I yelled out was please dear god, please dear god, don't kill me. Her name is Beth Keller. I thought I was about to die, and the only thing I could think about was her. Your story is compelling and universal. I believe you. We can't always change the way we feel. You have the all the right to feel however you wish, about whomever you want. I'm just saying that when you go around talking all about it and bringing negative attention to it, that is when you should stop.

Understood?" I said.

"Yeah, that is what I was going to try to do." He answered.

"Well, your very bad at it. Treat this then as the last time you will ever bring it up, for a long time. Not giving her space and pulling harder is not going to change anything right now. These things take time, years. Can you do that for me?" I asked.

"Yes."

"Thank you, man. It'll be alright. She does love you. She just can't see that right now, and you just do not need to be the one to tell her that. If she's ever ready she will come to you. Have hope."

Chapter 43

Hiking that day was strange. I kept passing this woman, and then falling behind her, and then passing her again. I didn't want her to think that I was following her or something like that. We were just going at a similar pace and I probably wandered off the trail, and we both kept taking breaks at different times and it just seemed like there was something going on but there wasn't.

I didn't get any cigarettes in Port Clinton for some reason, and I was running low, so once I came across a road, I pulled out Google maps to see how far away the nearest gas station was. It was about two miles, and I didn't have time for a four-mile detour. I was low on water though, and there was a restaurant, so I went in.

"Do y'all sell cigarettes?" I asked the bartender.

"Nope, sorry buddy."

I saw some familiar faces from the Fellowship having lunch, but I wasn't about to join them.

"Can I use your bathroom to fill up on water then?"

"You're going to have a hard time using that sink in there. Go around back and there is a faucet that you can use," the bartender replied.

Around back showed off the extent of this restaurant hotel hybrid. It was nice and rugged at the same time with a New Mexico clay desert vibe. Just a little unkempt, and I would have been honored to stay there but only because I'd been sleeping outside for the past while. It was definitely a hiker destination, just not mine.

Ares let me know that everybody was going to try and make it to the next hostel. The day was only about seventeen miles but when I showed up to the shelter there were no spaces available. Apparently, people were camping down on the land that was technically owned by the hostel. I didn't really have many high hopes but once I went down to the small pasture hidden by some trees there were about twenty people camping.

"Hey! sad guy! You made it." Ares cheered, as he

always did.

"Looks like it. I'm gonna set up my tent and eat before I come join all y'all."

You don't want to set up your tent in the dark. I grabbed the food I had and sat down in the large circle. There were some familiar faces and some new ones. Ares, Wild One, Xbox, Tonic and Feathers were enjoying themselves either eating or rolling cigarettes. There was a red-haired bearded mate who was quick to introduce himself to me.

"Hey man, I'm Auto."

"Nice to meet you. I'm Cheerio, but lately I'm going by sad guy."

"That's kinda confusing."

"Yeah, tell me about it. You can just call me Cheerio."

"This is sad guy!" Ares butted in and got everyone's attention.

"Pay no attention to him," I shook my head smiling.

There was one other British lad, who was somewhat dominant. He had a little bit of a monkey face and reminded me of a friend of mine that I had gotten into a physical disagreement with in college. I missed my old friend and knew not to cross this mate. He went by Harrison. I didn't have a stove, but Tonic was willing to help me out. Everyone had a lot of food to go around and I was happy to get whatever I could get my hands on. Everybody was making little dumb good old-fashioned jokes. I took that as my time to try and get acquainted with everyone and I didn't do half bad.

After about a half hour two people showed up. Their names were Ergon and Amazon. They were obviously a couple but were trying to hide it, however contradictory to my prior thought of Feathers being the head of the pack, Ergon was who was leading everyone. Amazon looked almost exactly like Wonder Woman in the movies. She was tall, tan and had black hair. Everyone almost treated Ergon like a god, but I knew he was just a hungry man and going on about how he was on the last of his Reese's peanut butter cups.

After he ate, he began to roll a cigarette.

"Yo, Mr. Peanut Butter Cup!" I smiled wide.

He didn't acknowledge me.

"Do you have a paper?"

"I'm sorry what?" He said, as though I had offended him.

"I was just wondering if you had a paper to spare. I was going to roll a spliff."

"Oh, um sure."

"You know the rules, Cheerio. If you are going to roll that you gotta share it with everyone." Ares said to me.

"I know. Y'all've been more than generous to me."

As I was rolling, I thought I would toy with Ergon's (Mr. Peanut Butter Cup) ego just a little bit.

"You know you sort of look like Adam Sandler." I said.

"Really? I've never gotten that before." He said.

Amazon laughed at my poke. "A little bit, I see it."

"So?" I nodded back at her. "Fifty First Dates eh?"

Harrison laughed. "God, his movies are awful."

"Not all of them," Ares said. "Just everything he does now."

You could tell Ergon was trying not to blush.

The woman who I had been playing tag with all day hiking showed up.

"Hey, what's up Ms. Ginger?" Ares said.

"I have the worst rash right under my pussy and up into my butthole."

We all broke out into laughter.

"I'm serious, I have to go to the hospital tomorrow."

"Do you think its poison Ivy?" Ergon asked.

"I don't know what the fuck it is, but it hurts." She said annoyingly.

It wasn't that late, but the evening began to unwind after that. Feathers said that they were going twenty-five miles the next day, so I thought I should get some rest too. Morning came, but I checked the clock and it was only around five am, so I decided to roll a little joint for myself in my tent before I got out of bed.

The night had been especially moist, and my tent and clothing were a little damp. When I got out, I aired everything out on some hiker poles. Everyone in the Fellowship had hiker poles except for me, and they do make a major difference. They take a lot of the weight off of your knees and put it into your arms, so you are more balanced in carrying your weight and not everything is forced into your legs. I hung out my wet tent on a pair of poles for them to dry.

This left me a little bit of free time that I didn't really want. I changed and a lot of people were getting a move on. I was not one of the last people to leave, but once again, not the first. The day of hiking was hard because the sun was out, so it was hot, and I drank a lot of water. I had also been hiking a higher amount of miles than I had been for the past couple of days and the trail was challenging.

The rocks were unforgiving, both in the sense that you had to climb over them, and they kept stubbing your toes. I thought I was doing pretty well but I was actively trying to go at a quicker pace than I had been going for the rest of the trip and I slipped and hit my head pretty badly. I was dizzy and worried that it might lead to a concussion since there was blood.

There was a shelter that I came across that Harrison, Ergon and two new fellows were eating lunch. Hansel and Gretel were brother and sister and were part of the Fellowship and seemed like really sweet people from Washington.

"Did you hit your head?" Ergon asked me a little worried.

"Yeah I slipped." I said.

"Do you feel alright? We should clean that up. I think I have an alcohol swab."

He went into his bag and pulled one out.

"Thanks man. I don't think it's too bad, I'm just gonna eat lunch with y'all if that's alright."

"Fine with me." Harrison said.

Lunch was nice because these people were so carefree from the world. Hanzel was playing music that I liked. He was about to start his first year of college. He played Bob Dylan which was telling of his character. Of course once we started getting into it, we started competing for who knew the most obscure band and I let him know that I was writing an album on the trail.

He dug it.

I took a poop in a toilet hole and when I got back, they were trying to see if they could jump over their hiking poles, laughing that if one broke they'd be buying each other new ones. I decided to get a move on, but they all seemed like they were wrapping up as well. I don't know. I liked these people a lot, I just knew I wasn't a part of them, and it was no use lying to myself that I was. These people had been hiking for almost a thousand miles together, and I had just shown up two days ago. It was good to be in their company since good company can keep you sane and safe on the trail, but why else?

After mile twenty of the day, Hanzel started to catch up with me but I didn't want to let him. Even though I had already taken one spill for the day I kept at an upbeat pace while listening to the Black-Eyed Peas and I'm sure his headphones were pushing him too. I can't believe that after all this distance I was still feeling so petty and competitive about my physical abilities. We were just close in stature and that usually instinctively happens to people. They test themselves against one another.

After the uneven rocks leveled out and once I was back on sturdy forest terrain, I began to feel my second wind come in. I let the music overcome me. All of sudden my feet were flying and instead of just hiking I was dancing through the trail. Each of my feet movements were taking me further along and I was stepping with intention, motion and discipline that only comes with years of training in the art of dance. Next thing I knew I was running. The power of music should never be underestimated. It was as if the entire physical benefit of walking miles upon miles day after day finally just surged through and I was weightless. I didn't even care about where I was going, I was doing the tango with the trees. I probably did a backflip and grabbed the next tree like it was my partner and swung into the campsite for the night.

Wild One and Feathers were already set up as

though they had been there for hours. I checked to see if there was space in the shelter and there was. I set my things up for the night and pulled out whatever food I had. I didn't want to bother anybody with using their stove, so I began to build a fire. It was easy to get one started, but I knew that I was going to need to prolong it for the night. No problem there, plenty of wood surrounding us in the woods.

Wild One was going on about his wife and how he was missing her. Feathers brought up the proposal that if I enjoyed hiking with all of them that I should just go with all of them to Maine. It was not only a kind offer that made me feel more part of the group, I took it into deep consideration. What the hell was there in New York? What the hell was there *anywhere* waiting for me. Nothing. Nothing and nobody waits for you. I couldn't let go of the fact that I was not doing all this for me. I was doing it for someone. Why shouldn't I take up the offer? I would have been more at home out here for the summer than I ever would be back in Carolina.

A few hikers came through who weren't stopping for the night. An older blond woman observed my stature, but I was too tired to give her the attention. I just began to stretch out my legs, which turned into me casually doing yoga.

"Those look like dancing legs," Harrison said.

"They are." I kept on stretching.

"You dance?"

"I did, when I was younger." I said.

I didn't need to be performing or bragging for all of them but six years of ballet if you are wondering. Ergon showed up with Amazon and let everybody know that Ares was going to stay the night with Tonic and Xbox at a restaurant a few miles back. Around dinner, he brought up that he had a lake house that he was going to let members of the Fellowship stay at. I didn't know if this included me, but I assumed it didn't.

Sensai was the last of the members of the Fellowship whom I was introduced to. The brilliant Thai immigrant was a photographer and a good sweet man. He shared his food with me, and we compared photos that we had taken. His English was very good apart from his accent. The wisdom from living in another country or his own looked as though it had served him well. He knew he could make everyone laugh the way he mispronounced certain words, like Appalachian.

The night unwound around the humble but burning fire I had built. Gretel put on the Rat Pack with Frank Sinatra, Dean Martin and Sammy Davis. Jr. The old tunes made love out of me. Sometimes our eyes can gaze just beyond what is close in front of us and it just looks alright. Likewise, Gretel was smooth and soft around the edges due to weeks of overgrown hair from not caring. We decided to dance together, which got others on their feet as well until we found out that apparently the Rat Pack were pretty racist to ol' Sammy. They weren't horrible by any stretch, but they would have been crucified by today's standards. I wanted to let Frank off the hook, but I wouldn't have been any better, at the same time it was the 40's.

I went to sleep with having put in plenty of miles. I did today's walk for myself and because I know everyone out there expects that much of themselves, and nothing less. Feathers was getting up at five and I was right behind him with the rest of us. Breakfast was simple but sweet. Just oatmeal but Wild One had an extra packet of honey, which made it all go down a little smoother. It was an easy eight miles or so to the first shelter where we rested for about an hour around nine in the morning. Some of us shit and others smoked. We talked about the map that said there was steep climbing up ahead. A man who was with his two boys told us to not drink any of the water coming up because of some pipeline problem, he also said there was a murder that happened near where we were passing.

The man and the map weren't lying and after we crossed a bridge, an area was roped off and surrounded by a team of police cars. We lingered but Feathers got us moving again. The path stopped from being just uphill to literally becoming rock climbing. The light beige boulders were bigger than my entire dorm in North Carolina. I dug in my fingers and hung on, pulling myself up with my upper body strength. We all watched for each other but had to look after ourselves first. It was dangerous and took everything. I wanted to throw up after a few moments out of height anxiety and just the pace at which we were moving.

Once we got to the top it overlooked an old factory town. I wasn't sure whether to feel sorry for it or stop off and visit it. It was probably trashy and not worth my time, but still I bet it made a good home for people struggling somewhere. The backbone of this country made themselves heard in the last election, but still, nobody really listens to them.

We stopped for lunch after that. It was Wild One, Harrison, Feathers and I. They all had generous meats and produce in what they were eating. I broke off stale ramen into two almost bread like pieces and turned that into a tuna cracker sandwich. They all looked at me disgusted.

"Jesus Christ man? That's what you're eating?" Feathers said, taken a little back.

"I don't know. It's not so bad," I crunched

"I wouldn't dare eat that," Harrison said with his thick British accent.

"Blimey, are you alright on food then?" Wild One asked.

"I suppose. I didn't leave with a lot of money when I left so I just have been sorta making do with what I got."

"Suit yourself, I've got enough pepperoni to share if you want some," Harrison said, making a burrito with Italian meats, carrots and lettuce.

"Whatever works." I said taking a little of everything.

I was intrigued about the history of the Fellowship and they were delighted to share. It seemed like it had been a long road. Each of the respective people having a specific relationship with one another.

"Nobody really got too deep into shit talking one another, yet." Feathers said.

"Well, Bobcat." Harrison replied.

"Yeah, but Bobcat is a fuckhead. I heard he yellow blazed just to keep up with us."

“I hear he was actually getting off the trail,” I spoke up. It was true, “I saw him right after I got dropped off at the trail outside of Port Clinton smoking a fresh packet of cigarettes and a Reese’s Peanut Butter Cup after our night of drinking. He told me so.” I said.

“When did he say this?” Feathers asked.

“Yesterday, I think.” I replied.

“Damn.” A silence between all of them.

“I’ll have to confirm this, but it sounds pretty accurate,” Feathers said, pulling out his phone. “He’s been talking about getting off the trail for some time now.” He finished stoically as though he had just seen one of his men shot down in battle.

A lone hiker came by with a dog.

“Y’all hear about the murder?” he asked.

“A little bit, we saw the cop cars.” Feathers appointed him.

“Yeah, apparently someone was stabbed to death just before the rocks.”

It was odd that at that moment someone should show up and talk about death. Whether someone physically dying or just the incapability of living life the way you wanted anymore (like in Bobcats’s case). The end of anything always leaves us all a little cold.

I rolled a small cigarette before we left, and I felt like more of a man than was good for me. These guys were at the front of the Fellowship. Hiking with them was not only like running a marathon, it was like being at a forefront sprint. It felt good, but I was glad I could take it on with a sense of calm. After lunch, the miles started to become much more poignant. Each step began to hurt and one of my legs felt especially out of place. I thought about the permanent damage I was doing to my knees for carrying so much weight up and down hills for so many miles, days on end, with no relief.

I kept up with them for as long as I could. We all were starting to make distances between us. I was in second place behind Feathers about fifteen feet or so around a bend, I saw him pause for a moment and then keep walking. I wondered what the hell he was staring at and I came around the corner quickly only to be greeted by a full-grown snake jump at me flashing its venomous fangs. I looked that fucker right in the eye, but we were both scared of each other and it raised its head but darted away at the last second. I nearly fell back on my ass, but luckily, I had been stretching my dancing legs and I was able to land upright to just strut away.

I wondered why Feathers had not said anything about it. It was such an adrenal shock that I stopped focusing on my painful knee since all the blood rushing to my head was almost bulging out of my eyeballs. Slowly the chemicals in my brain began to wear off and the exhaustion began to take hold. It wasn't long before I was at the back of the pack. I tried to not slip too far away from them, but the pain in my legs was overbearing. I screamed out once or twice in agony.

We got so spread apart that when I arrived at their last pit stop for the day, they were getting ready to make a move on. I had to take a seat. I thought about smoking some marijuana to ease the pain, and I did, but asked if any of them had any aspirin or something like that to help me out. Harrison had some pills that are basically the same thing as aspirin from across the pond.

The last stretch of that day was the worst of the entire trip. It was only about three miles, but it felt like three hundred. The drugs began to take effect, but it was no heaven. I had been doing a pretty good job of avoiding whatever I had left of that filthy lust. Dire times call for dire measures. I knew nobody was around, not even any snakes. I recalled my sweet little mischievous bag of powdered opium I got swindled into at Trail Days. I had only used so far to fix my hotel depression and physical distress was a situation as dire as any to get high.

I pulled everything out, dipped my finger in the yellow small bag of opiate like fun dip and took a sweet ol' sniff and rubbed it in my gums. Doogie Howser, I was swell after that. I could barely walk straight. I was sure I wouldn't be falling off the edge of any cliffs. Relax, it was good for me. The pain in my knee turned to a soft numb that was replaced with the tickling of the tall grass brushing up against my legs. I laughed like I was high on off about something, but really, I was just grasping at the nothingness that was there, thinking it as something new for me once again. It was like I was holding everything in my hands, and it was holding me. A warm feeling that carried me to where I needed to be. Of course, I felt a little guilty, but really things were out of my control at that point. Nothing to do but laugh, like you would with your dead relatives.

Chapter 44

I was too tired to set up camp once I got to the campsite. I just laid my backpack down next to a tree and grabbed my cigarettes and weed and got down to smoking to enhance any afterglow. Since we started hiking so early it was only about four o'clock and we were the first people at camp, so I wasn't too worried about finding a place to sleep. There was also a shelter in the vicinity, but water was a mile walk downhill, so that meant a mile uphill. I put that off for as long as I could.

Hansel and Gretel were only about twenty minutes behind us and Auto showed up after that, followed by Amazon. When you chain smoke, people get interested in just having a small taste for themselves. Wild One was the first to be guilty of this. He claimed he was getting a little antsy about being away from home and thought some marijuana would help ease him of his anxiety. I rolled a joint and he took a few puffs on it, and you could tell he'd been out of practice. He laughed pretty hard, and I laughed.

"Good lord, that's enough for me." And just like that he was on his ass. I didn't want to admit it to myself, but I was on my ass too. I couldn't tell if everyone noticed. Everyone eventually joined in as I just idly tried to regain strength and the ability to not seem so sedated. I'm sure it wasn't a good look, but I was basically in sad guy mode trying to brighten up. I sure as hell didn't look as good as Feathers who was going on about how he was looking for the most lightweight tents for his Pacific Coast trip he was doing next season (Cubin Fiber). He genuinely took himself too seriously.

"The clouds! Look at the clouds," Wild One said, lying on his back, looking up at the sky. We all looked at him like he was a bit mad.

"It looks like a room. Like you could just go up there and live up there."

Feathers and I locked eyes and cracked up. Harrison was on his phone and shook his head but not because of Wild One.

“Some criminals just took power in Parliament.” Harrison talked it over like a proposition.

“Yeah well, what can you do?” Wild One exhaled.

“Glad I’m in this country right now. England has gone to hell.”

“This country ain’t much better off,” I said.

“Well *my* country is run by thugs.” Harrison responded.

“I just don’t get the argument that immigrants take money from the American people,” Wild One said shaking his head, and Feathers looked up.

“Really, because I know a lot of Americans who might disagree with that notion.” I said.

“Why?”

“Greed and Prejudice,” I said. “An indignant truth.”

“We bring so much money into this country through travel and spend loads to boost this economy and all I hear about is how much we take from this bloody country,” Wild One said, making Harrison annoyed like he didn’t want to be on anyone’s side. I thought Wild One had a good point that I hadn’t acknowledged.

The walk down to water was not awful, but it was a lot of work for such a small stream. It probably took me about twenty minutes and the pain in my legs returned. I felt like crying, but I just took a deep breath, remembered how far I had gotten. It took another twenty minutes to fill up my water bottles and, on the walk back the path was crossed by another huge black snake. It just kept going and going and I’m sure it was the devil himself letting me know he was nearby.

The topic of height came up back at the campsite.

“Hanzel is shorter than you, Gretel. Isn’t he?” Harrison said who was quite tall himself.

“No, he isn’t. He’s five’ nine. Just as tall as me.”

“Well, I’m six foot three.” Harrison said.

“I’m the shortest person in the world,” Auto said to himself loudly enough for us all to hear.

“How tall are you?” Amazon asked Auto.

“Five foot six.” How bout you?” He asked Amazon.

“Five ten.”

They looked at me.

"About six four." I said sarcastically and it broke the tension.

Feathers didn't chime in, but he was no taller than six foot either. He was one hell of a good-looking man, though. It's not always about the height, it's how you use it. They all joked at Feathers that he was probably sexting a bunch of women which seemed oddly accurate but made me have a little distaste for the way technology was replacing human intimacy. I'm sure he was on a journey of self-discovery, but If you are just filling it up with bimbos sending you nudes, I feel like it would be hard to learn anything about yourself, but it probably wouldn't make it hard to love oneself.

Ergon showed up last to the campsite with a broken hiker pole. It very quickly became all about him and Amazon tried her hardest to refrain from physically comforting him. It was somewhat beautiful, but also odd to look at. No one seemed short on affection and that's what made it odd. Who knew who the hell these people were in their real lives and what luck to come across them without having to reveal myself. I was just sad to think they probably would look back at their own mirrors once all this was done and just see themselves, instead becoming different people. It really was none of my business.

I offered Ergon a spliff to ease his bones and we talked all about the day. He took the time to be a little interested, and in all honesty, I probably spoke with a little too much pride. The feeling was mutual. We weren't fighting for airtime, but we weren't really listening to the radio either. Everyone out there wasn't perfect, but the deep forest loved us, and it helped us learn to love one another. Something I still need to work on. He brought up that he was going to his lake house tomorrow and his mom was going to pick everybody up in town, he sort of included me in this conversation.

I waited too long to set up my tent and it was dark and everybody else had set their things up. I walked down to the shelter to see if there was room, but it was filled up. I mosied back to where I had spent the second half of the day and spent a long time setting up the tent and an even longer time looking for some flat ground to put it on. I never found one. I slept on a rock.

When morning came, I was one of the first people up, but I realized I had done a poor job of putting everything in my tent and was worried that I might've lost something last night while setting up. I just had to remind myself that I didn't need anything. I was doing alright for myself, I suppose, apart from a bad habit that was lurking. I didn't eat much for breakfast, but Harrison gave me an orange, so the vitamin C woke me up.

Ergon and Amazon were still in their tents when the rest of us left.

"Suppose they are trying to get a good shag in before this weekend eh?" Wild One poked at me.

The morning hike wasn't bad at all. My legs were used to the pain, and it was mainly downhill. Once the trail ended, we were by a small highway and it was supposedly a two mile walk into the town. We all tried to hitch in, but there were too many of us. I proposed we walk, and they followed until they all thought it might be worth the wait. I walked up to a man on his back porch and asked him if he would be willing to give some of us a lift into town. He claimed he was busy, and that town wasn't that far away.

Town wasn't that close. I had to put in a little extra effort before a possible zero weekend. I think it was Friday or Saturday morning and all the diners were open and I was in the mood to get some good food in my stomach. Instead, we stopped off at a gas station, and I grabbed a coffee. Feathers let everybody know that Ergon's mom was going to be picking people up at the Food Lion and they were all going to pitch in for the weekend.

We walked along some streets that were somewhat busy and posted up to wait for everyone to arrive. It was sort of funny. There was a table set out, and we all sat around it and pretty soon it looked like we were a bunch of hiker trash holding the store hostage. There was a small "festival", if you would call it that, organized outside of the store. It wasn't much, just a white tent and some flags. There was pizza out and I asked if I could have some and the lady running it said of course, "Tell your friends."

"There's 13 of us. I counted and that includes everyone." Feathers said, "If we all put in ten dollars that will be enough for booze, food and a good dessert. There was Feathers, Hanzel and Gretel, Wild One, Harrison, Auto, Sensei, and Amazon and Ergon.

And we were still waiting on Ares, Tonic and Xbox.

"Alright. Everybody put your money in." Feathers said.

I didn't really know if it was going to work, but I put in my ten dollars. Ergon looked at me as I did so, and I hoped to think nothing of it. I would have stealth camped on the beach just to come along. I waited as everybody shopped and got things outside with Feathers and Hanzel, charging our phones. Ergon's mom arrived and gave him a big hug and was excited to meet everyone. I tried to be as transparent as I could, but he pulled me aside.

"Hey man, listen. This is only for members of the Fellowship and it has been great hiking with you the past few days, it's just we've all been hiking together for a long time now, and we're just going to keep it between us. So, you can have your ten dollars back, but you can't come out to the lake house with us."

I understood but I was still hurt. He let me down easily, but I was still let down. It was my fault for getting my hopes up. I questioned if I just wasn't good enough for the world, but I hope, even lied to myself that that wasn't the problem. I'm not impervious to denial. No one is. I took it with stride, but it wasn't easy to watch everyone pile into the car. There was more than one trip, so I just waited pondering what I should do next. I wasn't dependent on these people, but they had made hiking a joy.

After all that mess, by the graces of god I saw Ares strutting up to the Food Lion, with a loose cigarette hanging from his lip.

"Need a light?" I asked him.

"Sure. Good to see you, sad guy."

"You too friend. Are you going to the lake house with all them?" I asked

"My dad and girlfriend are actually coming to stay out here for the weekend, so I got a hotel. Are you going?"

"About that," Feathers interjected. "I tried to include him, but Ergon said there wasn't really any room, and was trying to keep it just the Fellowship."

"Oh." Ares looked a little disappointed.

"Are you gonna stay in town for the weekend? I know Wild One is getting a hotel room for pretty cheap so he can have some time to call his family."

"I don't really know. I'm trying to save my money if I can."

"It's probably not that expensive. C'mon, I'm gonna walk by there now, you wanna come?" Ares asked me.

"Might as well." I didn't say goodbye to anybody as I left with Ares. It suddenly seemed like since I wasn't accepted by the great Ergon that they wanted to get rid of me. I wasn't sad that none of it meant anything. Social boundaries still existed all the way out here. As we walked, I tried to get over the small break up that just happened.

"I shouldn't have been lying to myself these last couple of days that I was really a part of the Fellowship."

"It's alright man, it's not you, it's just kinda like guidelines we have in the Fellowship. Like you know, Ms. Ginger?"

"Yeah."

"Well, she's been hiking with us for quite a while, but she isn't technically part of the Fellowship." I understood his point, but it didn't make me feel any better.

"I understand. It isn't that. I get that you all have been through a lot and for me to just barge through and think I'm part of anything would be foolish. It's just the thought that I was counted, in what felt like a sort of a public manner, strains a little bit on a more personal basis when it is individually revoked."

"Don't worry about it. You can just get back on the trail and keep going to New York."

"That's the other thing. I think I'm technically more North than NYC. I might just go due East and try and get there as quickly as possible."

"How far away is it?" He asked.

"Only about 100 miles. I could make that in a few days if I move quick."

"That is an idea. Let's just see if we can book you a room in the motel. Ok?"

Wild One was sitting outside on the phone.

"You coming to the lake house?" He asked me.

"Nah, I'm seeing if I can get a room. If not, I might just take the off roads all the way to New York."

"Blimey."

I walked through the door and went up to the lady clerk at the motel while Ares waited outside.

"How much for a room?"

"Sixty dollars a night."

"I don't have that."

"Then you're not staying here." She said.

"Fair enough. Thought I'd ask."

I went back outside less discouraged than I was before. Maybe this is what I had been looking for. The trail had become easy, and I knew how to navigate it.

"No luck?" Ares said as I walked out.

"Nope."

"Well, let's just go back to my hotel room and we can share a beer and think over a plan."

"Might as well," I said again.

"Would you mind taking a listen to one of my songs?" I asked him.

"I would love to. I'm a songwriter myself."

"You are?"

"Yeah, I went to school in England."

"Did you like it?"

"I loved it." He said.

"Why didn't you stay?" I asked, comparing my New York quest to his time abroad.

"I just didn't need to stay there. There was enough of everything I needed back home. Listen, my dad used to hate what I was doing, but now he couldn't be more proud of me. You have to think for yourself first, and everything and everyone else will come."

"Here just listen to this." I gave him my headphones and pressed play on *if I don't have Love*. When it ended he didn't say anything at first.

"That was really good man." He said.

"You think so?" I asked.

"Definitely, if you have songs like that, you'll do just fine in New York."

"But the whole reason I did all of this was over a girl."

"I think you'll find a few girls in New York that you'll like. Seriously, they put something in their water." He winked at me.

We laughed for a moment and arrived at the hotel he was staying at. His room was around back. Hotel rooms all look the same and yet can be so comforting and basic at the same time. I was anything but comfortable, I needed to figure what I was going to do, and quick.

"Here, have a beer." Ares said handing me a cold one.

"Thanks."

"Listen man, I wish you could stay here, it's just that that would defeat the whole purpose of seeing my girlfriend this weekend."

"I understand. Do you mind if I roll a spliff and we go outside and smoke it? I just need to get my shit together."

"Not at all."

I got everything out and mixed up some tobacco and weed and we went outside.

"Do you know what you are going to do?" Ares asked again.

"Kinda. I've been playing with a few ideas."

"Throw one out."

"Well, you know how I've been going on about this girl?"

"Sure yeah."

"Well, a long time ago while ago, I gave this girl my social security number, ya know, as a joke since we didn't have each other's phone numbers."

"Uh huh."

"Well, I was thinking. If I get to New York, I might as well try to set myself up there, but I'll need a job if I'm going to do that, and my father is not going to be in support of that in any way. So, I'll see if she still has my old social lying around somewhere and if she could give it to me and I could set myself up and get set up. It's sort of my last hope."

"I think that you should try and reason with your dad if you can. You shouldn't just call up some girl that you haven't talked to in a while asking for all that."

"I know, but you said throw out an idea and that's what I came up with. Listen, I just need to know if I'm doing this all for someone else, or for myself. If New York is where I can start over. If I can't figure that out, then I sure as hell don't know how to love someone. Sorry. I didn't plan on *any* of this at all. I probably shouldn't even be out here. Right now, this *is* just me getting my shit together," I said pointing at the beer and spliff.

"I don't know what to tell you. Only you can answer what is right for you."

"I think I'm just gonna walk from here towards New York due East and see if I make it there."

"You wanna go with that plan?" He asked sounding a little worried.

"Got any better one?"

"I can call Ergon, I'll explain the whole situation and see if he will let you stay over the weekend at the lake house," he said.

"No, I definitely don't want that." I answered

"Why not?"

"Because that would put a damper on the whole weekend and there would be way too much focus on me, and all the trouble I'd caused. I just don't think I could do that. For my sake and all yours." I said.

"I suppose I understand. So, you are just gonna walk it?"

"Looks like it. That was the idea from the start." I finished off the rest of my liquid courage.

"You've got a lot of heart man."

"I've been told that before."

"You got a lot of *something*. You're going to be alright."

"I just keep telling myself that." I said. I was hoping all of this might account for more than a big heart.

"You will be, and even if you aren't, you said it in your lyrics, you 'just don't care'."

It was strange to have someone tell me about myself something that I'd told myself in a song.

"That's right. I don't care, that doesn't mean I'm not trying. To hell with it. I should make a move on. It's still early in the day, I can probably make it pretty far If I get going now."

"Do you need anything? Here, I'll get you some Italian ice and then you can go." Ares said.

"I mean, I'm not going to turn down a treat like that. The ice will be good. It'll cool me off."

We went over to a cute Italian ice shop and I got key lime. I thought about the rich Italian heritage in my blood and the courage that had been bestowed upon me for generations. What I did then was an act of bravery, not fear, for once. It wasn't the first act of courage on the trip and it wasn't the last, but you never get used to throwing yourself out into the wind.

Ares gave me a strong hug before I left and by that point, he felt like a brother to me. I didn't care if I made it to New York at that point, I had found what I was looking for. Someone with just an inch of faith in me, and a reason to put that faith back into humanity.

I was here

Chapter 45

I had done it now. The only thing that kept me calm was that I had some *time* until it was going to get dark. Worst case scenario I would be stealth camping somewhere, but that opens up opportunity for the law to intervene and that is never good, especially since they seemed to be out and about. A road was closed off, with a cruiser blocking the road. I stayed my distance, but I was just walking so there was no apparent reason I couldn't pass. I didn't realize how badly I looked like a drifter.

Along the road there was a car for sale. It was asking for five hundred dollars and I wondered if my story would be compelling enough to possibly lower the price. I knocked on the door and who answered was much more compelling than any of this. It was an old man who was missing a leg. He had the flag up, waving on his porch. I didn't need to ask if he was a veteran.

"Can I help you?" He asked.

"Yeah, I was just wondering about that car?"

"Oh, it's my daughter's."

"Oh, I don't know if she would be willing to knock the price off of it at all, would she?"

"You'll have to talk with her. She gets off work at five."

"I'll just come back tomorrow." I said.

"Alright." There was a dog at the door who was barking as I walked away like the universe was telling me to wait. I still wonder if that could have been how I got my first car. Probably not. I wouldn't want one in New York anyways. I checked the weather since there were some daunting clouds in the far distance, although the day was still very sunny. I made it about another seven miles before I went through a suburban outlet. There was a man and his wife sitting out on their driveway.

"Where you going with all that?" The man called.

"New York. Coming from North Carolina."

"Are you taking the AT?"

"Not anymore." I said.

"What'cha gonna do? Just walk there?" He asked.

"Planning on it."

"Do you need anything to eat?" His wife asked.

"I wouldn't mind it if you've got something." I took my pack off my blistered shoulders.

"I can make you a sandwich, is ham fine?"

"Sounds lovely."

"Mayo, mustard? All the good stuff?" She continued.

"All the way, but do you mind if I stop here for a moment?" I asked the couple.

"You're fine," the man answered.

"Thanks."

"What are you going to do in New York?" The man said.

"I'm an artist."

"An artist eh? Alright, what do you do?"

"A writer, and a dancer and a singer." I answered.

"Where's your guitar?"

"You got one? Every time I find one, I write a song. I have a few recorded if you want to listen."

"Sure. Is it on YouTube?" He asked.

"Um, I can just play it from my phone."

"You know I'm in a band," He said, which was a little out of character for having a house and a wife.

"Oh yeah, what kind of music?"

"Heavy metal."

"Right on. You might not like my music then, it's sort of acoustic garbage."

"Let's hear it then."

I plugged my phone into the speakers. One of my songs started playing and it helped ease conversation, but I get a little uneasy hearing my own voice.

"Where you gonna stay?"

"Tonight, or in New York?"

"Either one."

"I'm sort of figuring that out right now. When I get to New York it isn't as much *me* that needs a place to stay, it is my backpack. I can't be carrying around a fifty-pound backpack going through Manhattan, I'll stick out like a sore thumb."

"You're thinking of staying in Manhattan?" He

asked.

"God no. Brooklyn is where I want to be. I've heard there are some art community living spaces." I said.

"Yeah, well, you don't want to be in Manhattan without a place to stay. It gets real tough real quick,"

"I've heard."

"Well what about tonight?"

"Well, hypothetically, would you let me pitch a tent on your lawn?" I proposed.

"No."

"Well, then I'm still figuring that out."

"Here's your sandwich. I made one for now, and one for later," the woman said, handing me two sandwiches in plastic bags.

"God bless."

A man pulled up into the driveway and a few kids jumped out of the car.

"Boys, are you going to say hello to our guest?" Their father said.

"Hi guys," I said.

The biggest and tubbiest one of the bunch came right under me.

"Why you got a backpack?" He got right under my nose.

"I'm a traveler." I shrugged.

"Like a real person who goes on adventures?"

"Haha, sort of."

"Are you on YouTube?" The boy asked.

"Haha, yeah."

"Are you famous?"

"Haha, not yet."

"How many subscribers do you have?"

"Like 50." I laughed.

"THEN YOU SHALL HAVE 51!" He raised his arm in astonishment.

He cracked me up. So young and interested in whatever the world was to him. There was another boy who was much quieter and had glasses, but I made sure to be kind to him as well. Another shorter man with long grey hair wearing sandals came over and I realized what it was. These were the guys, the boys and the family, you could tell. I hope someday to have something like that, if that isn't so much to ask.

They offered me a beer and we got to sharing.

"You know what the kid from *Into the Wild* did with his knife when he got to a city?" The one with a ponytail wearing sandals said.

"What?"

"He buried it."

The thought of me digging a hole in the middle of Central Park to bury a knife sounded like some sociopathic shit. I tried not to think about it. They were all kind, but you could tell they didn't have the kind of hospitality that only exists in the South. Both of the little boys gave me a hug before I left, and they played heavy metal as I walked off. The band was kinda rad, you're never too old to rock.

The further I walked from the suburban outlet, the more rural the land became and the bigger and farther apart the houses got. It was strange having never been in the East Coast before and this being my first exposure to it. It wasn't really what I expected. Part of me was glad for it. It wasn't dark yet, but the further I went, you could see people working out on their farms. I could just imagine walking up to a house and they would be the type of people to understand.

Those clouds in the distance were beginning to get a little closer and much darker. I didn't want to think about it, but it became apparent that it was going to rain. The clouds moved quickly over me, and it rapidly turned into heavy downpour. I didn't even have time to put any poncho (trash bag) over me, I just started running, hoping to find to shelter. There was a house with their front door open that looked into a warm living room with a few people there, but it was surrounded by a picket fence. I waved my arms and called, not wanting to go on the property, hoping they would see me or hear me over the rain.

A young woman looked up and touched her father. He got up and opened the glass front door at me in the midst of heavy rain.

"Hello?" He called over the sound of pouring rain.

"Yes, hello. I'm travelling to New York and I was wondering if there was any way you could help me get out of this rain?"

"Go into the barn. It's right around back, just go on in." He pointed.

"Thank you so very much. That's great." I quickly walked past the fence onto a gravel road that lead up to a barn. I pulled open the door and was astonished to see six or seven men all inside moving hay bales. I wasn't expecting company. I took a moment to sit down and compose myself. I wondered if the rest of the Fellowship had heard about my decision to go rogue and thought I was probably caught in a rainstorm. It didn't matter, I was just glad to be in a safe dry space.

The owner of the farm came in to inspect the situation.

"You alright?" He asked.

"I'm fine, thank you so much." I said.

"You're walking to New York?" He asked.

"Pretty much."

"Well you're welcome to stay in here until the storm passes over." He offered.

"That would mean so much to me."

"Alright then." He then went over to talk with one of the men who were piling the hay. He spoke with authority.

"I think we are going to have one more cart if we can get it in here quick, how quick can you empty this one?" He asked one of his workers.

"About twenty minutes," the muscular hay stacker said.

"Sounds good."

"I can help if you want." I stood up.

"That'd be great." He appointed me to one of his men.

I jumped up on the hay barrel and began pulling. They aren't light, around twenty pounds and the hay gets stuck to all your clothes. It was hard work.

"How much you get paid to do this an hour?" I asked the hay stacker who was wearing cowboy boots and an American flag on his sleeveless shirt.

"Ten."

"Not bad. How many hours a day?"

"Ten."

"Must get pretty strong doing all that."

"They speak for themselves." He didn't have to flex.

The first pile was finished, and a young man with a scar on his lip came in backing up the hay stack. He was able to maneuver the entire structure on a pivot from the tractor he was riding. It was sort of like watching Picasso paint, an art in its own right. It must've taken years of practice, and he not only did it perfectly, he was incredibly fast.

Me and the other lad climbed up on it and started pulling them off. It was sort of like an odd algorithm. Taking each hay bale off layer by layer. We broke into it taking everything off of one side, and then everything off the top, and then again vertically and finally off the top until there was nothing left. The hay was passed from one man to the next, me being the first, and then handed down onto a conveyor belt up to a much larger stack where it was being restacked and all of it was kept. One of the rowdier boys grabbed onto one of the haystacks and rode it up the conveyor belt.

Once we were all finished, the man with the scar came in with dinner and shared it with us. They were all good fellows, a little dirty and stinky, but I couldn't help but analyze the situation that maybe this was all I was good for. Hard labor. I longed to be inside with the owners over a cup of tea, but good artistry is all about knowing the time and place, and it wouldn't have been natural to just go and invite myself in.

The conversation of the dirty men was just as good. I didn't say much. They were interested in what I was doing but had seen a lot of hikers in their day. Some of them had girlfriends they talked about going home to. The others talked about getting booze for the night, and the conversation ended on who was the leader. The tallest of them pointed to the chap who drove the hay tractor and said, "This is the fucking man."

He was maybe five foot, but I valued what his consciousness had revered. They all drove off and I was left alone in the barn. The door was wide open though and the sound of the rain from a safe place soothed me.

The owner came back in on a golf cart to inspect the work. He was pleased.

"Are you gonna stay the night?" The owner asked me.

"If you would allow it."

"I don't see why not. I'll come back in a few hours before bed to check up on you."

"Thank you so much."

"No problem. There is a bathroom around the back, if you need it." He said as he drove off on his golf cart.

It was humbling to talk to a man who had so much. I would be lying if I said I didn't eye his daughter, who I'd seen out on the porch when we were working, but I'm sure all those dirty guys had been giving her the stink eye, so I thought best to not get wrapped up into anything silly. There was so much that extended from this man's life that even the scraps were all that I could have ever wanted. I cleared off a desk that was in the barn and took the time to journal.

Saturday night in some barn

Do you suppose that the people who know what they want end up with more, or is it just chance? These are age old questions that the likes of Mark Twain have been writing about since Tom Sawyer. Superstition and God. If there is a God, he must not like me very much, and if there isn't, I'm very lucky. I don't know why chaos is comforting to me. I couldn't ever just be complacent about things, although I contemplate a lot. Maybe someday I'll find all the answers, and maybe all the answers will find me. Every once and awhile, it's better to have no questions, no answers, just raw beautiful life that you can look at without it looking right back at you. The problem is we try to comprehend it all. Make sense of it, but no scientist or priest on the planet has ever understood what life is made of. The atom. Sounds just the same to me as Adam from the Bible. Just a compilation of random energy and ideas going nowhere and believed to have some sort of pattern. It is a good trait to be able to control and wield yourself properly, but it might just be in our nature to be uncontrollable. Let go. You will always have enough no matter what, just sometimes enough is never enough. I just wish I could be happy with so much less. I wonder if this man still knows how. All the things we do, no matter how big or small in the world, whether physically or in our head, mean something. Call it prayer, call it God, call it love, call it chance, coincidence or fate, we are all made of it, and what we name it makes us who we are. A person's thoughts are just as much who they are as what they look like. We can't hide from others only because we can't hide from ourselves.

The owner of the barn came in and told me about the lights in the old building, He flipped them all off at once and the place was pitch black. It was sort of bizarre.

"What time are you going to be out of here in the morning?" He asked.

"I can be gone by five am." I said.

"Well, you don't need to rush off at five. Let's say six o'clock. I've got a horseback riding event tomorrow being held here, and I will have to be tending to that."

"Thank you again for everything."

"Also, a neighbor of mine is going to stop by to give you breakfast."

"At six?"

"Around then, I'll probably see you."

"Until then, good sir. Goodnight."

Chapter 46

All the lights were turned off and the barn began to take an ominous feeling. I thought best to quickly brush my teeth. The bathroom was cute and had relics from a lifetime of horseback riding. I put two and two together and realized that this was a horse farm. It was late but I could see just down a hallway and saw the stables where the horses were kept. I treaded lightly as to not scare any of them this late at night. I let my eyes adjust and the outline of the gracious animal looked back at me, but it didn't talk.

I watched the sun rise to warm the whole barn with its love. We either see everything or just can't seem to see a thing. I wish I had paid more attention in geometry. Then maybe I could finally get those angles I'm looking for. The land was beautiful. Farmland with thick trees and well lived-in homes. The neighbor lady came by around six and gave me a few boxes of fig newtons. It was a good breakfast because I could eat it while I walked. I passed the sign that let me know I was leaving Pennsylvania. Looking up from its initial interest, was a real-life bear and it was looking at me for food.

"Get in." A woman pulled up in a SUV. "Where are you heading?"

"I'm just trying to make it to church this morning." I said.

"I can help you out with that. I was worried about you walking alongside the road."

"Eh, everything is just as scared of you as you are of it. Sometimes throwing a little danger into people's life does them good." I said idly for how dangerous a hungry bear could have been.

"Don't get too carried away, now." She eyed me.

"You're a lifesaver."

She drove across a beautiful river that made the streets wind and we were in New Jersey. The Garden State. I don't know why but nobody talks about all the flowers from here, smells lovely.

"I've heard they've had a wildlife problem in Jersey." I said.

"Bears get hungry." She said back.

I was about five minutes late to a Methodist service. Everybody eyed me as I walked in with my big backpack and I took a seat. There wasn't really a preacher. Or a service at all. It was more of a town hall meeting with a little prayer mixed in. The lady running the show was going on about how Prom was coming up, and when it was time to pray, she singled me out.

"Let us make sure that all of us do not fall into temptation, and that the Lord will feed us, and heal our poison ivy problems."

Enough of that. I come to hear the word for all of man, not just for my own sake. A community meeting my ass, this was a cult. They wanted me to join! I had to get the hell out of there, quick. I grabbed my backpack, but there was no good time to walk out. As I stood up, she talked louder to make sure I got the message.

"Let us not hide from ourselves our true desires, but never give into them for the Lord shall make us repent. The Lord will see all."

Everyone was stone cold silent as I slammed the door but was replaced with the morning chirping of the birds. There wasn't an ounce of luck in that whole building. I checked to see if there was a better way to get closer to God, and hallelujah, a Baptist church was down the street and had a service starting in ten minutes.

I don't know about you, but Jersey is damn beautiful. Hands down, just bloody gorgeous. Everyone was actually in their gardens, or on their porches reading the paper. The town was small enough and held on to an old style of life that I hadn't seen since my own hometown. The diners were brick and there were multiple parks. I peered through the school windows and thought back to my favorite time of life. It must've just been because it was Sunday morning, but I was in love with the place. Of course, that feeling of home, surely had to be ruined by a phone call from my father.

"Hello."

"Hello, son." He said solemnly.

"Hi."

"Looks like you are in Jersey."

"Looks like it. Nobody ever talked about how lovely this place is." I said.

"Jersey? Wait til you get to New York."

"Yeah, I've been thinking about that." I said.

"Well, we have to set up your living situation at school for next year right away."

"Yeah, about that..." I gulped.

"What about that?" He yelled back.

"I was thinking maybe, I could stay a few months out in New York, ya know. I've been talking about art school for years."

"If you think you would have a better chance getting student loans."

"I was just talking about for the summer."

"Still. That's stupid." He answered.

"What if it is? What if I *just don't care*," I said with fucking romance.

"Alright, great."

"Yes, it is."

"Alright. Well, it sounds like it's time to come home."

"Actually, I've got to get to church. You should *think* about doing the same thing."

"I'm serious. Nobody is going to take you seriously. You're a no-good-dirty rotten-young-man."

"Happy Sunday." We hung up.

I checked the time and church started in three minutes and I was about five away. I picked up the pace to a light jog, and I made it and was greeted by a kind black man with a moustache. He guided me to where to set my bags, and I walked in and could tell that this was where God was actually spending his Sunday morning. The people of the church were not especially kind but weren't put off by me being there. They smiled, and I started to see what Ares had been talking about with the water. I saw probably the most attractive man I'd ever seen in my entire life. He was six foot seven and had a sexy little mole on his blond upper lip.

In front of me were three daughters dressed so

gorgeously, it hurt to have to keep my nose up above the pillars vouching for that cross. The pastor was a tall bald man. He had the essence of a mad man hiding behind his eyes, and once he got to preaching it was apparent that he was in fact crazy. He just yelled and it felt so good. We sang for Chrissake and sang loudly. He preached about the gates of heaven. How when we all get there and the Lord asks us, if we have been good in our lives, if we will believe in the deepest of our hearts that we deserve to be welcomed. Buddha believed life was just pain. I think we all have to get through this hell we call life and we ought to be allowed into heaven. The only thing we are responsible for is our own lives, and even then, I believe we have a right to take it if we wish.

People have different tastes. These Baptists were glad to have me praying with them. I respect that people need their personal space and beliefs, but at any time when people gather, there is communal spirit for one another and peace to be given, and we pray together. That's why I go to different churches. All I can say is that, apart from the church being somewhat too small, this was what I describe as spirit. Hardwood walls, pews, a podium for the pastor and Jesus Christ sitting right there with all of us.

"Do you have a place to stay for the night?" An old woman turned to me.

"Not yet. It's still sort of early but if I was being honest with you, I'm exhausted."

"This is my husband, Vern. We would love to have you stay with us for the night." She smiled sweetly."Would you really?"

The thought of a warm meal and a cozy bed flashed across my eyes and I thought that God was probably throwing me a bone.

"Of course. Let's talk after church."

The church service continued, and all the players played their parts. We said "peace be with you" to each other in the church, which could only fit about forty people maximum. The handsome young man stood tall and proud, taking each part of the ceremony with deep leadership. Not only a man of God, but a good man at that. Once we all got outside, the lady who offered to let me stay for the night introduced me to the pastor who I told my whole story. He seemed interested, but hesitant to let me go with the old woman.

He pulled her over to the side and whispered some words to her.

He looked at me. "We'll take him." He said to the woman waving me over.

I wasn't going to fight it, but I felt that now this was a little bit out of my control. There was no need to overwork myself, and if this was the luck that I was having *not* being on the trail, I had nothing to worry about.

"Do you need your clothes washed?" The pastor asked me.

"In fact, I do. It has been much too long since I've seen a washing machine and I've been wearing the same shirt for the past week."

"CJ!" He called over to a tall young man wearing glasses.

"This is my son CJ. He will help you get some new clothes and you can give him your old ones."

"Nice to meet you, CJ. I'm Jack." I said meeting his gaze.

"Hello. Alright well, let's go upstairs and get you some clothes and then we'll eat lunch."

I looked at the pastor who was attending to other people at the church but was aware of all that was going on. Almost like he wanted the Lord to see the good tidings he was bestowing upon me. We went through the church and up the stairs above where the pulpit was. It had a forest green rug, costumes probably used for Christmas, and a few old VHS tapes.

"Give me any clothes you need washed, and the bathroom is right through there," CJ directed.

I will never understand why it is so comfortable for me to wear other people's clothing.

"Does 34 length work for you?"

"Sure. Those'll work fine."

"Yeah, these were mine before college."

"Thanks man."

"I'll see you in a few. No hurry." He went downstairs.

Now, I should have been grateful at that point for all the Lord had given me. The opportunity for a good night's rest, food to come, but I had that unknockable urge that sometimes rushes through our veins to endure just a little bit more pleasure than bargained for. I reached into my backpack and got out the yellow powdered bag, which didn't have that much left in it and in the bathroom. I clicked my finger on the bottom of it and out came a little hill to rail.

The shower was silky like baby lotion and hot like tequila tea. I knew I was being a little unorthodox and borderline anti-Christ-like, but at the same time, why would I have the opportunity to do such a thing if all the pieces hadn't been put in their place. I didn't feel guilty at all. I was very highly thankful. It was one of the times in this trip that I was completely comfortable to be dancing on the edge.

Scrub, scrub scrub, wash, wash, wash, clean, clean, clean out my butthole. Play with pee pee pee. Dance and dry and dance and cry, dry your eyes. Laugh in the mirror, hysterical. Contain and compose, blow your nose. The clothes clothes clothes I was wearing were oversized, but I liked it. They were like a perfect turtle shell that I could just sneak back into if things got too bad. I hoped that I was still able to talk without slurring my words, but I did some theater warm ups just in case. Unique You Nork. I boogied down the stairs worried about how much time had passed and at the bottom of the stairs, the pastor's wife was making lunch in her high heels.

"I hope you like burgers," she said to me. The whole scenery was almost too beautiful to look at. It wasn't like these people had a lot, but they had everything all the same. CJ entered from a discussion with his sister who was wearing bright lipstick in his room.

"I've got a belt for you." He opened his hands.

"Thanks."

In walked the bald tall pastor and everyone diverted their eyes.

"You're a long way from home, are you?" He asked me.

"Few hundred miles."

"And you aren't trying to hide from the Lord, now are you?"

"Hide from him? No." I said, swallowing my words and tightening my lips as to not creak a smile. "He's got a plan."

"A plan? Sounds to me like you are rushing to get into heaven."

He wasn't far off, but I wasn't about to give him the satisfaction.

"Well, we're all in God's Country."

"I just want to ask you one question."

I stood up a little bit.

"When all is said and done, will he forgive you?" He said looking into my soul.

"Yes."

"Well, you are going have to meet him, and explain that to him and whatever moment you think you've had with his peace is going to be questioned."

"I believe there will be an answer, and that answer will be grace."

He lightened up a bit. "So? You still think we have a population problem on this planet after all of God's country you've seen?"

"A good point. No. Not anymore, but I wouldn't want to go knocking down a bunch of forest animal's homes either."

"Then why have you come into my home?" He said in a frightening calm.

I wasn't going to let him get to me.

"You're the pastor. I can leave if that's what you want, but you said you were going to be the one to help me."

"That's not what I'm getting at, son. You already left where you came from. You didn't need help and now you do. What're you looking for?"

"Nothing too special, a nice meal, a warm bed, God and love, something worth crying about when all is said and done."

"Well you should have thought about that before you left."

I thought the conversation had ended and he was kicking me out.

"I did think about that when I left! I thought I was never going to get to see any of it." I tried use my rational brain.

"Then go home. I'm sure someone's worried about you."

"Them worrying about me doesn't do *me* a bit of good."

"Do you remember my sermon this morning?" He stood to his full height.

I couldn't remember my own name.

"Yes."

"What was it about?"

"Prayer."

"I ask this because I care about you, but the way it looks right now, I don't know if you are going to make it."

"I have heard that sentence so many times. You're not God. None of you men are." The whole room was quiet.

"God ain't a very funny man."

"Well My God has a sense of humor. I'm sure he's laughing right now at all this." I tried to lighten the mood.

"Do you really think getting into the gates of heaven is a laughing matter?"

"No. I don't." I sobered up my answer. "But it isn't your question to ask, it's mine."

"I'm going to ask you to pray with me, so that you, when you are gone and you see me waiting for you, I don't want to be the one to tell you I told you so."

"Should we do the Lord's Prayer, then?" I said as he watched.

I looked up at the ceiling. "Our Father who art in heaven, hallowed be thy name, thy kingdom come, thy will be done on earth as it is in heaven. Give us this day our daily bread and forgive us our trespasses as we forgive those who trespass against us. And lead us not into temptation, but deliver us from evil, for thine is the kingdom, the power and the glory. This we ask in Jesus's name. Amen."

One of those short pauses poured in. The whole family was watching from the stands. These were people who took this shit so seriously they lived in a fucking church.

The pastor looked over at his wife. "Let me just discuss it with my wife."

CJ butted in. "Let's go outside. You like basketball?"

"I've been a little out of practice, I'll need to warm up."

A young boy was sitting on a bench outside and stood up as we came by.

"Kyler. Come on and play basketball with us." CJ said to his brother.

He was interested in me as all kids are, but he couldn't tell if I was a good or bad guy right off the bat. The more I talked with him, about school, hobbies and even God, pretty soon we were laughing and taking trick shots for fun.

We had to stop for lunch, which we all ate outside as a family. Apart from me being lightly sedated, everybody in the family was extremely tall. The only one who was close to my height was Kyler. The pastor's wife was about my height with her heels on and his daughter who wore bright pink lipstick was also around my height, but the pastor, CJ, and the handsome one, Dane, towered over the lunch table.

The one who dominated the conversation was Dane. He was hard to not look at or listen to. I saw him during church go up at the front and ask for God's forgiveness, so I was skeptical if he had been keeping his nose clean in good Baptist faith. If this guy was a virgin, I'm a virgin. He went on about how all of his friends were getting married. He talked about the differences in the weddings, the small ones of just close friends and ones that were too big and lasted too long, and how him and his friends wondered if it was rude to leave early. He had another wedding coming up this weekend and it sounded like he hadn't taken a weekend off in a while. He questioned the scam of marriage, and how it might just be a facade, but his father told him that if he finds a lucky girl all that will change.

Dane eluded that CJ had already found the right girl, nodding to his sister who was sitting next to him. Both of them were quiet about the topic. I didn't want to bring up my love, because I was sure that I would have been crucified for any of the sexual things that I've done. I didn't really know what to think of all them, but I just ate as much as I could and was polite, and I still didn't know if I was going to be spending the night.

After lunch CJ said that he would take me for a ride through town and we could go to a Wawa. We got into CJ's pickup truck and began to talk. I liked CJ because you could tell that he was somewhat of the odd one out. He wasn't the favorite son, to say it blatantly.

He talked about growing up in Jersey and I let him know that I loved the place. I wished I could've stayed longer. We went to the Wawa and he bought me a large coffee shake, which was fun to drink because it got us going on some really good conversations. We got into addictions. He told me about how he used to be really into guns. All types of guns. He was obsessed with them to the point that it was all that he cared about. I asked him if he masturbated and he said he did, which was also something he struggled with. We pulled up to a park and sat down at a bench and drank our smoothies over conversation.

"Where'd you go to college?" I asked.

"Southern Cross- Engineering." He said.

"Did you like it?"

"I liked some of it, some people didn't take faith as seriously as they should have, and by the time my fourth year came around I changed my major, so it took me a long time to graduate."

"Nothing wrong with that. Most people never find out what they want to do with their lives."

"Haha, it wasn't easy." He said sipping his drink.

"I cannot imagine. My brain just doesn't think like that. I've always known what I've wanted to do, it's just doing it that's the hard part."

“It sort of gets hard to not think like you’re just doing what is expected of you, once it’s all you’ve ever known.” He said.

“Well, is it what you really wanted to do? I mean both your religion and your career.”

“Sort of, I did it for my family. I’m working here to help support my dad, since we could use the help.”

“Surely, you don’t want to be doing that forever?”

“No, just the next two years. I’ve got a great job out here and it isn’t bad staying at *home*.”

When he said the word, my body had a metaphysical reaction and I viewed the world around me and imagined I was right back in North Carolina. It was a painful discovery that I was indeed nowhere of the sort. I wished that I could have just gone home. Not in a given up sort of a way, just be back where I come from, and then maybe go back out or spend sometimes with my friends.

“You got a girlfriend?” I asked.

“One once, but she ended up being crazy.”

“What do you mean?” I smiled.

“Well, I liked her all through high school, but right before we left for college, she dyed her hair.”

“What’s wrong with that?”

“There was nothing wrong with it, it was just the way she went about it. She told me that she did it because her dad couldn’t do anything about it, and I don’t know if I could love a girl who would be that disrespectful to her father.” He said.

“Listen, I don’t want to shock you or anything, but most people don’t live in as strict of a household as your Baptist father. Honestly, I don’t think it is healthy to hold in what you are feeling. What she did was probably really freeing for her, and if she didn’t do it then, it might’ve come out in a worse way.” I suggested.

“Yeah, but that is exactly what I don’t want in a person. I don’t know.”

“You’re looking for a nun?” I poked.

“I don’t think I’m going to have a problem finding a girl. I have a job. She ran off with this shrimp guy anyways.”

I halted. “Is she happy?”

“She seems so.” You could tell he didn’t want her to be.

“And this guy she’s with now?”

“Nothing wrong with that. It’s just hard being hung up on a girl that I know if she found the Lord, she would be so much happier.” He said aloud not for the first time.

“And you think it’s your job to show that to her?”

“No. I just think I might be able to.”

“Not all of us are looking for God. You really believe everything in the Bible is real.”

“100%” He said.

“Noah’s Ark, Evolution being false, Lake of Fire? All that?”

“There have been real life size structures of the Ark created.”

“And all the animals just came out of the woods to have an orgy on a boat?” I said.

“I understand, how it could be hard to believe but I have no doubt in my mind that it is all accurate.”

“And Evolution?” I asked.

“Evolution can’t exist because if you look at chromosome mutations, which is the basis of evolution, you can’t create a chromosome. There has never been an account of one being created, only lost, and that is why people have disabilities. Are you in college?” CJ asked.

“At the moment?” I answered.

“You like it?”

“Yeah, but for probably all the reasons you didn’t like yours.” I finished my shake.

“What are you studying?”

“I wrote my own major about Race.”

“Oh ok, what do you think about Affirmative Action?”

“I think it is a good thing. We can’t just have years of discrimination and lowered opportunities for people and just expect things to be all good.” I said.

He didn’t say anything.

“What?” I pondered.

“I just don’t think you can solve racism with more racism.”

“It’s not *solving* racism with more *racism*. If we did nothing or it was more likely for a white student to get into college due to their race, that would be trying to solve racism with more racism.” I said.

“I just don’t think that way. If a person is going to be successful, they are going to be successful no matter what. My dad for instance, is one of the hardest workers I’ve ever met in my life. He worked his whole life to get what he has today, and he didn’t get any help.”

“But not everybody starts at the same point or moves at the same pace. Do you really think that every house I went to would just blindly let me in if I was a minority? Or would it be fair for me to try and race someone driving to New York. The answer is no. Not because I don’t want it to be that way, but if I’m being straight with you, I’m talking to someone who has prejudices, and that exists from individuals to systems.”

“I’m not racist. I love everybody the same and would welcome anybody into this church.”

“I’m talking about you as a generalization, as a statistic.” I said.

“Whenever I get into an argument. And I’m not saying that we are having an argument right now, but my mind always seeks out a flaw in the other person’s argument, until I am right.” He said.

“Don’t you see that that makes you just as wrong?” I asked.

“I’m not saying that I know, or even don’t believe in evolution, but I have a better understanding of why creation makes better sense to others.” He said.

“Hopefully, I have done the same to you for affirmative action.”

A young boy maybe thirteen came and sat next to us.

“Hey there fellow,” I said.

“Hey guys.” He said quietly.

“How you doing, what’s your name?”

“Beckett. I just want to say that both of you guys, whatever you are talking about, are extremely smart.” He said.

“Don’t worry man, by the time you're our age, you’ll

probably be smarter than us. Just stay away from the pot. Do you smoke?" I said, patting him on the shoulder.

"I do. Not that often." He said a little embarrassed.

"No problem with that, just stay focused on school and that girl I saw you running around with earlier." I said.

"I will." He smiled like he got what he was looking for and kept sitting next to us while we went back to our conversation.

"Now, neither of us is right or wrong, life is a beautiful thing that way. We can say that there are answers to everything, but faith or science either way, blind acceptance is what's dangerous. It goes along the same lines as power or ignorance." I said.

He checked his phone and the conversation began to calm down after that, we talked about good movies and actors, books. How that I should avoid guns if at all possible since he deeply believed they ruined his life. Guns can be substituted with any word for anything that we put too much time, energy and focus into. Any form of addiction.

We drove back to the church and there was an evening service. Whenever the bible is read to me, each passage is speaking directly about the feelings I have about something going on in my life. I was dabbling with making it to New York, what I wanted out of it, and still wondering what all of this was for.

When it ended, the pastor let me know that it was fine that I could spend the night. He gave me some suggestions on how to make it into the city. I learned the only way in on foot is by the George Washington Bridge. I had to go a little bit more North than I had anticipated, but it started to get so close that I could smell the garbage.

"Why do you want to go to New York?" The pastor asked me.

"Sounds romantic."

"Hahaha, well, after you get there, let me know how romantic it is."

I looked at the maps and found a town called Buttzville. That cracked me up. We all played basketball until it got dark and I asked if there was a guitar lying around anywhere that I could use. Kyler was quick to his feet and dug it out from their hybrid home. It had a dark blue shell and a light metallic tone. I played them a few of my songs that I had written on the road and even the sister with bright pink lipstick who was skeptical of me sat nearby.

Dinner was quesadillas, and the black man who greeted me this morning with the moustache stuck around and ate. He went by Mr. Ben and he made a lot of jokes. I accidentally made a political joke and like his beliefs in the church being very strong, his political views were the same. It upset him and he left. When Mr. Ben did return, he came with a cop. Mr. Ben had done it now. I played it cool and just fiddled on the guitar looking for some chords and lyrics to write for the night. I had made it this far with no trouble, there was no need to start any now. The cop asked to speak with me.

"What's your name son?" He asked.

"Jack Wright. I haven't done anything wrong."

"Relax. I'm not saying you're doing anything wrong. I've just got to make sure that you aren't running from anything."

I sat there as he ran through my history. The worst part about it was Kyler was looking at me, and this probably furthered his belief that I was some sort of bad guy.

"God, that's all I keep hearing about," I said under my breath.

"I ran your name. Nothing came up. You're clean. Does anybody know you are out here?"

"Me? Um, yeah. My dad does. Why?"

"Just checking, you're old enough to take care of yourself. What happened to your forehead?"

I touched the rough skin where the scab was.

"I fell in Pennsylvania. Hit my head against the rocks."

"You don't need any medical attention, do you?" He asked.

"I feel fine." My heart was beating out of my chest.

"Alright now, you have a good night. Here is my

number if you get yourself into any trouble, but you are with good people."

"I know that. They have been more than kind."

"Mr. Ben, I'll see you." The cop waved to him.

I looked back at Mr. Ben and he smiled like I was going to kill the president of the United States.

Chapter 47

We were in the Wawa around five thirty in the morning, since CJ was an engineer and had work early. It was more crowded than I expected it would be that early. Apparently, a lot of people have a lot of places to be. CJ bought me two sandwiches and we made small talk, which ended on him saying, "Nope man, I'm a Baptist, have never drank and never had sex, any of that." It was devastating, but it made me wonder what someone who was twenty-seven who never had sex was like and the answer was, pretty normal.

He dropped me off at the beginning of Buttzville and I walked along the morning road until I thought it was a good time to eat my first sandwich. It wasn't even six. I sat outside of an outdoors store and the owner, who was a woman, came out intrigued. I told her my story, and she told me that it was best if I left. I thought it was rather rude.

The layout of the land that I was travelling on was much different than the AT in the sense that it was constantly changing, unlike the forest which all starts to look the same after a while. I didn't not like it, I just didn't love it. Some parts of it were nicer than the AT, like the rich gated neighborhoods of Jersey. The little towns I would go through and stop off for water were sweet and charming. Every once in a while, I would walk by a construction site and the workers would all tip their hats my way, and I would do the same even though I no longer had a hat.

As the sun rose, the day became hot. Exceedingly hot. So extremely hot that I had to fill up my water every hour or so. I looked at a fountain and jumped in to cool myself off. It worked for about 45 minutes and by then all of the water had evaporated from my clothing and was replaced with my sweat again. For as far as I thought I could go, it just seemed to keep going further.

A man in a van pulled up to me.

"You Crazy!" He called from his vehicle.

"I know." I just looked ahead walking.

"You crazy in this heat! Let me get you out of this heat."

I thought about if it was a bad idea to get in a stranger's car, but I had been in so many ins and outs without any repercussions so I thought one more probably wouldn't hurt. I got in and threw my backpack in the back.

"I saw you for the past two hours. I went and did a job at one house and thought you were crazy then and now I see you again. Where are you going? You are going to die." He had a thick Polish accent.

"I'm walking to New York." I said as my breath filled the car with humidity.

"*Walking*? There is a train that comes out of my town every morning. Come, we will feed you, let you rest up."

"I don't know if I could just take a train into New York after walking all this way. I'm coming from North Carolina. Where are you from?"

"Originally, Germany. My name is Victor." He said with grit in his teeth.

It explained the accent and the generosity.

"Come, you come over, and we will feed you. If you want to leave after that, you can, but I cannot let you bake in this heat."

"Thank you."

"Oh no problem." He stopped talking and focused on driving again.

We pulled into his driveway, and he guided me in through his garage.

"You need to take a shower?" He offered.

"It wouldn't hurt."

"Ok. No problem. I'll get you a towel."

The garage led into the basement which had a large leather couch, a bar and a painting of Marlon Brando from the Godfather. It was extremely Jersey. I thought it was one of the nicest, most properly lived in spaces that I'd been in in a while. Their shower was magnificent. It reached deep into all my sore torn muscles which were quite defined at this time. I came out of the bathroom with nothing but a towel, and a beautiful woman with short dark greying hair stood before me. What a shock that my steamy body wasn't covered, but I was able to calm down most arousal.

"You are the travelling one?" She glanced up at me.

"Yes. Nice to meet you. I was just going to grab some clothing." I said behind the tight towel wrapped around my waist.

"Yes, I am making dinner for you, we have guests...Well more guests." She said with a European accent.

I changed and grazed to the upstairs living room in a clean, relaxing calm. I was at ease with what I had been given, and myself. After I changed, I sat at the table and Victor spoke with me about my journey. I told him all about what I had seen and how I had become somewhat of a songwriter on the road.

"I think we have guitar. Do we have guitar, dear?" He asked his wife.

"I think it is in Fletcher's, our youngest, room." He went down the hall and returned with an untuned small guitar.

"It isn't much, but it works." Victor said offering it to me.

While I was tuning it two more, well six, people came in. It was a husband and wife and their four children.

"Who's this?" A blond-haired young mother asked.

"He is walking to New York." Victor answered.

"No way! That is crazy. Hi, I'm Mimi, and this is my husband Mike." I shook Mike's hand and his fresh pair of dark brown eyes and shaped five o'clock shadow greeted me. Mike was the nephew of Victor's wife, Ana who was a European immigrant as well. Mimi was very interested in me. Her three toddler girls and one baby boy were entertained by riding a small truck by the coffee space that the kitchen overlooked while we talked. She was a good person to open up to, they all were. I began by showing off a few of my songs.

"That's so good. Do you have a following?" Mimi asked.

"Basically, just friends and family. I'm not really

doing any of this for fame. I'm still going through somewhat of a breakup, but I'm in love with someone else. It's complicated."

"There are hundreds of girls everywhere." She tapped the table without making much noise but a lot of social commotion to get her point into my head.

"Yeah, but it's the right one that counts, how did you two meet?" I asked.

"We met at a bar, five no, six years ago. We've been married for four years now. So, it's been a long time."

"Yeah, I was with my first girlfriend Austin for three years."

"Uh uh, he's getting sad. He's not over her, let's change the topic."

I rolled my eyes.

It was the best damn food I had on the trip and in my entire life. It was feta cheese on some bright orange tomato sauce with farfalle, with a garden salad, and a potato salad.

"This is incredible," I thanked Ana.

"Really, nobody around here thinks my cooking is any good." She smiled.

"Well, you spoil them," I looked over at Victor, who was on the couch. He was older and had let his hair grow a little long and I wondered if they were at the point in their marriage where he wouldn't really mind if I had a go at his wife. She seemed kindly interested in me, but I wasn't sure and wasn't going to ask or step over any boundaries on the likelihood that I might get murdered.

They all agreed I should avoid going through Newark. Mike was talking about taking a job in the Middle East, that Tom teased him about that he was going for too long and was going to die. Mimi was just so worried about being away from her husband for so long but compared herself to me to find strength and said that if I could go a month without being with anybody, so could she.

"I'm sorta worried about you," she looked at me. "Like you might have built up this shell that makes you impervious to feel anything."

"I'm not sure if that is exactly my problem, but this

trip has definitely made me a stronger person." I said.

She was sweet but broke my heart because she reminded me of Paris and how I just wished to be married someday. Would I have to be compromising my time spent in other countries to make more money after I was married? Why couldn't things just be simple. I didn't want that. I didn't really want any of this, but I had no choice. Mimi invited me to a birthday party, which sounded fun, but at the same time I had been going a long way and rest was not a bad choice. Fletcher came in and he looked a lot like Ana. He was beautiful and had long hair. He went straight to his room, and I didn't see him after that.

I took a quick nap out on their hammock for a while and when I woke up the sun was beginning to set. Victor said that he would go out and get me some food if I needed any. I was pretty set, but he insisted. When he left, I was alone with Ana in the basement. I wanted to talk with her so badly, she seemed so kind.

"How did you meet Victor?" Was my first question.

"Oh, we were friends when we were younger. I once had a birthday, when four separate boys all showed up thinking they were my date, Vic included."

"And he was the one who stole your heart?" I asked.

"Yes, but many years ago. He was my brother's best friend."

"And you guys moved out to here after that?"

"Yeah, growing up we didn't have any money. My mother saved her entire life so that me and my brothers and sisters could come to this country. I was the oldest, so I came out here when I was sixteen."

"What did you do after that?"

"I got married first, second - one moment." She got up from the bar stool and grabbed behind the bar a big white booklet and opened it up. It was the wedding pictures of her marriage. She was the most beautiful woman I had ever seen. Genuinely stunning and she looked so happy with her arm around a younger Victor, who in his youth was a very attractive man as well.

"You were so beautiful. You're still beautiful, but Jesus Christ. Gorgeous."

"Yeah, Victor wasn't bad looking either. Now not so much. We are just older, it was a long time ago."

"How old were you guys?" I asked.

"Twenty-two. Right after I went to college for art."

"You're an artist?"

"A very bad one."

"No one is a bad artist."

"Trust me, I'm not very good. One of my friends who I went to school with. He has made quite a good living making art. Let me see if I can find him."

She pulled out an iPad and showed off the work of a respectively brilliant artist. Not exactly my preference but it was good visual artwork of anime women and Rothko background textures."

"Did you finish art school?" I asked.

"No, that's why I am in school right now, and I feel bad because I am also very sick."

"Sick?"

I don't remember the disease she had, but it basically amounted to her bones were beginning to deteriorate and soon she wouldn't be able to walk, and the only solution was very expensive.

"If you are sick, why don't you just enjoy the rest of your time?" I said.

"I do. I just want to help however I can," she shrugged.

"I see and respect that."

"I respect you, and what you are doing. You know you can do whatever you want, but why not finish school?" She looked back at me.

"I never said I wasn't going to finish school." I said.

"Well, you can't live in New York and go to school in North Carolina."

"What about art school?" I asked.

"You'll never finish." She shook her head smiling. "You have so much time. You are so young, there is no need to rush to go to the places you want to go to, they will be there later."

"I'm not going to college for money and personally, I'm just not that happy."

"Nobody likes college, but Victor always say, I'd

rather cry in my Mercedes than on my bike."

"Ha, I would be happy to have a bike at this point in my life." I said.

"Just be careful. I don't want to hear about you on the news that you are dead."

"Eh, I probably wouldn't make it onto prime time if that happened."

"I don't care about any *prime time*. I care about you. And you should learn to do a little more of that yourself."

"I wish I knew how to."

Victor came in with groceries. It was a full supply of food. Tuna, Rice, Clif Bars, Oreos. Enough to eat for a week. The thing was, I already had a lot of food, but I wasn't about to not take it. Ana hugged me and went up for bed. Vic hung out with me on the couch and we watched television about some crime comedy. It made me feel good and laugh about the fact that I was having so much trouble letting go. If I ever did let go, it was that night, since I was only about thirty miles from New York, New York and a whole new life awaited me.

Chapter 48

"Ready to go?" Victor said, standing over me.

"I'm up!" I sprung up. "What time is it?" I asked rubbing my eyes.

"You said five o'clock."

"That's perfect."

"If you want to sleep in more, you can, I have two more hours before I need to be anywhere."

"No. Earlier is better. I might make it to the city today."

He took me out of his suburb to some heavier streets where you could tell cars might be commuting all the way into the city at this hour.

"30 miles down. How far I take you?"

"Just let me out here."

"Do you need any money?" He asked.

"No, really, I think I'll be alright."

"Alright, well here is my phone number. You call me for anything, anytime it is too dangerous, and I'll come get you."

"Thank you for everything."

I began walking on what I knew was going to be a long day. Google maps said that it was a little over thirty miles to the city but by the end of the day I probably travelled over a hundred. When the sun finally did show its neon glow across the tomato soup colored sky, the exhausted cars buzzed with a sense of possibility. I was this close to achieving my goal and nothing was going to stop me.

Google Maps kept leading me through highways and construction. Closed off streets and bridges you couldn't get around. Each time I came across a barrier I became more and more discouraged, until I realized why God had been leading me in such a winding way. At the end of one of the roadblocks there was a store, and outside of the store was a vintage Schwinn *la tour* bicycle for twenty-five dollars. It looked like it had two wheels that just needed to be filled up with air and it could fly. I went into the store and was directed to the owner of the bike. When I asked if that bike was for sale he responded.

"It's funny. I've had two bikes laying out there for two weeks and nobody has even come near them, now today, someone just came and bought the first one, and now you." He eyed me up and down, and I suspected my full backpack looked a bit suspicious. He analyzed me closer, almost sniffing out my story.

"Eh, let's call it ten bucks even, would you like that?"

WOOF

"It would not only make my day, it would make all my dreams possible."

"It's yours then."

I couldn't just get on it and ride it with over forty pounds on my back and two flat tires, but it worked fine. Google Maps said I was about ten miles away from a bike store. It was early in the day, so I knew it was doable to get downtown but was still going to be a hassle. I thought it was a good time to check in on the only possible limb I had for a place to stay in NYC. I texted my old neighbor John that I was about 30 miles away from the city and hoped that I could see him if it wouldn't be too much trouble. I had reached out to him before about the same idea when I was in Tennessee, but he never got back to me, so I wasn't expecting much.

He texted back right away excited to hear from me. He let me know that he didn't have a place for me to stay but that he would look around. I told him that it wasn't *me* that needed a place to stay, it was my backpack. He said he would look, but that it was unlikely. I remembered my belief from the beginning of this trip that if I was going to make it, I was going to make it on my own, and that was all I needed to rely on.

The day was just as hot as the last and finding a route to the bike shop turned from 8 miles, to 12 miles, to 7, to 10, so I thought I would put my thumb up. I knew my chances were slim since I needed a big car that could fit my bike as well, but I just held it up high until my arm got tired. Right before I wanted to give in, a guy veered out of the road and pulled over and popped his head out of the car.

"What's up man? You got a flat?"

"Sort of, it's a new bike that I need to get checked out before I take it into New York," I said.

"How far aways the bike shop?"

"About five miles."

"I can do that, here, help me get it in the back."

His car was not a pickup truck, but a sort of Vista Cruiser with a dog in a cage in the wide truck bed.

"We'll leave the window open so she doesn't get scared. Hey man, I'm Jo, but people just call me Black Bear."

"What's good man?"

"What's good. You going to the city?"

"Today's the day." My heart beat.

"Righteous man, how long have you been out here?"

"I honestly don't know."

"Gnarly."

"It has indeed been gnarly my dude."

He was hip and reminded me of one of the best poets I'll ever know in my lifetime. He wore sunglasses and was tan and worked to protect animals that were in parks. We got to talking about weed which made me want to smoke with him, but he had a strict "not on the job" mentality. I respected it. The problem was that when we showed up to the bike shop, it had been closed for about a year.

I asked the new store owners if they knew of one nearby and they said they did. The thing was, that bike shop was back where he picked me up, and he said that he had to go get a signature for his job before we went there. I wasn't really in a rush, too many things were in my favor. I waited in the parking lot while he did his business and apparently the bike shop was just down the road. The last thing we talked about before I left was his girlfriend. I brought up Instagram and he showed me his first and then he showed me his girlfriend's. She had 200 followers and he had 700.

Now I hope to god that we don't move towards a

world where people only look at a number to define a person's self-worth, but it often feels like we are moving in that direction. She also had anxiety attacks that they solved by using medical marijuana with. He seemed happy. In fact, they had just recently tied the knot after meeting where they worked. I was happy for him, for the world as a whole.

If I ever meet the right girl, I better not give a damn about how many Instagram followers she's got. It ain't about that. It's who someone is as a person and love should always be regarded as nothing less. I thanked him for the wild ride, and he asked me to let him know once I got into the city.

I walked into a quaint biker shop and the owner was behind the counter. I told him that I had just picked up my Schwinn *la tour* and didn't have money for much other than a few new innertubes. He said that he would take a look at it for me, and pretty soon he was cleaning that sucker's guts out. A man came in who looked like he was getting into avid biking and was looking for a new seat.

He bought a new seat, and I asked for his old seat. When I say my bike was vintage, I mean it. The total came out to thirty-five dollars for two new tires, a quick check up, a lock, and a free seat. He only asked that I put a good review on Facebook for him and his business.

I put my headphones in and the feeling of the wind brushing against me on the hot day brought life into my lungs. I was going to make it if it killed me. I had not adjusted however to riding a bike with that amount of weight on me and I had some trouble with some of the initial turns I was taking and had to get off and back on my feet to reassess.

Once you learn to ride a bike, you never forget and that was a lesson I had told myself about this whole trip. When I left, I had no idea how to fend for myself, I barely knew how to pitch a tent and I definitely didn't know how to sleep alone at night. Now that I had come this far, done all that, I could never forget how to survive in the wilderness. It made me at peace with much less in my life and I am glad from new gratitude.

The first glimpse of the city blew my mind. My heart came right out of my sore skeleton and I started to holler in excitement at the achievement for all the work that I had put into this. I had indeed already come out a better person because of this experience and if that was all anyone would ever want to accomplish, it would make them great.

At this point, I was able to pull out my phone and film myself viewing the city for the first time and God, it was glorious. I stopped listening to the maps and just started heading right in (with making a note I had to make it to the George Washington bridge). I kept going faster and faster on streets that seemed to continue to get steeper and steeper downhill.

The layout of the world changed, and you could tell that I was leaving Jersey. The buildings were older but there were a lot more of them. Kids getting out of school all looked so beautifully lost in their own lives. Urban kids are much more socially cultured than kids who grow up in the suburbs, probably because they are exposed to so much more, or possibly have more interesting backgrounds than married parents and a dog. The streets led me to a gas station that was the end of the road before it turned into a byway, if you would call it that. The road just picked up and I checked the map, and this was my best shot. I could not have gone on it on foot, and it probably wasn't legal for me to go on it on a bike, so I shoved my baggage in my sock, shoved everything else I had up my ass and took the leap.

I wanted to move as quickly as I could without getting hit by a car. The experience was so overreaching, literally reaching out and grabbing the reality of the towering buildings in the distance as they became more defined and taller. Getting into New York is quite tricky. I was now going over a river on a highway. I was just waiting to get stopped by a cruiser since someone had told me they were looking for hitchhikers heading into the city. But I, I was biking.

The highway turned off into what felt like a small island. It seemed lost in time or something, and I was not supposed to be there. The streets were empty and only construction sites occupied the space on this strange area I had come through. It looked like a construction ghost town. There would be long moments with no noise, injected with truck honks and cranes. I wasn't shy about being there though. I would go through gated areas as if I could see that there was a way out and I often got too close to construction sites.

"Ey! Get the fuck outta here!" A worker said as I came across heavy artillery carrying a long steel bar.

I wasn't sticking around. I pedaled as hard as I could and tried to find my way closer into New York. I used some time once I got back on a major road to reach out to people who I knew were in the city to see if they could either house me or would just want to get together. I asked my friend who goes to Cornell, that I knew was going to be staying in the city over the summer, and my old dance instructor who taught at Julliard, but I didn't hear from either of them right away.

It was no better on John's end either. The last pit stop I took was in a tiny little town right beside the city that seemed utterly unaffected by its obese neighbor. It seemed like it belonged somewhere in the South or Twentieth Century.

Luckily some fight or flight mentality broke in and it occurred to me that I have a distant aunt who lived on Long Island. I say distant not because I personally felt distant towards her in any way, but by my family sometimes kept their distance from her. I honestly feel closer to her than I do with much of my own family, as I do with a lot of my relatives. Aunt Kelley was just a little far out. She could see the paranormal.

Aunt Kelley was my mother's sister. However, I haven't talked with my mother in years. Things were not about to change, and I knew my father would be of little to no help, but I had to ask anyways. I let him know about the fact that I had indeed made it and achieved my goal, and you know what? He sounded happy for me and didn't make it seem like I was asking the whole world of him for a little help. I am not saying I am not a *difficult* person to be around. We have had our scuffles, but he genuinely cares. A dad is just as good as a bad mother.

I didn't have any set plans, but at least things were in motion. I had trouble finding my way onto the Washington Bridge, but once I did, I knew I was welcomed into the gates of heaven. No. Matter. What. I took my time as I rode across it. The wooden pillars bumped along my tires and it sounded like music. I saw two police officers, and although this city was notorious for having rough cops, I thought I might as well get off on the right foot with them.

"Could you take my picture, I just walked here from North Carolina."

"Yeah, buddy. I can take your picture if you did all that. That's insane."

The belief in an idea and bringing it to life was captured.

"Be safe now in the city."

Chapter 49

You can't write how good I felt. The buildings were white brick and all the streets were filled with cars with a new license plate. I wanted to scream out, "I made it!" to everybody I saw, so I did. Let's be real. The whole city is a cliché. Everyone looked like they were dying in some way or were already dead. They don't like people on bikes or people with big backpacks who think they are just going to show up full of life and stay a while.

I needed peace and I went to the one place in the world where no matter how awful it ever got, it always seems to help, McDonalds. Everybody said the city was loud, but it seems like everybody is constantly yelling at one another all the time. Conversation is an understatement. I was lovin' it until I realized there wasn't a dollar menu. Not only was I was petrified about the idea of my bike getting stolen within the first five minutes of it unattended, but *I* had been asked for money.

I joined two men outside while I ate. One was mid-seventies and the other was thirty. I didn't really take the time to explain all that I'd done because I wasn't about to just get on a soap box. You don't always have to be in the spotlight, and I think that a lot about living in big cities is learning to share that spotlight. There wasn't much to say, but we all held our cards close.

John told me that he got off at his music production internship around four and that I should meet him in Brooklyn. The bike ride from Harlem to Brooklyn is not a quick one for those of you who don't know. Eh, what was biking across Manhattan going to be after all this? It was hell. It was like being a chicken lost in that city. Crossing roads was not simple, but pretty quickly I realized that nobody gave a fuck about anybody. I just had to do my thing. Balance all that weight on my shoulders and hope I didn't hit something.

The numbers on the streets began to decrease and the layout changed from impoverish bodegas to metropolitan enterprises. Still, there weren't any less people anywhere, and this was probably the most dangerous part of my whole journey. I would wind in between cars, inches apart from getting knocked off and my only directions were from tattooed fellas and dime whores toward the Williamsburg Bridge.

Once I got through Midtown, the rush of New York settled in. There is an energy in that city that exists unlike anywhere else and you can physically feel it consume your body. I kept going just past Time Square and headed down East towards the bridge through NYU. The Williamsburg Bridge is a blessing and a curse. It is great for bikes to use, but the bike paths are very steep up to the center, so you are going uphill to get to the top no matter what, but once you do make it to that halfway point, it is smooth sailing.

Apparently, I was on the wrong side though, and some guy told me to use the other fucking side. This made me feel like I'd earned the right to tell anyone to fuck off after that. I was parched once I got into Brooklyn. Luckily, Arizona iced tea was still only 99 cents, but it wasn't that way everywhere. About 10 seconds after I bought it, it was finished, and I headed to McCarren Park where I was to meet John. I was a little early, but John and I have been walking to school together since middle school, so I expected him to be a little late.

I was cashed. Physically, mentally, emotionally, spiritually, you name it, I was drained of any energy left in this world and I just wanted to go under a tree and dig a six-foot-deep bed. John rolled up with a wide stride in his tight rolled up jeans, slicked back hair in a ponytail and his chucks. He is always rejuvenating to see, and his hug brought me back to life.

"S'up man, you made it." He said, casually and respectfully unsurprised.

"That bike in through Manhattan was almost the death of me. Nearly lost me gentlemen." I joked in an accent.

"Haha. Dude. The bike ride through Manhattan? What about the walk?"

"I could walk anywhere you could point to on a

map."

"Haha. What about the city man? Did you find a place to stay, yet?"

"I have an aunt who lives on Long Island which looks promising, but I'm thinking about sticking around for a while."

"Like living here?"

"Maybe, just for the summer."

"Dope man. Is your dad gonna be alright with that?"

"He didn't even want me to do any of this in the first place."

"Oooh. I knew it! Your dad doesn't just let you do shit like this."

"Hahaha, indeed not. Do you mind if I smoke?" I asked pulling out a cigarette.

"Wanna split a beer?" He said pulling a cold one out of his pocket.

"Sure, I'm sort of at that point where I'm like, why go back?"

"Dude, I know of a bunch of places that you could get for cheap."

This is what I love most about John. He doesn't second guess big ideas like that. That is most people's problem and I said this at the beginning. It's the reason why a lot of people don't do anything with their lives, they're always asking too many questions. I've always thought of him as a golden ticket and now was no different. Not to say that I was just trying to mooch off of him or live my life vicariously through him or anything, he's just a solid support that comes once in a lifetime.

I was a little bit in shock, so I went over the story for him. I couldn't focus on many details other than personal things you can tell your best friend. We finished our beer and cigarette and John offered that we go explore a little bit. I let him know I was pretty light on cash, but he said he could probably vouch for me, but I'd get the next tab.

Brooklyn, to this day, is my favorite part of New York. It is not just a giant picket fence like Manhattan, there was integral vandalism. Where you don't just have the rich and the poor, but instead a good place where hard working people make something of the world no matter what or where they come from. It breeds dignified humanity. It was the type of people that I wanted to be surrounded by that I don't find at college.

We went to his favorite restaurant in the whole world, a little French bistro and I knew that place meant as much to him as home did. When we ate, we laughed that there was a "help wanted" sign on the door but I said I'd rather just play in a band. We brought up the idea of getting together with some people from high school who were in town and joked about posting on our class Facebook page. Cher, his girlfriend, seemed to be doing well. They had lived together for almost a year by then and were on their way to Rome for a month.

My dad was trying to play the good guy after realizing that it really wasn't so much to ask to get in touch with my Aunt Kelley. I told him I felt like I was home, which felt true at the time. Uncle Dan, Kelley's husband, texted me not long after that, and was wondering what train I would be taking out to Long Island where they lived. I told him midnight. He said that he would be up. We walked the outskirts of Brooklyn along the rivers and enjoyed the rugged life that New York brought, continuing a buzz in the busiest town in the world.

"You like it out here?" I finally asked.

"I love it."

"Anywhere else you think about going to?"

"California."

I'd never been to California before, but I imagined the famous weather.

Chapter 50

Almost late to the train, I hopped on, pulling my bike along with my very wide backpack. I took this time to sit by myself and think of my family back home. I hoped they were all well wherever they were. I got off and onto a dark lit platform surrounded by suburban streetlights. My Uncle Dan stood next to a big grey Tahoe. He was not rough around the edges with dirt, but properly sculpted by a good character of man that made me glad to be in ties with him. In some ways, he symbolized a new standard of egotistical stature that I had accomplished.

"I bet you're tired of carrying that ol' thing around." He looked at my weight.

"You wouldn't believe." I said shaking his hand.

"Here, throw it in the trunk and you can follow me on your bike to our house, it's not that far away."

I followed him in the dark weaving through the streets until I pulled into the driveway.

"You can put your bike in the garage, next to Jake and Will's."

I pulled up the garage door. My new bike was getting to spend the night in such a nice place on my first day of having it. So was I, their home far exceeded any households that I had been in on my trip. It was well lived in, and properly decorated. Aunt Kelley waltzed down the steps and I was bombarded by the two golden retrievers coming from behind her.

"Hey, glad to see you," she looked up.

Lord knows I needed the affection, and I gave her a big hug. She seemed in a little disbelief.

"Oh my god, I just got off the phone with your dad, he told me you walked here? Aren't you hungry? It must've been an extremely long trip."

That was the moment I felt like I had accomplished what I set out to do physically, so my posture adjusted as such with pride. "I'll eat anything you've got." I slumped again from exhaustion.

"Do you like chicken and rice?" She asked.

"Fantastic."

We went into the kitchen as she began to reheat some dinner for me, and I couldn't be uncomfortable in her home. It was too nice. Long Island is just nice. However, what really made me feel at home was an old Christmas card from my family, hung up in their kitchen refrigerator. From many, many years ago, before the divorce. The black and white picture with me hanging on tight, with everyone was pinned into a corkboard.

All this time had gone by since then, and I'm sure Kelley didn't notice it every day, but the thought of being endeared was kind. Dan was occupied with where I was going to sleep, so I brought everything up to the attic. After that, Kelley and I caught up on the couch. It's hard for me to write this, but we didn't talk like a distant aunt and nephew. She sat and listened to me like I was her son. It wasn't what we said, just how it was said and how it was heard.

Romance is all well and good for what it's worth, the passion, the bravery. However, motherhood is something so much more subtle with its candor and compassion. It's hard when you tell yourself you're too old for that sort of thing, and just want to be a man instead. Words hurt, and not all the people around you think the same way about things. Kelley was known for having a drinking problem and rude sarcasm, and avoidance from our family should not be a modern solution. Maybe I say this just because I have so many problems of my own and expect the same from my siblings. The reason I resort to myself is because nobody *really* wants to be my family or my friend. I'm stuck with myself, who I am, and I wish I was someone else, but I can't help but see the world so differently, believe me, I don't want to be different. To be misinterpreted is to be loved.

Either that or I can't really be friends with people. I'm honestly surprised that anyone would want to listen to what I have to say. My art, though experimental at times, often elusive, downright unpolished, is only meant to help me feel closer to this world and the people in it, whoever, whenever, why ever. It's the only way I know how. Art is the longest relationship I have ever had, and I believe it will die only when I do. An artist is like being born stupid, in love, and afraid.

Chapter 51

Aunt Kelley told me that she would be up at five but didn't want me getting up like I had been every day the past week. I planned on getting up, but my body wouldn't let me. It was dead ass fucking raw aching hurting cracking sleep-inducing sore. I got up around ten and didn't want to spend the day in Long Island, so I thought I would bike into Brooklyn.

Kelley was in the basement when I came downstairs and I helped myself to breakfast in the kitchen. I got online and looked to see if there were any jobs, and a few looked promising. I sent out a few emails, formalized my resume and thought that was good enough for a job search on my first day. When she came up, she talked about how the boys wanted to see me, and how there was a concert tonight. I thought about going, but I had to leave open the opportunity that something might arise downtown.

She chuckled when I said I was biking to Brooklyn.

"Wear a helmet," and she lent me hers.

It was about a twenty-two-mile bike ride and since it was already pushing eleven o'clock, I wanted to bike as quickly as I could, and I got hit by a car in about two minutes. I didn't roll over the windshield or anything, I just was thrown off, slamming into a turning car. It sucked, but nothing was broken and the second I stood up the car drove off. I took that as a lesson to go a little slower.

I texted while I biked, organizing plans with John and my Jewish friend, Burk. I went through Jamaica, which was an interesting environment. It seemed like an urban desert consisting mainly of families with small shops or people who sold things on the streets for a living. I was just passing through but could spend a lifetime studying this culture if it would have me. I kicked it in the outskirts of Brooklyn for a while. Brooklyn had more to offer in its looser upscale environment.

For about an hour, just attending to the atmosphere wasn't that boring. Some people didn't seem like they wanted to be watched at all and others were screaming for it. The streets were laid out in a way that reminded me of the streets under the train and the shops ranged in class by how many people were inside verses outside asking for money. I went into a library while I waited for Burk and asked if I could become a member. If I had lived there it would have been as easy as signing my name, but since I didn't, the cost was a hundred dollars.

Burk was a friend of mine from middle school. We were sort of in separate cliques and were a little nasty to each other like everybody is at that age but had known each other well enough. He ended up with the more chic guys and all my friends were the musicians. No reason to not get together. I waited for him at an art community in front of a mural with vagrant colors.

I went outside and not too long after that, Burk came up and greeted me and I hugged him.

"What's good man?" He said to me with his kind smile.

"Nothing much. How long have you been here?" I asked.

"I've stayed here for about a week with a friend from Vancouver."

"Nice man."

"I'm leaving, like tomorrow, though. You walked here?! That's insane. You gotta tell me everything about it."

"Let's go sit down at a park and we can." I said.

I told him about the journey. We got to talking about relationships since he'd recently gone through a breakup himself.

"We just both realized that it was hurting both of us to stay together and so we let it go."

"Who broke up with who?" I asked.

"We just both thought it was time to see other people."

"Are you guys good?"

"Yeah, we're good."

"And you're doing good?"

"Yeah. I'm with a girl out here right now, anyways." Burk smiled.

"Word."

It's hard for me to fall in love with anyone when it seems impossible that you'd ever get be with them. Sometimes it's better to focus on what is in front of us, instead of chasing someone else.

"But dude, I think if you want to stay out here to act and sing, you should go for it."

"Who knows." I said.

"It probably wouldn't be too hard to find a guitar or an audition."

"I suppose not."

We chilled together for about another hour until he met up with this girl that he was staying with out here. It was their last night together. I got some good pictures of the skyline looking onto Manhattan, but I didn't really need to go in there. I biked around Brooklyn for the rest of the afternoon. I went into random places just to observe the art on the walls, strange clothing, and a dream of finding a family.

I went into Bushwick looking for young college students and offhand weed. It had started to get a little dark, but sure enough I asked a guy who was sitting out on his porch and he had some. I waited for a few minutes with his friend and we talked about other cities. He was from Jersey. Pretty quickly I was stoned in the city. The sunset on the buildings, the funny faces everybody had held me handicapped in giggling. What good was worrying about it all going to do me? I had everything at my fingertips and sure I should probably go about becoming a puppet of some sort, but I was just having much too good of a time being free.

I saw some musicians walk out of a building and asked if the place had spare guitars to use, and they said I should try and come back in the morning. I thought that was a good enough place to call it a day. I should have stayed out later, but I went back to the train station. I was unlocking my bike when a wise fellow came up to me.

"Hey, nice bike. Hey, listen, do you have a dollar?"

"Thanks man, I got it for ten bucks." I said.
"I ask if you have a dollar because you're standing in my spot."
"Your spot?"
"Yeah, this is where I usually panhandle." He said it with pride.
"Oh, sorry man, didn't know. You can have it back."
"Well, listen, do you have any weed?"
"I actually do, I just got some."
"Well, I might be trying to buy some."
"Oh yeah, how much?"
"Just a dime."
"Alright man, I can do that."
"But I wanna try it first..." He said.
I should've known better.
"I mean I can roll a joint, but I've got a train to catch."
"C'mon let's go over there."
We sat down at what seemed like a major focal point for police officers if I ever saw one. He was eying each one of them and let me know when it was clear.
"Give me some bud."
I gave him a little.
"Nah, man give me some *real* bud, I wanna roll."
I reached a little deeper and gave him enough for a joint.
"Hmm. "He said sniffing it. "Smells good, but you gotta be careful about that because they spray it."
"Uh huh."
He finished rolling and I was on edge. I didn't come all the way out here to get busted for a dime rendezvous. He hit it, and then hit it again, and again, and when I asked him to pass it he said he was still hitting it. Then his whole-body language changed.
"Man, this ain't weed. This is garbage!" He handed it back to me and started acting irrational.
I took the joint, hit it one time and threw it into the street.
"Thanks dude." I walked away and he continued to yell at me.
"It's *garbage*. Ain't even worth picking up!"

I really didn't care. I should have expected it when he came up to me with his cavalier attitude. On the train ride back, I talked with a much nicer man who was making a living for himself out in the city even though he didn't go to college. I double checked to see if it was good weed and he smelled it and looked up and smiled.

"That's great weed."

"That's what I'm saying."

When I got back to my Aunt Kelley's, Dan was up but looked like he was ready to go to bed. He showed me how to work the alarm and I wished him goodnight. Up in my little attic bedroom office that they were letting me stay in, I contemplated smoking. I thought I could blow it out the window, or go in a crawl space, but then I realized they had just showed me how to use the alarm, I might as well go outside.

I'm glad I didn't smoke inside, since there were young boys sleeping downstairs. When I got back upstairs, I put my knife away in the desk.

Chapter 52

Another day came, as usual. Visitors get real old real quick, and I thought I should get a move on myself, but it was probably just because my father had been yapping that it was rude to stay longer than two nights. I had an idea for a short art project where I would burn my last hundred-dollar bill on Wall Street and see what would happen for a week without any money. I let Kelley know about this, and she pressed that Will and Jake wanted to see me.

I compromised and said that I would stay the rest of the day until they got out of school and then I would go into the city. Three o' clock came around and I got to be part of the ritual of picking the boys up from the bus. It was only a walk to the end of the street, but when they saw me, Jake was excited and yelled my name and gave me a hug. Will was going through his "I know everything in the world because I'm twelve" stage.

By the end of the car ride neither of the boys could contain themselves as I talked about my trip and played video games with them. They were sad that I had to go into the city, but I promised them that I'd be seeing them again. It was not late, but half of the day had passed and if I was going to try out this little art project, today was the day. I left with just my smaller backpack, a few meals worth of food and went into the city, not sure when I would return to Long Island.

I went straight to the shittiest place on earth. Times Square. It is nice for about five seconds if you are passing through, but it is one hell of a shithole if you post up. There is a bench that you can sit on, and you feel like you are sitting in the middle of the universe, as if the whole city is just performing for you. I sat there with a sign up that read, "Walked from North Carolina. Take me home." It worked for the most part. People gave me money as they walked past, old women flirted with me, but pretty quickly it became late. I just tried to mediate through all of it. It was literally bright as a sunny day, even when I closed my eyes, it felt like I was sitting in the middle of a sunrise.

I meditated until about 3 am, because then I got really hungry. Someone had left me a green tea drink from Starbucks and that was all that I had eaten. Everything was open all the time. Once I got some food in me, I was getting sleepy. 1$ pizza. I felt bad that I couldn't make it a week with no money, let alone one night. The idea of living in New York with no money on top of all that I had done was ludicrous and would call for serious intervention.

Mediating in Times Square was not cutting it. I decided to walk towards Central Park since I hoped it was early enough that I wouldn't get in trouble for scouting. Once I got to the edge of the park, I was discouraged to see dozens of people sleeping on the street corners. I asked a man if he had a place to stay.

"You're looking at it."

Damn. I thought about laying down right next to him, but he told me that there were shelters in the cities that would help me get a room for a night if I needed it. One of which was specified to help minors. It was across the city, but it was my best bet and I really didn't have a better option. As I started walking through the late-night streets, I saw the usual things. Drunk people getting into cars, and beautiful women coming back from a long night, people sleeping on concrete.

When I got to the Covenant House, which was meant for people eighteen to twenty-one, they said that they were at capacity and that I needed to come back tomorrow. I was heartbroken. I was just so tired I wanted to sleep, but they directed me to another shelter, which was hard to find, and when I did find it, they slammed the door in my face.

My last resort was Bellevue Hospital. Apparently, there is always space there. I walked past it and it looked like something out of a horror film. Men screaming, shooting up in the dark corners, K9's and cops at the door with a metal detector. You could just tell that this was one of the darkest places on earth. I went up to the door, but there were multiple police officers about to manhandle me.

"If you have anything, you can throw it out now." An officer said to me.

When it came down to it, I needed a place to sleep more than anything. I went outside and trashed my weed, and yellow baggie, thinking it would all be there in the morning. Before you get a room, you have to go through a hell of a waiting period, and a lot more paperwork. I spent my night sleeping in the waiting room until about 5 am when the workers got back from their break. They did a little report on me, and when it was over, they told me that there was a room for me but breakfast was at 6. I had twenty minutes.

I snagged breakfast and I ate as quickly as I could. Waffles and orange juice. They let me sleep but not long, and when I peered out the door, I had been given a pink slip and was told to go meet Ken. Ken was one of those people who helped. He was good at what he did, and you could tell that he enjoyed doing what he could. He waited with me and called the Covenant House, and they said that they had a room available, but I needed to go there right away. He said he had to escort me off the property, but I said I needed to go to the bathroom. There was only one bathroom and all the men were in line for it. When it finally got to me, I had already shit my pants before I could make it.

It was such a disturbing moment. It was worse than what I ever imagined. There were no paper towels. I assessed the situation and took off all my clothes. The toilet was clean, and I dunked my shorts in the toilet to clean them and rung them out and took as close as I could get to a bath with the toilet and sink water.

When I came out sopping wet, and my eyes watering, Ken said that he was escorting me all the way off the property, he meant all the way, so I couldn't get my stash. The Covenant House was about 15 streets away and they felt long as hell. When I got there, I was graced with more paperwork.

"Let's cut the shit, are you high?" The seasoned woman at the desk asked me.

"No."

"Don't lie to me, Jack."

"No, I'm not fucking high. I swear to God." I felt like hell though.

"Alright, then we got a room for you."

I probably looked strung out, but in my deepest heart of hearts I knew I wasn't a junkie. The paperwork took an hour to fill out and I got a room. I was ready to sleep, only thing was, you weren't supposed to be in your room until 8 o'clock at night earliest. Everybody was just getting out of bed, so I had a long day ahead of me.

I chilled in the lounge which was discouraging, but you could do it. I had to be set up with a case manager, so I thought I might as well get it out of the way. While I was waiting in the lobby, a chill looking dude was also chilling.

"What's up my guy?" He asked.

"Sup, The name's Jack."

"Yo, you new here?" He asked.

"Yeah, just got in last night."

"To New York or to the Covenant House?"

"Pretty much the same thing."

"What's good man, I'm Cyrus."

"Nothin' I just walked here from North Carolina."

"Damn son, how long that take you?"

"Over a month."

"Valid."

"Thanks man, I'm just getting set up with a case manager now." I said.

"Word, if you go through the steps here, they will help you out big time."

"I hope someone can help me," I laughed.

"If you get a job, they will help you get grants to schools, and even help you pay for a place to stay."

"Dope. How long have you been in the city?" I asked.

"Just over a year now. I stole my mom's credit card and took a bus ride and have been here ever since."

"Damn, you glad you came out here?"

"Hell, yeah man, I mean the city definitely has its dark sides to it, but I'm gonna go to the library in about an hour and you are welcome to come with."

"They wouldn't let me in to one in Brooklyn."

"New York Public Library will help you out.

"Dude, nothing in the world sounds better."

"Word, take my number."

I checked my phone and who in the world had shot me a text, but Paris. I was flabbergasted. I had gone through so much agony over the way we left things, trying to get over her, maybe for the better. All of this hadn't been over just one girl, but how could I let go of something that I couldn't walk away from. I had nothing to hold on to. I had tried to let go of Paris. I had let her know we shouldn't communicate anymore, so that we would have a better chance of moving on. Obviously, neither of us could. It was probably my fault for doing this whole thing in the first place, but I always felt that way and shouldn't. We have a right to live our own lives. However, I was not unhappy to hear from her, it just put everything in a new perspective.

My case manager welcomed me into her office. She was young, beautiful, kind, had a great taste in music, and seemed genuinely interested in me. I spent the good half of an hour sharing my deep struggle. I explained it all. Forget walking. I was in love with three women. How I was foolish to ever break any one of their hearts, how dumb I was to put one up on a pedestal and just leave her there, and how greedy I'd been to have had wounded a dove. I didn't cry but I felt like it. My emotions were all over the place and I needed the comfort of a friend just as much as a lover. My case manager loved listening to me, like I was talking about some television drama or something. She gave me some Twilight fan fiction to read and it helped, about a vampire and a werewolf who were in love but had to break up. It didn't solve any of my answers, but it was good to read about a break up between two mystical creatures.

I texted Cyrus who said he was on his way to the library and we met up. We talked more about art and how he was a painter. It was good to be by his side, like we regarded each other as equals. I told him some poetry I wrote and about my songs.

Cyrus fucked with it and told me that if I even just showed that music off to a committee at the New School or Pratt Art Institute that I was not only likely to get in, but get money to go there too. I thought about it, but I really hadn't made much art besides that. Just a few songs and some poetry. I wasn't sure if investing a fresh four years of my life into an art school was the best option for me.

The New York Public Library was what I had been looking for. We might as well have been in a house of the Lord. Cyrus had a card, which let him check out a laptop that he gave to me as he wrote lyrics on pen and paper. It was that afternoon that I started working on my latest work.

What I got was a pretty rough draft of a prologue, and Cyrus said he didn't really like it and that the story needed more background text. We stayed there for about an hour and then left for dinner. When we went into the cafeteria, I was the only white guy besides one other dude who was sitting alone.

Cyrus, you could tell, wanted me to pay no attention to these facts and invited me to sit with him and his friends. They all had something going for them in a different way. There was an immigrant from Chad who had thousands of followers on Instagram and wise guy who went on about how much pussy he was getting, and a vegetarian.

I didn't really talk much, but I didn't not talk. I just didn't speak with the conviction that I had been going on about this whole trip. I was far more interested in these guys, but just wondered what got them there. Most of them were there by choice, and their main goal was to become discovered it seemed.

I was exhausted but the Covenant House was holding a dance after dinner, so I thought I might as well join. It was good music and I was dancing pretty hard with some girls and it felt alright.

Pretty quickly I realized that there were better things to do with some of the people. A few of us went outside and smoked. Two girls showed up, one short and light skinned with long braids and one tall dark girl who was funny. I was kicking it with Cyrus and his friend Roman who talked about getting so many girls it was probably illegal (it probably was), and he told me that he fucked with me more than the last white guy who came through.

We went down to a pier and they shared some alcohol with me and we rolled a blunt. We started freestyling. I was a little rusty, but I am definitely better than you might think. They laughed when I smoked but got real quiet when I drank. They told me I gave up my white privilege when I went there, and how I'm worse than black now.

It was interesting to watch them debate about power dynamics. I hoped I was able to solidify myself as a person apart from an idea of one, and by the end of the night, we drunkenly walked back to the Covenant House, linked arms, well past the time of curfew.

I was dead ass asleep in five minutes. It had been a good day. I was suffering from extreme exhaustion, but I hoped that I would catch up physically sooner rather than later. I let Aunt Kelley know that I had found a place to stay and she invited me back to stay and go to Jake's game on Saturday. I said that I would try to make it if I didn't have anything going on, but I didn't have a thing to do, and that feeling got really old really quick.

Chapter 53

New York, New York. There was so much of it, nothing stood out. I had been there a week and spent most of my days in the city with Cyrus. He was helping me get set up with a job as a food runner at a restaurant in the Village. After work he'd lent me his library card which I'd use to go to the library until it closed. Sticking around the Covenant House was not productive. Everyone would just spend whatever money they had on weed and would smoke. I was feeling uneasy and smoking constantly sinc I didn't have anything harder.

I took everything I had brought with me back from Long Island on to Manhattan and was given a lock to store my backpack in a closet. It was hard to live in the shelter. I had four roommates and one would spend most of his night on the phone to some girl explaining how he wasn't cheating, and he'd spend all day scouting.

I found peace with an old guitar they had. The strings were very old, but I restrung it for about 10 dollars. You couldn't leave the guitar lying around anywhere for too long because people would untune it, not knowing what they were doing. Facebook kept updating me about my friends who were in the city.

Some nights I would play the guitar, and some guys would sing with me. You could see their desire for fame in their eyes. As if singing along to someone playing a few chords was all they needed. The Covenant House trusted me with the guitar, and I would take it out and busk, and I made about thirty bucks on Saturdays. People seemed to like my songs, it was hard to sing over all the noise but if you could find a good place to do it, people would listen.

I would go back to Long Island to spend time with Aunt Kelley about once a week. It was a rainy day and Jake was playing lacrosse. Uncle Dan was the coach and he was the loudest person on their field, encouraging all the kids to play harder. I'm pretty sure their team still lost every game. I would hang back on the sidelines with Kelley, her son Will, and her housewife friends, and she would brag about my journey to them. I asked them all about how and why they got married and most of them talked about how their future husbands were recognized as New York's most eligible bachelors or made a lot of money. Kelley told me she was engaged to someone but then started having feelings for Dan and she couldn't marry someone if she was feeling that way about someone else.

Since Jake won his game, we all went out to dinner at a very nice Italian restaurant. I had a pretty early curfew, so it kept me from staying overnight anywhere else but the shelter. The dinner they took me out to probably cost more than everything I spent on the whole trip. I got something with a pink sauce.

I loved Kelley and Dan's boys more than you can ever imagine. They were so much fun and knew so many things about the world in ways I'd never looked at before. Before I left to go back into the city, we watched America's Funniest Home Videos, and I tell you, I never heard anyone laugh as hard as them. It was hard not to feel at home with them. I would have stayed in that city just for them.

At the end of the night Dan dropped me off at the train station and told me he would see me soon. I gave him a big hug and agreed but didn't know if I was sticking around much longer. Everything was fine and all, the suburbs reminded me of my hometown, the city reminded me of high school, but it just wasn't home.

I met up with my friend Noelle, from Cornell. She was studying psychology. Surprisingly, she told me that I should to stay in New York because if I didn't try, I would spend the rest of my life wondering what if and it would be detrimental to any progress that I was working toward. I was surprised since I always thought of her as someone who would tell me I might be taking up her spot in such a selective scene, but I don't think we were really talking about New York.

I talked to a few girls here and there, the right ones would talk about books and the wrong ones would talk about social media stars. I wasn't really looking for love, I just needed a place to put my hat. There was an improv show that one of my friends from high school was in. It was odd and fitting, but my mind was exhausted, thinking about love.

John and I met up to go see Ellen, our high school friend, perform in an improv show and she was the best in the lot. She has genuinely always been one of the nicest, and by far sunniest people I know. She's also a great writer. John and I sat in the back row and laughed. A woman passed through us, and exclaimed, "Wow, you're all so tall." It was a small theater. After the show we all stuck around to see Ellen come out and she greeted us with grace and charm. A lot people from my high school were there. It was bizarre. Again, I got that feeling of home away from home. The conversations began to split off.

I think everyone is lost in their own little New York City in their head. John and Ellen were going on about doing very well in their respective industries of music and show business. In all honesty, I was very proud of everyone, not that they needed my approval. My approval was just an alternative variable to arriving at the same place as a group of rather excellent people who wouldn't have to work to get there if they didn't want to, but they did.

John and I hung around a little afterwards and got tacos which didn't help any. My stomach was coming down with something else. This underlying feeling of being sick started to get persistent. As we walked the Highline, I brought up my longing for an old love. It was really something I couldn't ignore. He said that I could probably find new love out here. I was reassured, but I couldn't truly grasp the thought of just starting over. Our minds don't just forget everything at once no matter how much time passes or how many things you do. After we split it wasn't long before I started feeling like I was going to puke.

Perhaps it was a dazed state of mind, but as I tried to get back to the Covenant House, I saw someone. Or I thought I did. It was one of those girls you think you see right then and there. As if after all of this, if I ran into them, how much would any of this matter? I wondered how this wasn't really what I wanted. I can't help but feel something when I see her and I think that only proves I am human, but my body stopped working organically.

When I got back to the Covenant House, I was lime in the face, and I let them know that I had vomited. They told me that I could go to the nurses tomorrow, but that I was allowed to get some rest if I thought it would help. I thought it would, but this was something else. The struggle and pain of just breathing became apparent and persistent. My feet were cold, hell my whole body was cold, and I would go through heat rushes at the same time. It continued to get worse and lying in a bed only made the pain and sickness more apparent by allowing me to focus on each infinitesimal nauseous convulsion. I would throw up every few hours combined with a horrible shit. There was no doubt in my mind that this was vengeance of how I had been treating my body after what I had been putting it through.

The idea of food made me gag. I didn't eat dinner or breakfast for the rest of the week, which didn't help anything either. I waited in the nurse's clinic and they took my vitals and asked for a pee sample, which I wasn't enthusiastic about learning the results. It took a long time before I saw any doctor, two days in fact, and I wasn't getting any better.

The only thing that had been keeping me alive was the guitar. I'm pretty sure I looked mad, but I was clinging to it when the soothing doctor brushed in. Honesty is the core value that I was looking for in this city, and I wasn't sure if I ever found it, but if I did, it was in that office.

A man is only as good as his word, and the best thing he can do is fall in love. I didn't see a ring, but he told me all about his past in California as an art student and how afterwards he decided to get into medicine. It made me realize how wide and long and barren the vast time of a lifetime could be, and that I didn't need to rush to do everything I wanted to. I wanted to stay in the city, but this was probably the worst decision of my life and the most horrible I'd ever felt. In the dark of my room, I laid down once again. I swore the whole thing off. I don't want to live in New York, I wanted to die in New York.

All I had accomplished was that goal. I came to seek deep pain in this world, and wonder if it was still worth it to live. It was a little unfair. Humans look for life, and in the midst of a 7 million people population blizzard, I found more life and love from where I came from, than going anywhere. It didn't feel like it, but I did have something, somewhere. I had walked through North Carolina, laughed in Tennessee, danced through Virginia, climbed through Pennsylvania, lived in Jersey and died in New York.

Everyone thought that I was a goner. I tried to wait it out, to see if it would pass, but the longer I waited the worse it got. Anytime anyone saw me, which wasn't often, only when I could stomach an apple for breakfast just to throw it up by lunch, they would all ask if I was good.

I'm not good, I'm well.

Finally, my case manager asked if it was time for me to go. She said that it didn't look wonderful. Lying in bed alone with all the nightmares that only made me dream of how all the things I had previously thought about the world were now false. After walking nearly a thousand miles, at the end of the rainbow something stopped working. It wasn't drugs, it wasn't some sense of rejection, the only reason that I couldn't breathe was a torn heart.

ABOUT THE AUTHOR

Ben Bonkoske was born in Chicago in 1997. He attends the University of North Carolina, Asheville, where he has written his own major focusing on Inequality. He enjoys dancing and songwriting. This is his first novel.

You can find all of Ben's music referenced in this book, along with other works, at his website:

www.poetwithoutapen.com

Find Ben at:
Instagram: @bencbon
Email: BenBon@poetwithoutapen.com

Cover Illustrator: www.SarahGoodYear.com

Made in the USA
Lexington, KY
19 February 2019